A LADY'S FORTUNE

JANE DUNN

Boldwood

First published in Great Britain in 2024 by Boldwood Books Ltd.

Copyright © Jane Dunn, 2024

Cover Design by Alice Moore Design

Cover Photography: [Abigail Miles] / Arcangel / Alamy / Shutterstock

A CIP catalogue record for this book is available from the British Library.

Paperback ISBN 978-1-83533-552-9

Large Print ISBN 978-1-83533-548-2

Hardback ISBN 978-1-83533-547-5

Ebook ISBN 978-1-83533-545-1

Kindle ISBN 978-1-83533-546-8

Audio CD ISBN 978-1-83533-553-6

MP3 CD ISBN 978-1-83533-550-5

Digital audio download ISBN 978-1-83533-544-4

Boldwood Books Ltd
23 Bowerdean Street
London SW6 3TN
www.boldwoodbooks.com

To Nick,
reluctant Sancho to my Quixote,
supporting me in all my wildest schemes

CONTENTS

1

TWO STRANGERS COME TO HASTERLEIGH

It was a rare warm day in October and Leonora Appleby sat at the piano-forte playing an étude, but her mind was on other things. The full-length sash window was flung up and the garden with its late roses, penstemons and clematis beckoned. She heard a *hallo* and looking up, saw a young woman appear, one hand carrying a sheet of music and the other fluttering over the top of the box hedge that lined the path. The sun caught her fair hair. 'Leonora!' She waved.

'Oh, Lottie.' Leonora stopped playing. 'I'm glad you're early.' She stood up and walked to the window. 'I have a plan. Instead of your music lesson, let's go to the lake. Summer is over and perhaps it's our last chance to swim this year.'

Charlotte Blythe's face lit up with pleasure. 'Oh, yes! But I'll have to be careful leaving the house in my bathing dress. Mama Mildmay does not approve of girls swimming, particularly if I'm missing a lesson to do so.' She laughed.

Leonora was already dressed in the required blue calico bathing smock she had stitched for herself, with long sleeves and a high neck, copied from a print in *The Lady's Magazine*. 'Just wear an everyday cotton pelisse over the top. No one will guess what we intend.'

'I'll be back in five minutes.' Charlotte Blythe turned and ran back down the garden to the pretty gothic house adjoining the Manor's parkland. Both the Vicarage and the Manor were so rooted in the surrounding land that they seemed to have grown out of the soil and to have been there forever. Leonora walked into the garden. She was enveloped in scent and in the buzz of bees harvesting pollen with a busy diligence that suggested they also knew the days of bounty were numbered.

Leonora loved her childhood home. She gazed on the symmetry of its elegant stone façade with long sash windows opening to the garden. To one side, an ornamental orangery was filled with fruiting citrus trees and the fragrance of an exotic and warmer land. On her father's death two years before, the entailed estate had been inherited by a distant relation, but the lucky recipient had shown little interest in taking possession. However, that morning, a letter had been delivered from one George Lockwood, informing her in a measured hand that he would arrive the following Monday. Leonora could barely conceive that the Manor would no longer be her home; her settled world was beginning to tremble under her feet.

When Charlotte returned, the two young women set off down the lane. Hasterleigh was a downland village like many in the county of Berkshire, with church, vicarage and manor all in close proximity. Then slightly set apart was the big house of the neigh-bourhood, Rokeby Abbey, with its estate of some thousand acres of prime land. The forty or so tenanted farms provided the earls of Rokeby with the substantial income that funded a leisured, aristo-cratic mode of life, but the house had been uninhabited for years. Leonora led the way as they clambered over a broken-down section of stone wall and began to make their way through the fringing woodland. Full of ferns and moss with towering oak and beech trees hanging with lichen, the untended woods had a magical, other-worldly atmosphere.

The young women emerged from the cool shade as they reached the knoll, following the faint track curving through the grass until the dark water came into view, still and glassy in the late afternoon sun. At the sight of it, Leonora's heart began to beat faster. Trespassing on the Rokeby estate some years ago, she had stumbled upon the lake and discovered the surprising joy of swimming. Under an oak tree, they cast off their pelisses and walking shoes, pinned up their hair as high on their heads as they could and, slipping on some canvas pumps, waded into the lake.

Leonora pushed off into the chill water and gasped. The cold was less intense after the hot summer, but it was still breathtaking and hit her like a body blow. That first gliding stroke never failed to thrill as she breasted the still surface, drawing a cloak of ripples behind her, her whole being entirely alive. The euphoria that radiated from her heart to her limbs was close to love.

It was a pleasure too to find that Charlotte, her young friend and pupil, also enjoyed these clandestine expeditions. She was less bold and proficient in water and preferred to splash in the shallows while Leonora swam easily to the middle of the lake. No one knew how deep it was, but the thought of the inky depths below did not trouble her.

Bliss lay in the peace that descended, and in how the lake and surrounding woods were so unfrequented and still. She knew Earl Rokeby had left as a young man to fight as a hussar in the Peninsular War and had never returned. His younger brother had joined him, and it was rumoured that during the Battle of Corunna, Rokeby had died in his brother's arms. The house and estate had fallen into disrepair during the ensuing four years, and Leonora had come to treat the lake as her own domain.

Knowing she should not stay too long in the chill water, she turned to swim back to the shore where Lottie was well within her depth. Yet the meditative pleasure of the place was rudely broken by the appearance of a man. In the couple of years they had been visiting the lake, they had never seen another soul and it was a shock to find they were no longer alone. He was walking with purpose towards the farther bank. Leonora's heart quickened with apprehension. She sensed danger, as if a serpent had entered paradise and the certainties of her world had slightly shifted.

'Lottie, swim to me,' she urged, considering the water gave them the greatest protection.

The man shouted something and waved his arm. He looked unkempt, and Leonora turned with Charlotte to swim in the opposite direction towards their clothes, hoping to get there before he could walk round the lake's edge. Suddenly, the sound of a gunshot shattered the silence and birds flew skywards, squawking in alarm. Leonora felt the shock reverberate through her body and with it, anger and fear.

She turned, her eyes blazing, to see the man put down his flint-lock rifle. No longer feeling the cold, she was hot with rage. Her responsibility for Charlotte also weighed heavily as they swam on towards the oak tree while the man walked round to meet them. When Leonora was close to shore, she shouted, her anger still flaring: 'How dare you shoot at us!'

The man was nearer now, and she realised he was in his middle years and dressed in the worsted jacket and breeches of a gamekeeper. 'My lord don't care for trespassers.' His voice was loud and gruff and echoed over the water.

Leonora stood waist high in the lake, sheltering Charlotte behind her. 'So your orders are to shoot before asking any questions?'

'You ignored my shout. Discharged me trusty over yer heads to get yer attention.' The man seemed on the defensive.

Leonora was not certain if he had any authority in the matter. 'No one has been in residence for years. We thought the Earl had died at Corunna.'

'His brother's now the Earl. Escaped from Boney, didn't he? Now he's home, he don't care for company.'

'Well, will you tell your master that he will be troubled neither by Miss Appleby from the Manor nor by Miss Blythe from the Vicarage. Now please be gone so we can get dressed.'

The young women watched him turn on his heel, his gun over his shoulder, to walk back to where he had first emerged from the long tree-lined vista that led to the house. Once he had disappeared, Leonora said, 'I can hardly believe he fired his gun like that. Treating us no better than poachers.' She was still shaken. 'We're neighbours and do no harm. It's shameful!'

Charlotte waded out of the water but Leonora turned and looked longingly at the lake. She felt this secret place had been desecrated, but could not bear to think she would never be here again. 'I'm going to have one last swim to the middle and back. Wait for me under the tree, Lottie, I won't be long.' She set off with strong strokes to where the clouds were reflected on the dark still water. Only then was she ready to turn and swim back to shore.

Dressing in haste, Leonora and Charlotte headed to the fringing woodland and clambered back over the wall. They walked the hundred yards along the lane to the Manor, carrying their wet canvas shoes in their hands and keen to put on dry clothes again. Leonora struggled with a combination of outrage and sorrow that something she loved had been spoiled and snatched away. Emotion made her stride out, and Charlotte picked up her skirts so she could catch up with her friend. 'He seemed a giant of a man; do you think he would have aimed directly at us?'

'No, he wouldn't have shot us.' Leonora was reassuring but her own calm was fractured.

'But he has the power to stop us swimming in the lake?' Charlotte was puzzled.

'I'm not sure he was telling the truth about the Earl's return. I'd heard from Reverend Mildmay that the younger Rokeby brother had been killed too, or at least so badly wounded he could not survive. Nobody in Hasterleigh knew anything about this Rokeby heir, or even whether he lived.'

'Well, it seems he's back.'

In the next few days, the weather turned wet and stormy, and Leonora started to pack her books and treasures into a collection of old trunks which had been brought down from the attics. In his letter, Mr Lockwood had suggested that she could live in the Lodge, a smaller house on what was now his land, until she married and set up her own establishment. She began to wrap the portrait of her mother, who had died at the age of twenty-seven – Leonora's age now – and gazed into the blue eyes, large and full of sparkling life. It saddened her to think how little she knew of her, how little she remembered. There were other people's words: *Oh, what a beauty Mrs Appleby was!* and then often in an aside, how her young daughter looked more like her father, with her hazel eyes and russet-coloured hair. Leonora was denied even the feeling of connection in knowing she shared her mother's character and looks. Instead, her mother remained this angelic blue-eyed figure in memory, unknowable, unreachable. A pang clutched at Leonora's heart. How altered her world would have been if her mother had lived, and how livelier the Manor with perhaps a brother or sister too to rattle around its empty rooms, playing hide-and-seek.

She sat on her bed, pensive as she finished wrapping the portrait; if her own Captain Worth had not been killed two years before at Fuengirola then she would be married by now, perhaps with her own family, and the loss of this house would matter less.

There was a knock at the door and Charlotte appeared. 'Can I come in?' Her bright eyes alighted on the half-wrapped painting. 'I love that portrait of your mother. You are lucky to understand just where you've come from.' She sat heavily on the bed beside Leonora.

'I wish she were still alive. She died before I really knew her. When she was still just Mama.'

'But at least you have a memory of family, and knowledge of where you belong on your ancestral tree. I feel like a piece of this-tledown blown by the wind, with no sense of what I am or from where I've come.'

Leonora stood up. 'Enough gloomy talk. We are both young.' When Charlotte laughed, she continued: 'Well, *you* at least are young; I am a spinster of this parish at twenty-seven, but I have my music, I have you, and Nanny P, and the rest of the village to care about.'

'Oh, Leonora. What a difference it would have made if you had a brother to inherit, then you could have stayed and life would have continued in contentment.'

Leonora caught sight of herself in the looking glass and was shocked at how doleful she appeared. Her hands flew to her cheeks. She was not conventionally beautiful despite the attractive symmetry of her features. She had fine skin and waves of auburn hair that had made Captain Worth call her his wild Irish beauty, but now he was gone and her radiance with him, would she only ever be the unremarkable daughter of a tragic and beautiful mother?

Charlotte reached out to touch her arm. 'Is anything the matter?'

Leonora straightened her back and forced a smile. This was not how she liked to think of herself at all. She was proud of her brave approach to life and optimistic turn of mind. 'We have our health, good looks and warm hearts, there is no reason for either of us to be downcast.' But she still felt in the shadow of a dream she'd had the previous night when she had heard her Captain's voice calling *Leonora! Leonora!* She had woken suddenly, with a sob, knowing she would never see William Worth's smiling eyes again, or hear that soft Irish brogue call her name.

Charlotte returned to the Vicarage through the garden and Leonora went in search of her old nursemaid, Peg Priddy, whose calm, philosophic approach to life was soothing to every soul she encountered. She found her in the kitchen, a floury apron round her ample waist, her sleeves rolled up to her elbows, kneading pastry in a large earthenware bowl. 'Nanny P! I thought you'd be quilting in the morning room, but here you are taking over Cook's work.' She laughed.

At the sound of Leonora's voice, Mrs Priddy turned her rosy face to her. She was in her fifties, with a comfortable bosom that was too exuberant for unstructured modern fashions, so she favoured the more upholstered style of her youth. 'Oh, Nora my love, I'm making an apple pie. Cook's run off her trotters preparing dishes for Mr Lockwood tomorrow.'

Leonora hugged her.

'Don't get too close, my dear, I don't want flour on your pretty gown.'

Subsiding onto a kitchen chair, Leonora asked, 'So what can I do to help?'

She looked up to see Mrs Priddy's blue eyes fixed on her face. Nothing much missed her regard but she did not choose to query

Leonora's subdued demeanour. 'If you could collect some more windfalls from the orchard, that would save me the trouble. After this bad weather, there'll be drifts of apples in the grass. And bring me what blackberries you can find.'

'Of course. I'll be back in a minute for a basket.' Leonora ran upstairs to collect her walking boots and threw on her workaday pelisse of green linen with a hood, should the heavens decide to open once more. She whisked into the kitchen and collected a basket from the cupboard.

'Select the blush Bramleys if you can. They're the best for cooking,' Nanny Priddy called after Leonora who headed down the flagged kitchen corridor to the back door.

* * *

The Manor orchard was famous in the neighbourhood for the variety of apples, cherries and pears that flourished on its favourable site within old stone walls on the edge of a south-facing escarpment. It was a long-standing tradition inaugurated by Leonora's great-grandfather that everyone in the village could help themselves to the windfalls and, for as long as anyone could remember, the farmer at Manor Farm grazed his sheep under the trees to keep the grass cropped close.

The storms had indeed brought down swathes of apples, and Leonora collected all the big Bramleys which had not been half-gnawed by sheep or mice, or hollowed out by slugs. Just being in the orchard, with the blackbirds singing and the bees busy in the foxgloves and clover, never failed to lift her spirits. There were fat blackberries too and she made a makeshift container in the basket with dock leaves. With a lightened heart, Leonora began her short walk home, the basket heavy against her hip.

She was concentrating on avoiding the mud when she heard

the rattle of a coach being driven too fast for the rutted road. She glanced behind her and a smart black carriage pulled by a team of four black horses flashed past, straight through an enormous puddle, splattering sludge up her pelisse. 'Oh no!' she cried, watching with dismay the trails of mud dripping down her skirts. She looked up to see that the chaise had been brought to an abrupt halt, the horses whinnying and stamping, their breaths like puffs of smoke.

Walking alongside the carriage, Leonora saw the blind at the window roll up and found herself staring into the face of an enormous hairy hound. She stepped back with a gasp. A man's voice drawled from the dim interior. 'No need to be frightened, you know, Achille is only of danger if you're a wolf.'

Leonora was indignant. 'I'm not frightened of him. Only surprised!'

The voice continued with an amused languor. 'Tell me, Miss Green-Coat, do you live in the village?'

Leonora was astonished by the lack of an apology for the muddied state of her clothes. She gazed past the hound and into the interior where a man slouched in the farther seat, his curly-brimmed hat pulled low on his brow and a black patch over his left eye. Her chin went up and she answered in a crisp voice, 'I do. And my name is Leonora Appleby.'

With a supercilious air he replied, 'Well, Miss Appleby, can you tell me if there is anyone in the vicinity who can tune a piano-forte?'

She was taken aback by the request. Tuning a piano-forte was a complicated procedure, but she had learnt to do it in order to keep her own instrument in the best condition for playing.

'Yes. *I* can.' Her voice was wary.

The passenger was obviously disconcerted by this piece of

news as he sat up. 'You? It's not a harpsichord I need tuning, it's a piano-forte.'

Irritated by his superior air, Leonora was gratified to be able to tell him, 'Yes, I do know the difference. I was taught how to tune my Broadwood by one of the Broadwood sons, when I first bought the instrument.'

'By Jove, you were, were you? And where is this fancy beast kept?' He had forgotten some of his languor as he leant forward. She saw his face for the first time and had to suppress an instinctive recoil. The black leather patch covered part of a livid scar that ran from his temple to the edge of his lip. His one visible eye glittered almost black in a haggard handsome face.

Without any change in her manner or voice, Leonora said, 'I live at the Manor for a few more days and then I move with my piano-forte to Hasterleigh Lodge.'

The realisation that she was not just a village girl, despite her homely clothes and basket of apples, seemed to pique the stranger's interest. 'Well, I'm Rokeby. If you could see your way to tuning my piano-forte, I would be gratified,' he said stiffly, as if unwilling to be beholden to anyone. With the sound of his name, Leonora knew that the gamekeeper was right. The Earl had indeed returned. A ripple of excitement and alarm shivered through her veins; what difference would this make to the predictable pace of village life? His gaze alighted on her blackberry-stained fingers and she slipped them into the pockets of her pelisse.

Disconcerted at appearing such a country maid, Leonora nevertheless met his sardonic expression with a frank, unembarrassed face. She was used to being Queen Bee in Hasterleigh and was not going to be intimidated. 'It might take me a long afternoon. When do you need it to be tuned?'

'Tomorrow?' He seemed impatient.

'The heir to my father's estate is due tomorrow. But I could manage the following day?'

'I'm on my way to a friend's estate. I will be absent for a few days but my factotum, Stowe, will show you where the instrument is. Would two of the clock suit you?'

Leonora nodded and picked up her basket, which seemed to have grown heavier. Rokeby was about to rap on the roof of the carriage to tell his coachman to drive on when he turned to catch her eye again. 'That mud, was it my doing?' He gestured to the drying streaks splashed up her skirts.

'You were going rather fast, my lord, and a wheel hit a rut in the lane.'

A sudden smile broke his austere countenance and he tipped his hat. 'My apologies, Miss Appleby. Perhaps I should be more careful in future.' And with that the horses sprang forward, the blind went down and he was gone.

* * *

The following dawn was overcast and had the chill of autumn. Leonora had not slept well, troubled by the day ahead which marked the fissure in her life when her childhood home would be hers no longer and a new, less carefree, stage would begin. Mr Lockwood was expected by the afternoon. He was travelling some thirty miles from Mayfair, which should take the best part of the day. Cook and Nanny P were busy in the kitchens and Jack Clegg, their general manservant, was preparing the dining room for the evening meal. Daniel, the gardener, had brought in an armful of late-blooming roses, Michaelmas daisies and some rare pink Mexican dahlias, the tubers of which her mother had managed to charm from the head gardener of the royal estate at Kew.

Leonora decided to arrange the flowers herself for a large vase on the dining room table and one for the hall. She walked quickly into the garden to collect some more greenery to bulk the arrangements out. Busy cutting ferns in the boggy garden by the stream, she was hailed by Charlotte who swung through the gate from the adjoining Vicarage garden.

The girl's sweet face was downcast. Leonora straightened up from the fernery and joined her as she walked towards the Manor, asking, 'Why so dismal?'

Charlotte paused to look up at the house and said, 'I can't bear to think of you no longer living here. It's so encouraging to know you're just a garden away.'

'The Lodge is only a few hundred paces farther. You'll still be able to visit whenever you like.' Leonora smiled at the young woman. She had known her all her life from when she herself was eight, and had been caught up in the excitement as the news flared round the village that a foundling had been left on the Vicarage steps. Leonora's mother had died the previous year, leaving her alone with a distant father who immured himself in his library; the miraculous advent of this baby was somehow connected in her own childish imagination with a longing for a sister.

The unknown baby also brought a different dream of family to Reverend Mildmay and his wife Sarah. They had not been blessed with children and were long reconciled to their state, but when this newborn baby was delivered to their door, it seemed to have been by the Divine stork itself.

Charlotte Blythe was her name, given her by an unseen hand who had pinned it on a card to her swaddling cloth. Now, at eighteen, Leonora thought her as pretty as a picture. The two young women stood in the Manor gardens, both with their different thoughts. Charlotte was disconsolate, gazing back at the house. 'I hope the new heir will not change it. It's perfect as it is.'

Leonora took her arm and led her to a stone seat in the shade of an old yew tree. 'Lottie, I've been wondering if Mama Mildmay has mentioned presenting you for a Season in London?'

Charlotte looked surprised and not a little alarmed by the change in conversation. 'No. I don't think I have the breeding or they the funds for such a thing. They're only my foster parents, after all.' She grasped her friend's hand. 'You haven't been presented, Leonora, and you don't mind, do you?'

'Well, when I was your age my father was unwell and I could not leave him. I was also going to marry Captain Worth, don't forget. But then he was killed.' The baldness of those words and what they meant never failed to catch her breath. How could someone so young and full of life be snuffed out? Leonora sighed. 'So I am too old now for such thoughts.'

'You seem happy enough.'

'Oh, I am content. Happiness can be found for a while, at least if you venture everything, but I've come to consider contentment as the greater art. I have my music, and Nanny P, and you, and others in the village as friends.' She took her hand. 'But for you, so young, I'd hope a chance of a wider life, to marry and have your own family. And there is nowhere with more choice of fine young men than London in the Season.'

Charlotte had turned to look Leonora in the eye. 'I know the Captain was cruelly taken from you, but you can't mean you are resigned to not marrying?'

'I have enjoyed helping to manage the Manor estate all these years since my father's death. It is the loss of that that pains me more.'

Charlotte's face turned mischievous. 'Reverend Mildmay's new curate is looking for a wife. You know he's the son of Sir Roderick Fopling.'

Leonora gave a shout of laughter. 'Lottie, you can't be serious!

The best that can be said for Richard Fopling is that he is as unalike his sporting papa as anyone could be!'

'Oh, I know. What a bore Sir Roderick is. Always in his hunting clothes, mud-splattered and braying about his prowess in the field. He has no other talk!' Charlotte's face had fallen at the memory of how many meals she had sat through at the Vicarage as Sir Roderick talked at headache-inducing volume of his latest triumphs.

Their heads touched as they laughed. Leonora stood up. 'Come, I have to get on with the flower arrangements. You are joining us tonight at six, are you not?' She picked up her basket of ferns and some trailing ivy and they headed back to the house.

'Yes, it's very kind of you to include the Reverend and Mama Mildmay. And Curate Fopling too.'

'Well, I thought it useful for everyone to get to know the new owner of the Manor and for him to meet his neighbours.'

'I hope Nanny P will also be there.' Charlotte was handing Leonora the best pieces of trailing ivy to finish off the arrangement.

Leonora was firm in her response. 'She's the closest I have to a mama, and I don't care a jot if Mr Lockwood objects to sitting down with my old nurse.'

Charlotte recalled what she had wished to tell her friend. With an animated voice she said, 'Oh, the latest gossip! Everything comes to the Vicarage you know. The Earl of Rokeby has been seen in his black chaise. Well, they *think* it's him. The blind is always down but he has this great black-eyed dog which sticks its head out to survey the world and frighten the children.'

Leonora had begun to put the flowers into the vases when she looked up. 'Oh, I've actually spoken to him.'

'What? You should have told me! What's he like?'

'Well, he looks as if he's been very damaged by the war. He has an eye patch.'

'No! Did he say anything to you?' Charlotte was immediately intrigued.

'His coach was going so fast in Orchard Lane it splattered me with more mud than even the young pigs manage when they escape to the orchard. He didn't seem in the least concerned.'

'How inconsiderate! Surely he apologised?'

'He was more concerned to ask me if I knew of a piano-forte tuner.'

'You didn't offer to tune his, did you?' Charlotte's eyes were round with astonishment.

'Actually, I did. But don't trouble yourself, Lottie. I'll take Nanny P as a chaperone. Anyway, the Earl will still be away.'

'But it's complicated to do. I've watched you with yours. It'll take you all day.'

'I so like piano-fortes. They have different characters and I'm happy to get to know a new one.'

* * *

The evening did not get off to a good start. The Reverend and Mrs Mildmay arrived early, hurried there by Charlotte who wanted to help her friend. She was sensitive to the fact that Leonora, without the benefit of parent, spouse or sibling, was due to entertain the assembled guests and this unknown interloper who would claim her home and everything she had known. Curate Fopling was delayed, having been sent by the Reverend to administer spiritual comfort to a parishioner crushed by a cow. The hostess too was late and still dressing so Mrs Priddy, in her best navy brocade gown, showed them into the drawing room with the windows facing the garden, and offered refreshments. Mr Lockwood, the unknown heir, had been due in the afternoon but was yet to arrive.

Leonora hurried into her best gown of cornflower-blue silk, embellished by herself with tiny cream silk roses round the neck and hem. Milly was the general housemaid but could come to her aid as a lady's maid when needed, to lace or button clothes and lend a hand with Leonora's luxuriant hair. In the country, Leonora felt she did not have to concern herself with high sartorial standards, fortunate indeed given her natural character and lack of sophisticated help to call on.

She dashed down the stairs just as Richard Fopling was being shown into the house. He was a tall man like his father, but where Sir Roderick was broad, red-faced and blustery, his curate son was willowy and pale; where the father had a booming voice full of opinion, his son was soft-spoken and poetic in his sensibilities. He looked up, surprised, as Leonora, a vision in blue, welcomed him, a trifle breathless in her haste.

'Mr Fopling, I'm glad you have managed to join us.'

'So am I, Miss Appleby. My apologies for my lateness.' They walked into the drawing room where the Reverend and Mrs Mildmay stood looking out on the garden and Charlotte tinkled on the piano-forte in the middle of the room.

'I do apologise for not being here to welcome you.' Leonora took Sarah Mildmay's hand. The Mildmays were in their middle years, both shorter and plainer than Charlotte, the beauty who now towered over them with her own slender grace. Mrs Mildmay liked to say it was as if a pair of mallards had raised a swan and as she spoke, her genial face twinkled with gratitude – as if she still did not believe her good fortune.

Charlotte stood up and walked across from the piano-forte. 'Oh, Leonora, you look very well!' she said, beaming with admiration. Leonora Appleby was striking with her large expressive eyes, flecked it seemed with gold, and her lively face, full of intelligence and humour. 'Your hair looks different. How have you arranged it?'

Leonora laughed and then dropped her voice. 'Oh, it's probably still stiffened with pondweed from our swim.'

They both looked across at Mr Fopling in conversation with Nanny P who had poured him some whisky to fortify him. Mrs Priddy knew everyone in the village, was called Nanny P or Mrs P by most, and was indulgent of them all. The bad boys were merely expressing their animal spirits and needed some useful employment; she was not shy of asking them to clean the village pond of blanket weed, or collect the windfalls from the orchard and offer them to the elderly. Sulky girls she took under her wing and taught to quilt or collect wildflowers from the verges to press and set in sketchbooks. The adults whom she had known as children accepted that her opinion carried authority. In her small world, she reigned supreme.

With the continued absence of the heir, Leonora visited the kitchen to soothe Cook who was growing concerned for her *pièce de résistance*, a roast crown of beef. This she withdrew from the enormous oven and wrapped in cloths to keep warm. The fish soup would not spoil, pulled to one side on the range, and the celery, cauliflower and spinach from the walled garden were all washed and chopped and in their pots, ready to be boiled when Cook was alerted that the last guest had arrived.

As she dashed back up the kitchen stairs, Leonora heard the crunch of wheels on the cobbled drive and walked quickly into the hall to open the door herself. A vision of fashionable tailoring emerged from the smart blue coach, but as George Lockwood straightened up, she was amazed to see just how tall and broad he was. His large face and rosy cheeks would have looked more at home above a good, worsted jacket and buckskin breeches, but he was dressed in a close-fitting coat of finest inky-blue broadcloth and dark pantaloons with mirror-bright hessian boots. His expression was guarded as he walked into the porch.

Leonora was disconcerted by Mr Lockwood's dandy dress, in incongruous contrast with his broad bluff face and ox-like physique. Such finely accoutred metropolitan men were rare and intriguing sights in the vicinity of Hasterleigh. She came forward to greet him. 'Mr Lockwood, welcome to the Manor. I am Leonora Appleby.'

It was her visitor's turn to look disconcerted. 'Why, Miss Appleby! We are distantly related, are we not?' He took her hand and bowed. 'My apologies for being later than I hoped.'

She smiled. 'I'll ask Milly to show you to your room. Your valet can fit in with my servants.' A young man had struggled in with a smart leather trunk and Leonora called for Jack Clegg to help him transport it up the stairs. Milly led the way to the main guest bedroom at the back of the house.

When Leonora finally re-entered the drawing room, everyone turned curious faces to meet hers. Charlotte's question was on everyone's mind. 'Well, what's Mr Lockwood like?'

'He's very well-dressed.' Then with a mischievous laugh, she added, 'And he's enormous! The tallest, broadest man I've ever seen.'

Charlotte's eyes were wide. 'Even taller than that gamekeeper at the Rokeby estate?'

'Yes, by a good measure.'

Mrs Mildmay gasped and took Charlotte's arm. 'My dear, when were you ever in the way of Diggory Shrubb? He only ever concerns himself with poachers.'

The young woman met Leonora's eyes before responding airily, 'Oh, Mama Mildmay, Leonora and I sometimes cut through the park at the Abbey on our walks.'

'Well, my dear, no longer can you wander at will. The new Earl is back from the wars and not in a cheery mood, it would seem.'

'He's already asked Leonora to tune his piano-forte,' Charlotte said with a giggle.

Mrs Mildmay grasped her arm again and in a hushed voice exclaimed, 'No young woman is safe in Rokeby Abbey! The parties his father used to have! His sons were exposed to them too. Carriages full of disreputables would arrive from London. The profligacy went on for days. You would not have believed the servants' tales!'

Leonora intervened. 'Do not fear, the new Earl seems to be far from sociable. In fact, he will be absent all the while I am there.' With this, she seemed to soothe some of Sarah Mildmay's anxieties.

At the sight of George Lockwood in the doorway, Leonora crossed the room to introduce him to the assembled guests, and at last they could process into the dining room where Cook's special meal awaited. Leonora had decided it would be gracious to seat George Lockwood at the head of the table, but he declined. 'This is still your home, Miss Appleby.' He sat instead at her right hand with Mrs Mildmay beside him, and opposite Mr Fopling and Charlotte Blythe. Mrs Priddy and Reverend Mildmay took their places at the foot of the table. Everyone's eyes were on the new heir as he tucked into the beef.

He met their eyes and smiled. 'I think it will interest you all that I won't be taking possession of Hasterleigh Manor in the immediate future. I hope Miss Appleby will remain here at least until the summer.'

Charlotte could not contain her delight. She clapped her hands together. 'Oh, I'm so glad.' She turned to address the hostess with a question in her bright eyes. 'That means things can go on as usual?'

Leonora was more composed at the news and turned to Mr Lockwood with her own question. 'So do you wish me to continue overseeing the estate?'

'I would wish it to carry on as before, with you and your father's bailiff in charge. If that suits you, Miss Appleby?'

She nodded, a small bubble of happiness rising in her chest.

He continued, 'We'll formalise the arrangement while I'm here. You see, I'm busy with my father's estate in Oxfordshire. It's in a sorry state. And my stepfather insists I spend the Season in Town with him.' His face fell.

Mrs Mildmay asked him, her voice full of concern, 'Do you not care for London, sir?'

'I don't enjoy frittering my time with gaming and dancing and would much prefer country life. But first I have to find myself a wife.' George Lockwood gave a rueful smile. His bluff, honest way of speaking made Mrs Mildmay's eyes widen in surprise. He then turned back to Leonora, a certain tightness constraining his features. 'I'm looking forward to seeing over your father's estate. I'm impressed by how productive it appears to be from the figures your bailiff, Fleming, has sent me.' His candid blue eyes gazed into hers and she realised with relief he was not going to be the ogre she had feared.

There were other women around the table coming to similarly favourable conclusions about him. Mrs Priddy was listening to the Reverend's chatter about his parishioners, all of whom she knew or had helped bring into the world, but her attention was half on the top end of the table where her beloved Leonora sat with this new man to enter their world. He was rich and nice-looking enough, big and strong, a perfect country gentleman, but even better husband material.

Mrs Mildmay also approved of a man who was tired of London and preferred the country life. How much she wanted to see her beautiful foster daughter Charlotte happily settled. She looked sideways at George Lockwood. It was not in her nature to aim high, let alone scheme to achieve her ends, but she thought what a perfect son-in-law this man would make. Pity he was quite so tall – she and the Reverend were like pygmies beside him, but Mrs Mildmay was prepared to overlook that handicap given the kindness in his eyes and the largeness of his fortune.

Charlotte too eyed him with interest. She so wanted Leonora to be happy and married with a family of her own, and could not think of a more fairy-tale ending than the heir to the Hasterleigh estate marrying her dearest friend. This would mean she could remain the chatelaine of the house she had grown up in and loved so. She thought Mr Lockwood a fine figure of a man and liked his amused eyes, deciding he would most likely treat Leonora well.

But Leonora was watching Charlotte as she listened with rapt attention to their guest relating a story about his favourite hunting dog. Her eyes were sparkling with amusement at the story's denouement. Would it concern Mr Lockwood, Leonora wondered, if someone as beautiful and charming as Charlotte Blythe had unknown parentage? Surely her evident attractions would outweigh any disadvantage of illegitimacy?

George Lockwood, himself the focus of so much scrutiny and speculation, seemed unaware of the stir his presence created. He had been schooled by his stepfather to practise *sprezzatura,* the courtier's manner of studied carelessness and effortless superiority, which sat uneasily on his open nature. The tension between the sophisticated dandy he was required to project and the friendly giant he naturally was created a guarded care in his dealings with strangers he was meant to impress. Instead, he focussed on the meal, so appreciated after a tiring day's travel, and was particularly delighted with the quality of the beef he ate with such gusto.

What he'd seen of the house looked modest but handsome enough. He was not one to nit-pick and find fault in unexpected good fortune. And he was pleased to be in the company of two such attractive young women, both of whom were much more interesting and open in their manners than the schoolroom misses he had to court in Town. He liked the lack of airs of these country people and looked forward to the week he had allotted himself to explore his inheritance.

It had been some years since the small rural community of Hasterleigh had enjoyed so much excitement: in this one week they had not only seen the arrival of the new heir of the Manor, but also the unexpected return of the master of the big house, the mysterious new Earl of Rokeby.

When at last Leonora went to bed that night, her mind was restless with possibilities, not focussed on these unexpected arrivals in the neighbourhood, but on the fact that she could remain at the Manor for a few more months and continue to help run the estate alongside her father's bailiff, the redoubtable Ned Fleming.

When she came down to breakfast, Nanny P was already there, her knitting in her lap and a cup of coffee at her elbow. 'Good morning, child. I realise with Mr Lockwood in the house, you need me as chaperone. You know how the village gossips for the want of something better to do.' She looked up, her wise face wreathed in a knowing smile. 'I must say, dear, he seems a good man, and up to the job of running the estate. What do you think?'

'I hope that first impressions don't deceive. I'm just pleased I won't have to move into the Lodge just yet.' She helped herself to some toast and sat down beside the older woman. Leonora loved this room in the morning. Her mother had chosen to have it painted a rose pink and no one had ever wished to change it, despite it being a surprising colour for a dining room. It glowed in the morning sun that spilled through the birch tree in the court-yard, and never failed to lift her spirits.

'I approve of his liking for the country,' Mrs Priddy said mildly, not looking up from her speeding fingers.

Leonora laughed and leant towards her, to say in a confiding low voice, 'I know you well enough to recognise your match-making brain at work. If it's anyone I'd like to see well settled, it's Lottie.'

Nanny P stopped her work and looked up, a troubled expression on her face. 'My dear, you know her unknown parentage makes it more complicated, charming and beautiful as she is.'

Leonora grasped her old nanny's arm. 'Oh, it's so unfair! Why should the child pay for the transgressions of her parents? Charlotte Blythe's character and person are such that any man should be proud to call her his wife!'

'We know that, my dear, but Society is not so forgiving. She will marry, but it's a mistake to aim too high. I fear your Mr Lockwood's cheerful manner and fortune mean he has the choice of any number of well-born heiresses in Town.' Mrs Priddy put down her knitting and turned to face Leonora, her eyes intent. 'But you are a different matter, Nora. You are well-born with a small inheritance of your own. You have beauty and charm and every kind of accomplishment – your father and I made sure of that – and I can think of nothing better than your remaining at the Manor, the property that is rightfully yours.'

'You are incorrigible!' Leonora leant over to kiss her cheek. 'I'm afraid you're going to get a great deal of knitting done. I will need you to chaperone me this afternoon at the Abbey.'

'Oh, I'm looking forward to that. I haven't seen inside that great crumbling house since I went there when the two rapscallion boys were young.'

Leonora's interest was piqued. 'Really, Nanny P, why so?'

'Oh, their poor mama was beside herself. They were out of control, and encouraged to be thus by the old Earl. She felt in need of some advice.'

'No! What did you say?' Leonora was intrigued.

'Well, I just told the Countess they were good boys with an excess of animal spirits.'

'Of course you did! That's what you thought of all the roaring boys in the village. So what did you suggest would put them right?'

'I suggested they needed small jobs around the estate. Charles liked shooting so I thought he could work with Mr Shrubb, the gamekeeper, protecting the habitat for the nesting grouse.'

'What was the younger brother like?' Leonora remembered her abrupt meeting on the road with the arrogant Earl.

'He was quite different. He loved dogs and was very musical. Of course his father, the veriest rake if ever there was one, didn't appreciate his son playing the piano-forte, like a schoolroom miss, he used to say.'

'Well it's that very instrument the Earl wants tuned this afternoon. But he won't be there.'

'It may be more relaxed if he isn't,' Nanny P said in a way which made Leonora look at her again, wondering what it was she knew. Before she could ask, George Lockwood came into the room in search of breakfast.

Leonora sprang to her feet. 'Good morning, Mr Lockwood. I hope you slept well?' She was interested to see him dressed in his country clothes and looking so much more at home. His green broadcloth jacket was generously fitted around his broad shoulders and his buckskin breeches were a soft buttery yellow, but it was clear they were as finely tailored as the immaculate Town clothes he had arrived in.

He bowed to both women. 'I slept as in the arms of Morpheus. Thank you for giving me such a comfortable room.'

Mrs Priddy poured out some coffee for him and Leonora gestured to the cold ham and the bread. 'There's ale if you prefer. And sweet pastries on that plate by the window.'

They all sat down again at the table and George Lockwood extracted from his pocket a hand-drawn map of the Hasterleigh Estate that he spread between them. In between mouthfuls of bread and ham he pointed to the big hundred-acre field. 'Can I congratulate you, Miss Appleby, for this is a well-resourced estate. I'm intending to bring my father's less well-endowed land back into productivity, but yours has plentiful water. A boon indeed.' His forefinger traced the course of the Hester River that meandered through the Hasterleigh acreage, providing irrigation points for livestock and crops. 'I'm not surprised your arable and pastureland is as fertile as it is.' Mrs Priddy saw Leonora's stance soften under his praise of the estate and her care of it.

Mr Lockwood took another gulp of coffee. 'I am indeed grateful to you for offering to show me over the estate. Have you any free time today?' George Lockwood's frank face turned to Leonora, his blue eyes alight with anticipation. Nanny P had returned to her knitting but was alert to the conversation and change in the atmosphere.

'Yes, I can manage a couple of hours this morning but I'm busy later. My bailiff Ned Fleming will come with us and can accompany you in the afternoon.' She stood up and took her leave of him and Mrs Priddy. 'I can meet you here in twenty minutes, if that suits.'

* * *

As Leonora, Ned Fleming and Mr Lockwood strode down towards the woodland that fringed the western border of the Manor lands, George Lockwood threw back his head and inhaled the crisp clean air. 'If I never returned to London, I would be a happy man.'

Leonora looked across at him with some puzzlement. 'Why do you feel compelled to go then, sir?'

'I'm only there for the Season. In part to please my stepfather, Beau Beacham.'

Even Leonora in her country fastness had heard of the Beau. He was well known as a dandy and man about Town, striking for his elegance, charm and fast way of life. 'He married my mother when she was widowed, and was kind enough to adopt me before she herself died.' He looked across at her with a rueful smile. 'He has a high opinion of his place in Society and expects me to occupy a similarly elevated position, especially to find myself a suitably rich and noble wife to match his social pretensions. Then I'll be free of my obligations.'

Leonora felt a prickle of unease at being reminded of the gulf between the simple country life she and Charlotte enjoyed in Hasterleigh and the expectations and prejudices of London's *haut ton*. How foolish to even countenance the thought that Mr Lockwood and his family would consider her young friend as a suitable match.

They walked on through the lower field ready for the plough, Mr Fleming at a discreet distance. Mr Lockwood bent to crumble the soil between his fingers as he turned to the bailiff. 'This is good loamy soil?'

'Yessir, over a brashy clay.' Ned Fleming's eyes met Leonora's; he appeared pleased that this fancy Town gentleman seemed to not mind getting his hands dirty.

The new owner of the Manor estate then gestured to the neglected field on the other side of the drystone wall. 'Whose land abuts ours?'

Fleming replied, 'Oh that's the Rokeby Estate, sir. The Earl was killed fighting for Lord Wellington in Spain. It's been fallow ever since he left.'

'It's in a sorry state. Those tares and thistles migrate into our domain, I suspect?' He narrowed his eyes as he surveyed the distant fields. 'It would be easiest to traverse the Manor lands on horseback.' George Lockwood turned to Leonora with a warm smile. 'Do you have a mount big enough to carry me?'

Leonora was disconcerted and felt her cheeks grow warmer. It was considered impertinent to draw attention to someone's physical size, but he seemed to be quite unembarrassed and she thought she should be as frank. 'I'm afraid we don't. But our sporting neighbour, Sir Roderick Fopling, runs a whole stable of hunters. I'm sure he'd be happy to lend you one of his.'

'That would be very kind, Miss Appleby. Perhaps we could make a visit this afternoon?' He met her eyes with an enthusiastic gleam.

'I have a previous engagement so will not be able to accompany you, I'm afraid.' Her face brightened with a happy thought. 'But the Foplings are well known to Miss Blythe and her family, the vicar and his wife. I'm sure Charlotte Blythe would introduce you. It would be perfectly appropriate if Mr Fleming accompanied you both.'

The men set off to return to the Manor while Leonora headed for the Vicarage to call on Charlotte. The house had all the charm of its occupants. An old, honeyed-stone building over three floors, with symmetrical latticed windows placed three on each side of a porticoed front door. Late roses of golden yellow still bloomed on the trellis round the door and bees were busy in the red and purple hollyhocks, taller than Leonora. As she walked up the path, Charlotte opened the door, her face bright with the excitement of the previous night. 'I'm so glad it's you! Come in.'

'I can't stay. I have to get ready to go to Rokeby Abbey. But

Lottie, would you mind introducing Mr Lockwood to Sir Roderick Fopling? I hope he'll be able to borrow one of his hunters. He's too big for ours.'

'Of course I will. But what about last night?' Charlotte could not suppress her curiosity. 'What do you think of him?'

'I am pleasantly surprised that he seems to be such a countryman, despite his dandyish appearance.'

'Oh, no! You couldn't call him a dandy! He's just finely dressed, surely? But what about his character?'

'He seems perfectly amiable and I hope will be an excellent custodian of our beloved Manor estate.'

Charlotte was impatient with Leonora's prevarication. 'Of course he will! But did you like him?'

Leonora laughed. 'He seems well enough, but it's too soon to say if I like him. More to the point, do you?'

'Of course I like him. I think him really fine. He fills a room! Rarely do we have the pleasure of any personable young man in our midst.'

'This is why I think you should at least have a partial Season in Town to meet some other young men and realise the world is larger than Hasterleigh, however lovely it is here.' Leonora turned to go. 'Thank you, Lottie, for taking my place this afternoon. I think if you can charm a good hunter out of Sir Roderick, then Mr Lockwood will be happy to set off on his tour of the estate with our bailiff.'

She ran from the Vicarage, aware that she had to hurry if she was going to be punctual on her first visit to Rokeby Abbey.

2

MISS BLYTHE'S WORLD SHIFTS ON ITS AXIS

As Leonora ran into the Manor, she heard the church clock strike once and immediately went in search of Mrs Priddy. The older woman was busy pickling walnuts in the kitchen. She wiped her hands on her apron and looked up with a lively eye. 'Nora dearest, I do wish you would change your gown and wear something more charming. I don't like to see you hiding your light under such dowdy apparel.'

'Oh Nanny P, it's not a social call; the only person we will see is Stowe. I'm there to tune the piano-forte, that's all.' Leonora went to collect her case of tuning instruments, changed her shoes, and found a capacious apron to protect her dress from the dust from the internal stringing of such an instrument. She threw her old green pelisse over the offending plain blue dimity and with Mrs Priddy beside her, walked round to the stables. 'I thought it easier if we went in the gig. It's a bit far for you to walk, Nanny P,' she said, looking down fondly at the small bustling figure by her side.

Martin, the groom, was busy brushing mud from the fetlock of her grey mare when Leonora asked him to harness up Clover, their hack. She handed her elderly nanny onto the seat who then patted the wood beside her. 'Lucky it's not far. For someone as slender as you, my love, this is a hard seat to sit on for long. Luckily, I have natural cushioning.'

Leonora climbed into the gig, picked up the reins and they trotted out of the stable yard and onto the lane that led to Rokeby Abbey. She had only ever trespassed in the grounds and glimpsed the buildings through the encroaching woods, but had never actually approached the house from the main entrance. The drive passed through an avenue of overgrown chestnut trees, their lower branches bending to the ground and making it difficult to navigate. As they followed the sweeping bend, the mansion was slowly revealed to them. Leonora could not suppress a gasp. The ancient Abbey ruins loomed over the house, roofless, its great gothic windows empty of glass, ivy falling in curtains down its walls. The desolate atmosphere was intensified by a roost of ravens which had exploded into the sky, screaming their warning to a magnificent osprey circling in the warm air currents overhead.

Mrs Priddy felt Leonora flinch and put a hand on her knee. 'It's always had a rather forbidding aspect, but it's looking more derelict than I recall.'

Leonora drove the horse past the ruins to draw up outside the great house, built against the west wall of the old Abbey. The main wing was Elizabethan with three enormous windows adding elegance to the central section, the many panes of glass glittering like marcasite in the late summer sun. Ancient stone cloisters united the ruined Abbey with its tower at the farther end, and the stone portico round the front door to the house was distinguished by an old yew tree.

Leonora jumped down and walked around to help Mrs Priddy to the ground. Clover stood patiently while her mistress looped the reins over a rusty hook in the wall. 'I'll ask if the Rokeby groom can take her to the stables, as we'll be some time. You have your knitting, haven't you?' She pealed the doorbell and both women listened while it echoed through the house.

Eventually they heard footsteps and the locks drawn on the great oak door. It swung open slowly and an elderly man, his face the colour of parchment, stood uncertainly on the threshold. Mrs Priddy walked forward with a friendly greeting, 'Sam! You remember me? Peg Priddy.'

'Of course I do, Mrs P. I remember you coming here when the Countess was alive. In better days.' His face dropped further.

Leonora gave him a friendly smile. 'Good afternoon, Stowe. I'm Leonora Appleby. The Earl asked me to tune the piano-forte.'

The old man nodded and turned to lead them towards the back of the house, complaining to Nanny P about the state of the property, too long empty. Leonora, following in their wake and full of curiosity, was free to look around. The hallway was dark and cheerless, the ancient oak staircase rising in stately flights to the even dimmer recesses of the upper floors. Dried leaves had blown in and collected in small dusty piles.

All doors to other rooms were closed, which added to the sense of gloom and decay. How she longed to see what lay beyond those mahogany defences. Rokeby Abbey was so much grander than the Manor but lacked the colour, light and life of her own childhood home. And yet Leonora sensed this was a house just waiting to have windows and doors flung open, to be loved again.

She hurried to catch up with Stowe and Nanny P, just in time to see the farthest door opened into a drawing room filled with light. It ran along the back of the house and despite its vast size, seemed a more welcoming space. Five tall windows drew the eye to the overgrown garden with the distant glitter of the lake. Her lake. There were sofas on either side of a great ecclesiastical stone fireplace and the piano-forte stood at the far side in an alcove in the window.

Stowe walked with them towards it and lifted the lid, securing it open with its rosewood prop. A fire burned in the fireplace, which Nanny P eyed with gratitude.

'Thank you, Stowe,' Leonora said, placing her case of tuning instruments on the piano stool.

'May you take some tea?' His old eyes were looking distinctly more cheerful at the advent of these two ladies in his care.

Leonora answered, 'Thank you. I'm afraid tuning is a time-consuming business; we'll be here for some time.'

'You take as long as you need, Miss Appleby. It's good to have some life in the house.'

Leonora was inspecting the instrument when the retainer returned. He placed a silver tray with teapot, bowls and some small pastries on the table by Nanny P then caught Leonora's eye. 'His lordship was always keen on playing music. While he was a prisoner in France he found an old instrument there; kept 'im sane, he says.' As he turned away, he muttered, 'Don't know 'bout that – he's not what he was.'

With that enigmatic statement, he left the room, pulling the door to, but not quite catching it on the latch. Leonora wondered if he hoped to hear some of the music she would play, for nothing brought a house to life more quickly than the sound of a piano-forte echoing through empty rooms. Perhaps the silence, like the sombre light, lay as heavily on the servants as on visitors?

Mrs Priddy poured out the tea. 'Come, my dear, have some refreshment before you begin.' She nibbled on one of the pastries and wrinkled her nose. 'This is at least three days old. It's more like a rock cake,' she grumbled, but continued to eat.

'What did Stowe mean? The new Earl is not as he was?'

'Well, I haven't seen him since he's returned from the war but when I knew the Rokeby boys, they were thick as thieves, though so different in character. Perhaps his brother's death and the horrors of war have altered him.' Nanny P picked up another pastry and was lost in her own memories.

Leonora put on her apron. The inside of the instrument was filled with dead insects and wood dust, and Leonora picked up her small brush and whisked the debris from the strings, then sat down to play to see just how out of tune it had become. By the dereliction in the main house, she suspected it had not been played for many years.

She began Clementi's Sonatina in C major and winced as certain notes were so out of key that the jarring sound was almost painful. Even Nanny P looked up, an expression on her face like she had chewed on a piece of sourest lemon. 'My dear! What a jingling jangle. I hope it won't prove too difficult to put right.' She had settled deep into the sofa with her knitting in her lap. Leonora had asked what she was making but had only received the answer, 'a christening shawl'. Nanny P was using the finest gossamer thread and it seemed such a labour of love that any child would be full-grown by the time it was finished.

Starting on the central octave, Leonora picked up her rubber wedge and slipped it under the second string of middle C to damp off its sound while she worked on tuning the first. Her tuning wrench fitted over the wrest pin and as she struck the tuning fork, the thin sound filled the room. Playing the ivory key with her left hand, she turned the wrench with care until the two sounds aligned. In this way she worked from middle C to lower C and began to move down into the bass notes.

The occasional comments from Nanny P had ceased and Leonora glanced across to see her asleep in the glow of the firelight. Stowe brought in a candelabra ready for Leonora to light with a taper from the fire as the day began to fade, and put another couple of logs in the grate to keep the flames high.

Leonora was tired and hungry and thinking she might leave the last two higher octaves until another day. She played the Clementi through one last time, pleased that the necessary notes were those she had managed to retune. The music swelled forth and she imagined it echoing through the dusty house beyond. Making music was central to her life, it banished loneliness and filled the spaces in her heart with love. Leonora felt a quickening of excitement as she moved into the lyrical *Andante* section when a shaggy dog's head was laid lightly on her knee. She was so engrossed in the music that this unexpected interloper barely broke her concentration.

Little did she know that a man stood in the shadows by the door, watching. Lost to the music, Leonora played on for a minute or so until the natural break at the end of the *Andante*. From the doorway, her face could only be seen in profile, her skin luminous in the candlelight, her expression rapt as she listened closely for any anomalies in the notes. There was a smudge of dust on her cheek and her homely dress was covered by a plain calico apron. Her chestnut brown hair was piled in an untidy bun on her head, tendrils already escaping, which she brushed impatiently off her brow. The air still seemed to vibrate as the last notes died away.

Leonora paused, about to start the final *Vivace* section, and in that moment of quiet, noticed the dog. She looked up and turned towards the door with a gasp as she saw the Earl standing in the encroaching dusk.

'I'm sorry to have startled you, Miss Appleby.' His voice was quiet and amused. He did not sound in the least sorry as he walked towards her with a marked limp. 'You have wrought some sort of magic on that poor instrument of mine. Thank you. Even Achille seems soothed by the music.' In the flickering light of the candelabra, his face looked leaner, his scar more prominent, his eye patch, sinister. The great wolfhound padded to his side. The Earl's eye glittered as he watched Leonora's almost imperceptible recoil as she saw him fully for the first time. A grim smile twisted his mouth.

'I'm afraid I still have two of the upper octaves to tune, sir, but it's late and I must take Mrs Priddy home.' She nodded towards the sofa and Alistair Rokeby noticed for the first time the elderly figure asleep in the corner, her cap slightly askew.

His expression instantly lightened. 'Oh, how good to see Nanny Priddy again. She was but young when my distracted mother called her in for advice on my brother and me.' He walked towards the fire but seemed reluctant to wake her. Turning back to Leonora, he said, 'But we have all aged. And some have not survived the cruel exigencies of this world.'

Leonora was taken aback at his bleak tone. She sought to reassure him in a small way, saying, 'Mrs Priddy is remarkably well, you will be pleased to know.' She glanced back to meet his gaze. The severity had returned to his face.

He watched her ruffling the fur behind his hound's ears. 'You were playing the Clementi. Before you go, Miss Appleby, could you just let me hear the last section, the *Vivace,* I believe. Music so consoles the spirit, don't you think?'

Leonora was struck by the emotion in his voice. She was about to sit down on the stool again when she was arrested by a thought. 'My lord, I'd like it if *you* would play it. You can then tell me if you approve of my tuning.'

She moved away from the instrument as he looked at her, a question on his face. Then he smiled and took her place at the keyboard and began to play. Leonora watched his face transform, seeming to lose its years of suffering. As his fingers picked out the cascade of notes, his head moved with the music, his eyes closed, his mouth smiling with some fond memory. Abruptly, he stopped in the middle of a cadenza and looked up at her, the spell broken. 'I've forgotten what comes next.'

Leonora moved to stand behind him and leant over to play the next phrase. She was thinking only of the music but being so close to him, could not ignore the fiery energy radiating out to meet hers. She stepped back. Immediately, Lord Rokeby picked the tune up again and his hands continued the sparkling melody to the end. It was then Leonora noticed his damaged right hand and the rough stub where his middle finger should have been. It was shocking to see, and yet it did not impair his ability to play the notes with fluency.

Alistair Rokeby's voice was quiet. 'Thank you, Miss Appleby. The tone is as good as I remember it before I went to war.'

'There are still two more octaves to tune, if you'd like me to complete the task.'

He had sprung to his feet, his gruff, supercilious manner returned. 'I don't wish to trouble you further.' His dog stood tall by his side, its relaxed windswept look a foil to his master's tense demeanour.

'It is no trouble. It's a fine instrument and I enjoy its resonance. It's mellower than mine.' Leonora was not going to be cowed by his off-putting humour. 'I could come for a few hours tomorrow afternoon.'

Mrs Priddy stirred from her sleep and looked up. 'Nora my dear, are you finished?' She then noticed the brooding figure beside her mistress and struggled to her feet, straightening her cap. 'Master Alistair! How you've grown!' She saw his scarred face and for a moment her expression registered shock. Then, walking towards him, she apologised for her presumption of address. 'I mean, of course, Lord Rokeby.' And she dropped a quick curtsey.

His face lit up with a smile as he took her hand. 'You'll always be Nanny Priddy to me, and no doubt I'll always be Master Alistair to you, the wild, harum-scarum boy, despair of his family!'

Peg Priddy twinkled up into his face. She'd always had a soft spot for bad boys and this bad boy just looked all the more disreputable, having returned so altered by the war. With an indulgent chuckle, she said, 'You were just full of energy in need of occupation.'

'I wish you'd persuaded our tutor and Papa of your view. Both thought it wickedness which only the birch could purge.' His face became thunderous again at the memory. 'Not even my brother could save me.' He turned to bid farewell to Leonora. 'Miss Appleby, I am indeed grateful for your skill today. If I can presume on your time further, I'd be pleased if you could finish the task.'

He put out his right hand to her, with a challenging look in his eye. Without hesitation, Leonora placed her own in his mutilated one and he bowed. 'I'm afraid war makes brutes of men,' he murmured. She was disconcerted to see a spasm of pain cross his face. Turning to Mrs Priddy once more, Lord Rokeby offered his arm and led them out of the drawing room, limping slightly and carrying the candelabra to lighten the gloom of the hall. His loping hound followed in his wake.

Stowe appeared at the front door. 'I have asked the groom to bring your visitors' conveyance round from the stables, my lord.'

Lord Rokeby led the two women to the gig. The last rays of the setting sun would allow them just enough light to see their way home. The Earl helped Mrs Priddy up and then offered his hand to Leonora. 'I am in your debt, Miss Appleby. You will let me know a way to recompense you for your time?' He bowed and calling softly for his dog, turned back towards the house. It struck Leonora that Lord Rokeby was tense with the effort of minimising his limp as he strode away.

As she drove the gig towards the drive, she thought of the only thing the Earl could give her of value: permission to swim in his lake again.

* * *

Mrs Priddy had been thoughtful during the short journey home but as they turned into the stable yard at the Manor she said, 'Do you know, my love, something terrible has happened to that boy.'

''Tis cruel indeed the injuries he's suffered.'

'No, I'm not talking about the physical scars; there's something heavy and dark in his spirit. He was such a mischievous and naughty boy, so full of life and laughter. That has gone.'

'He said to me that war makes brutes of men. Is that perhaps what you mean?'

'We cannot imagine what happens to our brave men sent to the Peninsula. So many injured, too many killed. So young, too. And his brother dying in his arms.' Nanny P's voice was quiet with emotion. Leonora knew she was thinking of her own father, killed when she was eighteen, fighting in the American Revolutionary War and left to die on the battlefield at Lexington.

She leant across and squeezed her old nanny's hand. 'I know these experiences are beyond us. But Lord Rokeby has such a forbidding look and manner, he holds himself apart.'

'It was his brother Charles who held himself apart. Very honourable but conscious of his place in the world. I like to remember Master Alistair as the sparky boy he once was. Those boys had a cruel, unforgiving father and their mother, ailing and dying young. It was life's harsh schooling.' Mrs Priddy regained her brusque demeanour and stood up, bringing the bleak conversation to an end. Leonora picked up her skirts, sprang down from the gig and quickly walked round to help her down.

'Could you chaperone me again, tomorrow afternoon? Just for the few hours it'll take me to finish the tuning.'

Mrs Priddy smiled. 'Of course. I can get on with my knitting.'

They entered the Manor just as George Lockwood came stamping through the back door from the stables. He had been in the saddle all afternoon surveying his inheritance, and was dusty and dishevelled. Leonora noticed how comfortable he seemed, his face flushed from exposure to the weather. He came towards her, smiling. 'Miss Appleby, I have had such a capital time. I do commend you for the fine estate. I've so many ideas to improve it.' He called for his valet to remove his boots and turned to her. 'I've asked Miss Blythe to join us for dinner. I hope that is to your liking?'

'It's your house now, Mr Lockwood. You can ask whomsoever you will.' In fact she was always pleased to see Charlotte, but the realities of the passing of ownership to this new heir would continue to jar. She dashed upstairs to change, aware that her clothes appeared old-fashioned and dowdy next to George Lockwood's fine tailoring. Leonora's spirit, usually so optimistic, was unsettled by the sense of some momentous shift in the tectonic structure of her life since she had made the acquaintance of these two previously unknown men.

* * *

Charlotte Blythe arrived for dinner in an excited mood. Her youthful imagination was energised by the possibilities of change. She had enjoyed being the one to introduce George Lockwood to Sir Roderick Fopling, and her love of horses meant she helped too with the selection of a large hunter for him to borrow. Riding her own mare and accompanied by her groom, she had even joined the new heir on his initial exploration of the Manor lands and had been interested in his evolving plans. The thought of her dearest Leonora having to move down the lane to the Lodge seemed less tragic if such an amenable person was to take her place at the Manor. Change was not always to be so deplored, she assured herself.

Charlotte's most consequential news, though, she could not keep to herself for long. As she and Leonora, Mrs Priddy and Mr Lockwood gathered in the drawing room before dinner, she took her friend aside and in a low voice confided, 'Mama and Reverend Mildmay have had a note delivered from Rokeby Abbey. The new Earl has summoned them to an audience the day after tomorrow. Probably just to make their acquaintance, but poor Mama is in a fuss about what she should wear. She doesn't feel up to snuff at all.'

Leonora laughed and patted Charlotte's arm. 'Tell Mrs Mildmay not to trouble herself. From what I've seen, the Abbey is full of spiders, vermin too, no doubt; it's a sorry, neglected sight and Lord Rokeby is almost as unkempt. He's certainly no fashion plate like our own Mr Lockwood.' She gave the younger woman a conspiratorial smile.

Leonora asked George Lockwood to carve the roast chicken while she passed the dishes of braised cabbage, carrots and a plate of pickled cucumbers around the table. The Manor servants were minimal; Jack Clegg was willing to do most things, from opening the front door to visitors to waiting at the table, but it was all effected in an informal way which was considered totally lacking in appropriate style and deference by servants used to working in the great houses of Mayfair. Similarly, while Milly was a general housemaid who helped Leonora dress when necessary, she was not skilled in arranging her hair or embellishing gowns and bonnets. These were skills Leonora had been taught by Nanny P; she was wearing her favourite old yellow muslin with the silk primroses round the neckline and ribbons binding the bottom of the puff sleeves, appliqued by herself during the long winter evenings.

Leonora looked across the table at Charlotte who was attentive to Mrs Priddy, her pretty face inclined towards her as the elderly lady regaled her with tales of her mercy dash to the Abbey when the Rokeby boys were young. Charlotte's family relied on even fewer servants at the Vicarage, and Leonora recognised her blue muslin gown as one they had worked on together in the spring, plaiting cream silk ribbons then sewing them round the neck and hem to provide extra definition to its modest simplicity.

George Lockwood was less immaculate than when he had first arrived and the disarray of his hair and the outdoor colour on his skin suited him. He turned to Leonora and said in a cheerful way, 'I have had such an interesting day. I'm sorry I have to return to Town before the week is out. Wintering at my Oxfordshire estate, you know. All kinds of sporting weekends are booked with my friends.' He put a piece of chicken breast on her plate. 'I intend to move here more permanently after the London Season is over.'

Leonora smiled. 'I thought you were only released from the purgatory of London life once you'd found yourself a suitable wife?'

He let out a bark of laughter. 'That's the plan, or rather my stepfather's plan. Frankly, I don't think I could face a further Season. I'd rather spend my time working out a system of land management at Hasterleigh, new wife or not, than hang about any more London drawing rooms!'

Charlotte Blythe had overheard the end of the conversation. 'You have ideas for a new irrigation system too, using water from the river.' Her face was bright as she looked at him. Then turning to Leonora, she said, 'I suggested Mr Lockwood dam a part of the river to make a swimming lake.'

Leonora frowned at her. She did not care to have her love of swimming bruited to all.

Charlotte realised her unguarded tongue had displeased her friend and coloured, then with deftness, changed the subject. 'When we called on Sir Roderick to borrow a hunter, he was in the most irascible tweak. Poachers had been spotted with their dogs. He was foaming at the mouth, wasn't he, Mr Lockwood?'

'I don't think it was quite that theatrical, but he wasn't in a very welcoming mood, 'tis true.'

'He was yelling for his gamekeeper to dust off and grease the extra snares and mantraps! It's so wrong; people only seek to feed their families.' Charlotte's face was full of outraged feeling.

Leonora turned to George Lockwood. 'It's been a tradition since my grandfather's day that villagers can hunt rabbits for the pot for one day a month in winter on the estate. That way we find they respect the land the rest of the time.'

Her guest had a mouth full of chicken and could merely nod. After a while he said, 'I'm not going to be in a hurry to change any of your family's long-established habits, I assure you.'

The following afternoon, Leonora set off in the gig again with Mrs Priddy beside her. They left the Manor and turned towards the Abbey. Nanny P looked sideways at her and said in her knowing way, 'Nora my dear, how nice to see you spruced up a little. That blue chambray really suits you, makes your eyes look almost green.'

Leonora bridled. 'I haven't gone to any extra trouble. It's only an old day dress.' She encouraged Clover into a fast trot as they bowled along the lane, then into the overgrown drive of Rokeby Abbey. As they rounded the bend, the sprawling building before them looked as forbidding as ever, its north face in shadow, the ruined Abbey looming over the later mansion built beside it. Stowe greeted them at the door and let them through to the drawing room where the piano-forte awaited. Achille trotted towards Leonora to nuzzle her hand, but there was no sight or sound of his master. The dog walked over to Mrs Priddy and flopped down on the sheepskin laid on the Persian carpet in front of the fire, his great head resting on a footstool which seemed to be placed conveniently for this purpose.

Hound and elderly woman fell asleep and Leonora laboured on, tinkling at the higher notes, tightening the strings gradually to bring them into tune with each other and with the other notes in the octaves. Dressed in her calico apron and with her wrench in her hand ready to work on the last two strings, she was bending over the instrument when Achille got to his feet, yawned, stretched, and made his elegant way out of the room. The peaceful atmosphere was disturbed by a distant call and footsteps which echoed in the hall but did not approach. Leonora was disconcerted by the tremor of excitement and then disappointment she felt.

It was mid-afternoon by the time she had completed the tuning and as Mrs Priddy awoke, Leonora decided to play the *Adagio* from Pleyel's Sonata in B major, known for using most of the keyboard. She played it with greater gusto than usual, still hoping the Earl might appear to thank her, but only Stowe entered the room as she came to a flourishing end.

Leonora looked up. 'Oh Stowe, I've finished. Mrs Priddy and I will soon be on our way.'

He bowed. 'Miss Appleby, it's a pleasure indeed to have music filling the house once more.' As Leonora stood up, removed her apron and collected her tools, she glanced out of the window and in the distance saw a man on a magnificent black horse cantering in the parkland that led to the lake, Achille running by his side. The afternoon sun cast long shadows across the green sward and she watched for a moment as man, horse and dog moved from light to dark then light again, as if in a dream.

Nanny P had joined her in the window and realised what had held her attention. Carrying her knitting bag, she tucked her hand in Leonora's arm. In a quiet amused voice she said, 'He's a law unto himself, you know. Always has been.'

Leonora looked down sharply at her old nanny. Why did she say that, she wondered? She had no interest in the Earl beyond extracting permission to swim in his lake and not risk being shot by the irascible Mr Shrubb.

Leonora told Stowe they would walk round to the stables and collect Clover and the gig themselves. She was curious about the rest of the rambling place and thought it might be interesting to approach the stable yard through the ruined Abbey. The massive stone arches towered above their heads. It had been without a roof for more than two centuries and the great stone-flagged floor, once polished and waxed by its devout community, now had a carpet of moss and leaves and occasional saplings that had eluded the scythe. The atmosphere of peace and welcome belied its forbidding demeanour and the two women gazed about them with some wonder. 'Isn't this lovely?' Leonora turned to Nanny P.

'I don't think I've ever seen it from inside before. What a miscreant king, old Henry was! All that despoiling of the monasteries. And yet he was father to our great queen.'

Leonora laughed. 'Does that mean you will forgive the tyrant anything for the fact he begat Elizabeth?' Mrs Priddy responded with a chuckle as they turned into the stable yard. Leonora's eyes widened further. If the house appeared unloved and half-forgotten, the stables were smart and clean and bustling with activity. Boys were busy shovelling the dirty straw into wheelbarrows while the grooms were brushing and fussing over teams of magnificent horses: four matched bays, another set of black horses as glossy as glass. And a grey hunter with a ghostly tail and mane that floated like a cloud around his handsome head. Leonora gasped. 'Well, the Earl certainly loves his bloodstock.'

Compared with the magnificence on show, the little hack pony, Clover, and the gig parked in the shade of a spreading beech tree at the entrance to the yard, were like country dowds out of place at a grand society ball.

A groom approached and Leonora explained she had come to collect her carriage. He bowed. 'I'm Roddy, his lordship's chief groom,' and he handed both women into their gig. As Leonora drove Clover down the drive, she looked back at Rokeby Abbey and considered its austere façade, now less dark and sinister, and more enticing every time she saw it.

Just as Leonora arrived back at the Manor, Charlotte Blythe appeared through the garden gate, as if she had been waiting for a sign that her friend had returned. 'It's so dull at the Vicarage, do you mind if I read my book here with you?' she asked with a winning smile.

'Of course not. I've just got to do some mending. I've torn my favourite blue muslin on that thorny rose by the front of the house.'

'I thought Nanny P was expert at any needlework.'

'Oh, she is!' Leonora smiled. 'She's expert at everything but I want to show her I can manage without her, sometimes!'

Charlotte settled into the sofa and opened the book she held in her hands.

Leonora looked across, her needle poised. 'What are you reading?'

Charlotte waved it in the air. '*Belinda*! It's so charming, I'm reluctant to put it down.'

'Has Mrs Mildmay read it?' Leonora was aware how carefully Charlotte had been brought up, and restricting her reading matter was part of her foster parents' protective cloak.

Charlotte giggled. 'Actually no. But the bishop's wife recommended it to her maid and this Mama Mildmay took as proof of it being morally impeccable. No woman in her right mind, she declared, would allow her maid to be corrupted by unsuitable literature!'

'And have you yet found anything unsuitable in those pages?'

'Not yet, but I'm ever hopeful.' Both young women giggled.

Leonora stitched on while her young guest read a few more pages of her novel. She lifted her fair head and asked in an innocent voice, 'Is Mr Lockwood still out riding?'

'I presume so.' Leonora gave her friend a quizzical look.

'He's less stuffy than he appears. In fact, he's rather charming in his straightforward way.'

'He's quite a catch, you know.' Leonora met Charlotte's startled brown eyes.

'But not for me, Leonora. I thought it would be better if you married him, then you wouldn't have to leave your childhood home.'

Leonora put down her needle and thread and said with a smirk, 'Miss Charlotte, you're reading too many romance novels. I've told you, I'm past marrying, and I'm quite reconciled to leaving my home.' She paused, then decided to confide her thoughts. 'But it would warm my heart if *you* were to live here instead. Then I could visit all the time. As you do now!'

Charlotte gasped and a blush suffused her neck and cheeks. 'You can't mean that. Like you, I'd rather not think of marriage at all, but just go on as we do.'

The light was beginning to fade when there was a commotion at the back door and the sound of men's boots and the shuffling patter of animal paws. Leonora sprang to her feet and dashed into the corridor to see Achille disappearing into the kitchen and George Lockwood standing in his stockinged feet, having just removed his muddy boots.

There was a scream from Cook. 'Get this great clumsy cur from my kitchen!' And she ran into the utility room carrying a leg of lamb above her head.

'He followed me back. I think he'd been hunting on our land.' Mr Lockwood looked apologetic as he tried to grab the hound by his collar.

Charlotte had also joined them. 'He's huge,' she said, her eyes wide.

Leonora called, 'Achille, come!' and the dog trotted out of the kitchen to her side. 'This is Lord Rokeby's dog. Was Ned Fleming with you while you explored the estate?' She looked at George Lockwood. 'I'll ask him to take him back to the Abbey.'

'I'm sure he'll find his own way home.' George Lockwood looked at Achille speculatively.

'No!' Charlotte's voice was urgent. 'The Fopling gamekeeper shoots any dog he finds on their land, and they abut the Manor estate. You can't risk it.'

'I left Ned investigating a broken fence in the lower field.' Mr Lockwood's face assumed an amused, put-upon expression. 'I suppose I'll have to take this preposterous animal home.' Achille stood patiently by Leonora's side, looking from one face to the other. George Lockwood struggled back into his boots and called the dog's name and together they stepped into the twilight.

Cook resumed her preparations for the evening meal and the young women returned to the drawing room where Leonora's piano-forte stood expectantly in the far window. 'You have your lesson tomorrow. I hope you've been practising that variation on *Logie O'Buchan*.' Leonora looked at her young pupil who nodded, an uncertain smile on her lips. They sat on the piano stool side by side. Leonora said with a twinkle, 'I thought it may be a good idea to give a small concert here to entertain our friends in the winter months. I've found a composition by Mr Field arranged as a duet for four hands and it would be amusing for us to play together, don't you think?'

'Oh no, I don't think I'm skilled enough.' Charlotte flushed at the thought.

'You will be. And everyone will be delighted. There's so little to divert our neighbours in the dark months. It also gives us something to work towards in our lessons.'

'Will it be the last winter you will enjoy at the Manor?' Charlotte looked at her friend, her face full of sympathy mixed with her own sorrow.

'It will. And I'd like to mark the end of this stage of my life and the beginning of another.' Leonora could not hide the emotion she felt. She was alarmed by how featureless the future seemed, but knew she had yet to discover what awaited in that hazy void.

Charlotte fixed her mischievous gaze on her friend's face. 'If we do have a concert, will you ask the Earl?'

'I very much doubt he will come. Even his staff say he eschews company. Though music seems to be important in his life...' Her voice faded as she remembered the fleeting sight of him riding away on his horse.

Charlotte sat on the sofa and opened her book, and Leonora returned to her sewing. When Charlotte finished her chapter, she looked up. 'Perhaps I'd better get practising.' With her book in her hand, she headed in the direction of the garden door. Again, the usual quiet of the Manor was shaken by the banging of the back door and both women turned to see George Lockwood enter the stone-flagged corridor a second time, stamping the mud from his boots.

'He's insufferably rude!' he expostulated. It was surprising to see such a usually phlegmatic man so discomposed. 'You'd think that doing a neighbour a good turn might have elicited some gratitude. But no! Lord Rokeby almost accused me of stealing his dog!'

Leonora started forward. 'Did he know that you're the new owner of the Manor?'

'He didn't give me a chance to introduce myself. Just took the hound, gave me back the bridle rope I'd fashioned into a lead, and stalked off.'

'I'm sorry I suggested it, Mr Lockwood. Apparently, Lord Rokeby's not the same after his experiences in the war. We had all heard he'd been so badly injured he had died at Corunna along with his brother. Then he suddenly arrived home, scarred as you see.'

'From his behaviour, the worst scars are not what we see,' Mr Lockwood muttered, still put out by the high-handed treatment he had just endured. He then caught sight of Charlotte on her way out. 'Miss Blythe, while I'm still in my boots, may I escort you home?'

Charlotte coloured slightly at this unexpected offer. 'I go via the garden. There's a convenient clicket gate Leonora and I use, so we don't need to use the lane. So I thank you, Mr Lockwood, but it's quite unnecessary.'

He bowed and Charlotte Blythe curtsied quickly and left.

Excited by the idea of creating a winter concert for their neighbours, Leonora opened the piano-forte and began to play the various compositions she thought may prove entertaining. Her mind ranged over who might be prepared to sing a few country songs, accompanied by her if necessary. Just as the new heir was about to disappear up the stairs, she called to him, 'Mr Lockwood, do you sing?'

He paused by the drawing room door. 'I can do. Why?' He looked wary.

'I'm thinking of organising a concert at the Manor and I wondered if you would attend. Better still, take part?'

He walked into the room and said in a ruminative voice, 'Well, I'm not averse to singing. But I'd have to come across from my estate in Oxfordshire. When would this be?'

'Perhaps in the New Year before you head back to London for the Season?'

'That's a possibility. A little brightness before the dark.' He grimaced. 'I could come to your soirée on my way to London, although it's a bit of a detour. Are you or Miss Blythe going to London for the Season?'

'Goodness, no! But that does not mean we need to be dull in the country.' Leonora smiled at him.

'Not dull at all,' he said as he turned to continue his way upstairs.

Leonora went back to the demanding arpeggio of a Pleyel sonata.

* * *

The following morning, Leonora woke early. She was restless; her usual equanimity of heart had been disturbed for days with thoughts of loss and the instability of change. Overall was the sadness that William Worth lay in a foreign land, his resting place unmarked, never to grow to maturity with her as they had dreamed. Lord Rokeby's return had reminded her again of the suffering of war. Now the night was passed, she decided to head towards the garden to restore her spirits with the promise of a new day.

She was too early for the pitcher of steaming water brought up each morning by Milly, so instead scrambled unwashed into her morning dress of grey checked cotton and dragged a comb through her thick wavy hair. Barely pausing to glance in the looking glass, Leonora pinned up her chestnut curls and, slipping a shawl over her shoulders, ran down the stairs, through the drawing room and out into the waiting garden. Within moments, the heavy dew drenched her pumps and the hem of her gown, but the sounds and scents drew her on towards the river that meandered through the low mist at the end of the lawn.

The flowers were dressed in nothing but the light, and the scent of late roses was sweet on the air as they pressed through the white Michaelmas daisies and the flowering mint tangled in their beds. There too were her mother's precious dahlias; they bloomed with all the exuberance of their nature and lifted her spirits as she thought of her gentle mother, never quite robust enough for the world.

As she approached the river, the susurration of the water rippling over stones added to the rich layers that filled her senses; how these interleaving scents and sounds reminded her of music. Leonora felt herself and the morning brimming with life.

As she bent her head to sniff the palest pink damask roses growing in profusion by the riverbank, she heard the creak of the garden gate. Who was up so early? she wondered. Who but the inhabitants of the Vicarage ever used this private access to the Manor?

In the misty sun, the tall, fair-haired figure of Richard Fopling appeared almost ghostly in the milky light. He was wearing his curate's surplice, ready for the morning service, and this added to his otherworldliness. He started when he saw her. 'Oh, Miss Appleby, my apologies for intruding. I was just delivering a note to the house before beginning the morning's devotions.'

In his hand was a folded sheet of white paper sealed with a

dab of red wax. She walked towards him smiling and took the note. 'I was so lost in my thoughts you startled me. I didn't think anyone else would be abroad so early.'

His pale blue eyes were on her face, then he glanced around the bounty of the late summer garden and said, 'This is like a prayer.' Leonora was surprised by his fervour. Mr Fopling continued in his quiet reverential voice, 'God is made visible in the beauty of His creation, the reaching heavenwards of all living things.' He paused, then continued, 'For me, everything is intentional, even that drifting cloud.' He pointed towards the brightening horizon where a single cloud appeared as ragged as a shred of sheep's wool suspended in the sky. He bowed his head, preparing to take his leave.

'Before you go, Mr Fopling, I'm thinking of having a small concert here in the winter months and hope you'd attend?'

'It will depend on a number of things.' His eyes searched hers again before he saluted her. 'Good day, Miss Appleby.' He turned on his heel to walk back into the Vicarage garden. Puzzled, Leonora opened the note in her hands. There in neat black ink were the words:

Dear Miss Appleby,
> *Would you be so kind as to grant me an audience at The Manor,*
tomorrow at three?
> *Richard Fopling*

Leonora suspected this was a portent and her heart sank. She stuffed the note into her pocket and began cutting with increased vigour the dead flowers from the roses, her fragile equilibrium once more unsettled.

After breakfast, she returned to her piano-forte; Charlotte was expected later for her lesson and she wanted to begin practising the melody part of the John Field duet she hoped they could play together.

It was mid-afternoon when the door to the garden was flung open and Charlotte dashed into the Manor, a wild look in her eyes. 'Come quickly! Mama Mildmay and the Reverend are just back from Rokeby Abbey and they're in such dismay! Please come and help calm them. They fear they're going to lose me.'

'What on earth do you mean, Lottie? How could they ever lose you?'

'Come. Tell them that. They won't listen to me.' The girl grabbed Leonora's arm and hurried her into the garden and through the gate.

The Vicarage was a serene and symmetrical stone house but, on this afternoon, it housed a maelstrom of emotion. Mrs Mildmay, always the most reasonable of women, greeted Leonora, her eyes streaming with tears and her nose red with blowing. Reverend Mildmay was pacing in the drawing room, attempting to remonstrate with his wife to cease her crying. Leonora ran to her side and put her arms around the distraught woman. 'Mrs Mildmay, my dear, what can be the matter?'

Between hiccuping sobs, the story tumbled out. 'It's Lord Rokeby. He asked us to come and see him. He told us our beautiful child, the baby we found on our doorstep whom we thought had been sent by the Lord for us to care for and love, actually belongs to the Rokeby family.'

Leonora was astounded. She looked from her to Charlotte, who also had tears in her eyes. 'What can he mean?'

Charlotte then spoke to save her mother further pain. 'Lord Rokeby told them that his brother, the Earl, charged him in his dying breath to put right a wrong. He had fathered a child with a maid. That baby was me, left on the doorstep of the Vicarage in the hopes that I would be cared for, and the young Earl was immediately sent to war by his father. He had organised financial support and always intended to tell me the truth when I was eighteen. But he never came home again.'

Mrs Mildmay had collapsed onto the sofa and looked up at Leonora with a tragic expression. 'Of course the Rokeby family will claim Lottie. We have no rights, you see. We always knew she was too good for us. A beautiful spirit come to live with two country clods as we are. Even our own child could never have compared with the angel we had been sent. We always feared this day would come.'

'No! No, Mama. No one can ever claim my heart when you have given me all the love a mother could.' Charlotte threw herself onto the sofa beside Mrs Mildmay and buried her head in her bosom.

Reverend Mildmay paused his pacing to add, 'The new Earl wished that it would be us who broke the news to Charlotte. He wants to see her in two days' time to explain his brother's wishes to her directly. Mrs Mildmay is unwilling to go through any more upset and we hoped you would accompany her, Miss Leonora, as her chaperone?' His anguished eyes were on her face and she could only nod.

This news was astounding to her too. It changed everything. Leonora looked across at her friend whose face was pale with shock, her eyes pricked with sympathetic tears as her foster mother silently wept beside her on the sofa.

Leonora sat on Mrs Mildmay's other side and placed a hand on her arm. 'I will be happy to act as Charlotte's chaperone. Although I know nothing of what is in the Earl's mind, I can be certain that you will never lose the love of a daughter who has known only you as her mother. She has been lucky enough to be the focus of all your goodness.'

Charlotte took her other hand and kissed her wet cheek.

'Mama, no one could have loved me better or given me a greater sense of happiness and safety than you and the Reverend.'

Reverend Mildmay, unable to deal with the turbulent emotions that had taken over his sitting room and his own heart, escaped to the calm of the kitchen where he asked Cook for a pot of tea and some of the newly baked almond cake to be sent through to the mistress and her guest. He then walked into his library and closed the door.

3

SHAKING THE STATUS QUO

The tea and almond cake at the Vicarage settled everyone's nerves and in the temporary lull, Reverend Mildmay joined the women to talk about the hymns for the following Sunday's service. However, when Leonora arrived home, her heart was still in turmoil at the import and uncertainty of this unexpected news.

'Nanny P!' she called as she entered through the garden door.

She found Mrs Priddy in the small morning room, sitting by the fire, sewing the guipure lace border to a fine linen tablecloth. She looked up. 'My dear, what is it?'

'I've just come from the Vicarage. They are in disarray thanks to Lord Rokeby.'

'Not for the first time, that scampish boy! What now?'

'It's not about him, it's his dead brother. He's Charlotte's father!' Leonora subsided onto the chair opposite her old nanny. 'The Mildmays and Lottie are distressed by what this might portend.'

'I've always wondered about that girl's parentage.' She nodded in a way that suggested she knew more than she was saying.

Leonora leant forward and said with urgency, 'What? You mean you knew all this time?'

'No, I didn't *know*, but I thought it significant that Lord Rokeby was sent off very quickly to the army, and at such a young age. I always thought his inclination was to manage his estate. But his father was a hard man who, despite his own profligate ways, would brook no scandal attached to his heir.'

'Why didn't you tell me?' Leonora's face was aghast.

'Because it was only rumour and I don't like tittle-tattle.'

'But it's not tittle-tattle when you tell *me*,' Leonora protested.

'If I'd told you my suspicions, then that would have altered your friendship with Miss Charlotte. How could it not have been a secret that burdened you? No, I was right not to speak of it.' Mrs Priddy had put down her sewing and folded her hands in her lap, a serene expression on her face.

'It will alter my relationship with her anyway. This is what upsets me; how can we go on the same?'

'Well, you have yet to know what, if anything, the Rokeby family will suggest. She will always be the same person you know.'

'Is that true, Nanny P? People are altered by their circum-stances, are they not?'

'Just wait and see. Charlotte is not a giddy girl, and not about to become one.' Then Mrs Priddy continued in a ruminative way, 'How often the quiet ones surprise us most! Charles was at heart the responsible heir, and Alistair, the boy who continually kicked over the traces.'

Leonora answered, 'Well, the younger son is now Earl, and the Mildmays want me to act as Charlotte's chaperone when she goes to see him the day after tomorrow.'

'That's good, then you'll know for yourself what, if anything, will change.'

Leonora's heart was agitated in the most disconcerting way. All her certainties seemed to be shifting. Charlotte's astonishing news was not the only thing that threatened to dislodge one of the props supporting her life. Even though she did not wish to entertain Mr Fopling's proposal – for that was surely the purpose of his visit tomorrow – it was vexing to have to think about things that had been so long out of mind. She reached out to take one of Mrs Priddy's small plump hands. 'Early this morning, Richard Fopling surprised me in the garden. He had come with a note, hoping for an audience tomorrow afternoon. Will you chaperone me?'

Leonora's face was glum and her old nanny, who loved her better than anyone, squeezed her hand and smiled. 'Nora my dear, it's not so gloomy being courted by a personable young man, surely?'

'He's perfectly amiable, I'm sure, but I prefer my life with you, able to please myself with my friends, my music, and the garden. Why would I trade that for life with a man whom I might grow to esteem but never love?'

'For children and a family of your own?' Mrs Priddy said in a voice soft with emotion.

Leonora knew what her nanny had given up to care for her, how much she would love to see her with her own children and be central in the care of them. 'Oh, Nanny P, you know if there were a man who would love me and whom I could love in return, I would happily unite my life with his. As I longed to do with Captain Worth. But my chance of love and the hope of a family died with him.' She broke off, overcome by a stab of memory. All she had of his was one letter that survived the journey back from the camp in Spain, and she clung to it as the last connection with the man she had loved.

Leonora turned back to address Nanny P again. 'I am content with my life. I'm luckier than most women, as long as you are happy to live with me.' She smiled into the wise eyes of the woman she had known all her life, disconcerted to see a shadow of sadness cross her face.

Mrs Priddy was not one to dissemble and said, 'I know you for your passionate heart, my love, and I think you need more than mere contentment.' Leonora hugged her, tears suddenly springing to her eyes as she realised the truth of her old nanny's words.

She walked briskly into the library and was surprised by a man sitting at her father's desk, a large sheet of paper spread in front of him. 'Mr Lockwood, I thought you were still exploring the estate.'

He looked up, his face alight with enthusiasm. He had taken off his jacket and rolled up his sleeves, and Leonora was taken aback to see just how broad and beefy his forearms were as he leant forwards, a stick of drawing charcoal in his hand. 'I'm really interested in your splendid trees in the field that abuts the river.' He had sketched out a plan of the area and had drawn in representations of the oak, elm, willow and maple that already existed in the space. 'My father was a friend of Lord Greville. They were at school together and Uncle William, as I called him, often had me to stay at Dropmore Park where he began planting every type of tree that would thrive in our temperate land.'

Leonora was intrigued. She had loved trees ever since she was a child climbing into their canopies to hide or dream, but not many people she knew thought of them beyond their utility as shelter or timber for building and fuel. 'That big oak in the middle of the field has a platform built amongst the branches. My father had that made for me, and then added a rope ladder. I spent many happy hours high up with the birds, with no one aware of where I was.'

'Miss Blythe pointed it out to me on my first ride. But she said the rope ladder had rotted away.'

'When she was little, I taught her how to climb trees. I don't think she needs a rope ladder any more.' Leonora chuckled and then noticed George Lockwood was watching her with amusement.

'She speaks of you with much admiration, you know.'

'She's been as close as any family could be.'

'I heard the servants chattering; what's this revelation about her parentage?' He had a querying expression on his face.

Leonora's surprise turned to amused resignation, for she realised nothing much escaped the servants' notice. 'Mr Lockwood, I know you wouldn't expect me to engage in gossip. Surely it's for Charlotte to tell you herself?'

'She's rather shy in my company.'

'She's young. And I think she is regretful about not having me living next door when you take over the Manor.' Leonora's frank gaze met his more ambivalent one.

He looked away. 'I realise that my inheriting your father's estate causes all kinds of anxiety and some distress to those who would like things to remain as they were. But I assure you that any changes will be for the good of the estate and for the good of those who work here.'

'I believe that.'

'This morning, whilst exploring the village, I came across Hasterleigh Lodge and it appears a commodious dwelling.' His voice was expressionless, but he looked to her for some response.

Leonora spoke with composure. 'I shall be very comfortable there, I'm sure.'

He turned to gaze out of the window and seemed lost in his own thoughts. 'After my father's death, my mother married Beau Beacham and I had to leave my family home. I found that difficult.'

'How old were you, Mr Lockwood?'

'I was fourteen, enduring Eton, longing for home.'

'Had you not inherited the house and estate you loved on your father's death?'

'I had, but was too young to live there.' He let out a great gust of laughter. 'But I would so much have preferred to be there on my own with the old servants than with Mama and the Beau in Davies Street.'

Just at that moment, the door opened and Charlotte stood on the threshold, swinging her bonnet by its ribbons. She had expected to find Leonora reading in her favourite chair in the window and was startled to see George Lockwood sitting at Mr Appleby's old desk, as if he owned the place. She coloured when she remembered that he *did* in fact own the place and suddenly felt an intruder. 'Oh! My apologies, Mr Lockwood. I thought I'd find Leonora alone.' She looked ruffled and distracted and Leonora walked towards her with concern.

'Lottie, I forgot. Are you here for our lesson?' She took her arm.

'Yes. I thought we should practise that Field duet you want us to play at your musical evening.'

They nodded to George Lockwood and walked through to the drawing room where Charlotte blurted out, 'Everything I've taken for granted has changed. I was content, living with Mama Mildmay and the Reverend, next door to you. Now I may be about to know more about who I am, but not where I belong. And you're having to move, and things just cannot be the same ever again!' Her speech ended in a wail.

Leonora hugged her and led her to the piano-forte. 'Come now, I'm just moving down the lane, I won't be far away. The Mild-mays aren't going anywhere and will always love you, whatever transpires. We'll learn more when we go to Rokeby Abbey and see the Earl.' She opened up the lid of the Broadwood and they sat together on the stool.

Charlotte hung her head. 'But you're going to marry Mr

Fopling and move to his new parish, so we won't even be in the same village.'

Leonora was shocked. 'Where did you hear that? I've certainly got no plans to marry anyone or go anywhere, I assure you.' She began to run her fingers over the keys to ease her own agitation.

Charlotte answered quickly, 'I was passing the Reverend's door and Mr Fopling was discussing his curacy and hopes to move to Wetherleigh parish to be in charge of his own church. He said he intended to go with his wife.' She was shy at mentioning it, not wanting to be thought an eavesdropper, but her eyes were defiant and bright with tears.

'Well, I can assure you I will not be that wife Mr Fopling intends.'

In a rush Charlotte continued, 'You've been everything that a sister could be and I don't want to lose you.' Her words ended with a sharp intake of breath.

Leonora stopped playing and placed her hand on Charlotte's, clasped tightly in her lap. 'And you have been everything that a sister could be to me too. Nothing will alter that.'

Both young women sat together, their heads bowed, shoulders touching, Leonora's loose bun of glossy chestnut brown contrasting with Charlotte's fine fair hair, naturally straight and teased rather inexpertly into curls. They began to play, with hesitation at first and then more fluently, the balm of music calming their feelings. Soon they were swaying together, laughing at their mistakes.

Aware of a change in the atmosphere, they both looked up to see George Lockwood's large frame leaning against the door jamb. He was watching them, a smile on his face. 'I didn't want to interrupt you.' His light brown hair was in natural disarray, so different from the pomaded dishevelment of dandy fashion, and it suited him greatly, as did the informality of his loosely tied neckcloth. 'I think I'll go back to the field where I hope to plant the trees. Have to check the lie of the land. I'll be back for dinner.'

* * *

Leonora awoke the next morning to the sound of rain. It was soft and light but enough to make the climbing rose round her bedroom window rustle and sigh. She lay in her bed listening to the sounds of birdsong in the garden beyond. The creaking wings of the pair of swans added their own rhythm when they took off from the river and flew overhead. The rain made her feel cosy, enveloped as she was in a feather bed and a mound of bedclothes. This had been her room since childhood and Leonora loved the sprigged wallpaper of buff and pink flowers, unchanged in all these years.

She rose, washed, and dressed for the chilly day, pulling on for extra warmth a fur-trimmed woollen spencer over her morning dress. She was aware that Mr Fopling was due in the afternoon and felt shamefaced at knowing little about him, despite his being the curate in the village for three years. His manner was so quiet and unassuming that he was easily effaced by the cross bonhomie of his father, Sir Roderick, or the more obvious charm of virtually everyone else in the room. But on the few occasions when Richard Fopling had spoken, Leonora was surprised by how beguiling his meditative view of the world was.

She hurried through breakfast. Mr Lockwood was already out, making the most of his last full day before returning to Oxfordshire, and Mrs Priddy was busy with Cook planning the week's menus, so Leonora settled down with her old friend, the pianoforte. Exploring the repertoire for her musical evening was a welcome distraction that even reading her current novel could not supply.

Realising how quickly time had flown and that the hour of three approached, Leonora ran upstairs to put on her afternoon dress of pale primrose cambric with long tucked sleeves. She flung her best India shawl over her shoulders, slipped her feet into pale pumps and paused for a moment to gaze at her reflection in the looking glass. She had always liked her face, not pretty like Charlotte's but handsome with an elegant nose, and distinguished by large intelligent eyes and a wide mouth expressive of her wit and warmth. Her hair was her best feature, waving round her face and luxurious enough to fashion into a number of flattering styles without much effort or expertise from her or her maid. She had not the time now to brush it out and redo it but replaced her combs in an attempt to look passably tidy.

Glancing out the window at the rain that had begun to fall again, Leonora was surprised to see Richard Fopling standing under the maple tree, listening to the resident blackbird's mellifluous song. Even without an umbrella, he seemed oblivious to the weather. She called to Nanny P to chaperone her as she descended the stairs and hurried to the front door to open it herself. Mr Fopling turned from his rapt attention and, seeing her, tipped his hat. 'Miss Appleby, each little bird sings in its own Latin.'

'That is a nice conceit, sir.'

'It is indeed, but not mine, I confess. I have been reading the great poetry of William of Aquitaine.' He stood on the doorstep, in no hurry to come in from the wet. 'What a blessing, this rain.' He looked up, even as it fell on his face. 'You can almost hear the earth cleave as the tree roots stretch ever outwards.'

'Mr Fopling, your hat and coat are drenched!' Mrs Priddy took his redingote and hat to hang by the range in the kitchen while Leonora led him through to the drawing room.

'Can I offer you any refreshment?' she asked as she gestured to the chair by the fire. He shook his head as he sat down, crossing his legs. Leonora perched on the edge of the seat opposite just as Mrs Priddy entered the room to take the window seat, her book in her hand.

Richard Fopling met Leonora's eyes, his face made lively with the cold and the rain still on his cheek. 'Miss Appleby, I have admired you ever since I first met you. Your kindness to the Reverend and his family flows as a constant spring which far surpasses the measured offerings of others.'

This disarmed Leonora. He had obviously paid more attention to her than she had to him, and it touched her heart. 'I thank you. It is no hardship to care about them, as you can imagine.'

'I watched the pair of swans fly over the Manor this morning. High, just below the clouds, they seemed like two angels streaming across the sky, their wings outstretched, in perfect synchrony.'

The curate looked towards the window and Leonora saw Nanny P glance at her, a puzzled expression on her face. Leonora thought it fell to her to respond. 'I heard them pass over the roofs this morning. I wondered if it was the young ones forced to leave and claim their own piece of river.'

Richard Fopling's grave regard alighted on her face once more. 'I have been offered the parish at Wetherleigh. The vicarage is prodigious fine with many rooms. The parish too has souls hungry for the kindest touch...' His voice trailed off.

Leonora came to his aid and said, 'Wetherleigh village is upstream from here, is it not? I wonder if the swans were headed there.'

'You are perceptive, Miss Appleby. I did identify with them, 'tis true.' He took a breath and continued in a voice quiet with emotion, 'But they were a pair. I have known loneliness. I have known disregard, but with God as my guide and a wife beside me I

believe I can make a difference in this world.' His refined symmetrical face softened with a tentative smile as he leant forward to
take her hand. 'There are angels who visit us, if we have an open
heart to receive them.' His fingers held hers with a lightness of
touch that tingled.

Leonora's heart was beating faster; how to turn him down
without hurting his fragile sense of self? She was touched by his
poetic sensibility and did not wish to trample on his feelings.
Luckily, a more robust individual was about to intervene. The door
swung open with a crash and both looked up, startled to see
George Lockwood, his hair wet and wild from the blustery rain,
still wearing his muddy boots, a thunderous expression on his
face. 'That damned dog!'

Both Leonora and Richard Fopling disentangled their hands
as they sprang to their feet. 'Which dog?' Leonora came towards
him with concern.

'The damned Earl's great hairy hound!'

The curate gasped in disapproval at his swearing and Mr Lockwood coloured.

'My apologies, ladies, Curate Fopling, for my intemperate
language, but that dog is a menace.'

'What happened?' Leonora took his arm, her voice urgent.

'Our herd of red deer was grazing peaceably under the copse
of oak when suddenly that infernal cur burst out of the woodland
that separates our land from the Abbey's!'

'None were mauled?' Leonora's face was drawn as she
wondered whether she should get the gun used to despatch any
grievously wounded animal.

'No. They scattered in fright and that galumphing hound
appeared to want to chase rather than kill. But fright can kill a
deer.'

'Indeed. Terror alone can make a deer's heart burst.' Richard

Fopling's voice trembled with feeling. 'We too can die of fright, until we learn how to survive.' And in that moment, Leonora understood that here was a man whose childhood had instilled such fear in him that he passed through the world as inconspicuously as possible. He walked towards Leonora, his face haunted by some memory she could not know. He took her hand and bowed. 'I'll leave you to deal with the disturbed herd and I'll return to my restive flock.' He managed a slight smile. 'Forgive me, Miss Appleby. I have made a mistake in troubling you. I fear I have nothing to offer.' He saluted Mrs Priddy and Mr Lockwood and left as unobtrusively as he had come.

George Lockwood recovered his good humour. 'I do apologise for bursting in like this: my manners are deplorable. I hope I haven't hastened away your visitor. It is still your home. Forgive me.' He took Leonora's hand and squeezed it in a friendly manner.

But Leonora's mind was on the incident in the field. 'Is there anything to be done? Are the deer settled? Where is Achille now?'

'I chased him back into the woods. Probably returned from whence he came. And good riddance, I say! After I did his lordship the courtesy of returning his dog yesterday and was greeted with such insolence, I'm disinclined to do him any more favours.' He stamped off to the back of the house to remove his boots, and then extracted from the inside of his coat the folded plan of his tree-planting scheme which he had sought to protect from the rain.

Nanny P took Leonora's arm. 'Well! What a to-do. That dog seems as intractable as his master.'

'If the occasion arises, I might mention his roaming hound to the Earl when I accompany Miss Charlotte to the Abbey tomorrow.'

'Oh, Master Alistair never liked being chastised for anything. He was the most stubborn of boys, only really respected his brother.'

'And you too, Nanny P?' Leonora looked at the elderly woman with a mischievous smile.

'Oh, tush now!' As Mrs Priddy drew Leonora back into the drawing room and closed the door, she asked the one pressing question on her mind. 'Nora dear, was that a proposal from the young curate, do you think?'

'Perhaps he was just strengthening his resolve to do the deed,' she said with a wry smile. 'But I don't know if in his mind that pair of homing swans included me or whether he was happy enough to fly alone.'

'He's a good man. My dear, he would treat you well, you know. Don't dismiss him out of hand.'

'I think Mr Fopling's full of sympathetic feeling, but he doesn't seem equipped for the hurly-burly of the world.'

'That wicked father of his had any spirit beaten out of him. He was the same with his dogs.'

Leonora's heart contracted with horror at the thought, but she was then distracted by her name being called. Charlotte dashed in through the garden door. Mrs Priddy grumbled, 'This house has become like a well-oiled turngate, so many alarums and excursions, comings and goings.'

Under her breath, Leonora protested, 'Nanny P, Charlotte has every reason to be unsettled after the recent turn of events.'

'Well, you'll know more tomorrow, so there's no use in awful contemplation.' Mrs Priddy smiled and nodded at Charlotte as she turned for the kitchen in search of Cook.

'Oh Leonora! I saw Mr Fopling walk past so lost in thought he didn't even see me. Did he propose?'

'Come through to the morning room. Mr Lockwood's in the library completing his arboreal planting scheme.' Once they were sitting together on the sofa in the window, Leonora answered her friend's anxious question. 'I think he was about to when Mr Lockwood burst in complaining about the Earl's dog upsetting our deer herd. In that second of distraction, he thought better of it.'

'The Earl seems to have a capacity to upset everyone! He banned us from swimming, he's visited grief on my family, his rudeness has made an enemy of Mr Lockwood. Only Nanny P looks on him with kindness.'

'Lottie!' Leonora laughed. 'It's not that bad. Don't get yourself into a state about him. I like the fact he cares for his piano-forte and plays well and is a fine swimmer. Rumour has it, like Lord Byron, he's crossed the Hellespont.' Her eyes were sparkling at the thought of such a heroic swim.

Charlotte's eye fell on her copy of *Belinda* still open on the table by the fire. 'Oh good, 'tis here. I've been missing it. I love her character. She makes me think of my own life and how I want to live.'

'I'm reading Mrs Burney's *Camilla* and the antics of what I call the Typhoid family.'

Charlotte gave a gasp of laughter. 'They're the Tyrold family, not the Typhoids!'

'That's better. I like to see you laugh.'

'In *Belinda* there's a character who is very like you, Miss Appleby. She spreads light and warmth wherever she goes. Mama Mildmay could not have been kinder but she is timid and afraid of the world, and you are not. You encourage me to be brave. Since reading *Belinda* I have lost patience with the idea that women exist at the mercy of men's wills.'

Leonora was surprised at her young friend's growing independence of thought and chuckled as she said, 'See, there are good reasons to read! Thus we inhabit other lives and begin to think in new ways.' Charlotte had been a reluctant reader, preferring the outdoors in summer and attempts at dressmaking and bonnet trimming in winter, but her view of life and relationships were very much moulded by the Mildmays' careful nurture. Leonora was pleased to see her horizons expanding.

Charlotte was looking at her hands when she said, 'Mr Lockwood leaves tomorrow. With his schemes and enthusiasm, he's brought extra interest to our daily lives at Hatherleigh.'

Leonora suspected a growing restlessness in her friend and said, 'He has indeed. Life in the village is a bit tedious for someone as young and full of spirit as you, is it not?'

'No, no!' Charlotte was quick to demur. 'It's just it's been pleasant to hear about his plans. I don't feel as sad about your moving to the Lodge.'

'Well, that is a good thing, wouldn't you say?' Leonora's hopes that Charlotte and George Lockwood might discover a love for each other were very much alive. 'Would you like to join us this evening for his last meal with us?'

'Thank you, but I think I should dine with Mama and the Reverend as they're so anxious about what will transpire when I meet the Earl with you tomorrow.'

'Mr Lockwood is due to leave at noon, so come by and wish him farewell.'

Leonora was matter-of-fact but Charlotte's voice was less certain. 'Then we'll have to go to Rokeby Abbey in the afternoon. But why am I full of foreboding?'

They were walking towards the front door, Charlotte's pretty face tight with anxiety. Leonora gave her a quick hug. 'Now remember how much you like the character of Belinda in your novel. How she rises above adversity and thinks the best of things. Borrow some of her cheerful spirit and let's just wait and see what the Earl has to say.'

'Belinda would tell us change brings opportunities undreamt of.' Charlotte's face had cleared, and she was smiling again.

Leonora looked surprised. 'Would she, indeed?'

'Well if she didn't in the book, she would in real life!' They both laughed as Leonora embraced her young friend at the door and waved her off to walk the few paces to the Vicarage porch.

* * *

The next morning, Leonora found Nanny P and a letter waiting for her amongst the toast, eggs and pastries on the breakfast table. She didn't have the range of clothes or social occasions to support changing her costume three or four times a day, but was aware that she needed to look more sophisticated than usual when she accompanied Charlotte to Rokeby Abbey; so she dressed in her best gown of lilac twilled sarsenet embroidered with tiny sprigs of cream flowers. Leonora had added a close-fitting spencer in a soft purple with cream frogging and felt at her most attractive and confident.

'Goodness, my dear! What a treat for my old eyes.' Mrs Priddy got to her feet to kiss her cheek. 'Look! A very distinguished letter has arrived for you.'

Leonora picked it up. The thick paper was folded and affixed with dark red wax impressed with a very important-looking seal with a coronet. The black writing was distinctive and Leonora recognised it immediately. 'Oh! This is from Lord Dearlove.' She felt a small skip in her heart as she opened it. 'Look, Nanny P, he's expecting his friend Captain Ormonde to spend Christmas with him at Monkton estate.' She looked up, her face shining. 'I can ask him and the Captain to attend my musical evening. It will be so good to see him again.'

'Was the last time you saw Lord Dearlove when your young Mr Worth was killed? He was your beau's best friend, was he not?'

As Leonora read the letter to the end, her expression grew less ecstatic. 'Oh no! He's with his sister, Lady Livia. She's so haughty and grand she'll freeze any party spirit we might manage at the Manor.'

'Is she the lady your dear Captain Worth used to call the Honourable Livid Ne'er Loved?'

Leonora gulped with surprised laughter. 'I had forgotten that!' With a small shiver she turned her attention back to Mrs Priddy's question. 'Yes, she's the Honourable Livia Dearlove, with an inheritance large enough to make prospective suitors overlook her disagreeable temper.'

Her old nanny enclosed her hand in her small plump ones and said, 'I recall her visiting with her brother when Captain Worth was courting you, my love. She was a Mistress Princum-Prancum to be sure, so set on being treated with the deference her rank demanded.'

'Well, if they all come, it will add a certain excitement to the evening.' Leonora was suddenly fatigued by the emotion that had sprung up from the past and subsided onto a chair.

Mrs Priddy poured out a cup of coffee and handed it to her. 'The fact tragedy denied you happiness once doesn't mean you have to deny yourself happiness again.'

'Oh, Nanny P, I'm not going to argue the case. But just look at you, we don't all need to marry and have children to be happy and useful. In fact, you have been most precious to me in ways which would not have been possible if you were married with your own family.' Leonora suddenly realised how selfish that sounded and grasped both the elderly woman's hands and kissed them. 'You have made all the difference to my happiness, even before Mama died.'

Mrs Priddy brushed a tear from her eye, then became once more her sensible self. 'Enough of that, dear Nora. Eat your breakfast and then we have to bid farewell to Mr Lockwood.'

'Has he already breakfasted?'

'Yes, and he has taken his borrowed hunter back to Sir Roderick Fopling's stable. He wanted to thank Sir Roderick himself for the loan of his horse.'

* * *

George Lockwood walked back along the lane from the Fopling mansion and caught up with Charlotte as she was leaving the Vicarage, tying her bonnet strings. 'Miss Blythe, I'm so glad to see you before I leave.'

She blushed. It was only a short walk to the Manor but she was aware that she was unchaperoned. She glanced up at him, so tall in his driving coat, the capes ruffling from his shoulders making him seem even broader. 'Oh Mr Lockwood. I'm on my way to see Miss Leonora and bid you farewell.'

'It has been an unexpected pleasure to get to know the Hasterleigh estate and the neighbours. You have added to that pleasure immeasurably.'

Charlotte was glad to be walking beside George Lockwood as he spoke rather than being addressed face to face. In the time she had grown to know him better she recognised his frank nature and lack of artifice and how a compliment from him mattered more than from a practised charmer.

'I have been pleased to make your acquaintance too. I no longer feel quite so sad that Miss Leonora will have to leave her home now I know you will care for the Manor as she does.'

Before he could answer, they had walked down the short drive to where the honey-coloured manor house seemed to rise like a dream in its well-established parkland. The herd of deer could just be seen in the distance cropping the grass in the protective shade of the mighty Hasterleigh oak, its ancient branches almost reaching to the ground.

Jack Clegg had opened the great front door and Charlotte walked into the cool stone-flagged hall. She undid her bonnet and, as she had for years, placed it on the carved Elizabethan coffer that had stood black and solid since time immemorial in the alcove where the oak stairs curved upwards. Everything for her was now filtered through an elegiac light. How much a part of her life this house had become; since very young she had loved coming here to see Leonora and play in the gardens, running back and forth through the lychgate between the Vicarage and Manor lands. A melancholy gripped her heart.

There was a clatter at the front door and a flash of blue as the Lockwood groom brought up the carriage and horses ready for the return journey to Oxfordshire. The handsome team of bays were fresh after being turned out into the fertile paddock and rested for a few days and were whinnying, ready to go.

Leonora with Mrs Priddy emerged from the back of the house. She came forward to greet Charlotte and take George Lockwood's hand. He said in his unaffected way, 'Thank you, Miss Appleby, for your hospitality. I have seldom been more content than these few days exploring the estate and meeting you and the charming neighbours.' He glanced across at Charlotte with a smile.

Leonora bowed her head in acknowledgement. 'I have been pleased to make your acquaintance, Mr Lockwood, and am reassured now I know the estate's future will be in safe hands.'

'I hope you won't move just yet. I will not be able to take up residence until after the Season, perhaps even by next Michaelmas.' Then a thought occurred to him. 'If the Lodge needs any improvements to make it suitable for your future home you just have to let me know, either at Dracott, my Oxfordshire estate, or in Town at Beacham's house in Davies Street. Or failing that, at Brooks's, my club.'

'You're a man of many parts, Mr Lockwood.'

'It sounds like it, I fear, but having been introduced to Hasterleigh, I know now it's the only place I want to be.' His voice was surprisingly emotional, and Leonora looked at him and realised how the guarded expression she had noticed so clearly when he first arrived had relaxed into clear-browed bonhomie. 'I'll see you after Christmas at your musical evening.' He bowed and climbed into his chaise with a wave.

Leonora watched Charlotte, standing on the drive waving until the carriage turned out into the lane and disappeared from view. She remained still and pensive for a moment and then turned to catch Leonora's eye. Leonora put out her hand and said, 'We could walk to the Abbey this afternoon, it's not so far.' Charlotte looked doubtful so she continued, 'Or we could get Clover harnessed up to the gig. It worked well when Nanny P and I went there last. Clover was very impressed by the magnificent stables.'

'You mean *you* were impressed by the stables!'

'I was indeed. They're in so much better condition than the poor neglected house. It's obvious the Earl values his bloodstock more highly than himself, or his visitors.'

Charlotte cast Leonora an anxious look as she said, 'I'd prefer if we could go in the gig. I'd rather not arrive hot and bothered when I'm already feeling inadequate to the occasion.'

'You are the most beautiful and charming person I know. Adequate to any occasion! The Rokebys are lucky to have you as part of their family.' Leonora hugged her, hoping to instil some confidence into her slight frame.

* * *

So it was that Charlotte, dressed in her best yellow cambric afternoon gown, pelisse and matching bonnet, was driven by Leonora in the gig to meet her destiny. She was quiet as Clover

clip-clopped along the lane and then turned into the long mossy
drive that led to Rokeby Abbey. For eighteen years, she had known
nothing of her blood family and in her wildest dreams, could not
have imagined that she could belong to such an ancient and noble
line. As the drive swept towards the house, the imposing ruins of
the Abbey loomed ahead, the soaring arches, marking the ancestral might of the Rokeby dynasty.

'Oh, Leonora, I've not seen it before. We've never trespassed
this far. The size of it! Look at those huge windows glinting like
diamonds. The ruins make it quite forbidding.'

'Don't be alarmed. I was at first but even the ruined Abbey has
a welcoming feel once you enter. The house is just sleeping.'

'To be kissed awake?' Charlotte's mischievous cast of mind
could not be suppressed for long.

'I think it might take a lot of kissing!' Leonora had clambered
down from the gig, careful not to mark her fine dress on the dirty
wheel. She pulled her pelisse close and walked with Charlotte to
the front door. The clang of the bell echoed in the deep recesses of
the house and the heavy oak door swung open to reveal Stowe.

His expression lightened at the sight of Leonora. 'Didn't expect
you to come too, Miss Appleby.' He took the women's bonnets and
pelisses and with little ceremony, cast them onto the great hall
chair.

Leonora smiled. 'Good afternoon, Stowe. I'm accompanying
Miss Blythe. Would you be so kind to ask one of the grooms to
take Clover to the stable yard?' He bowed and led the way. The last
time Leonora had been to Rokeby Abbey, the hall had been ill-lit
and gloomy with every door closed against prying eyes. Now light
spilled from the long gallery on the right where one of the lofty
windows spangled shafts of sunlight onto the dusty wooden floor.

The neglected, unloved atmosphere had lifted as the distant
sound of music echoed through the empty hall. Achille emerged

and padded along in their wake. The two young women followed
Stowe and the music became louder as they approached the
drawing room. Leonora did not recognise the melody but it was
slow and elegiac. Stowe opened the door and sound and light
washed like a wave over them. The music stopped abruptly. 'Miss
Appleby and Miss Blythe, my lord.'

The Earl stood up, his face in shadow. In contrast, the garden
and the lake through the window behind him were brilliant with
sunlight which bounced off his shoulders and caught the curling
fronds of his dark, undressed hair. His scar and eye patch were
barely visible and Leonora was surprised at how fine-looking,
even noble, he appeared.

Lord Rokeby approached them with a faint smile of welcome
and as the light fell more harshly on his face, Leonora heard Charlotte's intake of breath. The raised jagged line that crossed from
temple to lip was unmistakeable, as was the leather patch.
Leonora had warned her young friend the Earl had returned
wounded and scarred from the battlefield, but seeing the damage
in the flesh for the first time was still difficult. So much death and
destruction were wrought by the years of war against Napoleon,
yet the higher echelons of the beau monde were shielded from the
full horror of disability and disfiguration. Most of their injured
officers did not appear much in polite society.

Leonora noticed again how Lord Rokeby attempted to
minimise his limp as he walked towards them. He put out his right
hand to take hers in greeting.

She smiled. 'Good day, sir. This is Miss Charlotte Blythe.'

He turned to Charlotte and noticing the shocked expression in
her eyes, took her proffered hand with his undamaged left hand
instead.

'Welcome to Rokeby Abbey.' He was formal in his manner and
Charlotte, slightly cowed by the situation, bobbed a curtsey.

'Thank you, my lord.'

He inclined his head. 'Come to the fire. May I offer you some refreshments?' Charlotte declined but Leonora said, 'I'll have whatever you're drinking,' nodding towards the amber liquid in a decanter that sat on the sideboard with a couple of handsome rummers beside it.

Lord Rokeby cast her an amused expression and poured out two glasses, handing one to her. 'It's my best French brandy. That and Achille were the only good things I salvaged from the war.' He gestured to his dog stretched out on his sheepskin rug by the fire.

The women sat together on the sofa and he in the wing chair opposite. It looked well-worn and comfortable but Lord Rokeby did not settle into its depths. His voice was intense. 'I owe you an explanation of your birth, Miss Blythe.'

Leonora took a tentative sip of her brandy and coughed as its fieriness hit the back of her throat. Charlotte clasped her hands together in her lap and waited. 'Charles was two years older than me, a hero figure in many ways. He was brought up with the knowledge he would inherit this ancient title and the extensive estate that gilded his name. I will show you the portrait of him afterwards.'

The Earl took a gulp of brandy and looked at Charlotte with a keen eye. 'You are fair where he was dark, but you have the Rokeby look in your eyes. I hope you have been spared the Rokeby temperament though!' He looked down into his glass, lost for a moment in thought. 'Father was proud of Charles. Less so of me.' His face grimaced for an instant. Then he glanced at Charlotte. 'You have every reason yourself to be proud of your father, despite the irregularity of your birth.'

Lord Rokeby took a deep breath. 'When Charles was eighteen, he had a liaison with one of my mother's maids. I don't recall her name but when she was with child, no one knew. Both she and

Charles were afraid of the consequences. I think my brother really cared about your mother and, in a romantic moment, thought he might be able to marry her and legitimise you. But future Earls of Rokeby were not allowed the indulgences of the heart afforded lesser mortals.' He gave a rueful smile.

Charlotte's quiet voice cut through his reverie. 'So my mother was loved by my father?'

Lord Rokeby looked at her and a fleeting softness suffused his features. 'I believe so, Miss Blythe.'

'That means a great deal to me. Thank you.' She smiled. 'Do you know where she is now? I hope to find her too.'

He shifted in his chair and Achille raised his head from the footstool at the Earl's feet. 'Your birth was unexpected and there was quite a stir in the servants' quarters. As your presence could no longer be kept a secret, the butler thought it his duty to tell my fierce papa. I'm afraid the old Earl decreed that the infant should be left on the Vicarage doorstep and that Charles should be immediately despatched to the army. He purchased a commission for his son and heir in the 15th King's Regiment. Your mother was dismissed and placed in another noble house in London, and my brother went to war.'

'So in one fell swoop you lost your brother, and Charlotte lost her mother and father.' Leonora shivered.

'Indeed. But with a family like mine, the individuals are not important; it is the family, its name, history and land that matter. And no one is allowed to risk that, even such a favourite son as Charles.'

'So, after eighteen years of silence and ignorance as to my parentage, why tell me now?' Charlotte had recovered her poise and forgotten her shyness, so great was her desire to know.

'I followed my brother into the regiment as soon as I could.' His face darkened with the memory. 'Then five years ago, mortally injured in the field of battle, Charles imparted to me his most urgent wishes. I had to find you and tell you the truth.' He was watching Charlotte's face closely. 'He had intended to do so when you were grown but of course never returned. I was then captured and only now have the opportunity to relay his instructions.' He got to his feet. 'Before I continue, come and see your father's portrait.'

Leonora and Charlotte followed him to the picture gallery they had passed as they entered the house. Walking into the long room washed with light from two great Elizabethan windows, they were presented with the grandeur of oak-panelled walls hung with ancestral portraits. Pale faces loomed out of dark interiors, stiff complex ruffs giving way as they moved through the centuries to waterfalls of snowy lace for the men and sumptuous silk and creamy bosoms for the women. The sunlight filtered through in bands, dust motes dancing in the air, and the atmosphere was heavy with history and the past lives of those who had gone before, a great continuum of Rokebys watching their progress down the room.

They stopped in front of a life-size portrait hung over the grand fireplace. Leonora and Charlotte gazed up into the proud face of Charles Rokeby in full Light Dragoons uniform, mounted on his black charger. They could not suppress a gasp of surprise and wonder. The young man was indeed handsome, a certain swagger in his inky eyes, his dark hair mostly covered by an impressive Tarleton cap of black silk and fur, chained in silver with a snowy white plume of feathers. His dolman was blue and also braided in silver, his fur-lined pelisse slung over his left shoulder. He looked magnificent, as the artist intended, a young man astride not just his war horse but the world he inhabited, a misty vision of Rokeby Abbey, its ruins and parkland behind him.

Leonora looked from the portrait to the new Earl and said, 'It's clear he's your brother.'

A swift grimace crossed his face. 'I'm glad you think so, Miss Appleby, even after the depredations of war.'

Lord Rokeby then led the way to the library where he gestured to the chairs on the other side of the desk while he withdrew some papers from the central drawer. Leonora was not immune to the attractions of the room. It smelt of leather, dust and woodsmoke. The walls were lined in dark oak shelves interrupted with regular reeded piers surmounted by carved heads of horses. Serried ranks of leather spines added their fascination. So many worlds, so many lives contained within their pages, within this room. She felt a flutter of excitement. How she longed to explore its treasures, but Lord Rokeby's voice returned her to the momentous matter in hand.

'Miss Blythe, I am pleased to welcome you to the Rokeby family; in fact, as my niece – as novel a thought for me as it must be for you.'

He sat down and passed a document across to her. 'Charles's dying wish was that you should be introduced to our grand-mother, the Countess of Bucklebury, who has a house in Brook Street in Mayfair. He wanted you to have a Season in Town, spon-sored by her. He was her favourite and she is keen to meet you.'

Charlotte was overwhelmed with the thought of being presented to London Society. Nothing had been further from her mind and she felt utterly ill-equipped for such an ordeal. She stut-tered, 'Sir, I am so unprepared. I never dreamed of such a future.'

Lord Rokeby looked at her closely. 'Can you dance, and engage in light inconsequential conversation? It would help if you can play the piano-forte passably and sing a little.'

Leonora was less shocked than Charlotte by this suggestion. Once she knew of her friend's noble parentage, she had expected that she would be launched on Society in some way as befitted her family's rank. She leant forward and said, 'Miss Blythe is a fine musician and can both play and sing. I have been teaching her these last five years.'

His dark gaze settled on Leonora's face. 'Then I am confident she will be most proficient in the drawing room arts.'

'I have had dancing lessons too. Mama Mildmay has been scrupulous in her care of me.'

'I'm glad to hear it. My brother assured me he left instructions with his banker, Drummonds, to send the Reverend a yearly sum for your upkeep. Drummonds are noted for their discretion in such matters.' He then pushed the piece of paper across the desk towards Charlotte. 'I would like you to read this and if you agree, I will ask the local attorney to attend. This too is your father's wish that you should have a dowry of ten thousand pounds.'

Charlotte gasped. She had never even heard talk of such a fortune before and for it to be attached to her on the occasion of her marriage astonished and alarmed her. 'But my lord, that is beyond imagination!' Her hands had flown to her cheeks which were rosy with the emotion of the afternoon.

'It's a generous portion, but not too generous for the daughter of an Earl with a significant estate.'

'But I am not his legitimate daughter.'

'No, but I am proud to belong to a family which historically has treated its irregular progeny as if they were legitimate.'

Leonora knew that Charlotte was overwhelmed by the enormity of the situation and so felt she herself should point out certain practical considerations. 'Lord Rokeby, Miss Blythe will need some new clothes if she is to attend the parties next Season.'

His lordship smiled at her intervention. 'I had thought of this, Miss Appleby. My mother's modiste in Windsor is still operating her business. Mrs Marmery will know just what is needed. Just mention me to her and she will know I will honour all the bills.'

In a breathless voice, Charlotte asked, 'When would your grandmama wish me to arrive?'

'Lady Bucklebury has suggested ten days after Epiphany. I have a letter from her for you.' He rifled through the papers on his desk and pulled out a folded and sealed missive, addressed in an elaborate hand. 'She can be fierce but she is not a stickler for convention. She had an unconstrained youth when social mores were less prescriptive than today. I think she's amused by the thought she has a great-granddaughter whose existence was a mystery to her. You're also her connection with her lost favourite, your father.'

Both young women looked at each other, unsettled in different ways by the unfolding realisation of just how much Charlotte's life was changing. Excitement and alarm were the salient emotions in Charlotte's breast and in Leonora's heart was a confusion of feeling. On the surface was joy for her young friend, knowing her father at last and being embraced by a family of such significance to open undreamed-of possibilities. But under the bubbling excitement was a sense of loss, of the easy balance of her friendship with the girl she had known since babyhood.

Lord Rokeby was watching both their faces, an inscrutable gleam in his eye. 'Miss Blythe, is there anyone who could accompany you to London?'

Charlotte was suddenly animated and leant forward. 'My lord, I have no lady's maid, but I would be much consoled if I could go to London in the company of Miss Appleby.'

For a moment Lord Rokeby looked disconcerted and glanced at Leonora with a curl of amusement on his lips. 'What? Deprive me of my best piano-forte tuner?'

Leonora was taken aback by both Charlotte's request and his

lordship's not entirely ironic reply. She was uncertain whether she wished to go to London to join the glittering social whirl, but she was nevertheless growing impatient with her life of quiet contentment and narrowed horizons. Now a voice long suppressed, a cry for adventure and the thrill of the new, quickened her pulse. She was aware of Lord Rokeby's gaze on her face. 'What say you, Miss Appleby? Do you exchange the solid known pleasures of Hasterleigh for the meretricious diversions of the city?' He seemed amused at the dilemma.

'If I can take Mrs Priddy then I might care to see what London has to offer,' Leonora answered carefully. 'It would be novel to see sights of which I have only ever read.'

'Well, I'm disappointed in you, Miss Appleby. I took you for a steadier type, but now know you are as giddy as the next feather-brained miss!' And he chuckled. Achille had walked to his side and was nudging his arm with his long shaggy snout. Lord Rokeby ruffled his hound's ears and murmured, *'J'arrive tout de suite, mon ami.'* Turning to his visitors, he said in a business-like way, 'I've probably given you enough to consider for now, Miss Blythe. Take this document concerning your dowry and the Countess's letter addressed to you. We'll meet again and I can answer any more questions you might have then.'

Lord Rokeby accompanied Charlotte and Leonora to the stables, Achille loping beside him. He explained that his dog had grown used to him accompanying him as he rode out in the late afternoon, and made a fuss if this routine was ignored. 'Jupiter will be saddled up ready. The grooms are as much in thrall to Achille as I am.'

'I am impressed by your stables, Lord Rokeby.' Leonora's eyes rested on the beautiful horses in various degrees of activity, from grooming to being ridden out for exercise by the stablemen and rubbed down on their return.

Lord Rokeby looked across at Jupiter, his magnificent black hunter, fully saddled up and waiting with some impatience, pawing the ground. 'My favourite warhorse was also black and called Jupiter, and he was cut down in the same cavalry charge that felled my brother and myself. A soldier's love for his charger can never be surpassed. But as my first Jupiter died, my second was being born in the stables here. He and Achille are the loves of my life.' Despite the emotion of his words, Lord Rokeby's voice was quiet and cool.

Clover was again found loosely tethered under the tree and the Earl offered his hand to help Charlotte climb onto the seat. Just as Leonora was about to climb up herself, he put out his hand to her. She hesitated then took it, and his other hand grasped her waist to assist her effortless ascent into the gig. The gesture took Leonora aback; the pressure of his hand against her hip, even through her pelisse, conveyed an unexpected strength and the fleeting intimacy of his touch sent a frisson through her. She glanced at him; had he too felt this or was it just her fancy? she wondered. His gaze met hers for a second and then he nodded in farewell. Both women waved goodbye as Clover trotted out of the stable yard towards the drive. Leonora looked back and saw Lord Rokeby spring into Jupiter's saddle. With Achille by his side, his horse's hooves clattered over the cobbles, his tail raised like a jaunty flag, as man, horse and hound headed towards the ruins and the great parterre that led to the lake.

4

PERILS OF THE COUNTRY AND ATTRACTIONS OF TOWN

The journey back to the Manor was silent for different reasons from those on the way out. Both Leonora and Charlotte were not quite sure what had transpired but were aware their worlds had tilted on their axes. Charlotte stole a glance at Leonora. 'I'm sorry to have blurted out that I hoped you'd come with me to London. I should have asked you first.'

Leonora still had her eyes on the road, manoeuvring Clover past a cart overfilled with hay. 'I quite understand that you were as much taken by surprise as I was.' Only when they had returned to Hasterleigh Manor and Martin had taken Clover back to the stables were the young women able to talk properly about the afternoon's revelations.

They settled in the snug sitting room by the kitchen and Cook brought in a pot of tea and some ginger biscuits, still warm from the stove. Both looked a little pale and sipped some tea before Leonora said, 'Well! What a change of course in your life.'

Charlotte's words tumbled out in a rush. 'I'm gratified indeed to know who my father is. I'd always wondered about who I was and where I came from; children in the village claimed I'd been delivered by the stork which made me feel somehow strange. Now I know half my real story, it gives me the foundation I have always longed for.' She was quiet for a minute. 'But I wish he weren't of such noble birth, with all the extra complications. And I wish he were still alive and I could know him.' She paused to take a bite of her biscuit. 'And I really wonder now about my mother. How I would love to know her and hope she has been happy.'

'Well, you can get to know your father's brother and grand-mother, so that will give you more of a connection with the Rokeby side of the family.'

'Lord Rokeby is so forbidding and severe. So injured too. And how fearsome his grandmother sounds; even Lord Rokeby says it, and he's been to war!'

Leonora pointed out reasonably, 'Perhaps you'll discover the Rokebys are more fearsome in reputation and demeanour than in deed.'

'Perhaps, but even my father's portrait shows him accoutred for war and unapproachable. A hero figure, which excites me, but how could someone like me be interesting to someone like him?'

'Come now, Lottie. You have this chance for a life different from anything you may have dreamed. You are young and beau-tiful and will now be an excellent marriage prospect!'

'Oh dear!' Her head drooped.

'Why "oh dear"? It will be good for you to be courted. To be married with your own household and family would be a fine thing.'

'Why not for you too then?'

'You know that had Captain Worth lived, I would be married, likely with my own family. But it was not to be.' She poured out another cup of tea and changed the subject with a brusque tone in her voice. 'You have a London Season to prepare for. We have to be practical. First, we must sort out your wardrobe. See what dresses we can refurbish and trim with braid, lace and ribbons, new buttons, tassels and every kind of frill and furbelow. I've heard dresses are getting flouncier.'

'Ah, but you'll have to do the same with *your* wardrobe! You'll be attending all the balls and parties too.' Charlotte's expression had recovered its mischief.

'Thank you, Lottie, for ejecting me from my comfortable life in the country!'

'Well, a part of me too would rather stay here, where I'm happy and known.'

'That is no longer your choice it seems. We'll have to go to Windsor soon to order some new fashionable clothes.' Leonora ticked off on her fingers until she ran out of digits: 'Morning and afternoon gowns, walking dresses, riding habits, ball gowns, every kind of tippet, pelisse, spencer, cloak and shawl. Not to mention your stays, petticoats, nightwear and bonnets and caps. Oh and I forgot, footwear for every occasion.'

'My heart fails me!' Charlotte groaned as her head fell to her hand.

'You wouldn't be a proper heroine of one of those novels you enjoy so much if your heart didn't quicken at the thought. Come now, make a list of what you have already which we can alter and trim, with Nanny P's help.'

Mrs Priddy came into the room carrying her needlework. 'Do I hear my name promised for some enterprise?' Her blue eyes looked from one young face to the other.

'As you're the finest needlewoman either of us know, I hope you'll be able to help us make more fashionable and freshen some of our old gowns. Charlotte is going to London!'

'Oh la! I expected as much,' she said with some satisfaction at her powers of deduction.

'Well, did you also expect me to have to accompany her?'

Leonora's eyes were fixed on her old nanny's face with a challenging gleam. Mrs Priddy nodded with a smug look. 'And did you also foresee that you were coming with us?'

Peg Priddy put down the linen she was embroidering. 'What makes you think I will? I was last in London when I was a girl and did not care for it. So clamorous, noisome and dirty, and the behaviour of the populace was not much better!'

'I know you'll come, because you're the most important person in my life, and both of us depend on your good counsel.'

Mrs Priddy batted this compliment away just as there was a knock at the door and Jack Clegg peered into the room. 'Miss Leonora, Ned Fleming wishes to see you.'

Leonora got up in a hurry; her bailiff was the most competent of men and rarely bothered her outside the hours allotted for their weekly meetings. She followed Jack Clegg to the back door where Ned Fleming stood, his weather-beaten face looking more anxious than usual. 'Pardon my interrupting you at this time but I am concerned.'

'Come in, Mr Fleming.' Leonora led him into the office by the pantry. 'What has happened?'

'I'm afraid Silas Sproat, the son of your tenant who farms the acres which lie alongside Fopling land, has been shot for poaching.'

Leonora's heart plummeted with shock. The Sproats were a good hard-working family and Silas was their eldest, a fine strapping boy of about sixteen. 'Oh no! Is he still alive?'

'It's a flesh wound in his forearm, but the Fopling gamekeeper killed his dog.'

'Not Molly!'

'I'm afraid so. She just managed to escape with Silas but collapsed from blood loss when they got home and died on the kitchen floor.'

'This is terrible. Has Silas had any medical assistance?'

'No. His family don't want Sir Roderick to be able to track him down. You know what a ferocious Justice of the Peace he is.'

'What can we do? Do they have any medicine that might stop the wound festering?'

'Mrs Sproat's so successful healing with herbs that people think her a witch. She has immediately strapped up her boy with a honey bandage and given him clove water and wild marjoram. But she has nothing to heal a broken heart. Molly was his pride and joy.'

Leonora felt a spasm of sympathetic grief for Silas. 'She was the best of dogs. But why did he risk poaching on Fopling land? He knows we allow the villagers to hunt for rabbits for the pot. The family could always come to us if they were in need.'

'He's a rumbustious boy and I think was poaching for the fun of it, Miss Leonora.'

'At least he wasn't caught in one of those fiendish mantraps Fopling employs in his woods. I can hardly believe they are still allowed. So destructive of man and beast!'

'Your grandfather banned them from ever being used on Hasterleigh land.' Ned Fleming turned to go. 'I'll get back to the fencing I'm repairing along our southern boundary.'

'If you see the Sproats, tell them I'll visit tomorrow with a basket of food.'

'Don't draw any special attention to them for a few days, ma'am. Fopling's man will be looking for clues.'

'I'm surprised Silas's red hair wasn't enough to identify him.'

Leonora returned to see Charlotte in conversation with Mrs Priddy who was sewing a hem on some linen cloth. She said in distress, 'I'm afraid Silas Sproat has been wounded poaching on Sir Roderick's land. And Molly's been killed.'

Both women looked at her, horrified. Molly was loved in the

village for her sweet nature and beauty. Her speckled coat of blue and white splotches stood out as she pranced beside Silas down the village street. Silas too was a fine, high-spirited young man, and no one liked to think of him in pain and danger. 'I'll take some food over to the family tomorrow, but we are to be careful not to draw attention to their cottage; the Fopling gamekeeper is on the rampage and they intend to prosecute.'

Charlotte's face grew pale. 'He doesn't risk deportation or—' she paused with a bleak expression '—or death?'

Mrs Priddy put a hand on her arm. 'More likely it'll be imprisonment these days. The law is not as draconian as in my youth.'

Leonora was less sanguine. 'But with Sir Roderick Fopling in charge of the local courts, don't expect moderation or mercy. He'll likely call for the death sentence for the stealing of a rabbit.'

Dusk was already falling, and Charlotte decided it was time to go home to explain the latest plans to Mama Mildmay and the Reverend. 'I'll go the garden way,' she said as she embraced Leonora and squeezed Mrs Priddy's hand.

Leonora was just about to go upstairs when there was a knock on the front door. Jack Clegg opened it to the young curate standing on the doorstep, his clerical hat in his hand. She hailed him. 'Come in, Mr Fopling.' Aware of propriety's demands, she led him through to the small sitting room where Nanny P was still busy with her sewing.

'Good evening, Mrs Priddy.' He nodded his greeting and took Leonora's hand in his. 'I have just seen Mrs Sproat and Silas on my weekly visit to my parishioners. I know Jack Fleming will have told you about Silas and Molly. I wanted you to know what I told them, that I may be Sir Roderick's son, but I do not share his vengeful spirit. Their secret is safe with me.'

Leonora felt a swell of affection for this mild-mannered, gentle man. 'Thank you for letting me know.' He seemed reconciled to the fact that Leonora would not be his wife and their main concern now was with the Sproats. 'How are they?'

'Silas asked me to pray for Molly. He wanted to know if she was in Heaven.'

'Could you say anything to console him?'

'Only what I believe. That all living creatures have their own souls.' He paused as Mrs Priddy looked up with a smile in her eyes. 'Molly is not gone from us forever, but is part of that other world that is everywhere.'

All were silent for a moment, then Leonora asked, 'Is Silas going to bury her in the woods she loved so?'

'Yes, deep enough to outfox the foxes.'

'I will go and see the family tomorrow, but I realise we need to be discreet.'

'It may be a hopeful sign that my father and his man do not seem to know that they wounded someone and killed his dog. As long as Silas lies low until he can use his arm and pull his sleeve over his wound.'

'Well, I thank you for your care of the family.' Leonora met his eyes.

'We are all equal before God,' he said, turning to her with a pale smile. 'From the Sproats to the mighty Earl of Rokeby.'

Leonora smiled and led him to the door. They stood listening to the birds in the beech tree opposite and Richard Fopling murmured, 'We find the truth of that equality in the blackbird's song and the sighing of the wind.' With that quiet riposte, he stepped lightly back into the lane.

* * *

After another restless night, Leonora awoke to a clear fresh morning. The breeze was building into a gale that animated the

branches of the gnarled old rose growing up the back wall of the
Manor. It tapped against her window an insistent rhythm that
seemed to her sleep-starved brain to be a message from the
natural world. What was the rose trying to tell her? she wondered
in her drowsy state. She dragged herself from bed, determined to
take her grey mare, Dione, out for a canter in the parkland that led
to the river. Dressing in her favourite riding habit, she was aware
how tired it looked now that she knew she would have to take it to
Town for the Season, and made a mental note to replace the military frogging and braid. The shape was still very becoming and
the fine blue broadcloth, smart and crisp. She decided against
wearing a hat as nobody would see her and she would soon be
home.

Having eaten a quick breakfast, Leonora headed for the stables
where Martin was already saddling her mare. Dione was excited,
sidling and stamping and sniffing the air. Martin tossed Leonora
up into the side-saddle and before she had even properly arranged
her skirts Dione was off, straining to leave the stable yard and
head for the park. Leonora loved her horse as a friend. She had
been bought for her by her father as a twenty-first birthday
present and her loneliness as William Worth went to war was
assuaged. Dione was the most responsive of animals; her lustrous
dark eyes with their white lashes had gazed deeply into Leonora's
anguished face when the news of William's death reached her. The
mare understood Leonora's heart and this morning, was agitated
and excited. Clouds were racing across the sky and the wind was
whisking up Dione's tail and making her long mane ripple like
water.

Given her head, the horse took off towards the river, kicking off
her heels and soon breaking into a fluid gallop. Leonora was a
good horsewoman but had never jumped fences as some of the
bolder women did when out with the Fopling pack of hounds.

Galloping on Dione's back was the limit of her equestrian bravery and she held tight to the pommel, feeling her horse's exhilaration through the reins and the beating of her own heart. As they approached the river, Leonora wheeled Dione towards the woods that marked the boundary between Rokeby and Manor lands. She was windswept and her cheeks were pink as she urged her horse towards home. But a cry made her turn. There was a distant figure of a man on a big black horse emerging from the woods, cantering towards her; tall in the saddle, his hair unruly and coat tails flying, the unmistakeable figure of Lord Rokeby. As he came closer, Leonora realised she was so used to his scarred face she barely noticed the damage; instead, it was the man and his emotions that she saw. As he brought Jupiter to ride beside her, she was struck by how distraught he seemed. Barely pausing to greet her, he blurted out, 'I heard a dog was shot last night.'

'Yes. One of our tenants'. Molly, a sweet hound.' She saw relief flood the Earl's face then realised that Achille, his constant companion, was not with him, and her heart turned over with foreboding.

'Have you seen Achille? Hasn't been home since he set off on the scent of something, heading this way. He was with me on my ride yesterday, after you and Miss Blythe had left.'

'That's very concerning. Has he ever gone missing before?'

'No, never. He's a lazy vagabond who likes home comforts.'

A cold trickle of fear caught Leonora unawares. 'Sir Roderick Fopling's land abuts ours. He's on a one-man mission to destroy all poachers and has had his gamekeeper set mantraps throughout his woods.'

'The Devil take him!'

'I'm afraid the law's on his side and in these parts, he is the law!' The agitation was back in Lord Rokeby's face, and Leonora leant across to touch his arm in consolation. 'Let's find my bailiff who's mending the fences in the next field along. He knows most of what happens hereabouts.' She trotted towards the field gate and they passed through to find Ned Fleming working on the far boundary. Cantering towards him, their horses side by side, they thundered down through the lush grass.

'Ned, have you seen Lord Rokeby's dog? A wolfhound, grey and white marled coat.' Leonora was breathless.

'He's been missing since yesterday evening.' Lord Rokeby's voice was harsh with emotion.

Ned Fleming put down his mallet, a gloomy look on his face. 'That's a worry, my lord.' He rubbed his chin. ''Fraid we're close here to the Fopling estate, a veritable circle of hell for dogs; none escape with their lives.'

'Oh Ned, hush your doom-mongering!'

'No, Miss Appleby. I fear your man may be right. That dog has never left my side since I rescued him from the battlefield.'

'I did hear an animal cry last night; I thought it might have been a fox. But it is lethal to enter those woods in the dark. There are steel traps everywhere. The Justice is at war and doesn't mind who he hurts.'

Lord Rokeby had sprung down from his horse. 'Then I'm going to have to go in there.'

Leonora cried out, 'No! You'll end up with your leg mangled in one of those fearsome things.'

'My body is already mangled, one more injury barely matters.' He glanced at her, a mordant smile on his lips. 'How can I leave Achille to die? He would never have abandoned me.'

'I'll come with you, sir. I know where some of the worst are hidden.' Ned Fleming took his fence-cutting hatchet and fashioned two staves from his stash of wood. 'We'll take a big stick each to spring the traps before we step on them.'

Leonora interrupted their preparations. 'Just a moment, my

lord. Would it not be more polite and indeed sensible if you went to Sir Roderick Fopling first and asked permission to search for your dog? I'm sure his gamekeeper would know exactly where he had placed the traps?'

'You will come to realise, Miss Appleby, that I am neither polite nor sensible. Time is of the essence and I consider this a necessary reconnaissance.' Lord Rokeby walked round to help Leonora dismount. His humour had revived now there was a plan of action.

He raised his arms to catch her as she unhooked her leg from the pommel and slid down Dione's side. Leonora felt his hands grip her waist to place her feet on the ground and she looked into his face. She had never been this close to him before and was surprised how much taller he was than she. His undamaged eye was as dark and deep as Dione's and seemed to sparkle with a mysterious light as he met her upturned gaze. She recalled Nanny P's words – *he is a law unto himself* – and she shivered at the thought of how far that lawlessness might go.

His gaze was unwavering. 'Can you manage both horses, Miss Appleby, while Mr Fleming and I take a cursory look? I think Achille may be reassured if he can hear my voice.' Both Jupiter and Dione started cropping the grass and Leonora stood with their reins loose in her hand, feeling increasingly anxious for the fate of Achille and, to her surprise, his master too. She strained to listen as the men proceeded carefully into the wood, Lord Rokeby calling Achille's name, then silence. She heard sticks breaking under foot, then the chilling distant clang as a trap was sprung, she hoped by the judicious use of one of Ned's staves.

Leonora was growing cold and began to stamp her feet to keep the blood circulating to her toes. Suddenly she heard a faint yelp and the sound of a man's shout. It seemed an age but was only a matter of minutes before Lord Rokeby and Ned Fleming emerged carrying a prone Achille between them. The Earl had stripped off his jacket and riding coat to cover his hound's body.

Leonora left the horses and ran forward, stumbling over the tussocks. 'Is he alive?' she called out, breathless with tension.

Lord Rokeby's face was grim. 'Just about. He was caught by the leg, and I don't know yet the full damage. But he's frozen through. I must get him home.'

Her father's illness and death had made Leonora capable and decisive in a crisis. 'Don't lay him down in the wet field; I'll fetch the farm cart. Martin can saddle Clover up in moments.' She led Dione to a fallen stump to use as a mounting block and lacking all ladylike decorum, scrambled into the saddle to set off at a fast trot up the field.

Within five minutes, she and the cart had returned. With great care, the men laid Achille on the bed of straw on the back. It was the first time Leonora had seen the dog properly and he looked in a fearful state. His eyes were closed, and his back leg had the skin torn so badly that the bone and tendons were exposed in a bloody mess. She shuddered.

Lord Rokeby turned to Ned Fleming. 'Could you take Jupiter up to the Manor stables?' He looked questioningly at Leonora. 'I presume, Miss Appleby, that is acceptable? Then I'll walk round later to pick him up.'

The bailiff said, 'I'll happily ride him back to the Abbey for you, my lord.'

A grim smile lifted the corners of Lord Rokeby's mouth. 'That's very kind, Mr Fleming, but I'm afraid Jupiter is a spirited ride, and he would not be as sanguine as you about the matter. It's better if I return later, if your mistress concurs with that plan?'

'Of course.' Leonora was still on the seat of the cart and watched Lord Rokeby climb in beside his dog. He was in such a state of dishevelment with his hair whipped by the wind which had made an equal mess of hers, she felt sure. His cravat was askew and his fine white linen shirt besmirched with mud, snagged by the undergrowth they had pressed through, and smeared with blood.

The Earl turned back to Ned Fleming who was holding Jupiter by the reins. 'Thank you for all your help this morning. If I didn't need to get Achille home, I'd drive right round to Sir Roderick Fopling and demand he banish all traps from his land.' Leonora saw his rage gush up from some deep well then recede as fast as it had come. He turned to her, his cheeks still flushed with feeling, but said in a controlled voice, 'Thank you, Miss Appleby. We should get Achille back to Rokeby Abbey.'

* * *

As Leonora stopped the cart in front of the great door of the Abbey, she was aware for the first time what a country wench she must appear to any casual onlooker. She was hatless, virtually in déshabillé, her hair blown loose by the wind that was still tempestuous and threatening rain; her riding habit, never overly smart, was made all the more disreputable by the gobbets of mud and grass stains where she had run through the park to reach the two men bringing Achille out of the woods. In a hurried movement, she tried to stick the pins back in her hair but was soon surrounded by Stowe and assorted grooms come to carry the dog into the house. No one was concerned with how she looked and she quickly abandoned any such concern herself.

The hound was laid on his favourite sheepskin rug by the fire in the drawing room, hurriedly banked up to provide more warmth. Rokeby's cook brought up warm salted water to bathe the gash, and his valet collected the bag of bandages, herbal tinctures and pastes that every soldier knew how to use to treat wounds on the battlefield.

Leonora felt superfluous and exposed, unchaperoned as she was and as untidy as a washerwoman, and was about to make her farewells, when the Earl looked up from his ministrations and smiled. 'Thank you for everything, Miss Appleby. Achille's limb is not broken and I know how to treat such lacerations, so given some luck, he will live.'

She met his relieved gaze. 'That is the best of news.'

'I am grateful for all your help today. One further imposition, Miss Appleby: will you keep Jupiter in your stables until tomorrow? It'll be dark before I've finished here.'

Leonora nodded. 'Of course, whatever I can do to help.' Her emotions felt shredded and raw. Lord Rokeby got to his feet to take Leonora's hand in a brief salute before accompanying her through to the stables. The wind had dropped and the dying sun had stained the clouds a fiery pink. Horses were settling for the night and Clover waited patiently. The Earl seemed distracted as he helped her up into the cart seat, untied Clover's reins and handed them to her. 'Goodnight, Miss Appleby. I won't bother you in the morning when I collect my horse. You've been troubled enough by me and my concerns.'

As she turned Clover to trot towards the drive, the Earl put out a hand. 'I forget my manners. Apologies. I owe you so many favours, Miss Appleby. Please tell me what I can do to make amends.'

Leonora was unprepared for the question and paused. Then she recalled the joy of swimming in the Rokeby lake. 'Oh! Yes, there is something, Lord Rokeby. I would be happy to have your permission to swim in your lake.'

He looked shocked. 'You swim?' She nodded. He continued,

'Real swimming, not just paddling in the shallows as ladies do at Brighton?'

'I surprised myself with how much I love to swim. I learnt in your lake.'

'So you've been there before?'

Leonora felt her cheeks colour. 'I'm afraid I have. We used to trespass when we thought the house uninhabited.'

'We? Who else?' His face had become increasingly amused as the conversation continued.

'Miss Blythe, although she is not such a keen swimmer.'

He surprised Leonora with a bark of laughter, his teeth gleaming. 'Ah, so I've had two trespassing Nereids! May I ask what stopped you?'

'Your gamekeeper threatened to shoot us!' Leonora could not prevent a note of outrage entering her voice.

'What! Diggory Shrubb? No! He looks fearsome, 'tis true, but he'd never harm a woman – even less so a water nymph!'

'That may be so, but he did discharge his rifle over our heads. And tell us you were back and did not care for company.'

'Well, he's right enough there. But surely it's too late in the year for you to swim?'

She did not want to be deflected from her mission and asked again, 'When it's warmer again I would be gratified if you could give your permission?'

Lord Rokeby looked at Leonora with a speculative expression. 'I too like to swim, but in the afternoon. You have my permission to go to the lake in the morning before I've risen from my bed.'

'Thank you, my lord.' She felt a bubble of joy expand at the thought she could once again strike out in that cold clear water.

His brisk voice broke into her reverie. 'But you must never go to the lake alone. There are all kinds of hidden dangers. When the valley was flooded in my great-grandfather's day, a section of woodland was drowned and the trees remain, petrified just under the surface on the eastern side.'

Leonora nodded. 'I will always have someone with me.'

'Fare thee well, Miss Appleby.' Lord Rokeby stepped away to let her go, turning back to the house, his anxieties about Achille uppermost in his mind once more.

* * *

The next morning Leonora was up early, determined to visit the Sproats without risking the attention of Sir Roderick Fopling and his men. She donned her cloak and bonnet and slung a basket on her arm with food from the kitchen. Mrs Priddy had taught Silas his letters when he was younger and so she joined Leonora's mission of mercy.

Silas was much more concerned about the death of Molly than about his own wound which was healing well. He seethed with resentment and Leonora was anxious the young hotspur might do something stupid. 'Silas, you know it's dangerous to trespass on Sir Roderick's land. You can always ask us for a rabbit for the family.'

'That's what I told 'im, Miss Appleby!' Mrs Sproat was exasperated and banged the birch besom against the wall as she swept the floor with vigour.

'They didn't have to shoot Molly!' Silas's red hair was sticking up like a flame around his freckled face, which was flushed with feeling. 'She was the best hound in the world. There'll never be a better.' Tears sprang into his eyes.

Mrs Priddy bustled forward and asked to see his arm. Examining the scabbed wound which had no tell-tale signs of inflammation, she nodded and caught his mother's eye. 'That's looking good. Mrs Sproat, your potions seem to have done the trick.'

Mrs Sproat put down her broom and crossed her arms,

looking pleased. 'My medicine is the wisdom of the country folk. Yet to let me down.'

Leonora had unpacked the contents of the basket and turned to Silas. 'Did you know that the Vazeys' dog has just had puppies?'

'Yes, but she's nothing like as prime a dog as Molly.' He was sulky.

'I know. No one could be. But they're good-looking puppies and I'm sure you'd train one up to be almost as good as Molly.' She knew not to press the point but to leave it, hopefully to tantalise Silas enough that he would go and see them. No one could resist a puppy, she thought with a smile.

'Please, no more trespassing on Fopling land. You've escaped this time, but it's too dangerous if you're caught. Silas, come to us if your family needs anything,' Leonora added as she turned to go.

Mrs Sproat came forward, a smile lifting her careworn features. 'Always grand to see you Mistress Priddy. And thank you, Miss Appleby. These victuals and your care are much appreciated. I'll make sure the lad stays within bounds.'

* * *

The two women were almost at the Manor when Curate Fopling emerged from the alley to the almshouses, walking fast. He nearly bumped into them and tipped his hat. 'Apologies, ladies.' His pale kindly eyes glanced at Leonora, then quickly flickered away. The morning sun was bright on the bare branches of trees that had given up their last leaves to the wind. 'Yesterday's storm has purged the air to bring us such clarity of light.' He met her eyes again. 'Such certainty is rare, wouldn't you agree, Miss Appleby?' Then he tipped his hat again and walked off towards the church.

'I can't make that young man out,' Mrs Priddy tutted as they entered the house. 'He will obscure everything in poetic observation.' They removed their cloaks and bonnets to be greeted by Charlotte's *hallo* from the small sitting room. Turning, they saw their visitor looking charming in a morning dress of palest blue cotton, her fair hair more carefully confected into curls than usual, a handwritten list in her hand.

'Lottie! You're early. Have you breakfasted?' Leonora went forward to embrace her.

'Yes, I've been up hours, making lists of my clothes so we can decide what we can improve and what we need to order from Windsor.'

'Aha! Well, we'll need Nanny P's excellent needlework skills.' Leonora turned to the elderly woman who was about to head for the kitchens in search of Cook.

Mrs Priddy laughed. 'I'll do what I can, but I also have my dear Nora to think about. She will need some new gowns too.'

'Oh no! This is Miss Charlotte's Season, I'll just be acting as her unremarkable chaperone.'

Charlotte grasped her friend's arm and said, 'It's imperative that you come as my sister, dressed to the same height of fashion.'

They went through to the room and sat together on the sofa. 'That's very kind of you Lottie, but I am twenty-seven, no longer an attractive marriage partner, and you are eighteen and at your prime. You are also the daughter of a nobleman and a hero of the Peninsular War. We are going to have to dress you appropriately.'

'But I'm not the Earl's legitimate child.' Charlotte's voice was quiet.

Leonora took her hand. 'You are going to behave as if you were, with all the pride in your blood. Do not give others reason to pity or shame you. Now let me see your list.'

'I have only listed the clothes that are in good enough condition, or appealing enough, to merit embellishment.' Charlotte had carefully noted every morning gown, walking dress, riding habit, evening gown and even one ball gown, together with matching pelisses, spencers, tippets, muffs and a single fur-edged velvet cloak and redingote for when the weather was grim.

'This is so helpful. I had no idea you had so many clothes, and a ball dress too!'

'Yes, Mama Mildmay has admitted she had an annual allowance from my mystery father to spend on clothes and she wanted me to be prepared for anything. I wish she had confided in me. It would have meant much to know my father cared enough to stay in contact, even if just through the bank.'

'How goes it with you, now you've discovered something about him?'

'I don't really know. I'm afraid of the person he wished me to become and the life I'm to inhabit. I've had no training to enter Society and feel such a country mouse.'

'Most young women who come up to Town for their first Season have lived secluded country lives. Your kind nature and talents will charm everyone, from your great-grandmother to the exacting Society Dames, to every young man about Town.'

Charlotte threw her arms around Leonora and said, 'I'm grateful you and Nanny P will be there too. Mama Mildmay says she cannot leave the Reverend and the parish responsibilities, but truly she is overwhelmed by this change in my affairs.'

'Well, we have to be practical now. I think we must travel to Windsor as soon as we can and order some new clothes. Have you thought about Mrs Marmery, your grandmother's modiste?'

'I've already written to her. Her shop's in Peascod Street just down from the Castle and I've asked for an appointment next week.'

'Good. Now we need to have some idea of what we'd like to ask her to make.'

'I have the latest *La Belle Assemblée* for that purpose. Mama

Mildmay borrowed it from the Dean's wife and it's full of beautiful gowns.' Charlotte gestured to a magazine beside her, filled with fine coloured prints of engravings of fashionable women in elaborate dresses and accessories.

As Leonora talked clothes and commented on Charlotte's choices, poring with her over the exquisite pages of the magazine, she realised she was on tenterhooks listening out for the sound of horses' hooves from the stable yard. She reasoned it was only because she was anxious to hear about Achille, but really she knew it was the Earl she hoped to see again.

Charlotte's voice recalled her to the subject of their wardrobes. 'Do you think my blue sarsenet would do if I lowered the neckline and added a ribbon trim?'

'I think it's most becoming as it is.'

'Ah, but look here.' She tapped a page with an engraving of *A Gauze Evening Gown from Paris*. 'See how the neckline is much lower and wider and as I don't have a beautiful necklace, I think it needs more embellishment.'

'Excuse me, Lottie, I must check something.' Leonora picked up her skirts and hurried down the stone-flagged corridor to the kitchens to open the back door to the stable yard. She heard the clatter of hooves on the cobbles and turned to see a large black horse mounted by a tall man dressed in black riding away towards the drive. Lord Rokeby had come for Jupiter and was disappearing into the hazy morning sun. She had missed him.

Cross with herself for feeling so dejected, Leonora returned to Charlotte and the discussion of the competing merits of cambric muslin, jaconet and silk, and whether there was anything finer than gauze and satin ribbons with which to confect a ball dress. With some reluctance, she also realised she must address her own deficient wardrobe and work out with Nanny P what she could modify to make it fashionable and acceptable for Town. She knew she would need to order a couple of special garments from Mrs Marmery for herself and was grateful for the small legacy her mother had left her.

* * *

The day for the journey to Windsor began clear and crisp. Martin was excited by the trip; it was not often that he had to dust down the Hasterleigh coach and harness up the carriage bays. It was ten miles away and the horses would be able to do both journeys in a leisurely fashion, allowing the young ladies enough time with the modiste and still managing to return before nightfall.

Leonora and Charlotte climbed into the coach, dressed for the cold in walking dress, spencer, pelisse and cloak. Their best winter bonnets trimmed with velvet were on their heads and each carried large rabbit-fur muffs. There was an old fur blanket on the floor and Mrs Priddy had heated up two bricks in the oven to be placed by Martin to warm their feet. For the young women, this was an exciting expedition, for they did not often go much farther than the local market town and had never been as close to London before. The Dean's wife had told Mrs Mildmay with some trepidation that this week, the Prince Regent was expected to be in residence at the Castle, which added an extra zest to their visit. Where the Prince Regent roamed, his wild set followed.

Charlotte and Leonora gazed out at the countryside as they passed through rolling rural landscapes with villages, coaching inns and scattered farms the only habitation. In the distance to the north was the blue blur of the Chiltern Hills, undulating and mottled with woodland. They had set out early and the sun was still low and pallid, casting faint shadows across the carriage as the horses trotted on. Soon they were travelling along the Bath Road through the Thames valley heading for London, and the traffic of horsemen, private vehicles and stagecoaches had increased. Ox carts laden with late-harvested hay or scavenged firewood trundled in front of them and it was difficult sometimes to pass as there were mail coaches and private vehicles rattling towards them, heading in the opposite direction.

As they approached the Windsor Road, Leonora was surprised to see so many smart curricles driven by fashionable young men. They were passed by one, the magnificent matched greys straining forward, their necks outstretched, nostrils flaring, and Leonora was struck with unexpected excitement. There was a young man driving, his long whip in hand and his passenger beside him. They were wearing their driving coats against the cold, the capes rippling in the wind, their curly-brimmed beavers pulled low, and their faces muffled to the eyes with long woollen scarves. Behind the driver perched his tiger with the horn used to summon the turnpike keepers to let them through without delay.

Charlotte had noticed these sporting drivers and was intrigued. 'Do you think those are the kind of young men we will meet during the Season?' The excitement in her voice made Leonora smile, relieved that her young friend's spirit of adventure was beginning to overcome her natural fear of the social ordeal ahead.

Leonora too was strangely thrilled by the sight. This world of the rich and noble male was alien to her but seductive in its freedoms and swagger. True, she had now met the Earl of Rokeby who had the same advantages of nobility and wealth but had chosen to go to war, and perhaps that entitled swagger was gone. During his army leave he would have lived the indulgent life of a buck about Town, gaming, racing and drinking, but Leonora mused at how he seemed to have missed out on learning the elaborate courtesies of his class; he was brusque and not practised in sly charm and flowery talk. As Nanny P always insisted with some admiration, he marched to a different drum.

'No doubt there will be many dashing young men who drive their curricles too fast,' Leonora laughed. 'But there'll be others who are more dangerous to young women of fortune.'

Charlotte turned back from the window, a look of surprise on her face. 'Surely I am not one of those?'

'If the Earl intends to settle a substantial marriage portion on you then you will indeed be one of those heiresses.'

'Despite my irregular birth?'

'I think the nobility of your father's line will matter more, and the Countess of Bucklebury's patronage tells the world she accepts you as part of her family. A great-granddaughter in fact!' The carriage had turned off the Bath Road and they were now travelling towards Windsor on a track that made the old springs creak as the wheels juddered in and out of the large ruts and ridges left by recent rains.

'Look, I think we can just see the Castle.' Leonora pointed across the low-lying green of the valley. The ancient grey crenellations, misty in the distance, contrasted with the pastoral vision before them: hazel, oak and apple trees clumped on the perimeter of a smallholding where a couple of pigs wallowed in mud.

The novelty of the journey was wearing thin and both young women longed to see Windsor for themselves, this growing town enriched by its royal connections. Soon the horses pulled up in Peascod Street, outside a pretty bow-windowed shop, its display dominated by an aquamarine pelisse edged in ermine.

Martin opened the door to hand the two young women out. Leonora had never seen such a fascinating mix of people promenading up the road towards the Castle. There were officers in their red jackets, women dressed in the height of fashion with their showy bonnets with plumes of bright feathers and pelisses of satin and velvet. They passed in a gust of chatter and laughter.

Martin did not seem amused. He tipped his hat. 'Miss Leonora, Mr Fleming asked me to warn you that there is a barracks in Windsor which attracts a certain type of disreputable woman and some bawdy behaviour from the soldiers.' His face was suffused with embarrassment at bringing up such an indelicate subject but the Manor bailiff, Ned Fleming, had known Leonora since she was a baby and felt a certain fatherly responsibility towards her.

'Thank you, Martin, for your and Mr Fleming's concern. I think Miss Blythe and I have so much business to conduct with the modiste we'll barely have time to see any of the passing show.'

'I'll water and feed the horses at the Star and Garter tavern just down the street.' He pointed to a large building three doors down. 'We need to leave after three hours in order to get home by dusk.'

A bell tinkled as Leonora and Charlotte entered the shop and an elderly bird-like woman emerged through a curtain at the back. Mrs Marmery had intelligent eyes in a sharp lined face. Wearing a pea-green satin turban with a purple cockade, her thin body was not flattered by the fashions of the time and so she had chosen a beautifully tailored spencer of violet silk, fastened to the throat by silver braid sewn to make it look like a hussar's. Her eyes flickered from Leonora to Charlotte, whom she approached, then dropped a quick curtsey. 'I presume you are Miss Charlotte Blythe. I remember your grandmother well. You have a look of the Countess.' Charlotte coloured and dropped her eyes while Mrs Marmery summoned a young assistant. 'Would you like some tea after your journey?'

Leonora was feeling in great need of refreshment and inclined her head in acquiescence. 'My name is Miss Appleby; I will be accompanying Miss Blythe to London. And thank you, Mrs Marmery, tea would be most welcome.'

The modiste motioned them to the sofa and said in a business-like way, 'We don't have much time to create your wardrobe, so I suggest we discuss the most important aspects of your apparel first. How many ball dresses and evening gowns would you like me to make?'

Charlotte removed her list from her reticule and handed it over. Mrs Marmery looked up with a speculative eye. 'I've just had a bolt of gold silk gauze delivered from Paris. With your colouring, I think a ball dress in that would be most becoming.' She clapped her hands and a young seamstress emerged blinking into the showroom. 'Delia, please bring us the new gold gauze.' This sparkling airy cloth was unrolled and whisked under Charlotte's chin; it did indeed somehow intensify her dark eyes and the lustrous contrast of her fair hair.

Then followed a dizzying parade of fabrics of every weight and colour: Venetian crape, cambric, sarsenet, silky China crape, chambray, airy tiffany, jaconet, muslin, worked point gauzes and a variety of pretty workaday sprigged cottons. Luckily, Mrs Marmery was decisive and seemed to have an unerring eye for what most flattered her young client. The fabric chosen and detail of the pattern was noted down carefully in a book by Delia. Measurements were taken and accessories discussed.

Charlotte was beginning to tire of the rich cornucopia of fabrics, patterns and details, all of which needed rapid decisions. She turned to Leonora and said, 'You too will need some special dresses.'

Mrs Marmery's eyes sparkled. 'I've just been looking at your colouring, Miss Appleby, and I have the perfect evening gown for you. It's already made up for a client who then eloped before she could do the Season, so her heartbroken mama cancelled the order.' She turned to the diligent young seamstress who had just finished sketching the detail agreed for the last gown for Charlotte and clapped her hands. 'Delia, fetch the silver gown. I'd like to see if it fits Miss Appleby.'

The dress was carried into the room and both young women gasped. In Delia's arms it looked like she had caught a wave of silver foam. Charlotte said in excitement, 'It looks beautiful! Please try it on.' Leonora was led behind a screen and the young woman helped her unlace her dress and slip into this new one. Leonora had never had much opportunity for fashionable dressing or even thinking about clothes. Now, as she stepped into the matching silk chemise and then slipped on the gauze overdress, she felt entirely different and straightened her shoulders and lifted her chin.

If Shakespeare was right that *apparel oft proclaims the man,* then she felt shaken enough by this new feeling to declare that *clothing maketh the woman.* She gazed at herself in the looking glass and barely recognised the image reflected back. The bodice fitted as if it had been made for her, lowcut and wide which flattered her breasts and neck and the creamy colour of her skin. The puff sleeves were ribbed with tiny tucks and the hem was lightly wired so it stood out from her ankles. She could not believe this vision in silvery gauze was herself.

Leonora, with a sudden shyness, slipped out from behind the screen to see Charlotte's eyes fly open as she clapped her hands in pleasure. 'You look *ravissante,* Leonora! You must have that lovely dress.'

Mrs Marmery's face also lit up. She was a master of her craft and the pleasure of sending young women into Society looking as beautifully dressed as possible affirmed her pre-eminent place amongst the most skilled modistes. 'Miss Appleby, it could not suit you better,' she declared.

Leonora twirled and then stopped, embarrassed, shocked that her love for this garment and pleasure in her appearance displayed the very girlish sensibility she had so disdained. Mrs

Marmery stepped forward and took Leonora's hand. 'Trust me, Miss Appleby, that design is most flattering. The bodice is the perfect proportion for your height and the low, wide neckline shows off your shapely bosom in a suitably modest but revealing way. No one could accuse you of looking vulgar, my dear.'

Leonora stole another look at herself in the glass and was astounded by how a fine gown could transform a woman's idea of herself and her place in the world. For the first time she felt beautiful, even noble. She met Mrs Marmery's amused eyes and said, 'I'd be very pleased if I can purchase this gown. And could you make me two more to the same design; one in that cornflower-blue silk crape you showed us and a second in the pale rose-pink tiffany. I like the lightness of the fabric.'

Just as both young women were fading after the excitement of the day, they heard the blessed sound of wheels clanking on the cobbles and the clopping of horses' hooves as Martin drew their coach to a halt outside the window.

Charlotte grasped Mrs Marmery's hand. 'Thank you, Madame, for helping me with my clothes for the Season. I no longer feel quite so unprepared.'

'You will both be as well-dressed as anyone.'

'Thank you for your help, Mrs Marmery, and Delia.' Leonora saluted them from the door. They scrambled into the carriage with their gayly striped boxes complete with one dress each that was ready-made, together with a whole gallimaufry of ribbons, beads and braids, feathers, flounces and fur, with which to refurbish their old wardrobe of garments and bonnets.

As they headed back through the green valley of the Thames again, Charlotte leant back against the squab cushions and sighed. 'I hadn't realised what a difference lovely clothes make. I am no longer afraid of going to London; in fact, I'm quite excited, as long as I have you and Mrs Priddy – and Mrs Marmery's creations as my shield.'

'It's quite a revelation. Even *I* felt positively beautiful. It's rather shaming, don't you think, when one has prided oneself on not caring about such things? How do we stop ourselves becoming the simpering Society ninnies we deplore?' They laughed.

Charlotte was pensive for a while then said with some wonder, 'Knowing who my father was and the family that I belong to has given me a centre I've never had before.' She held her head up with pride.

'Could it be that at last you have that sense of belonging you've sought all your life?'

'I know now where I've come from and although I can't ever know my father, I know what has made him, and made me too. But I must find my mother. Perhaps she will explain another side of me.' They both laid their heads back on the cushions as the coach rattled home.

5

MUSICAL CHAIRS AT HASTERLEIGH

Leonora hung up the silver gauze evening dress and contemplated it, wondering if it had some kind of talismanic power. She was twenty-seven and had been happy with the limitations of her existence in Hasterleigh, but this dress sparkled in the morning light, and it whispered that there was another world she could inhabit, if only for a time.

She descended the stairs to breakfast with an excitement of spirit. She was going to grasp whatever chances came her way. Leonora took a piece of writing paper from the desk in the library, dipped her quill in the inkwell and wrote in her fluent hand:

Dear Lord Rokeby,

Charlotte Blythe and I returned yesterday from a successful visit to your mother's modiste, Mrs Marmery of Windsor. I have been wondering how Achille has been. Did he pass a good night?

With greetings from your neighbour,

Leonora Appleby

She folded it and sealed it with a blob of warm wax impressed with her father's seal and carried it through to the kitchen where Jack Clegg was eating toast with Cook. 'Good morning to you both.' Turning to Jack, she said, 'When you've finished, would you deliver this to the Abbey?' He stood up, wiping his hands on his breeches, his mouth full, and with a twinkle in his eyes could only nod.

Mrs Priddy was drinking her coffee when Leonora walked into the breakfast room. Her old nanny's blue eyes missed little as she glanced sideways. 'Nora my dear, how are you after yesterday's excursion?'

'I feel quite restored,' she said as she took a newly baked roll from the basket on the table. 'Is this your bramble jam?' Leonora asked as she slathered a teaspoon of the glistening jelly onto the fresh bread.

'It is indeed. You and Charlotte picked me that trug-full from the hedgerow.' She was not going to be deflected and continued, 'You're up to something. Have you heard from Mr Lockwood since he's been gone to Oxfordshire?'

Leonora had barely thought of George Lockwood since he had left and looked surprised. 'No. But he has said he'll come for the musical evening I'm planning. I've also asked Lord Dearlove and his friend Captain Ormonde.'

'I liked his lordship when he visited your dear William. He was very attentive after Captain Worth died.'

'He was very kind to me, 'tis true. Pity he's also with his sister who believes any act of unkindness, however small, is never wasted.'

'Really, Nora my dear, it's not like you to be so sharp. Remember that young woman does not have your advantages of beauty and talent.'

Leonora snorted with laughter. 'Nanny P, you are irrepressible! You'd excuse the Devil himself by pointing out he was in need of food or a good sleep. Lady Livia has every advantage. She's an heiress, she's elegant, she's high-born. She just relishes being unkind to others less elevated than herself.'

Mrs Priddy tutted and changed the subject. 'Do you think that Lord Rokeby will grace us with his presence at your party?'

Leonora still felt like teasing her old nanny and nudged her arm. 'He was another of your bad boys who just needed understanding and love to be turned to the good.' But the humour left her face as she added, 'I think the war and loss of his brother has erased for ever the mischievous young man you used to know.' As she spoke, Jack Clegg knocked on the door.

He entered and handed over a piece of paper scrawled in black with her name. 'His lordship asked me to deliver a response.'

'Thank you.' Leonora opened the roughly folded scrap of paper torn from the bottom of her letter. She read out loud. '*Miss Appleby, Achille had a rough night and so did his master. I'd be grateful if you could come today at three with Mrs Priddy. Her wisdom in these matters might be useful.* Then he's signed it with a scrawled *R*.' Leonora looked up and met Nanny P's eyes. 'That sounds like an order.'

'Prevaricating charm was never his strong suit.'

'I hope you're happy to accompany me?'

* * *

So it was that at a quarter to three, Leonora and Mrs Priddy set off in the gig. Clover was getting used to this short journey to Rokeby Abbey and would have found her way there unbidden. To her shame, Leonora changed into her finest afternoon gown, more formal than she had worn before on her working visits, but it was particularly flattering to her figure and colouring. Charlotte had joked that it made her look like a piece of Mr Wedgewood's blue jasper-ware figured in white, but she felt confident in the fine blue wool that fitted so well. Mrs Priddy had brought with her a linen bag filled with dried chamomile flowers and lavender, together with fresh comfrey leaves she had picked from the orchard that afternoon. She had also included a jar of Hasterleigh honey.

The great Abbey door was opened by Stowe looking more lugubrious than usual. From the depths of the house they heard the Earl's angry voice curse, 'Shut that damned door!' Stowe took the women's cloaks and led the way into the drawing room where a banked-up fire crackled in the medieval fireplace. The Earl looked startled to see them. His sleeves rolled up and his face pale and strained, he came towards them, his hand outstretched. 'Apologies ladies, for my language. I forgot the time. I haven't slept with worry.' He gestured to where his large dog lay on his sheepskin, his eyes half-closed. Achille lifted his head and gave a weak wag of his tail before subsiding again.

Mrs Priddy walked towards the invalid. 'Is the wound infected?'

Lord Rokeby hung his head. 'I've seen so many infected wounds in the Peninsula, and it does not end well.' Everyone gazed down at the torn back leg which was swollen right to the pads of the foot. The area around the wound was red, the wound itself weeping.

'I've brought some herbs to mix with honey as a dressing when we bandage it afresh. But first it must be cleaned.' Mrs Priddy knelt beside Achille while his master strode for the door, his limp pronounced, as he called for Stowe.

Leonora felt her heart lurch with sympathy for the great hound and for his master who looked haunted with exhaustion and fear. She stroked Achille's back, murmuring to him in encouragement but did not want to be in the way and retired to the window seat.

Kneeling on the floor beside Achille, Peg Priddy mixed her dried herbs and the comfrey in a pestle brought to her by Stowe. She added a dollop of honey as the Earl, on the other side of his dog, cleaned the wound. His face was contorted with memory and words started to tumble from him as if a dam had been breached. Leonora's attention was rapt at the unexpected rawness of emotion. 'Achille getting wounded thus and the dread night just passed, when I faced his death, transported me back to the desperate clash of men and horses at Corunna.' He shuddered. 'The horrors of battle.'

Mrs Priddy worked on quietly, making her healing paste, their eyes not meeting. Lord Rokeby's voice was urgent, as if exhaustion had loosed his bonds and at last he could tell of his agony. 'I couldn't talk to anyone and thought I should push it away and forget. The suffering and blood, voices crying for their mothers or God, the nauseating stench of blood.' With delicacy he was washing the pus from the wound and his dog, seeming to know it was for his good, lay still, barely whimpering. The Earl looked up suddenly and caught Mrs Priddy's eye. 'When Marshal Soult's cavalry kept on coming, wave on wave, our men and horses were cut down and trampled in the gore; it was as if we'd stumbled into hell.'

He was staring into the fire. 'The cries of men begging to be killed rather than remain in such agony. The dying horses staggering and snorting.' His hands fleetingly covered his face as if to block out the sight. His voice was cracked as he continued. 'And I was cradling my brother who had been slashed with a sabre from his collarbone to his stomach. I was trying to hold his chest together, stop his guts from spilling out. He was bleeding to death in my arms.'

Peg Priddy gently extricated the clean linen bandage from his grip and started to bind Achille's injured leg over the sticky unguent of herbs and honey. As if breaking from a dream, Lord Rokeby shook his head and said with an air of embarrassment and apology, 'It's unconscionable to have burdened you with this, Mrs Priddy, but you're the kindest, wisest person I know.' He bowed over her hand. 'Thank you.' His hound lifted his head and gazed at his master, full of empathic feeling. 'Yes, you understand, don't you, Achille,' he murmured with tenderness as he stroked his neck. 'You'll be all right, my friend. You have to survive for us both.'

Mrs Priddy said in her pragmatic way, 'Well, my lord, Achille is not going to die. And you too have survived.' Their eyes met and an understanding passed between them. 'You have work to do and a life to live.' She was a straightforward woman who believed in service to others and that the gift of being on God's earth should not be squandered.

Mrs Priddy had put back in her bag her remaining herbs and honey. Lord Rokeby got to his feet and as he noticed Leonora in the window seat, a look of mortification crossed his face. 'Miss Appleby, I do apologise for my lack of control. I hope my words didn't shock you. I hadn't slept much and I think for a while was losing my mind.' With a rueful smile he walked towards her. She had sat too long in the draughty window and his anguished description of battle had shocked her to the core, filling her heart with pity for all men at war and for the waste of war.

When he took her hand, his warm touch felt as if he were transferring some of his life force to her. 'I'm sorry, you seem to have grown cold, sitting too far from the fire.' He squeezed her hand gently then drew it fleetingly to his face. 'The old country saying round here "Cold hands, warm heart"– I hope it's true for you.' His spirit seemed lighter than she had previously known. He continued with a wry smile, 'And I hope the converse is not true for me.'

He helped her up before releasing her hand. Leonora remembered her belief in the power of music to heal and feeling shy, turned to face him. 'My lord, I'm organising a musical party at the Manor on Twelfth Night. I wondered if you would grace us with your presence? I think a friend of yours will be attending, a Captain Ormonde. He's staying with a friend of my family, another soldier, Lord Dearlove.'

'Pleased as I always am to see you and Miss Blythe, and Mrs Priddy...' He nodded to her as she joined them, then continued, 'You've been warned by Diggory Shrubb already, I'm a recluse who does not care for company.' He met Mrs Priddy's admonitory gaze and added, 'Well, perhaps I *have* been a recluse who does not care for company but now shall have to make more effort. It may be, Miss Appleby, that I will have to practise my social skills after a lifetime as a rough soldier.' He paused and his face darkened. 'I wouldn't want you to think that Ormonde is a friend. I have met Dearlove, I have no objection to him. Perhaps I'll manage a short visit as part of my rehabilitation. I warn you though, my appearance and forbidding mien cast a pall over most gatherings.'

He sounded amused but Leonora noticed a bleakness in his face. Without thinking, she put out a hand and touched his; for a few seconds their fingers entwined, thrilling her with the unexpected intimacy. She glanced up with a startled expression and met his own watchful eye.

Mrs Priddy noticed this barely perceptible interchange with a knowing expression on her face. Lord Rokeby and Leonora's hands slipped apart as he led the way to the door. 'My thanks to you both for your help with Achille. I will send a note of his progress.' His voice was formal again. 'I'll accompany you to pick up your horse and gig.' They walked the long way, through the ruined Abbey, the ancient atmosphere once again settling on Leonora's shoulders like a benign hand. All the agitation of her thoughts and heart seemed to evaporate as she stepped on the springy moss, gazing up at the soaring arches of stone. Then her eyes alighted on Lord Rokeby's figure ahead, still only in his shirt with sleeves rolled up and forearms bare, fatigue making his limp more pronounced, and her heart flipped over.

* * *

Leonora was due the following afternoon for tea at the Vicarage. Before she set out, she had managed to transform her riding habit with some new silver braid for the military-style jacket and to retrim her favourite riding hat with its plume of green feathers. She walked through the Vicarage garden and entered the house to the sound of laughter. Charlotte was twirling in one of her refurbished gowns, an evening dress in shell-pink silk on which she had painstakingly stitched three narrow ribbons of gold gauze in parallel along the hem and then added ruffled ribbon to the neckline and cuffs of the sleeve. She was proud of her handiwork. Mrs Mildmay clapped her hands in pleasure as her beautiful foster daughter spun in the sunshine, her face alight.

Leonora joined in the laughter. 'Lottie, that looks as lovely as any Parisian gown. You *are* clever!'

Leonora took Mrs Mildmay's hands in greeting and sat beside her on the sofa. 'Are you feeling reconciled to Charlotte doing the Season?'

'I am so gratified that you are happy to accompany her, Miss Leonora. I think she will have a happy and successful time, don't you?' Her soft doughy face had relaxed since the anguish caused just a week ago by the news of Charlotte's parentage.

'Oh indeed. She will be the toast of the Season!'

At that moment, Reverend Mildmay and his curate came into the room. Richard Fopling took Leonora aside and in a quiet voice told her, 'I saw Silas Sproat this morning. He's working again and has a new young dog.'

Leonora grasped his arm. 'I'm so pleased to hear that, Mr Fopling. Is it one of the Vazey puppies?'

'I think so. A handsome dog, not going to be tall but intelligent. And Silas seems himself again. We watched the creature, full of joy, scampering through the wet grass, his silvery trail the picture of simple happiness in the world.'

Leonora was struck by the image and asked him, 'Mr Fopling, do you think we too have a duty to make happiness visible?'

He turned his pale eyes towards her and smiled. 'Not duty, Miss Appleby. Just by being. Consider the mighty sun; nothing is more wonderful than the way each evening it floats towards the horizon, then on the morrow, without pause, rises out of the darkness.' The tea had arrived and Mrs Mildmay poured it while Charlotte emerged from the kitchen with a plate of currant buns she had just baked. The young curate took his leave. 'Excuse me, I have a couple of parishioners to see who are suffering from the ague. May I take two of your cakes, Miss Blythe? They would tempt the weakest appetites.'

Charlotte nodded. 'Of course.' She wrapped them in a cloth napkin to give to him as he slipped from the room and out into the lane, barely disturbing the air as he went.

Mrs Mildmay looked across at Leonora and shook her head in sorrow. 'That young man needs a practical wife to handle the everyday.'

'He seems very attentive to the villagers, and surely good at his vocation? I find his view of the world refreshing.' Leonora took a bite of Charlotte's currant bun but did not miss the look that passed between Mrs Mildmay and her husband. She laughed. 'No, you are mistaken, I would not make Mr Fopling a good wife and I don't believe he even requires one like me.'

Reverend Mildmay answered before his wife, 'There you're wrong. The neighbouring parish he is being offered requires him to take a wife. As Mrs Mildmay knows, a good wife allows a man of God to attend to his ministry while she organises the home and pastoral care of the village.'

Leonora met his glance. 'Mr Fopling strikes me as particularly well-suited himself to the pastoral care of his parishioners. Of course, he is Sir Roderick's heir and so will in time come into a fortune. Which perhaps gives him some power to resist the bishop.'

A wry smile lifted Mrs Mildmay's expression. 'He may come into his inheritance sooner than expected. The reckless way that father of his hunts in the field! It won't be long before a terrible accident befalls him.'

'Well, the village poachers and their dogs will not be sorry to see him go,' Leonora muttered under her breath. She looked across at Charlotte whose golden head was bent over her stitching. 'Lottie, I wondered if you'd come with me tomorrow to the orchard to collect ivy, laurel and holly berries.'

'Of course. We can help each other dress the Manor, the church and the Vicarage for Christmas.'

'And the decorations will last until Twelfth Night for our musical soirée.' Leonora turned to Mrs Mildmay. 'You and the Reverend will certainly join us for Christmas dinner and for Epiphany, won't you?'

* * *

Christmas was like every other Christmas in the village of Hasterleigh, but this year there was added excitement and specu-lation. The Reverend and the curate, with the help of Mrs Mild-may, were much involved with religious services and ministering to the flock. Lord Rokeby caused a stir on Christmas morning by turning up to matins. The Rokeby pew had not been used for a decade and he sat in brooding solitude, Achille by his side.

Leonora was not there to see him as she had attended the midnight service so she could spend Christmas morning helping Nanny P and Cook prepare the feast for the dinner that evening. They had asked Charlotte and the Mildmays, Mr Fopling and the widow Mrs Chetwode and her daughter, Jane, who had recently moved into the Grove and were not well-acquainted yet with the community.

Richard Fopling also caused a ripple of surprise and some gossip by acquiring a dog himself. Miss Vazey, the daughter of the family whose bitch had whelped, had asked the curate to care for the puppy that no one wanted. Little Grace – for that's what he called her – was the runt of the litter, small and easily bullied by the bigger puppies. Leonora came upon her, trotting faithfully behind Mr Fopling as he went from house to house bearing seasonal victuals to the neediest parishioners. 'A dog! You too, Mr Fopling?' She waylaid him by the market cross and bent to ruffle the puppy's ears.

The curate's face registered wry surprise. 'Indeed, Miss Appleby, she has brought such grace to my life.'

'I thought you had wanted to be free of worldly preoccupations. What made you change your mind?'

'Vazey's daughter is a persuasive young woman.' He looked down at the small creature sitting at his feet and smiled. Leonora knew the Vazey family well. They were one of the Manor's best tenant farmers and Ernest Vazey, an intelligent and hard-working man. His daughter, Rose, was a quiet, self-contained girl with a gentle demeanour and vivid amber eyes. 'As you know, Miss Vazey's our own St Francis of Assisi; wounded animals and birds come to her door and she sends them back to the wild, restored.

She told me Little Grace needed me and I needed her. Who was I to disagree?'

Leonora met his eyes and recognised in that moment how right it was when a wounded soul met another and both felt they had come home. 'Well, she is fortunate to have found you.' She inclined her head. 'Goodbye, Mr Fopling; goodbye, Little Grace.'

* * *

Twelfth Night arrived on the back of a storm. From midnight, the wind roared through the trees outside the Manor and rattled the ancient windows in their casements. The force of the air swirling round the roofs made the chimneys whistle, and the rain sent gobbets of soot splattering into the grates in the fireplaces. Leonora could not sleep. She had organised the party herself and in the depths of the night she ran the details through her mind: the food was cooked, the cellar full, she had bought up every beeswax candle from the local chandler; with Charlotte's help the vases were overflowing with pussy willow and hellebore just coming into flower. Leonora had been particularly pleased to find wintersweet in the woods, its bare branches decorated with yellow waxy flowers, filling the air with its exotic heady scent. The bedrooms had been made ready for George Lockwood, Lord Dearlove, his sister Livia and her maid.

After such a wild night, the morning dawned rosy and clear, the early sun casting a calm pale light over the swirls of leaves and branches strewn across the park. George Lockwood had written that he would arrive early as he wished to catch up with Ned Fleming's activities on the estate. Leonora dressed in her morning gown, newly trimmed with ribbons by Nanny P, and was just brushing out her long tawny hair to twist into a loose chignon when she heard Charlotte's voice in the hall. She too was wearing one of her newly refurbished dresses and looked charming in pale primrose. They embraced. 'The Manor looks so beautiful with all this greenery, everything sparkling in the sun.'

Leonora grasped a cup of coffee and a bun, and they went through to the drawing room and sat together on the music stool to run through a final practice of the compositions they would play. Deep in the John Field duet, both young women were startled to see the tall figure of George Lockwood looming in the doorway. He laughed at their expressions. 'Forgive me, but Clegg seems to think the house is mine so he can leave me to come and go at will.'

Charlotte, in some excitement, exclaimed, 'Mr Lockwood! It is good to see you.'

He strode into the room to take her hand and bow. 'It is reward for my hellish journey to find you and Miss Appleby with sunlight in your hair, producing such sublime music.'

He reached out for Leonora's hand too and she could not supress a laugh. 'Mr Lockwood, you can leave your flowery London manners behind when you're with us!'

Charlotte protested. 'Leonora! I like Mr Lockwood's mannerliness. It makes such a refreshing change from what we are used to.'

George Lockwood was amused himself. 'If you think I'm overly mannerly, you wait until you meet my stepfather, Beau Beacham! He could charm a fortune from miser Daniel Dancer and a laugh from La Gioconda.' Despite Mr Lockwood's obvious admiration for the Beau, Leonora determined to dislike the man on sight, not least because he imposed his own Town tastes on his country-loving stepson. She looked him up and down and was disappointed that once again his large broad form was tightly buttoned into dandy clothes that made him look so uncomfortable.

'Well, now *my* manners are lacking, Mr Lockwood. You must

be hungry and tired. Can I offer you some refreshment?' She moved towards the door.

'No, thank you. I haven't much time before I need to get ready for the evening's jollities. I'll change and grab some bread and cheese from Cook and then find Ned Fleming.'

'When last here, you committed to sing a ballad for us tonight. I wondered if you have chosen one?'

'What about 'The Whitby Lad'? Or I could sing everyone's old favourite, 'Scarborough Fair'?'

Leonora thought for a moment. 'The Whitby Lad' had a rumbustious tune but the story of a young man's deportation for theft rather lowered the spirits. 'I think 'Scarborough Fair' would be best. It has such charm, and some of your audience might sing along.'

She and Charlotte went in search of the last candelabras and candlesticks to be found in the house, searching the pantry and laundry, and gathered them in the kitchen. After a quick polish they were filled with even more candles; the Manor would glow with myriad lights and look at its very best. Time was fleeing and they dashed their separate ways to dress for the evening's entertainments.

Leonora washed and slipped into the new silver gauze evening dress for the first time since she had brought it home from Windsor. It felt so silky and cool, and it rustled when she walked. She had asked Milly to help and the girl stared at her mistress, her mouth open. 'You look as beautiful as an angel, Miss Leonora!' she said in her honest country way.

'That's very kind, Milly, but I think when you see her, you'll find Miss Charlotte looks more the angel.' As Milly plaited and coiled Leonora's glossy chestnut hair, piling it on top of her head in a passable imitation of a classical goddess's coiffure, Leonora

looked at her own reflection in the looking glass with some pleasure and amazement.

The Mildmays were the first to arrive, exclaiming at the beauty
of the house and its decorations. The fires were blazing and the
hundreds of lit candles cast their soft light over faces and flowers,
and added a flickering lustre to the piano-forte sitting in its central
place in the drawing room. Mrs Mildmay hurried to the kitchen,
keen to help Cook and Nanny P put the food ready for a buffet in
the dining room. The Reverend manned the champagne until Jack
Clegg could take over, once his duty at the front door was done.

Charlotte did indeed look like an angel in a finely stitched
white gown overlaid with shell-pink gauze, her fair hair curled
and soft round her face with tendrils falling to her shoulders and a
twisted knot on her head, interlaced with ribbons. 'You look lovely,
Lottie.' Leonora took her arm and led her through to where their
new neighbours, Mrs Chetwode and her daughter were standing
slightly apart by the window. Charlotte collected a glass of champagne for Mrs Chetwode and Mrs Priddy's lemon and elderflower
cordial for Miss Chetwode and herself.

George Lockwood, immaculate in dark evening coat and pale
satin breeches, strolled over to talk to the women. His bluff kindness penetrated Miss Chetwode's shyness and she smiled, a blush
stealing up her pale cheeks. He then excused himself to offer his
services to Leonora as a joint host.

There was a sudden stir as three glittering personages entered
the hall, the men stripping off their gloves, top hats and travelling
cloaks to hand them to Jack Clegg, who looked suitably impressed.
With them was an imperious young woman, tall and stately and
dressed in a striking apple-green evening dress, with a daring, lowcut neckline, the bodice scintillating with matching bugle beads. A
green plume of feathers nodded from the complex construction of

her glossy dark hair. Leonora came towards them, her hand out in greeting. 'Lady Livia, how good of you to come.'

Her hand was taken in the lightest of grips and Livia Dearlove looked around the drawing room then down at Leonora from her greater height and murmured, 'How charming,' in a voice that did not sound charmed in the least. Just as Leonora was feeling the *froideur* seep up from her fingers, a young man with unruly brown hair and a sparkling expression pushed forward to grasp both her hands. 'Miss Appleby! It is a treat to see you after so long.' His genuine ebullience and pleasure at meeting her again made Leonora wonder if he was about to forget etiquette entirely and embrace her.

Lord Dearlove had always been an optimistic, enthusiastic energy who lifted her heart and made her laugh. She felt herself colour with delight at seeing him again and being reminded of happy times with her beloved. Rufus Dearlove turned to introduce Leonora to a lean-faced man, distinguished in his regimentals. 'Captain Ormonde, may I introduce you to Miss Appleby. Miss Appleby, Guy Ormonde is a captain in the Light Dragoons.' The stranger bowed deeply over her hand and as his narrow cynical eyes flickered over her face and down her person, his face broke into one of the most charming smiles she had ever seen. Leonora found it disconcerting to have such chilliness and warmth present in the same face.

All eyes were drawn to his braided red jacket and military swagger, and she was glad he had come to add extra distinction to the evening. In the country, entertainments were home-made and a musical soirée like hers was bound to strike sophisticated Town bloods as amateurish and tame. Lord Dearlove seemed free of such reservations and bounded into the room full of eager friendliness. He immediately engaged Charlotte and Jane Chet-wode in light conversation and both shy young women began to feel charming themselves in the warmth of his flirtatious attention.

His sister declined any refreshment and chose the best chair by the fire to await the musical performance. She surveyed the room with a faintly disdainful air, then her eyes alighted on George Lockwood for a few seconds before returning to her haughty regard of the company.

The last to arrive were Sir Roderick and Richard Fopling, the father red in the face from too much wassail and his son so pale and refined in comparison, it seemed impossible to think they were of the same genealogical tree. In an idle moment, Leonora had hoped that the long-deceased Lady Fopling had found solace and some respite from her husband in the arms of a sensitive lover. Seeing father and son together emphasised this polar difference of looks and character.

The chairs were arranged in a semi-circle facing the pianoforte. Once everyone had a glass in their hands, they took their seats and Charlotte sat down to play and sing the first piece, 'The Ballad of Barbara Allen'. Everyone knew this song well and they swayed to the melody before most of the guests joined in with the final verse.

Charlotte's performance was clapped with enthusiasm. Her lovely face registered delight and surprise; speaking in a quiet voice, she introduced next the slow movement of Pleyel's Sonata in the key of B major. As she began to play, people relaxed, accepting more champagne or burgundy from Jack Clegg and Mrs Priddy. Leonora was standing by the door, watchful and waiting. She wondered at her agitation then realised she was hoping Lord Rokeby would come, if just for a while. After all, it would be an opportunity to support his newly acquired niece and see her shine. She was shocked how deflated she felt at his absence even as the evening appeared to be such a success.

Aware of a tingling sense of danger, Leonora turned her head to find herself staring into the narrowed eyes of Captain Ormonde. He was standing behind her, slightly too close. 'Captain! You startled me,' she said under her breath, not wishing to distract from the music.

'My apologies, Miss Appleby. It is a most enjoyable evening. Lord Dearlove tells me your betrothed was a hero who died at Fuengirola.' His smile did not reach his eyes as he continued in an insinuating voice, 'More of a hero than your neighbour, the rake-hell Rokeby, methinks.'

Leonora turned again to meet his eyes, hers wide with astonishment. 'Sir, I think it dishonourable to besmirch the reputation of another officer, not here to defend himself.'

His face was cold with not a hint of his earlier flashing charm. 'Why is the Earl not here, pray? Could it be he knew I would be?' Leonora was hesitant for a moment. It was true, she had told Lord Rokeby that a friend of his would be attending and he had pointed out, rather coldly himself, that he did not consider Ormonde a friend.

'Excuse me, I have to accompany Mr Lockwood.' She bowed her head and walked to the piano-forte where Charlotte was just finishing the last *rallentando*. The clapping again was appreciative, and Charlotte stood up and bowed as Mrs Mildmay flew to her side to kiss her cheek.

Leonora addressed her guests. 'Before we pause for food and refreshments, Mr George Lockwood, new heir of the Manor estate, will sing 'Scarborough Fair' to my accompaniment.' She sat down and started to play the lovely melody everyone had learnt as a child. George Lockwood was unselfconscious, and his warm baritone flowed out of him as naturally as breathing. His height and broad chest gave his voice a richness of sound that caught the heart.

Leonora knew the music so well she could glance round the faces of her guests.

Most striking was the way Lady Livia watched George Lockwood as he sang, her dark eyes wide and unblinking, with an almost-smile on her lips. Charlotte too was attentive, the colour high on her cheeks. This was the first time she had heard the beauty of his voice, and it obviously touched her too. With a slight incline of her head, Leonora invited Charlotte to join in with the refrain. They had sung 'Scarborough Fair' together many times. Charlotte approached Mr Lockwood tentatively and stood by his side. When he looked down from his great height with an encouraging smile, she joined him with the sinuous refrain.

'*O, where are you going?*' he sang and she sang in response, '*To Scarborough Fair.*'

Then together their voices entwined in harmony:

> '*Parsley, sage, rosemary and thyme,*
> *Remember me to a lass who lives there,*
> *For once she was a true love of mine.*'

This was such a favourite that there were calls for them to repeat it, which Mr Lockwood, Leonora and Charlotte duly did, with more gusto, and some of their guests joined in, Rufus Dearlove's tenor being the most noticeable addition.

When it was time to pause for food, George Lockwood was about to escort Charlotte through to the dining room when Livia Dearlove slipped her arm through his and said in her lisping voice, 'It's a pleasure to be escorted into dinner by such a tall man.' Her soft sibilance meant men leaned closer and inclined their heads to catch her words. The childlike voice made them protective and unwary. Leonora watched this performance with interest and realised that a simple honest man such as Mr Lockwood was

as malleable as mastic in Livia Dearlove's hands. She saw him cast
Charlotte an apologetic glance as he was borne away.

Mrs Priddy came up to Leonora with a beaming smile. 'This is
splendid, my dear Nora. Everything better than could be hoped.'
They walked through to the dining room. Leonora surveyed the
table, laden with the best that Cook and Mrs Priddy could
manage. At the centre of the feast were a glistening baked ham
studded with cloves and a haunch of venison, both being carved
with some finesse by Jack Clegg. The potato pie was steaming and
the sweet pastries Cook had laboured over for days were quickly
disappearing. At one end, a pyramid of candied fruits made up for
the lack of any fresh ones beyond their own stored apples and
pears.

Richard Fopling glided up to her. 'What a sublime evening,
Miss Appleby. Good music expresses the perfect harmony of
things, as our blackbirds and robins know full well already.' He
smiled.

Leonora took his arm and laughed. 'Mr Fopling, I thought the
robin and blackbird sang with such ferocious beauty to mark their
territory and warn off other birds?'

'Ah, 'tis true, but their deeper message is joy in the world and
their attraction to others. This is why it transmits so clearly to us.'

Leonora looked across at his father, cheeks red and waistcoat
straining. 'I hope Sir Roderick appreciates what a superior being
you are.' His pale eyes met hers with wry amusement; no words
were necessary. He was a changeling child in a crassly sporting
family, yet somehow had survived.

'And you, my dear Miss Appleby, are a woman of the water. You
have the vitality of the tumbling stream.'

Leonora was taken aback. He had reminded her of her love of
swimming, and how much she missed it. But also, he made her
realise the elemental force of these two men who had stormed into

Hasterleigh's measured way of life. George Lockwood was obviously of the earth, and Lord Rokeby most certainly was fire.

'And you, Mr Fopling, are of the air.' She put her hand on his arm. 'But even aerial creatures need to eat. Come.'

* * *

When everyone was back in the drawing room, seated with glasses topped up, the chatter became noisier and more ebullient. Leonora and Charlotte made their way to the piano-forte. 'Miss Blythe and I are going to play for you as the finale tonight Mr Field's duet, Nocturne No. 5 in B flat major.' Just as they were about to begin, the hundreds of candles in the candelabras and central chandelier guttered as one. The front door had opened and a gust of wind blew through the house. Leonora looked towards the drawing room door which was pushed ajar by the snout of a huge shaggy hound who padded towards her. She leapt to her feet, her heart suddenly beating with the thrill of a prayer answered.

In the doorway stood the tall figure of the Earl of Rokeby. He looked more commanding and dishevelled than Leonora had ever seen him, as if he had ridden the storm. His scar was livid against his face, made all the paler by his black riding coat that he had not yet removed. His eye patch seemed to add to the air of menace and mystery. In the room, there was a communal intake of breath. Everyone seemed suddenly to have sobered up. All eyes were upon him and his hound when Sir Roderick's stentorian voice boomed out, 'The dog, sir! To the stables with 'im! Have respect for a lady's drawing room!'

Lord Rokeby turned sharply to address him. 'Who, pray, are you, sir? Are you master of this house?'

'Sir Roderick Fopling of the neighbouring estate.'

'Well, my hound goes everywhere with me since he almost

died in one of your traps.' He turned back to look at Leonora. 'Miss Appleby helped in his rescue and I have not been aware of any objections from her.'

Leonora had indeed begun to run towards the Earl before checking herself to transfer her unseemly delight to Achille instead. The dog's head was resting on her hand, his large dark eyes looking deep into hers. The Earl then bowed.

'My apologies for coming so late to your soirée, Miss Appleby. Don't let me interrupt the entertainment.' His dark gaze fell on the assembled company and when he saw Captain Ormonde, flashy in his gold-braided red coat, a sneer made his face more alarming. He turned back to the hall to divest himself of his coat as Leonora and Charlotte sat again at the piano-forte.

The relaxed bonhomie had become more subdued but with a hidden tremor of excitement, as if they were in the presence of danger. The young women began to play and as the lovely familiar arpeggios enchanted the room, Leonora was aware of Lord Rokeby slipping into the chair next to Nanny P. Achille had returned to Leonora's side and sat with his heavy head on her lap as she concentrated on seamlessly blending her higher register of notes with Charlotte's rippling lower cadences. In all the weeks of practising, Leonora and Charlotte had never played the nocturne better than they did that night. When they came to the end, there was a moment's silence, followed by enthusiastic clapping. Leonora stood up and asked if anyone else wished to contribute a song or piece of music.

Lord Dearlove sprang to his feet and said, 'Happen, I'll sing "Greensleeves" if someone will accompany me.' Leonora was not certain she was practised enough with the tune and hesitated. Well-lubricated with alcohol, he cast a bold glance at Charlotte, inviting her to step forward. She coloured and dropped her head, then to everyone's surprise, the Earl stood up. 'I will play for you.

"Greensleeves" reminded me of home when I was captured in Spain.' As he walked to the Broadwood, Leonora noticed he was careful to disguise his limp. She realised he was a proud man who did not care for pity.

The two men were both born to land and title and yet their demeanour could not have been more different. Rufus Dearlove's face was open and smiling. He looked like a man blessed by angels at his cradle with every good fortune: wealth, health, and nobility, aligned with a handsomeness of mien and a light-hearted nature that drew friends and hangers-on wherever he went. His voice too was a light and lyrical tenor. It seemed no hardship had shadowed his life.

Lord Rokeby, on the other hand, crouched at the piano-forte as if coiled to pounce. His brow was dark, his face scarred, his expression haunted by memories of hell. He too had been born with every advantage, until war had taken what was most precious. Lord Rokeby played the age-old ballad as an elegy for lost love, and Lord Dearlove was uneasy with the plaintive pace; he tried to speed it up to be closer to the drinking song it had been at Oxford, where his youth had been dissipated in alcohol and pleasure.

Dearlove was as day to Lord Rokeby's night, yet Leonora found she could not take her eyes from the Earl's face as he scowled over the keys. She was aware how most young men had frittered away their youth while Alistair Rokeby accompanied his beloved brother to defend his country in bloody battle. A feeling of shame washed over her; since her Captain's death, she had barely given much thought to the other young military men sacrificing life and limb so the rest could pursue their lives as they pleased. She looked across at Captain Ormonde, engaging Charlotte in flirtatious glances, with renewed respect.

The awkward musical collaboration came to an end, with guests joining in with the song with tipsy good humour, favouring the more upbeat interpretation Lord Dearlove had attempted to impose. There was a rush to refill glasses and seek out packs of cards.

Charlotte too had been arrested by the sight of the two lords at the piano-forte, but it was Rufus Dearlove who drew her eye with his merry countenance and lyrical voice. She had thought no one could sing as beautifully as Mr Lockwood, but here in one night was another. She glanced at the Captain beside her and her heart skipped; how exciting to have three young men in her orbit, appealing in quite different ways. London and the Season seemed suddenly to be filled with unforeseen promise and adventure.

Watching Lord Rokeby too was Captain Ormonde. Leonora was puzzled by the evident animosity between these fellow officers, but her reverie was interrupted by the Mildmays who were leaving. Richard Fopling also bowed over Leonora's hand. 'Thank you, Miss Appleby, for such a fine evening's entertainment. I don't wish to leave Little Grace for too long. She's still so young, she relies on me.' He smiled and walked out into the moonlight.

Leonora returned from the hall to the drawing room where Lord Rokeby was waiting for her. He drew her into the window recess and they sat together on the small sofa, still part of the party but secluded and intimate. He turned to her and said in a quiet voice, 'I do commend you for your teaching of Miss Blythe. She is a charming young woman.'

'Thank you, my lord, but I have only taught her music.'

Mrs Priddy had seen the Earl draw Leonora away and keen to protect her reputation, had approached and sat in an adjacent chair to provide a modicum of chaperonage. Lord Rokeby put his hand fleetingly on Leonora's. 'I know your friendship has been influential in much more than her music.' Then his manner became more practical. 'When are you leaving for London and my grandmother's house?'

'We go in a sennight. The clothes from your mother's modiste are due tomorrow and then we spend the following days packing.' Her smile was rueful. 'It is a great rigmarole I'm unused to, but I am happy to do what I can to help Charlotte.'

'May I offer you the Rokeby coach and a team of my horses so you can travel in comfort? I'll stable more horses for you at the posting inns on the road which will speed your journey.'

Leonora turned to look him full in the face. 'That's very generous, Lord Rokeby.' She had a questioning look in her eyes, not daring to hope that he had spent any time thinking about her and her comfort.

His penetrating gaze held hers for a moment and she felt the same thrill as when she submerged herself in the lake, jolted into intense life. Leonora was disturbed at how often her thoughts turned to him, wishing to be more in his company. And all the while she reminded herself she was deluded in hoping he even noticed her beyond her usefulness. She was a nobody in his world, with not even great beauty to commend her; he, on the other hand, with title and wealth, could have the pick of beauties, heiresses and the well-born, should he so choose.

Lord Rokeby appeared unaware of the turmoil in her heart and when he answered it was not to declare his thoughts for her, but his sense of propriety over Charlotte. 'Well, Miss Blythe is a member of the family; it seems the right thing to do,' was his reasonable reply.

Leonora's disappointment was fleeting and replaced with amusement at her own presumption. Achille had been lying across their feet and stirred; the Earl laid his hand on his head and sprang up. 'Forgive me for keeping you from your guests for so long. I should head home. I'll collect Jupiter from your stables. There's just enough of a moon and it's barely a mile.'

He was about to leave when Leonora put out a hand to stay him. 'Lord Rokeby, what made you decide to come tonight?'

He paused and gave her a surprisingly sweet smile despite the scar that gave it a devilish edge. 'How could I let you down when I owe you so much?'

'I am particularly pleased that you overrode your stated desire to eschew all society.' She smiled at him.

'Miss Appleby, your society is very different from the kind of society represented by men like the Captain over there.'

Leonora looked across to where Guy Ormonde had both Charlotte and Jane Chetwode hanging on his conversation, fragments of which could be heard with talk of cavalry charges and feats of courage and endurance. She laughed and glanced up into his face with some mischief. 'Oh, so the Captain was right. He suggested you would stay away because of him.'

The sweetness vanished in an instant and the thunderous look returned. 'That man's a blackguard and you must not believe a word he says!' he muttered in a fierce whisper. 'Who can trust such a popinjay who flaunts his regimental colours at a country soirée as if it's fancy dress! War is not for men of straw to use as calling cards to bed women...' He broke off and bowed. 'My apologies, Miss Appleby, I forget myself. As I said, war makes brutes of men.'

'War also makes heroes,' Leonora said, her hand inadvertently brushing his as they both fondled Achille's ears.

'Oh! If only that were true. The mere throw of a dice determines whether one is a hero or villain, a braveheart or poltroon.' He clicked his heels together as if transported back to the regiment himself, took Leonora's hand and pressed it fleetingly to his lips. He turned to take Mrs Priddy's hand, then bowed in farewell to Charlotte, George Lockwood, Lord Dearlove and the Honourable Livia Dearlove, and he and Achille headed for the door.

Soon after, Charlotte flung her arms around Leonora to wish her an excited goodnight and left through the garden to return to the Vicarage. It had been the best evening's entertainment of her young life. The remaining guests settled down to some light-hearted card games. Even more alcohol was imbibed, and laughter filled the room. The Dearloves and Mr Lockwood were staying at the Manor and Captain Ormonde residing with a local friend whose house was only a short walk away. Leonora realised it would be a long night. Fatigue threatened to overwhelm her as she forced herself to remain a further hour but increasingly struggled to stay awake. The gossip turned to the dramatic arrival of Lord Rokeby and Lord Dearlove, lubricated by alcohol, was talking loudly. 'So mortally wounded, it's a miracle he didn't die on the battlefield alongside his brother.'

Captain Ormonde's voice was sober and cold. 'Saved by a French doxy, it's said. He's either hellishly lucky or has the charm of the Devil.'

Lord Dearlove dealt the cards and laughed. 'I don't think Rokeby has ever been overendowed with charm!' This conversation jolted Leonora into agitated wakefulness. Alistair Rokeby had been saved from certain death by a woman? Who? Why? As her feelings for him deepened, the mysteries around him seemed to multiply.

The conversation moved on to racing fixtures at Newmarket, and Leonora's fatigue could no longer be resisted. She told Nanny P that she thought they could excuse themselves and leave George Lockwood in charge as the host of the night. She waited until a game of whist had come to an end and drew him to one side. 'Mr Lockwood, Mrs Priddy and I are going to retire. May I leave you to see our guests out and those who are staying to their rooms?'

'Of course. I will take care of them all. I'm not as deep in my cups as most.'

Leonora and Nanny P went round the party wishing them a good sleep and set off to their beds. On the chest in the hall, Leonora noticed a letter glowing white upon a silver salver, with a distinguished hand she recognised. *Miss LEONORA Appleby* was scrawled in black ink with speed blots under the strong curling line. Seeing her given name so distinctive in capitals made her long to hear his voice call her *Leonora*; the intimacy of it made her shiver. She opened the note to find just two lines:

> *My piano-forte will miss you. Please come and tune it one more time before you leave for London.*

Leonora folded it carefully along its original creases and carried it upstairs to slip into her dressing table drawer to lie beside her precious only letter from her lost love.

6

THE FRENCH CONNECTION

Leonora knew that her guests would not be down early for breakfast and so set off into the village to visit the tenant farmers and tell them she would be in London until the summer. Luckily Ned Fleming had been in charge of the Hasterleigh Manor estate since he was a young man, trained up by her father. He was more than capable of dealing with any immediate problem and both George Lockwood and Leonora were available by letter.

The morning was fresh and brisk and the puddles in the lane had dried to sludge. Leonora knew everyone and greeted them as she passed on her way to the Sproats' house. She had put on her walking boots and workaday cloak over one of her prettier morning gowns, with the warmth of a spencer fastened close across her bosom. Gloves and a simple bonnet completed her outfit.

The puddles may have receded, but muddy traps were every-where. She was just navigating one when she looked up to see Rose Vazey coming towards her with her own dog and Mr Fopling's Little Grace. A moment's inattention meant Leonora slid down the sodden bank at the edge of the lane and landed in the muddy cart track she'd been trying to avoid. 'Oh, Miss Appleby!' The girl hurried forward and offered an arm.

Leonora grabbed Miss Vazey's hand and squelched out of the mire to stand looking down at her boots. 'Oh dear,' she laughed. 'I now look thoroughly disreputable, and I have smart Town guests at the Manor.'

Rose Vazey laughed with her. 'Should have put on your pattens, miss. They would have saved you from the worst of it.' She was an unusual young woman who, since childhood, had shown an uncanny understanding of animals and all living things; as Richard Fopling said, she was Hasterleigh's own St Francis. Everyone knew the uses of plants for treating ailments but for intractable problems, it was to Rose that her neighbours went for advice. She was also the person to nurse any wounded creature, and dogs gravitated to her as if they were charmed. Leonora looked into Miss Vazey's amber eyes, surprised how speckled and like a plover's egg in colouring they were. She said, 'I'm glad you persuaded Mr Fopling to take on Little Grace.'

'She has flourished under his care.'

'As he seems to do under hers,' Leonora said with feeling.

'He belongs more to nature and the empyrean air than most men. A wife would tether him to earth and teach him the pleasures of the everyday.' Rose Vazey spoke in such an emphatic and down-to-earth way that Leonora looked askance at her. The young woman smiled and explained, 'You look shocked, Miss Appleby. But you may not know I can see the future for some people, and he is one.'

'What a useful gift, Miss Vazey!' Her light-hearted words died on her lips as she met the young woman's eyes.

'It can be a curse, Miss Appleby.' Then, appearing to check herself, added with a lilt in her voice, 'But for Mr Fopling, my future-sight is a blessing. For he will marry me.'

Leonora could not hide her astonishment. 'Does Mr Fopling know?' she asked in a quiet voice.

Rose Vazey gave a warm chuckle. 'What man ever knew what was best for him? But he will soon. His father is not long for this world.'

Leonora put a hand on her arm once again and in an urgent voice said, 'Now you're alarming me with your witchery, Miss Vazey.'

'Do not fear. What people call witchery is merely being close to the other world, separated from us by our own refusal to see.'

Leonora heard the church clock strike ten and knew she had run out of time to visit the Sproats, and had to return to the Manor to care for her guests. Shaken, yet somehow consoled by her meeting with Miss Vazey, she turned to her and took her hand. 'I must return home now, but wish you every good fortune. I'm off to London to accompany Miss Charlotte and won't be back until the summer.'

'I think you may be back before then, Miss Appleby. The heart has its reasons which reason cannot know.' And with that, Rose Vazey had gathered her skirts and walked away back down the lane, the two dogs trotting behind her like attendant spirits. Leonora stood there startled. What was she to make of it all?

Leonora walked back to the Manor and entered to the sound of laughter from the breakfast room. She had hoped her guests would still be abed but now had to greet them without time to change. She slipped her muddy boots off in the hall and ran up the stairs to find her slippers. Glancing in the looking glass, she noticed her hair was untidy and there was a smear of mud on her hem, but she thought it would have to do.

As she caught sight of the Dearloves, her heart sank. She wished she had taken more trouble as Lord Rufus lounged in the chair, immaculately turned out for Town in his close-fitting coat of dark superfine wool, his white linen neckcloth intricately folded, pale pantaloons and onyx-black shiny hessian boots, a cup of coffee at his elbow. Neither did his sister's appearance make any concessions to country life. Livia Dearlove was dressed as if about to set off on a shopping expedition down Bond Street, in palest pink tiffany with a smart rose spencer fastened with silver braid. Leonora was relieved to see George Lockwood wearing his country clothes. He stood by the fireplace, his hair tousled, and his broadcloth jacket cut to a more accommodating fit for his broad shoulders.

When Lord Dearlove saw Leonora, he sprang to his feet. 'Miss Appleby, we were just saying what an enjoyable evening's entertainment that was.' He offered her his own chair by the table where breakfast was the remains of the baked ham from the previous night, together with rolls and jam, bread, cheese and jugs of ale and coffee.

'Good morning. I hope everyone slept well?' Leonora looked around the room as George Lockwood came forward to take her hand. She noticed Lady Livia's gaze travel to the hem of her gown where she was sure clung all kinds of inelegant remnants of her walk.

'It looks like you've been round the estate already before we'd even risen from our beds.' George Lockwood poured her a cup of coffee.

'I set out to see a few of our tenants to tell them I was off to London.' She paused, embarrassed by her presumption, now that the estate was his. 'I meant, that *we* were off to London.'

George Lockwood laughed. 'You know I have yet to claim my primacy here and until then it is for you to do and say as you like, Miss Appleby.'

Lady Livia's eyes rested on Leonora's face. 'Where may you live, Miss Appleby, once Mr Lockwood moves into the Manor?'

'Hasterleigh Lodge is a pretty house on the estate that Mr Lockwood has designated as my home for as long as I wish.'

'That is indeed generous. There is some embarrassment I presume being still on the estate when the heir moves in, perhaps with his new bride, to become the master and mistress of a property that has been yours?' Her voice was soft and innocent like a girl's, but her words carried bite.

Leonora felt herself stiffen. This had touched a nerve, for indeed there was an aching sense of loss in being deposed from a house that had been her home since birth, intensified no doubt when Mr Lockwood installed his new wife to become, as she had been, mistress of the estate. But her pride and natural distrust of this lady made her hide any vulnerability. She summoned a sunny smile. 'Indeed, it is generous, but I shall be delighted to see Mr Lockwood's plans put into action. I know he will care for the Manor estate as I have done.'

Lord Dearlove broke into this conversation in his cheerful way. 'Miss Appleby, as you know, we set off for London and the jolly Season. When will we have the pleasure of the company of you and Miss Blythe?' Leonora understood just why he had been such a favourite of William's; she also marvelled, not for the first time, that Rufus and Livia Dearlove were siblings when they seemed to exhibit such opposing characters.

She was not looking forward with unalloyed pleasure to this departure, but felt she should hide her misgivings and mirror his lightness of spirit. 'We set off in four days' time. Miss Blythe's great-grandmother, the Countess of Bucklebury, has invited us to stay with her in Brook Street.'

Lord Dearlove's face clouded for a moment. 'I hope that Rokeby won't be gracing the London Season with his forbidding presence. He has one of the best houses in Grosvenor Square, which hasn't been lived in since the brothers went to war. But I trust he has no intention of removing the dust sheets; he rather throws a pall over everything, don't you think?'

Leonora was immediately defensive on the Earl's part. 'He's a hero, my lord. He's been through a war to protect us and seen horrors and suffering we cannot imagine.'

'I don't doubt that. But nobody wants to be reminded of the dirt and pain of battle. A gentleman owes it to Society to present his best face rather than his worst.'

'Especially when his worst is so much worse than most,' Lady Livia said, her soft lisp masking the malice.

George Lockwood then entered the fray and to Leonora's surprise, defended the Earl. 'He was damnably rude to me when I took his straying hound back to him, but I've since heard from my friend Gully Grantham in the War Office that they're going to give his brother the Army Gold Cross posthumously, for bravery. Both brothers were exploring officers, infiltrating behind enemy lines to glean intelligence on troop movements: the most dangerous job in the campaigns.'

This silenced the Dearloves for a moment. The rich young noblemen who stayed at home to gamble, dance and fritter their fortunes on horses, courtesans and cards were made uneasy by the contrast with the young officers who endured the cauldron of war. Rufus Dearlove frowned. He did not like this unfamiliar feeling of being overshadowed by the gilded reputations of others. He muttered, 'Alistair and Charles Rokeby were in the same regiment as my friend, Ormonde, who accompanied us here last night. He can't countenance either of them. Denies there's anything heroic about the Rokeby brothers, despite their fame to the contrary.'

Leonora regretted the turn this conversation had taken but could not refrain from a sharp riposte, 'Well, I think the Earl returns that disdain!' Everyone looked at her with surprise and she coloured. She did not like to be thought indiscreet or, worse still, sharp-tongued, so turned to the table of food and cut herself some ham. 'Can I offer you anything more to eat?'

George Lockwood was by her side in a trice. 'Let me carve some of that. I'll have a slice; anything more for you, Dearlove?'

'Yes, please. We have a long journey ahead.' Rufus Dearlove walked to the table with his plate and George Lockwood placed two slices of ham in the middle, alongside a knob of bread and pile of pickle. Leonora was struck again by his lordship's good looks, heightened by the colour in his cheeks and his dark auburn hair, worn long and curly to the collar. His greenish eyes were habitually crinkled in amusement.

Lady Livia had also walked to the table and stood close to George Lockwood. 'Sir, when do you head off for London, and to what destination?'

He looked down at her with a smile. 'I too go today, after breakfast. Home for the Season is my stepfather's mansion in Davies Street.'

'Well, with Miss Appleby and Miss Blythe in Brook Street and Livia and me in the ancestral cot in Berkeley Square, we'll be near neighbours.' Lord Dearlove was thoughtful for a moment. 'Captain Ormonde used to live in Berkeley Square too, but he's been living too fast and flying too high.'

'He's an Icarus, his wings melted by alcohol fumes and the heat of excess.' George Lockwood seemed unsympathetic as he dismissed him.

Lord Dearlove was more forgiving. 'You could say that. Certainly his rackety life has caught up with him and his debts; he's now in rented rooms in Audley Street. But his charm seems to rescue him time and again.'

Lady Livia put a hand on Leonora's arm and enquired in a solicitous way, 'I hear you're accompanying Miss Blythe during her

Season. Why, pray, are the heroic Rokeby family taking such an interest in her?'

Leonora knew the truth would soon be clear once Charlotte was launched on Society and thought honesty might defuse some of the negative gossip. She turned to face Livia Dearlove. 'Charlotte Blythe is the natural daughter of the previous Earl, Charles Rokeby.'

'Oh yes, the daughter of a hero.' Rufus Dearlove snorted.

'Yes, the daughter of a hero and she has been embraced by the family.' Leonora stood as tall as she could, her chin high.

'And awarded a huge dowry no doubt so that prospective suitors overlook her dubious parentage.'

'Lord Dearlove! I consider that comment beneath a gentleman's honour. Charlotte is beautiful, accomplished, and kind. Any man would be fortunate to win her as a wife, fortune or not!' Leonora felt blood rush to her cheeks. This was the first time she had come up against the snobberies of the *haut ton*, which she and Charlotte were about to enter.

George Lockwood had moved to stand beside her in solidarity as Lord Dearlove continued in his amused and suave manner, 'Admirably said, Miss Appleby, but you cannot be so naive to think that beauty and charm alone will merit a girl a good marriage. The marriage mart is just that: a transaction where money and breeding are the necessary currencies.'

Livia Dearlove had not sheathed her rapier which now went straight to the weakest point. In her silky lisp she asked, 'Pray tell me, Miss Appleby, who is Charlotte Blythe's mother?'

George Lockwood's good nature had been tried long enough. He stepped forward and with some exasperation answered, 'I agree with Miss Appleby, the best of men will seek out the most affectionate and amenable of women. Should she also have wit and beauty then that is a bonus. Fortune and breeding are merely the bloom on the apple, the icing on the cake. Charlotte Blythe will make a fond husband very happy indeed.'

This seemed to break up the breakfast party, and everyone went to their rooms to prepare for their return to London. Leonora heard the jingling of harnesses as the Lockwood and Dearlove coachmen and grooms drove two coaches and their teams of horses up to the door.

Lord Dearlove grasped Leonora's hand. 'Miss Appleby, thank you for the exquisite entertainment last night and your impeccable hospitality. My sister and I look forward to reciprocating once you are in Town.' His sunniness had returned and his face shone with the good looks and charm for which he was lauded.

His sister smiled and inclined her head as she took Leonora's hand. She had put on a bonnet of the finest Leghorn straw, and the flaring brim and Italian silk trim in a fetching shade of periwinkle blue so flattered her she had become almost attractive, animated with a sly humour. 'Miss Appleby, I shall look forward to introducing you and Miss Blythe to a suitable set of acquaintances. Do not hesitate to call on me for any entrées into the intimate circles of the more select hostesses.'

George Lockwood was the last to leave and he took Leonora aside. 'I will be honoured to be a *cavalier servant* to you or Miss Blythe should you ever need me. The Season is full of venom, and I would be sorry if either of you lost your unmannered charm.' He glanced across at the Dearloves about to climb into their coach, then continued with feeling, 'Your spontaneous goodness of heart is rare in Society, and you will discover why I cannot wait to dust the dirt of London from my heels and become a true country gentleman at last.'

He was so tall that Leonora had to tilt her head to meet his eyes. 'I think I too will be impatient to return to my measured life in Hasterleigh.' She smiled and he brought her hand to his lips.

'Farewell then, Miss Appleby. I'll see you once you're settled. Now I must just drop by the Vicarage as I need to take my leave of Miss Blythe and the Mildmays. It's a most congenial community we have here. I shall miss it.'

* * *

The next two days were a hive of activity at both the Manor and the Vicarage. The gowns and accessories had arrived from Mrs Marmery. These gorgeous creations were carefully unpacked from their nests of interleaved tissue paper to cries of delight. Charlotte had the full wardrobe, and she held the gowns up against her and twirled in front of the looking glass. 'How amazing the power of clothes!' she exclaimed in wonder. 'I have not changed and yet with these clothes on my back I feel beautiful! I now feel undaunted by what lies ahead.'

Leonora unpacked the few new gowns that were for her, one for each time of day and activity. She held an evening dress in oyster-pink gauze under her chin and gazed at her reflection, smiling. It was true: such creative needlework made her feel beautiful too. Having tried on and discussed every garment with excitement, the clothes then had to be repacked into travelling trunks to transport to London. The rustle of tissue paper and the scent of dried lavender dominated both houses as Milly and Mrs Priddy helped their young mistresses to make sure nothing was left behind.

It had been two days since the musical soirée and Leonora was surprised at how unsettled she felt. This uneasiness increased as the day approached to visit Rokeby Abbey one last time to tune the Broadwood piano-forte and to say goodbye to Alistair Rokeby. Once again, at the designated time of two in the afternoon, Leonora, with Mrs Priddy beside her, pulled up outside the ancient oak door to be greeted by Stowe. As they entered, Achille padded towards Leonora, still with a slight limp.

They divested themselves of bonnets and pelisses and Leonora followed the old retainer, her tuning tools and protective apron in a bag. She was wearing one of her favourite afternoon gowns made of lavender sprigged muslin with pale primrose cording and ribbons round the hem and neck, newly trimmed by her. They entered the drawing room where the Earl sat by the fire, a book open in his lap. He looked up, his expression softer and more reflective than Leonora had seen before. As he rose to his feet to greet them, his face resumed its usual cast of controlled politeness. He led both women to the fire and Stowe went in search of tea.

Alistair Rokeby inclined his head and murmured, 'I haven't seen you since your evening of entertainment. Thank you, Miss Appleby, for encouraging me to be more sociable.'

'It was our pleasure but I'm not so sure it was yours?' Leonora smiled.

'You are a perceptive woman. As you know I have little patience with flashy coxcombs like Ormonde, but then he has little time for prosy stiffrumps like me.' His demeanour darkened. 'Since returning from France I feel increasingly out of step with life. War has separated me from the world of the living.' His face was so full of pain Leonora had to stop herself from reaching across to touch his arm.

Nanny P was not constrained in the same way by propriety between the sexes. She moved to sit beside him on the sofa and placed her small hand on his knee. 'Master Alistair, you have survived against the odds. Your brother Charles would not wish you to let your life slip away on a river of grief and regret.'

'I accept that with my mind, but my unruly heart does not obey. But do not fear, Mrs Priddy, my music, my dog and my horses secure me to life. And thanks to you and Miss Appleby, my dog and my music are restored to me in health.' He smiled as he looked across at Leonora. 'I've been playing the Broadwood every day. Music expresses the inexpressible, don't you think?'

Leonora felt a leap in her spirit. Here was someone who felt as she did. 'Indeed, I've come to think that music is love in search of a word,' she said, then coloured. She had not meant to say so frankly what was in her heart.

Lord Rokeby's gaze held hers for a moment then he continued in his unruffled way, 'I would be grateful if you could wave your tuning fork once more before you go.'

Leonora finished her tea, slipped on her apron, and walked with him across to the instrument where the lid was already open. She sat down to play through the scales as Lord Rokeby leant over to watch. 'I should learn from you how to tune it myself,' he said as he sat down beside her on the stool.

Leonora continued to play, listening for any dissonance between the notes, but acutely aware of the energy pulsing through the body beside her. The stool was narrow and his thigh was pressed closely to hers. Mrs Priddy was sitting by the fire in the old-fashioned wing chair which blocked draughts and the possibility of overhearing most conversations. Alistair Rokeby glanced across at her, intent on her complex knitting pattern, and put a hand on Leonora's. It was the lightest of touches but she felt as if she had been branded. The back of her hand was so sensitised she stopped playing and looked at him, her cheeks flushing.

'Forgive my raising this, Miss Appleby, but I need to thank you for accompanying Miss Blythe to London. My mind is at rest knowing you and Mrs Priddy will be with her.' He sighed. 'Sadly, the fortune I have settled upon her might attract the wrong kind of attention. I just wanted to alert you to the world you are about to enter, full of blackguards and wastrels out for their own ends, and Devil take the consequences!' His voice softened as he said, 'I'm just concerned I may be making Miss Blythe vulnerable to these fortune-hunting mountebanks.'

Leonora looked at him with some alarm. 'I'm sure your grandmother will protect her too?'

'The Countess is more cynical than most. She traded her beauty for an unhappy marriage to a brute with a title and great fortune. I don't know I can trust her to protect Miss Blythe from similar predatory intent.'

'My lord, you paint such a forbidding picture. I wonder your brother should have wished for his daughter to be exposed to such danger.'

'Ah, Miss Appleby, you are as generous-hearted as she. But who would she marry if she stayed in the country? The pallid curate? His oaf of a father? God forbid! That misplaced dandy who's your father's heir? No! Miss Blythe is a Rokeby, if an irregular one, and as part of this noble family she is to marry someone of equal rank.'

Indignation rose in Leonora's breast. 'Lord Rokeby! I object to your own cynical view of the curate, Mr Fopling, and indeed of Mr Lockwood. Richard Fopling is as rare a spirit as anyone I know, and my father's heir as good a man as I could wish to inherit the Manor estate.' Mrs Priddy could not but hear Leonora's voice raised in protestation and she looked up from counting stitches, smiled, then returned to her intricate pattern of scallop shells.

The Earl had been watching Leonora's face and appeared to be struggling not to smile in a patronising way. 'I like your spirit, Miss Appleby. Indeed, you're right; I have been harsh. I'm just a sour, disappointed misanthrope in need of your flame to lighten my darkness.' He cast her a rueful look. 'All I meant to say is the Season is the gauntlet that every young woman of breeding has to run in order to gain the life for which she was born.'

'Well, Miss Charlotte was born into ignorance and ignominy.'
She sounded more reproachful than she meant.

He was unconcerned as he laughed. 'Ah, but her blood is half-
thoroughbred.'

'If you're thinking in terms of horseflesh then I'm just a moorland pony and there'll be no thoroughbred as a match for me in
Town.' Leonora had responded without thinking in a light-hearted
way but she was shocked that she had spoken thus, admitting to
him, and herself, that she still harboured hopes of marriage.
Embarrassed at being so frank, she began to run her fingers over
the keys from the bass notes to the treble. Glancing up, she said, 'It
seems to be still in tune. Is the top octave a little sharp? What do
you think, my lord?'

'I was just thinking that there's something irresistibly spirited
and sweet about a moorland pony.' Leonora cast a startled glance
at him, met his mischievous gleam and laughed. Their attention
returned to the piano-forte and Alistair Rokeby's voice was once
again serious. 'Perhaps it would be useful anyway to see how you
alter the notes. I should learn to care for my own piano-forte.'

Achille padded over from the fireside to lay his head on his
master's knee and Leonora stood up to reach the wrest-pins. As
she worked, she was aware that Achille's and the Earl's regard did
not waver from her face. When she had finished, she sat down
again on the stool with a triumphant smile. 'There! I think that
should do. Until I'm back again or you have taught yourself, Lord
Rokeby. I can leave you my tools if you would like?' Leonora met
his gaze and for some moments could not look away.

He broke the tension by running his hands over the keys. 'I feel
you've begun to retune *me*, Miss Appleby. The jangling notes
rearranged to a kind of music.' He gave a soft laugh. 'If not yet a
symphony.'

Acutely aware of the beating of her heart, Leonora looked

down at their hands, and slowly Lord Rokeby started to play. She recognised the base melody that undulated like a lullaby: it was the duet they had played before. She picked up the treble part that so sinuously intertwined with his.

Sitting so close, their bodies as one, their hands moving together then apart, crossing, brushing fingers, it felt akin to an elaborate courtship. She glanced at him, wondering if their thoughts too had merged, whether he felt the same pulse of recognition, but his face was intent on the keyboard. When they had stopped playing, he said quietly, 'It's the inner harmony that matters most; I feel that when we play.' So sensitised was Leonora, she shivered. They continued to sit side by side, silent, barely breathing. Lord Rokeby took her hands in his. He began to speak with some hesitation. 'Miss Appleby, I cannot bear...' But before he could finish his sentence there was a discordant banging of the front door and the moment was shattered. Both looked up as a woman burst into the room, followed by a flustered Stowe. 'Alistair, *mon trésor! Enfin je t'ai trouvé!'*

Lord Rokeby sprang to his feet and strode towards the visitor, his hands out. She flew into his arms and they held each other in a fierce embrace that spoke of an intense intimacy. Leonora, roughly awoken from her romantic dream, could barely believe her eyes. She and Mrs Priddy stood up; each caught the other's startled expression and looked away. Too shocked to think, Leonora placed her tuning tools in the bag and left them on the stool for Lord Rokeby. She removed her apron. Mrs Priddy too folded up her baby shawl, needles and wool, and stowed it all away as they prepared to go.

The Earl whirled round to face Leonora. 'My apologies, Miss Appleby, and Mrs Priddy.' He looked across to Nanny P who walked to take Leonora's arm. 'Let me introduce Madame Claudette Dupré to you. She was employed by the *Grande Armée* as a *vivandière,* running the canteen for the soldiers in the front line. She found me on the battlefield. And saved my life.'

He looked across to the young woman and translated, '*Tu m'as sauvé la vie.*' His face was alive with feeling.

Leonora gazed with some wonder and despair at this exotic woman who stood so full of life before her. She wore a striped jacket in red, white and blue, in the manner of the Paris revolutionaries a generation before. Her skirt was a simple blue calico, and an Indian shawl was tied round her shoulders and crossed over her breast to be knotted in the small of her back. But it was her face and hair that were most striking. Strongly boned and handsome, she had a fine nose and dark lively eyes. Her olive skin appeared gilded by the sun and she wore her cloud of wavy hair in the most informal manner, merely pulled back and tied in a luxuriant pigtail that reached half way down her back.

She laughed and punched Lord Rokeby playfully on the arm, speaking in a strong French accent. 'You know I understand Angleesh! And you, Alistair, had *embrassé la mort* as I drag you off that *sanglant* field, how you say? Blooded field!'

Lord Rokeby turned to Leonora. 'She says I embraced death; I was in fact embracing my brother who had just died in my arms. But Madame Dupré is right, when she found me, I did not wish to live.' He then took Leonora's hand and squeezed her fingers so lightly she wasn't sure if she had imagined the pressure. Turning to Madame Dupré, he said, 'Claudette, I want you to meet Miss Appleby who is about to go to London for the Season, *la saison sociale,* and her *compagne,* Mrs Priddy, who will accompany her and my young niece.'

Leonora and Claudette Dupré were guarded as they met each other's gaze, each uncertain of the character of the other or the nature of her relationship with Lord Rokeby. Leonora was struck by how free the Frenchwoman appeared in dress and manner,

A Lady's Fortune

159

astonished by her vitality and comradely ease with the Earl. She so envied her that. Madame Dupré's courage and competence as a woman working on the front line was almost unimaginable to her and made her own life seem so small in comparison.

Claudette Dupré grasped her hand with disarming spontaneity. 'M'selle Appleby, perhaps I see you *à Londres*? I go there in charge of the *cuisine* for the new French *ambassadeur*, le marquis de La Châtre. *Pouf! Il est vieux* but he likes parties and dancing.' She shrugged and then laughed.

Leonora was surprised yet again. Here was a woman with a job who seemed full of the kind of breezy confidence she expected from ennobled men. She found this *joie de vivre* immensely attractive and responded in as friendly a way as possible, 'I should like that, Madame. We will be staying with the Earl's grandmother in Brook Street.'

'La! He is not "the Earl" to me!' She laughed. 'He's *un vilain coquin*, how you say, Alistair? A rascal, who spent too much time with his horses, the cards and *les filles de la nuit*.'

Lord Rokeby interjected in mock indignation, 'Madame! Do not blacken my name.' He caught Leonora's eye and continued, ''Tis true, as an officer, there were certain freedoms, but not all the ones Madame Dupré suggests!'

His words were serious but his expression more roguish than Leonora had seen before. This unconventional visitor had reminded him of his spirit of old and a life Leonora could not know. She was shocked by the envy she felt of Claudette Dupré's part in this life. It had been many years since Leonora had experienced such a tumult of emotion and she was ashamed of her jealousy. Uppermost was the sinking feeling that she could never know Lord Rokeby as well. Claudette Dupré had saved his life; how could she, a naive countrywoman, with only their shared love of Hasterleigh, of music and swimming, ever compete with such a momentous history as that? How could a well-behaved Englishwoman like herself ever compare to such a force of nature with her free and easy manner, her unembarrassed passions, her animal energy and joy?

Leonora just wanted to get away and taking Mrs Priddy's arm, bade her farewells, inclining her head to Lord Rokeby. 'Thank you, my lord, for warning of the pitfalls that await Miss Charlotte and me in London.' They collected the gig and set Clover off at a brisk trot for home. Only once out of sight did Leonora feel she could exhale. Nanny P glanced across at her and gave voice to her outrage. 'Well, what a hoyden girl! Her hair! Her clothes! And the way she embraced Master Alistair! Who does she think she is?'

Despite her own tremulous heart, Leonora could not suppress an amused gasp. 'Oh, Nanny P! She's French and they're all revolutionaries now.'

'That may well be, my dear, but who is she to burst into the Abbey and treat him as if she has rights over his life and limb?'

'Well, he owes her his life. That is a considerable bond, you know.' Her light-heartedness had receded and her voice was flat.

Mrs Priddy gave her a sharp look. 'Nora! I understand you well enough by now to know your feelings are stirred by Lord Rokeby, but you are not to feel cast down. He's not proof against your charms, my dear; I'm experienced enough in the ways of men to know that at least!'

'But what presumption that a no-longer-young woman from Hasterleigh could ever think such a man would love her.' The full absurdity of the idea struck Leonora with greater force as she made her thoughts public; at the same time, she was aware of the cruel irony that in the incandescence of Claudette Dupré's arrival, her own amorous heart, so long denied, had sprung to life and settled unequivocally upon Lord Rokeby. With that precious gift of clarity, however, came the pain of jealousy and fear of loss.

She pulled up the gig in the stable yard at the Manor and as she helped Mrs Priddy down, her beloved nanny said, 'There's no accounting for the human heart. And we cannot know what life has in store for us. You are off to London in two days where every kind of adventure awaits.'

'To believe Lord Rokeby, it's more where every kind of predator, fortune hunter and libertine lies in wait!'

* * *

The two days that remained sped by in a flurry of activity. Leonora had no time to think of what had transpired at Rokeby Abbey and what might be happening there now. She had overheard some scurrilous servants' gossip about a wild French lass but for the sake of her own peace of mind, had tried to suppress any lurid imaginings.

Her only letter from Captain Worth had been her constant companion and a reminder of how much she had once been loved. Read and reread countless times, the folds were beginning to tear, so she decided not to take it with her to London. Leonora sat at her dressing table and drew it from the drawer to read one last time before she left.

My Beloved,

Death is ever near. Bleakness everywhere and I so far from all I hold Dear. My Thoughts of You, the glowing centre of my Nights, the Reason I can face the Day. How I long for this War to be over. And at last I can hold you in my Arms to never let you go. I fear I can no longer Live without You near – my Soul's a Desert, my Heart in Flames. I long to kiss your Hands, your Lips, your Throat. Oh! how I lose my Wits in Longing.

*Know that You are loved beyond Everything. May I call you My
Leonora? Most beloved of Names. Wait for Me my Dearest Love.*
    From your own Devoted Will

As she folded the precious letter, Leonora could not suppress a
sob. She had feared her heart would remain folded into this sheet
of paper for ever. But Nanny P had said to Lord Rokeby – and it
was as true for her too – *'you have survived, and it is your duty to
live'*.

*   *   *

The Friday morning they were due to travel began crisp and cold.
They were lucky the day was bright and free of rain. As promised,
the Rokeby coach rolled up at the portico of the Manor. It was
grand, painted a smart green and boasting the Rokeby crest on the
door, an eagle alighting on a turreted castle surmounting a sword
in a mailed fist. The motto *Pietas et Fortitudo* was painted in gold on
the banner flying from the turret. *Duty and Courage*; for a fleeting
moment Leonora wondered which quality Alistair Rokeby most
embodied.

Breakfast was eaten in haste while all the trunks were stowed
in the back of the coach by Jack Clegg. He bustled out with the hot
bricks which he placed under the blankets on the floor. The
Reverend and Mrs Mildmay had arrived early to see them off.
'Thank you, Miss Leonora, for taking care of our beloved Charlotte.' Mrs Mildmay embraced Leonora, tears pricking her eyes.
She had not been farther than Maidenhead in her life and the
thought of her beautiful Charlotte in the mysterious, dangerous
whirlpool of London filled her with nameless dread.

Leonora quickly grabbed her best bonnet and was just about
to join Charlotte and Mrs Priddy in the coach when there was a

clatter of approaching hooves. She glanced down the lane and saw Jupiter trotting towards them. On his back was the Earl with Achille running beside them. Leonora was aware of her breathing becoming suddenly shallow and fast. He dismounted and doffed his hat. 'Good morning.' He nodded to them all in turn. 'I hoped to catch you in time. To wish you a safe journey and a most successful Season.'

Lord Rokeby put his hand in his pocket and withdrew a blue velvet pouch. He took Charlotte's hand and dropped it into her palm. 'I wanted you to have one of your grandmother's favourite necklaces.'

Charlotte coloured with pleasure as she looked down at the bag and with care withdrew a scintillating river of cornflower-blue stones. She gasped. 'For me?' She looked into Lord Rokeby's face.

'Of course. It's part of a parure with matching earrings and a bracelet too. The rest of her jewellery will go to my countess one day, if I ever find someone willing to marry me.' His smile was crooked.

Charlotte appeared quite overcome with emotion, her eyes shining and her cheeks flushed. 'Thank you, thank you, my lord. I have never had anything so beautiful.'

He took her hand. 'They are but your due.'

Then Alistair Rokeby turned to Leonora and lifted her reluctant hand from her side. He held it lightly in his and gazed at her downturned face. 'Please look at me, Miss Appleby. I wish to thank you for everything you have done, and it is quite difficult talking to a bonnet and feathers, however charmingly trimmed.'

Leonora did not wish to give the impression she was sulking and lifted her head and smiled. He still had hold of her gloved hand and pressed it fleetingly to his lips. His face was serious and he did not release her. 'I have never properly thanked you for all the work you have done making my piano-forte a pleasure to play again.'

She answered in a formal way. 'I am pleased to be able to help.' It was hard to remain aloof when Achille was standing beside her, nuzzling her hand, waiting for her to scratch behind his ears.

Lord Rokeby was watching her face closely as if trying to understand what she really felt. Then he took a breath and said in a voice quiet and full of feeling, 'I want you to know that Madame Dupré saved my life, but it is you alone, Miss Appleby, who has made me want to live.' Their eyes met in an intense moment of recognition. Leonora knew by the pressure of his fingers on hers that he had felt it too. It quickly flared, then was gone. He saluted them all and sprang into the saddle. She watched him trot away into the morning sun, back to the Abbey and Madame Dupré.

7

DELIGHT, DANGER AND DESIRE

Leonora, Charlotte and Nanny P settled themselves into the comfortable interior of the Rokeby coach. Leonora was so exhausted with all the preparatory work and the tide of emotion that she did not even have the energy to read. She gazed out of the window at the landscape of bare swooping downland and valleys with sparse copses of leafless trees, everywhere cold and bleak with January frost.

Charlotte was onto the last volume of *Belinda* but even she was distracted by the thought of London. Only Nanny P seemed untroubled. Charlotte looked across at where she sat, a mound of what looked like white fine lace in her lap. 'Nanny P, what are you knitting?'

Mrs Priddy was in the middle of counting stitches and without looking up said, 'A shawl for a baby.'

'It's very intricate. Which baby is it for?'

Peg Priddy looked up with a vague smile. 'Oh, no baby in particular but by the time I finish knitting one of my shawls, there's always a newborn infant in need of it.'

A mischievous smile lit up Charlotte's face as she said, 'Well, I think Mr Fopling and Miss Vazey will be needing that shawl in a year or so.'

'Lottie!' Leonora was intrigued by what had prompted this comment, remembering her unexpected conversation with Miss Vazey in the lane. 'What makes you think that, may I ask?'

'Well, I saw Mr Fopling and Little Grace disappearing into the Vazey cottage, then heard him later asking the Reverend about when the living at Wetherleigh becomes vacant. They're both so unworldly, I think they'll suit each other well.'

Mrs Priddy ignored this diversion and her kindly blue eyes rested on Charlotte's face. 'In fact, the first I knitted was to this pattern. I had no idea who it would be for and then, as I was crocheting the lace border, you, Miss Blythe, arrived on the Vicarage doorstep. It was as if an angel had brought you to where you were needed most. And my shawl was ready to welcome you.'

Charlotte's face was suddenly close to tears. 'Mama Mildmay and the Reverend could not have been kinder to me. But to know at least who my father was has given me a sense of belonging.' She blew her nose then turned to Mrs Priddy. 'You remember my father when he was young. What was he like?'

'Well Master Charles and his younger brother were as close as brothers could be, but oh, so different. Master Charles, full of larks but steady and sensible underneath, then Master Alistair, wild and adventurous. He would always climb a tree higher than anyone and then have to be rescued by his elder brother. If anyone was going to get into trouble, I'd always have bet my money on it being Master Alistair.' Mrs Priddy put down her knitting, a sign that she was about to say something serious. 'Master Charles always protected little Alistair from their cruel father, but he could not save their mother. Lady Venetia asked for my advice more than once about her sons' behaviour and then died when they were barely grown. From that point on, the Abbey really lacked a woman's sensibility.' She leant across and took Charlotte's hand. 'Perhaps that's why your father looked to other women for love?' Charlotte squeezed Nanny P's hand in thanks, leant back on the cushions and closed her eyes.

The frozen landscape began to grow greener and less frost-bitten as they left the rural downland and fields for scattered villages and market gardens that proliferated closer to the city. Excitement for the adventure ahead began to replace anxious anticipation. They changed horses at The King's Head at Maidenhead where the day before, Lord Rokeby had had his grooms deliver the next team of fresh horses to make their onward journey swifter and more comfortable.

By the time the sun was low in the sky, they had left the villages of Kensington and Knightsbridge behind with their pretty cottages and occasional grand brick manor houses. Leonora peered out of the window and saw the beginning of the terraces of symmetrical houses built in pale stone. The sun glinted off their tall windows and she was struck by the orderly beauty of these recently constructed streets and squares with trees and gardens. Charlotte let out a cry as they glimpsed Hyde Park. 'Oh look, countryside of a kind!'

Leonora replied, 'The Countess of Bucklebury's house is at the Grosvenor Square end of Brook Street, so we'll be in easy walking distance of somewhere to stroll and ride.' The carriage came to a halt outside a mansion, six windows across with a grand portico and a shiny blue door.

Charlotte grasped Leonora's hand. 'Oh, I'm afraid. What if she doesn't approve of me? Thinks I'm just a country dowd, and ill-begotten too.' Her face was drawn with anxiety.

'Come on, Lottie. You're the Countess's only great-grandchild and you're beautiful and accomplished and kind. She's lucky to have someone like you in her family and I'm sure that's what she'll think. The new Earl has accepted you wholeheartedly and even given you his mother's necklace.'

'And he has settled a large sum of money on you too,' Mrs Priddy added as she put away her knitting. 'You are an heiress now, young woman, and need to start behaving as one! No more wilting violet but a proud rose. Come now, my dear.'

The Rokeby coachman had opened the door and handed Mrs Priddy down. Leonora and Charlotte followed. The door of Bucklebury House swung open and a footman in full livery of gold braid and green descended to escort them up the steps. Leonora exchanged a look with Charlotte and they found each other's gloved hands to cling together for a moment.

The hallway of Bucklebury House was as impressive as its façade. Spacious, with a wide stone staircase rising to the left in a sinuous curve, it was floored in polished limestone and had the faded grandeur of the previous century. The cerulean blue of the silk-lined walls had been bleached by age to a misty aquamarine on which large ancestral portraits hung. Their pale faces and dark eyes seemed to gaze accusingly from the canvas, watching Leonora with unblinking stares. Some wore ruffs as big as wheels and others, towering wigs with circles of rouge on their cheeks. The Bucklebury servants too were silent and austere, so different from the easy-going informality of the countryfolk who worked at the Manor.

Leonora, Charlotte and Mrs Priddy were divested of their cloaks, bonnets and pelisses and led up the grand staircase, past more watching ancestors, some shining in armour or poised in mid-charge on the back of a rearing warhorse. Cobwebs hung from the chandelier and dust motes danced in the cool light from the tall north window on the landing. The house was silent apart from the ticking of a clock somewhere. They reached the first floor and the footman knocked on a pair of gilded double doors.

'Come!' was the call from within.

'My lady, Miss Blythe, Miss Appleby and Mrs Priddy to see you.' He opened both the doors and they walked in. The drawing room was even more impressive than the hallway. For a moment Leonora could not see where the voice had come from as her eye was overwhelmed with the opulence of her surroundings. The walls painted ochre with gilded mouldings emitted their own glow and the jostle of sofas and chairs were upholstered in faded tapestries of purples and pinks. A square piano-forte sat in the window and Leonora longed to investigate it.

'Come in, come in. And close the doors. It's cold enough as it is.' A querulous voice arose from the sofa by the nearest of two blazing fires. There, sitting in splendour, was the most extraordinary person Leonora had ever seen. Frail and very old, the Countess of Bucklebury sat among her blue brocade skirts with a white lace fichu foaming at her neck; she, like her house, favoured the last century.

The women approached with deference and one by one took the hand that was proffered. She looked imperious, the remnants of her beauty displayed in the fine cheekbones and large dark eyes. Her lips and cheeks were rouged, and her hair covered by an elaborate lace and ribbon cap tied under the chin. The surroundings and her manner were so regal that Leonora found herself bobbing a quick curtsey, followed by Charlotte, her face suffused by a blush.

'Now, there's no need for that!' the Countess said in a surprisingly strong and brusque voice. 'I presume you are Charlotte?' She had hold of Charlotte's hand and examined her with beady eyes that appeared almost black, and missing nothing. 'You appear charming enough, my dear. Luckily the country maid look is all the rage this year, in London, if not in Paris.' She pulled her closer. 'But beware of confusing outer appearance with character. I disdain any gal who thinks it's charming to play the milksop in person.'

Leonora saw Charlotte's shoulders slump. This was damning with faint praise, she thought, and felt a stab of protective indignation on the younger woman's behalf. 'Thank you, Lady Bucklebury, I will strive to overcome any timidity.' Charlotte bowed her head.

'Tush! You may call me Grandmama. I know I'm your great-grandmama but that sounds so ageing.' She peered closer at the young woman's face and softened her manner. 'In fact, you have the look of my daughter, Venetia, about you. You are a beauty, but I hope your character will have more firmness than hers.'

The dark eyes then moved to Leonora. 'You, Miss Appleby, are here as a companion and friend to Charlotte?' When Leonora nodded, she continued in her terse way, 'Of course, every kind of scapegrace and fortune hunter will be attracted to my grand-daughter now Alistair has decided to bestow such a handsome dowry upon her.' She patted Leonora's hand. 'I'm assured by Lord Rokeby that you have all the sterling qualities to protect her reputation and fortune.'

Leonora smiled and said, 'I will do my best, Lady Bucklebury. I have known Charlotte all her life and she is as precious as a sister to me.'

The Countess looked impatient. 'That is admirable from a sentimental point of view, my dear, but in my experience, we are all selfish beings and I would hope that you will also find yourself a husband while you are under my protection.' One bony finger tapped Leonora's cheek. 'You're handsome enough, Miss Appleby, to attract a fortune adequate to live a good life.' When Leonora showed doubt, her colour rising, the old lady became tetchy. 'Save me girlish chatter about love,' she scoffed. 'We all know an unmarried woman has a narrow, circumscribed existence, unless she is very rich or of highest birth when she can make her own life and take her pleasure where she will.' Leonora felt thoroughly put in her place and wondered what it was going to be like living under this old termagant's wing for the duration of the Season.

Lady Bucklebury then turned her attention to Mrs Priddy and her face cracked into a rare smile revealing blackened teeth. 'Mrs P, I remember you from when you used to help my poor Venetia with those wicked sons of hers! I'm pleased to make your acquaintance again.' She patted the satin beside her, suggesting she join her on the sofa. 'I know that these girls will be in safe hands with you around.' She even managed a laugh. She gestured to Leonora and Charlotte to sit as her footman brought in a tray of tea and macaroons.

'It is indeed good to see you again, m'lady, and in such health.' Mrs Priddy poured out the tea. Lady Bucklebury settled back against the cushions, her face growing softer in the firelight. 'I must say this will prove to be diverting. At my age there is not much to entertain me apart from my memories. But they are rich pickings. At your age I was wild indeed!' Her eyes sparkled at her recall of youthful exploits. 'It was a much more libertine age. La! How prosy and particular Society has become! I was lucky enough to attract the attention of a very rich marquis and I married him. I had fallen in love with his house!' She cackled with laughter. 'Putting up with the blunderhead was not too onerous if I could live in this house and his very nice estate in Worcestershire.'

'By the time I met you, Lady Bucklebury, the Marquis had died in a hunting accident, I think?' Nanny P enquired as she handed round the plate of macaroons.

'Oh yes! Fate intervened! Bucklebury gave me my child – although Venetia was always a little below par – then was propelled from his saddle taking a five-bar gate!' She chuckled with amusement, then noticed Leonora's and Charlotte's shocked faces. 'Oh don't be ninnies, this is the reality of life. The heart just complicates things. If I had loved my lord then I would have wailed my life was over. All that's required for success is a certain charm, some luck, and a lot of land.' Her voice had an edge of triumph. 'Aged thirty, I was left with half Bucklebury's fortune and the freedom to do as I pleased.'

Leonora regained her equilibrium by concentrating on a favourite melody in her mind as her attention turned to the piano-forte. Curiosity overcame her shyness. 'Lady Bucklebury, is your piano-forte a Broadwood or a Clementi?'

The dark eyes fixed on her face. 'It is a Clementi. Do you or Charlotte play?'

'We both do. I've been teaching Charlotte and she's a very proficient musician. She has a pleasing singing voice too.'

Lady Bucklebury leant forward and said, 'I don't think I can host a party here for you as it's too disruptive, but I'm able to obtain vouchers from Almack's and I'm sure there will be many parties and balls in other establishments that you will be invited to.' She settled back in her seat. 'And of course I am happy for your friends to come to visit you here as long as Mrs Priddy chaperones you. I have strict instructions from the Earl.'

Charlotte surprised everyone, including herself, by saying, 'Lord Rokeby has been very kind to me.'

'I'm consoled to hear that, my dear. I can only regret that if one of the Rokeby brothers had to be sacrificed in defence of the country, it should be your father and not Alistair who was killed.'

There was a communal gasp and Leonora felt emotion surge up into her chest and without thinking, she erupted, 'Lady Bucklebury! I think that is an unconscionable thing to say!'

The Countess was quite unruffled. 'How so, my dear? I only speak the truth. Both of his parents would have said the same. Charles was everything that a nobleman should be, especially as the head of such an eminent family. Alistair was always recalci-trant, and look at him now! Returned half blind, lame, scarred, so damaged from war not even his dog can consider him a hero now.'

'Well, both Achille and I think him so,' Leonora muttered. It seemed only Charlotte heard as Lady Bucklebury clapped her hands and said, 'I think we should eat. I'll meet you in the dining room in an hour. My maid will show you to your rooms.' She got to her feet with a grimace of pain and accepting Mrs Priddy's arm, walked with the aid of a cane to the door. As she left them to go and dress for dinner she said, 'I am a selfish old woman who has lived too long alone. Forgive any lapse of social grace.' Her sly smile belied the contrition of her words.

The meal was a subdued affair. Both Leonora and Charlotte were still reeling from the broadsides as to their looks and general prospects. They felt their new clothes, with which they had been so delighted, probably erred on the side of 'milksop'. The food itself was meagre, the main dish being potatoes and a rabbit stew, and it became obvious that as Lady Bucklebury barely ate herself, she was unconcerned with providing a lavish table for her guests, expecting them to share her abstemious habits. Mrs Priddy kept the conversation alive by enquiring about elderly acquaintances, but everyone soon beat an early retreat.

Their bedchambers and dressing rooms were on the second floor, above the drawing room, and they congregated in Leonora's. When the door was closed, she threw herself on the bed. 'Well! I've never known such an unmannerly woman!'

'Now, now, Nora dear, it won't do to get uppity. She's from a different age, and wealth has removed her from the usual niceties of manner.'

'Nanny P, if you suggest Lady B's sour temper is just due to lack of food or sleep, I shall scream!' Leonora sprang off the bed and they all laughed.

'I'm afraid if I show mere kindly manners and politeness, the Countess will dismiss me as a milksop, which she considers worse than a jezebel or cockish wench!' Charlotte's fair skin had flared with emotion.

'Now Miss Charlotte, you are not to use such vulgar terms.' Mrs Priddy wagged her finger. 'It's just about acceptable to talk in such an informal way when you're in the country but not here. And not under Lady Bucklebury's roof!'

'At least I won't be accused of being a *milksop*! I was so pleased to belong to this family but now I see such a Lady Virago at its head, I'm not so sure.'

'We're all tired. Let's to bed and everything will seem better in the morning.' Peg Priddy straightened her skirts and kissed Leonora and Charlotte on the cheek.

Leonora pulled her close. 'I'm so glad you're with us, Nanny P. You put everything in its place. Of course things will look better tomorrow. For a start I want to explore Hyde Park.'

'I'll come with you!' Charlotte said, her face brighter and her sense of adventure restored.

'The Park is safe enough if you two stay together. Beware there are pickpockets and other ruffians, and young men exercise their horses first thing, so perhaps go out a little later.' Nanny P did not see the lively look that passed between the two young women. 'Good night, everyone.'

Leonora woke early after a deep untroubled sleep. She was still on country time and wondered what a suitable hour was to surface for breakfast. As she lay in a deep feather mattress, her gaze travelled around the palatial bedroom, the details just visible now the pale light was beginning to seep through the curtains. Her four-poster bed was hung with silk curtains frayed into ribbons at the edges but once beautiful. Pale yellow and embroidered with flowers and bees, they looked too fragile to pull closed and she feared she'd be enveloped in a cloud of dust if she did. The room itself was panelled and painted a pearl grey to which time only added an attractive smoky patina. It was restful to lie there warm and safe, and Leonora's mind returned to her beloved Hasterleigh and the Earl.

Her jealousy of Claudette Dupré and fears about her importance in Lord Rokeby's life had given way to a fierce protectiveness after Lady Bucklebury's harsh dismissal of him the day before. She knew Society and the Countess herself would consider it ludicrous if they knew her secret longing, a longing she barely managed to acknowledge to herself. But she held close to her heart what Lord Rokeby had said, so surprising she was not certain she had heard it right. *You alone have made me want to live.* Had she made that up in a reverie of wishful thinking? Surely such words could not be true?

Leonora refused to enter the maze of speculation and instead, reminded herself she was here on Charlotte's adventure; her young friend was to be given a chance of marriage that had been denied to herself with the death in Spain of her beloved Captain Worth. This was a noble cause and she and Nanny P would do their utmost to help her attain it. There was a soft tap at the door and a young maid entered with a jug of steaming water which she carried through to the dressing room and placed beside a large, chipped Delft bowl on the marble-topped table. 'Good morning, Miss Appleby. I'm Amy.'

Leonora knew it was probably time to struggle out of bed. Gazing towards the morning light suffused through the grimy glass of the window, she thought how entering London Society was akin to entering enemy territory, where pitfalls and Society

queens like Livia Dearlove lay in wait to undermine women like
her, neither rich, high-bred nor beautiful. But there was entertainment and opportunity too. She knew she and Charlotte had to be
prepared for anything.

Energised by the thought, Leonora was impatient to see more
of the city, and explore the great park. She dressed hurriedly in
her new walking dress of dark green twill with a matching pelisse,
fastened becomingly with silver toggles. She picked up a lilac-
trimmed bonnet to match her calfskin boots and knocked on
Charlotte's door.

Charlotte was dressed already, looking pretty in her walking
gown of primrose yellow cambric lawn. 'Let's have a hasty breakfast.' Leonora led the way downstairs, drawn by the smell of coffee.

After toast and honey and a cup of coffee, Charlotte looked
across at Leonora and with a mischievous smile said, 'Do you
think this is too early to set out, seeing Nanny P has warned us
about the risks of meeting young men exercising their steeds?'

They both laughed and Leonora stood up. 'I'm sure we'll be
safe from any untoward attention. Come on, Lottie.'

The quickest route to Grosvenor Gate was through Grosvenor
Square and both young women scrutinised with awe this grandest
of structures. Houses of pale stone stood in four proud ranks
around the large oval sweep of grass and trees in the centre. The
largest houses had pilasters rising from the first floor to the attics
and Leonora found herself thinking about the lives behind those
glinting tall windows. She wondered which was the Rokeby
mansion. Everywhere was bustle and activity as carts delivered
vegetables and meat, the carters shouting their wares and the
delivery boys scampering up and down the front steps leading to
the basements of the towering houses above.

The Grosvenor Gate entrance into the Park was thronged with
early horsemen leaving while carriages and curricles, wishing to

take the crisp morning air, swept in with a flourish. It was all so new and exciting that Charlotte hung on tight to Leonora's arm. The frosty grass was punctuated by gravelled avenues and copses of bare trees as far as the eye could see. The distant glint of water drew them towards the Serpentine and they walked down the well-trodden track, careful to avoid the centre where horses' hooves had churned the earth to mud.

The low sun made everything sparkle and Leonora and Charlotte felt their cheeks tingling in the chill air. Riders mounted on flashy stallions eyed the young women appreciatively as they passed; some were more forward, leaning out of their saddles to doff their hats and ogle. Leonora drew Charlotte close and said, 'When a man does that to you, just turn your head away smartly to give him "the cut". Now practise it with the next one.' They laughed and quickened their pace.

They approached the Serpentine's edge where noisy children and dogs gambolled amongst the reeds when Leonora's eye was caught by an enormous black horse emerging from the trees. The rider, sitting tall astride his magnificent steed, appeared to be a giant. She nudged Charlotte who recognised him and cried out, 'It's Mr Lockwood!' Relief at meeting someone so familiar in this unfamiliar place flooded them both. They waved.

He trotted up and reined in his horse, seeming to loom over them as they gazed up into his smiling face. He had swept his hat off his head, and his hair was unruly.

'Oh, we're so glad to see you!' Charlotte was the first to speak, her voice warm with feeling.

George Lockwood laughed as he dismounted. 'Why? Are you tired of London already?'

'No! We've only just arrived but it's good to see a friendly face, Mr Lockwood.' Leonora put out her hand.

'Well, I am inordinately pleased to see you, Miss Blythe, Miss

Appleby.' He bowed. 'You are happy reminders of my favourite place. And unlike you, I am definitely tired of London!'

His reins were looped over his arm as he allowed his horse to nuzzle his ear. 'This fine beast is Titan. I shall bring him with me to Hasterleigh after the Season is over. I think he longs for those rolling acres almost as much as I do.' In a companionable group, they walked round the Serpentine. 'Tell me then of your first impressions.'

Charlotte spoke first. 'We're staying with my dragonish great-grandmama in her ancient lair in Brook Street and she is full of opinions.'

'Not least that we look like country dowds!' Leonora's eyes flashed. 'Even with our newly bought fashions!'

Mr Lockwood looked down at them. 'If that's the case, I'm all for country dowds. To my eye, you both look entirely charming, no one better.'

Charlotte's indignation was still raw. 'And she said that my father was more worthy to survive at Corunna and it should have been Lord Rokeby to be killed! Leonora scolded her for saying such a thing.' Leonora was sorry that Charlotte had brought this up. It was still so shocking to her she did not wish to give it any more thought.

George Lockwood looked across at Leonora's pained face and said in an equable way, 'Any death in war is a tragedy. Those of us who have not been through that particular horror have little right to opine on it, I would think.'

Leonora was grateful to him for his measured reply, and they all walked on in companionable silence, Titan clip-clopping peaceably beside them. George Lockwood stopped. 'It's just occurred to me. My stepfather, Beau Beacham, holds a monthly party with dancing and cards during the Season and his first is at the end of the month. I usually escape to my club but if you'll attend, it becomes a much more attractive proposition.'

Charlotte's bright face broke into the widest smile. 'Oh good! We have no invitations yet. Grandmama will be pleased.'

George Lockwood let out a snort of laughter. 'It depends how much of a stickler she is. The Beau runs with a raffish crowd; not everyone he invites would delight a matron seeking a match for a beloved relation.'

Charlotte replied, 'I don't think Lady Bucklebury would deem me a "beloved relation" by any measure.'

Leonora's responsibility for Charlotte settled more heavily on her shoulders. 'Will Lord Dearlove be there?' She hoped to put her mind at ease with the presence of some respectable attendees.

'My stepfather is nothing if not up to all the tricks. He attaches himself to whomsoever might do him good by reputation or deed. Yes, Rufus Dearlove is likely to be there. Beau's cellar is legendary.'

'And Captain Ormonde?'

'That dapper dog seems to turn up wherever there's free champagne and pretty women. My stepfather rates him highly for his charm. I think he'd prefer him for a son; I'm afraid I'm an eternal disappointment to him.' They had reached Grosvenor Gate and the Park was filling up with horses and carriages. 'Would you like me to escort you back to Brook Street?'

'It's such a short walk from here, I think we'll manage. Thank you, Mr Lockwood.'

Leonora turned towards Grosvenor Square, but Charlotte seemed reluctant to leave his side and looked up eagerly into his face as she said, 'It has been so good to see you again, Mr Lockwood. You will be at Mr Beacham's ball, won't you?'

His blue eyes met hers, limpid and dark brown, in striking contrast with her fair skin and hair. He paused and did not answer or look away, as if for that moment mesmerised. Charlotte touched his arm and with an imperceptible shake of his head, he responded, 'I will indeed. I shall look forward to seeing you both then. The Beau lives in Davies Street, with an unmistakeable silver front door.' Doffing his hat, he mounted Titan and trotted off, a dark, imperious silhouette against the sun.

Leonora had watched this exchange and was intrigued. Was that the point when George Lockwood really saw Charlotte for who she was? She hugged herself, not just due to the cold. They walked back as briskly as they could, suddenly longing for some warming drink and a pastry. As they entered the Bucklebury mansion, they were delighted to find that breakfast was still in progress, with Mrs Priddy sitting with a cup of coffee talking in a desultory way to the Countess. The lady appeared much less imperious in her undress, wearing just a man's navy-blue silk banyan, tied at the front, with her nightcap still on her head.

Tossing off her bonnet and pelisse, Charlotte rushed into the breakfast room. 'We have our first invitation!'

Mrs Priddy put down her cup. 'Good morning, Miss Charlotte; Nora my dear.' Her voice was as close as it ever came to admonishment.

Charlotte blushed. 'Oh apologies, Grandmama and Nanny P. Good morning, I hope you both slept well?'

'Tolerably, my dear.' Lady Bucklebury indicated the coffee pot. 'Do help yourself to more breakfast. We won't eat again until this evening.'

Leonora kissed Nanny P on the cheek and wished Lady Bucklebury a good morning. As she took a chair she said, 'Hyde Park is full of interest and activity.'

'So I surmise.' Lady Bucklebury's voice was dry. 'So who did you meet and where is this party to be held?'

Charlotte reached for a roll and said, 'We met Mr Lockwood who is the heir to Miss Appleby's father's estate at Hasterleigh. His stepfather Beau Beacham has a monthly rout, the first one is at the end of the month. And we're invited!'

The Countess's mouth turned down. 'Well, my dear, this is only partially good news. Beacham's gatherings are half beau monde and half disreputables. I can only countenance your going if you are closely accompanied by Mrs Priddy. Miss Appleby is chaperone enough in safe environments, but Beau Beacham's world is full of libertines and reprobates and you need a more experienced chaperone.'

Both young women glanced at Nanny P whose face was inscrutable. The Countess continued. 'Mrs Priddy suggested I may have been a bit harsh yesterday in my assessment of your prospects. I have lived so long and seen so many innocent bright-faced girls brought to disappointment, in some cases ruin, that I wished to disabuse you of any romantic fancies you might have.'

'We are grateful, Lady Bucklebury, for your care towards us and realise we have much to learn.' Leonora noticed Nanny P nodding as she spoke. She poured a cup of coffee for herself and Charlotte as Lady Bucklebury's brilliant eyes settled on her great-granddaughter's face.

'My goodness, your cheeks are so rosy you look quite bucolic. I think a touch of lilac powder will give you a more flattering pallor. I'll get Amy to pass on some of mine.'

Leonora and Charlotte caught each other's eyes, widened with surprise. Their cheeks were pink from the cold but they were used to looking 'healthy', as Nanny P called it. It seemed the Countess was not done yet with her improvements and advice. 'When a man is introduced to you, it is not advised that you meet his eyes directly. Men are like dogs; it's challenging to have a new acquaintance stare into their faces. Turn your head slightly and look askance, through your eyelashes. This is a more becoming address for a young woman.'

Leonora and Charlotte tried hard to suppress a giggle. Leonora
turned to Nanny P, her head drooping slightly as she glanced at
her through her eyelashes. Mrs Priddy gave her a reproving frown.

The Countess folded her hands as she continued, 'Now finally,
a more delicate matter.'

Leonora froze. What embarrassment had they committed
now? Lady Bucklebury sipped her coffee, then said, 'Charlotte,
your undergarments could be improved. I wish you to pay a visit
to Madame Maurice in Bond Street. I have an account there and
she stocks the best stays from Paris. So much more flattering, my
dear. The English stays flatten the breasts while the French know
how to present them higher and better formed. It's the difference
between...'

'Between a mountain and a molehill?' Leonora said sweetly.

Charlotte gasped at her temerity but Lady Bucklebury gave an
unexpected laugh. 'Exactly, pert miss! But this is a serious matter!'
Her words were brusque but her face wrinkled with amusement. 'I
have promised my grandson I will find a suitable husband for you,
and we need every weapon we can muster.'

'This sounds like war, Grandmama,' Charlotte said.

'Well war it is. And all good wars need discipline and strategy.'

* * *

Leonora and Charlotte went up to their bedchambers to collect
their reading books and Mrs Priddy followed them to Leonora's
room where the young women threw themselves laughing onto the
bed. Leonora put out a hand for her old nanny. 'Lady Bucklebury is
so *exhausting*! All these things we have to remember to do! Powder
our cheeks, place our bosoms on a plate, flutter our eyelashes and
never look a man straight in the eye in case he becomes a rabid dog!'

'My dears, she means well. Don't forget she's very old and her heyday was in a different century.'

'But she makes us feel there's no hope for us!' Charlotte climbed off the bed, flopped onto the sofa and sighed.

'No, Charlotte, not at all. You and Nora are charming as you are and that's all you can be. Now I suggest we make your great-grandmother happy by buying these fancy French stays in Bond Street this afternoon. Then we'll walk on to the circulating library at number forty-five to borrow some new reading matter.'

They all set out in the afternoon, warmly dressed and bonneted, with Mrs Priddy wearing a wool tippet over her shoulders for added warmth. The journey was entertaining for two young women just up from the country as it involved walking almost the full length of the New and Old Bond Streets as far as Piccadilly. As this was one of the main areas for shopping and promenading, Leonora and Charlotte gazed wide-eyed from one sight to the next.

The shops alone were like jewel boxes, with their most attractive and brightly coloured goods brilliant in the windows. Displays of parasols, gloves, bonnets and gowns of every fabric and hue added their rainbow charm to the view. They walked past the mantua makers, jewellers and cake shops. The narrow pavements were thronged with young women out shopping with their mamas and chaperones, and groups of finely dressed dandies come to promenade and ogle the ladies.

Leonora pointed out a group of more sombrely dressed men coming and going from an establishment at no. 14. 'Nanny P, is that a gentlemen's club?'

'It is of a specialist kind, I suppose. Although the main gentlemen's clubs are in St James's. This is Jackson's famous Boxing Academy where the nobility spar with the heroes of the ring. I heard that Lord Rokeby and his brother were habitués on the few occasions they were home from the war.'

Leonora noticed a handsome man at the centre of a group of swaggering laughing swells. With a jolt she recognised Captain Ormonde but did not want to attract his attention. She turned away, knowing the brim of her bonnet would obscure her face, even should he have remembered her.

They walked on, attracting some attention from the strutting beaus with their canes and quizzing glasses. Men on horseback and smart curricles thronged the street, splashing mud on the pedestrians' shoes, and young women hurried past, their maids laden with various bandboxes.

'Look, there's Madame Maurice's.' Leonora saw the bow window with a yellow and lilac evening robe and an array of lace caps displayed like a bouquet of flowers. They entered, to be met by Madame Maurice herself, a tall, austere woman with clever, calculating eyes. Ushered into a discreet room towards the back of the shop, Madame measured Charlotte and her assistant brought out a selection of three French stays. These were so elegant in their soft seamed cotton and lace that Leonora thought it a pity they would be hidden from general view.

'Oh! I feel so pretty!' Charlotte invited Leonora behind the screen to see. 'Won't you try one for yourself too?'

Leonora shook her head. 'You do look very pretty indeed, but we are on a shopping trip for you, Lottie. This whole palaver is to launch you on Society, don't forget.'

The stays were packaged in pink tissue and tied with cream ribbon and placed in a striped box inscribed *Madame Maurice, Modiste of Distinction*. They set off down the front steps and hurried on into Old Bond Street. Opposite Stafford Street was a double-fronted shop with the sign *Mr Hookhams's Circulating Library* painted the width of its frontage. The bow windows were filled with books, some open at a particularly attractive illustration, displayed on various shelves and in decorative stacks on a variety of small tables, with the painted backdrop depicting a fireplace complete with blazing fire.

Inside was full of books and customers, mostly women, reading books. Leonora walked up to the central desk. 'Would you have any musical scores for piano I could borrow? Some of John Field's shorter works, perhaps?'

Charlotte requested *The Heroine,* a satiric novel that had been a great success, and glanced across at Mrs Priddy who had picked up a magazine. 'Is that *The Lady's Magazine,* Nanny P?'

'It is, or to give it its proper title,' Mrs Priddy read out, putting on a mock pompous voice, '*Entertaining Companion for the Fair Sex, Appropriated Solely to Their Use and Amusement.*' She examined it and then made her decision. 'It costs sixpence, I think I'll buy it. There's so much to read, we will all find something of interest in it, I'm sure.'

Just as Leonora was signing her name against the loan slip for John Field's sonatas, she heard a sibilant voice behind her. 'Miss Appleby and Miss Blythe, how charming.'

She turned to greet the only woman with such a deceptive way of speaking. 'Lady Livia, what a pleasant surprise!' Leonora looked up into the pale face of the most disobliging woman she had ever met, only too aware of her own unfashionably glowing cheeks and country demeanour. Was Livia Dearlove's pallor due to lilac powder, good breeding, or natural malice? Leonora wondered. She certainly looked exquisitely pearlescent in her dove grey pelisse, lined with ermine. Charlotte joined them, all three volumes of *The Heroine* in the crook of her arm.

Lady Livia lisped, 'I'm just collecting a book of Mr Pope's poetry and then meeting a friend in Bond Street.' Leonora could see Livia Dearlove's chaperone lurking at the front of the library, and she suddenly had the clear apprehension that the noble lady was set on a clandestine meeting with Captain Ormonde. The women all bade their farewells and Leonora watched Lady Livia's elegant back sway towards the exit.

She took Nanny P's arm. 'Why does she make me feel so unsettled and demeaned?'

'Come, let's walk home. The fresh air will blow these unwelcome feelings away. Just remember, my dear, it's not Lady Livia who demeans you but your lack of appreciation of yourself. Despite what you may think, you have so many more advantages than she.'

'Oh Nanny P.' Leonora squeezed her old nanny's plump arm. 'That's easy to say when you care for me as you do.' Charlotte grasped Mrs Priddy's other arm, and they left Hookham's and walked briskly north towards Brook Street, and a different kind of disquiet.

8

THE HEART OF THE MATTER

Lady Bucklebury had sent her grooms down to Rokeby Abbey to bring back two of the Earl's horses suitable for the young women in her charge to ride in Hyde Park. She met Leonora and Charlotte at breakfast. 'Good morning, my dears. I always think a good ride in the Park clears the heart and mind. I have two of Rokeby's palfreys in the stables, needing to be ridden. Would you take them out this afternoon?' It was couched as a question but both young women knew it was closer to an order. 'All the best of Society is on display there on a sunny afternoon.'

By two o'clock, Charlotte and Leonora were dressed in their newly embellished riding habits, and on their heads wore their smart top hats sporting plumes of feathers. They waited for the sound of hooves as the groom brought the horses round from the stables to the front door. Davy was the Bucklebury groom and was young and cheerful, dressed in livery that appeared to have been made for a bigger man. He rode up on his own chestnut horse with the reins of the two Rokeby mares for the young women. One was black and one was a grey, and both were finely built and glossy with good health.

Leonora cheered up at the sight of these magnificent animals. Her homesickness had been in part due to missing her beautiful Dione and the freedom to ride.

'They are very fine horses. What are their names?' Leonora asked as she descended the front steps.

Davy grinned. 'The grey is Iris, the black mare is Minerva.' Leonora and Charlotte were just gazing into their fine lustrous eyes, wondering which horse each should claim, when the groom said, 'The Earl of Rokeby suggested Iris for Miss Blythe and Minerva for Miss Appleby.'

'Well that simplifies matters,' Charlotte said, stroking the forehead of her pretty mare before accepting Davy's hand to help her into the side-saddle. Leonora's heart was once more troubled by mention of Lord Rokeby's name. And why would he designate which horse she should ride? Minerva, goddess of wisdom; was there any significance in this? She shook her head. How foolish to look for omens in every simple thing; how missish of her to let her thoughts be so dominated by him.

Davy helped Leonora mount and immediately she knew she was sitting on a lively mare who was keen for adventure. She had to rein her back as Davy, astride his chestnut gelding, led the way to the Park. Her overactive brain would not be stilled; she wondered whether it was because the Earl thought her a more experienced horsewoman that he had suggested this spirited ride for her. She knew she had to protect her peace of mind from these fruitless speculations, resolutely guarding her imagination from fearful images of Lord Rokeby embracing Claudette Dupré.

It was exciting entering at Grosvenor Gate where a crush of men and some women with their grooms were mounted on flashy steeds, chatting to acquaintances and trotting off in twos and threes along the rides radiating out towards the Serpentine and trees. Others entered the Park in a flourish, driving curricles and phaetons with their passengers beside them dressed for display in pelisses and bonnets, tigers perched behind them. The arrival of two good-looking young women on a pair of the handsomest horses to be seen in the Park caused quite a stir. Leonora had known that Lord Rokeby loved his horses and ran a large stable of the finest bloodstock, but she did not realise until now how distinguished the horses were and how much attention they attracted.

The day was bright and the afternoon sun had melted the frost from the grass, but the breath of horses and riders still wreathed in misty ribbons in the air. They were trotting in an orderly fashion when a small pack of feral dogs surrounded them. One nipped the fetlock of Charlotte's mount. In the melee, the horse took off in fright, galloping towards a distant copse of trees. Davy immediately spurred his horse in pursuit; a bolting horse could be dangerous to itself, its rider and anyone else in the vicinity.

Charlotte struggled to suppress her fear, clinging onto the pommel to try and prevent herself being thrown out of the saddle. Iris was unresponsive to any pressure on the reins and Charlotte could only hope the horse would exhaust her primitive need for flight. Davy was just beginning to close on her when a group of horsemen loomed out of the trees ahead. One, in a red jacket, broke away and galloped towards Charlotte. He took a wide loop to enable him to ride alongside her horse and lean across to grasp the reins, pulling Iris up as he reined in his own horse. Charlotte sagged in the saddle, overcome by her ordeal. Close to tears, her voice was a sob. 'Thank you, Captain Ormonde.'

Leonora had followed, full of concern, and she and her horse arrived at the small group. 'Charlotte, are you all right? Do you wish to dismount and walk a while?' Still pale, Charlotte shook her head. Leonora did not care for the proprietorial way Guy Ormonde still had hold of the reins of Charlotte's horse.

There was the sound of a cheery *hallo* and three more riders

cantered up. George Lockwood was in the company of Rufus and
Livia Dearlove. Lord Dearlove cast a roguish glance at Charlotte
and asked, 'Was that you I saw galloping, Miss Blythe, against the
express proscriptions of the Royal Parks?'

'Sir, don't be such a blockhead! You know Miss Blythe's horse
bolted and that her life was in danger,' Captain Ormonde drawled.

George Lockwood wheeled his horse around and trotted up
beside Charlotte. 'I saw your headlong dash and no doubt you're a
trifle shaken up. This elegant creature isn't your own mare though,
is she?'

'No, Lord Rokeby sent two mounts from his stable for Miss
Leonora and me to ride.'

Charlotte had placed her hand on Mr Lockwood's as if for
reassurance, then withdrew it as Captain Ormonde scoffed, 'I
wouldn't think Rokeby's likely to have any prancers suitable for
young ladies to ride. He's known for his high-bred bloodstock, not
everyday palfreys. No wonder one bolted.'

Leonora could not stay silent. 'I completely trust the Earl's
judgement on equine matters. He would not have sent two
unmanageable mounts for us. Charlotte's horse was bitten by a
dog. The reaction was to be expected.' She leant forwards to pat
Minerva's neck as if to prove her own horse's docility.

Lord Dearlove clapped Captain Ormonde on the back.
'Lighten up, old friend. I have a capital suggestion. The Duchess
of Hungerford's ball next week is one of the best of the Season
and I'm determined to get Miss Appleby and Miss Blythe
invited.'

'How will you do that? She's notoriously sharp-eyed about
whom she allows into the hallowed halls of Hungerford House,'
Captain Ormonde said as he released Charlotte's horse's reins, and
she coaxed Iris to Leonora's side.

'I have a particular power over the Duchess.' Rufus Dearlove's smile was knowing. 'She's determined I marry her daughter and agrees to most of my requests.'

Captain Ormonde scoffed again, 'Well, if that's the case, she's not going to be happy to include in her guest list two attractive young women as competition.'

George Lockwood smiled. 'From what Lady Livia has told me, I surmise that Dearlove has his own particular means of persuasion.'

Livia Dearlove had ridden up alongside Mr Lockwood and cast him a quelling look, as if he had said more than she thought he should. She greeted Leonora and Charlotte with an elegant incline of her neck and lisped, 'The Duchess's balls are always very grand but rather dull affairs. She doesn't allow card tables so the men sulk, and we women have to work all the harder to appear alluring enough for them to deign to dance and charm.' She made a small grimace then looked up into George Lockwood's face with a delicate pout.

He glanced at the assembled party. 'I think we and the beasts are getting chilled; let's head off towards the Serpentine and let our horses canter a while.' He led the way on his hunter, with Livia Dearlove close behind and Captain Ormonde and Lord Dearlove with Charlotte and Leonora, accompanied by Davy their groom. They thundered down towards the water glittering through the birch trees.

They reined in their horses and the groups reassembled with Leonora and George Lockwood riding slightly apart. 'Will you be going to the Duchess's famous ball?' she asked, rather anxious at the thought of not having his reassuring presence as a human lighthouse in a storm.

'I will be. I'm a trifle concerned about Miss Blythe.'

This startled Leonora. 'In what way, pray, sir? She seems to have survived the fright of her horse bolting quite well.'

'Well, she has, although there can be a delayed shock. But I know you can watch out for that.' His face looked troubled and he hesitated, as if he were not sure whether to confide in her. 'I'm afraid I'm worried about something less obvious.'

Leonora put out a hand and caught his arm. 'What? Mr Lockwood, I am here to mind her; what should I know?'

'I'm suspicious of Captain Ormonde. He's naturally charming and attentive but I fear he is more interested in Miss Blythe's fortune than her happiness.'

'But she is not a fool. She's also underage and cannot ally herself with anyone without permission from the Earl, whom I presume is her guardian.'

Lady Livia rode up to join them and Leonora and Mr Lockwood broke off their conversation. 'Mr Lockwood, the afternoon is growing colder, I think Lord Rufus and I will be riding back to Grosvenor Square.' Her regard had fallen on George Lockwood and she seemed to be hesitating, as if hoping he would decide to join her and her brother.

He did not move and instead tipped his hat. 'Thank you, Lady Livia, for your company. I look forward to seeing you at the Duchess's ball next week.'

Leonora and Charlotte also bade them farewell as Lord Dearlove called to them over his shoulder, 'I'll deliver your invitations tomorrow.'

Captain Ormonde and George Lockwood accompanied the young women back to Bucklebury House. They rode in silence, Davy keeping a discreet distance at the rear. The men were hailed by various riders and drivers as they passed, which would have piqued Leonora's interest had she not been so concerned with how subdued Charlotte had become. The men dismounted and Captain Ormonde went to Charlotte's side to help her down. She gave him a polite smile as she unhooked her leg from the pommel and slid down Iris's side. He put up his hands and caught her firmly round the waist and swung her to the ground. Holding her for a moment close, he looked meaningfully into her face and gave one of his dazzling smiles. 'Farewell then, Miss Blythe,' he said, bringing her hand to his lips.

George Lockwood offered to help Leonora dismount and once she was standing before him, took her hand in farewell. 'We will meet again, at the Hungerford ball, it seems.' His expression was wry and seemed to Leonora to convey a variety of thoughts: that he had much more he wished to say; would rather he did not have to bother with attending another Society ball; and was concerned about Charlotte. Davy led their horses back to the stables and Leonora and Charlotte ran up the front steps and entered the house.

Leonora drew Charlotte into the morning room and closed the door. She took her hands and asked her urgently, 'Are you recovered from your fright?' They sat down together on the small sofa in the window.

'Oh yes, it's just I'm missing Mama Mildmay and home. I really don't care for all this fuss about parties and balls and what I can and cannot do. I don't want to be an heiress, it just complicates matters. And I don't want to be married...' Charlotte's voice tailed off.

'I know. It's all new and is a challenge when we have lived such a simple life and largely pleased ourselves. But surely you'd like to have your own family? And be mistress of your own household, not always living in the homes of others?'

Charlotte hung her head. 'I would. But would rather marry someone who lives near Hasterleigh, so I can visit you still. Someone who loves the country as we do.'

'Well, you may well find such a person in Town. Every country gentleman comes to London to do the Season and that is when you are most likely to meet him. What do you think of Lord Dearlove?'

'He's amiable enough. And very handsome, 'tis true. But he doesn't seem to take anything but his cards and horses seriously. I don't think he'd be a very attentive husband.' Her face had grown even more doleful.

Leonora squeezed her hand. 'Someone who seems very attentive is Captain Ormonde.'

Charlotte suddenly blushed. 'He is. He's very charming and talks to me as if what I have to say is of interest to him. But he does not have a fortune and I doubt Lord Rokeby would give his permission for us to marry.'

This startled Leonora. Had things progressed so far? 'Do you wish to marry him?' She looked into her face with a searching gaze.

Charlotte pulled her hand away. 'No! I told you I don't want to marry anyone, but I fear he'll be the person most interested in marrying me!' A tear rolled down her cheek. 'I feel that if I don't manage to find a husband during this Season, I'll be a failure. It's all so confusing.'

'I know it is. But you are not to feel a failure. Look at me, I don't feel thus.'

'But I have been given this dowry and Grandmama has opened her house to me to effect such an outcome. If I fail it will be solely because of me.'

Leonora patted her arm in sympathy. 'We are only at the beginning of something we said we'd consider an adventure. Now, let's find your courageous self again.' A glimmer of Charlotte's customary brightness of spirit returned. Leonora continued, 'What about Mr Lockwood? He is a man who loves the country and will live in the heart of Hasterleigh.'

'He's the best man of them all but,' she hesitated, 'you know I've always thought that he was meant for you.'

Leonora laughed. 'Oh, dear Lottie. Remember my father's favourite saying? *The best-laid schemes of mice and men often go awry.* We fondly think we know what is best only to be soon confounded.' Her face turned pensive. 'I too have had my hopes shown up as foolish. We can only try to live like Curate Fopling, at one with the creatures of the natural world. To find who we are and what will make us happy.'

Charlotte brightened and grasped her friend's hand. 'Mama Mildmay's last letter had some interesting news.' She extracted it from her reticule. 'Mr Fopling is often seen on his parish duties with Little Grace, accompanied by Miss Vazey and her dog. Silas too is completely recovered from his gunshot wound and his new dog is almost as well trained as his beloved Molly. And Jane Chetwode.' Charlotte looked up and said, 'You remember she and her mother moved into the Grove and you asked them to our musical evening.' She returned to the letter to read, '*She's assumed responsibility from Reverend Mildmay for the Sunday school, which is a relief.*' She smiled. 'Oh, how I miss the comfortable certainties of home.'

'Why don't you rest, and I'll go and tell the Countess about the ride in the Park and the promise of invitations for the Hungerford ball.'

'Oh, thank you! I haven't got the energy for Grandmama.'

Leonora did not know that she had the energy either, but she was keen to see Mrs Priddy, whose presence alone calmed her spirit. She knocked and walked into the drawing room, still wearing her riding habit and no doubt looking a trifle dishevelled. 'Lady Bucklebury, Mrs Priddy, good afternoon,' she greeted them. Mrs Priddy rose from her seat in the window, 'Nora my dear, how was the expedition to Hyde Park?'

'It was so good to be riding again. Lord Rokeby's horses are beautiful. Thank you, Lady Bucklebury, for being so thoughtful as to send for them.'

Lady Bucklebury was sitting by the fire and her eyes flickered over Leonora, appraising her outfit and person. 'I'm so glad they are up to snuff but I assure you it wasn't my idea to send for them. The Earl decided you should both have some fine mounts to ride while you are here.'

'Unfortunately, one of the Park dogs bit Miss Charlotte's horse, and she bolted.'

Mrs Priddy took Leonora's arm in alarm. 'Is she all right? One of your father's tenants was killed when his horse bolted through a wood and he was knocked off by a branch, stone dead.'

'Nanny P! Luckily Captain Ormonde appeared and helped rein her mare in.' Leonora then turned to Lady Bucklebury. 'Lord Dearlove and his sister were also there, and he said he could obtain for us invitations to the Duchess of Hungerford's ball.'

'Goodness! That would be remarkable. That lady operates a very fine mesh that allows few to slip through. Just being seen attending will be the most valuable imprimatur for dear Charlotte, particularly given her irregular parentage.'

Leonora was surprised to hear that one woman could have so much sway, but she advised caution. 'Lord Dearlove may have been swaggering a trifle. I don't know if he'll be successful.'

Lady Bucklebury's paper-thin hands clapped together with delight. 'Oh, I think that young charmer may well succeed. From what I hear he's somewhat more than a favourite with the Duchess who, like Lady Melbourne, believes in keeping her enemies close but her lovers closer. She intends him to be affianced to her daughter, you know.'

Leonora looked at Mrs Priddy for clarification of what she thought Lady Bucklebury meant, but only Nanny P's widening of eyes revealed that she thought this a little irregular. Lady Bucklebury struggled to her feet and Mrs Priddy hurried to offer an arm in support. Together they walked to the door and the Countess turned to say to Leonora, 'I'm just off to dress for dinner. I hope to see you two young women in an hour or so.'

The next morning was cloudless and still. Leonora climbed out of bed, opened her curtains and surveyed the brightening view. She hoped the sky was as blue over Hasterleigh. She wondered what was happening with Curate Fopling and Little Grace and whether he had accepted the living at the neighbouring parish; she wondered about the Mildmays and their foreboding over their beloved Charlotte; she wondered if Silas Sproat was being careful not to trespass. Most of all, Leonora wondered what was happening at Rokeby Abbey, desperate to know how things were with the Earl.

She dressed for the day in one of her refurbished gowns of sprigged cotton and was admiring her handiwork in the looking glass when she heard a knock at the door, and Charlotte entered. 'Good morning, Leonora, are you ready to go downstairs for breakfast?'

'Good morning, Lottie. You look more cheerful.'

'I've remembered what you said, to treat this as an adventure, not see it as a test of my worthiness to be someone's wife.'

Charlotte looked particularly pretty in one of her new morning gowns made by Mrs Marmery in French cambric in a pale cerulean blue. The young women linked arms and descended the stairs to find, to their surprise and some dismay, Lady Bucklebury already there, her lace cap sightly awry. 'Good morning, ma'am,' both said in unison.

'Oh, my dears, you do look charming. I myself feel less than charming this morning; sleep eludes me.'

'Oh, Lady Bucklebury, I'm sorry to hear that. I hope my playing the piano-forte in the evening did not keep you from your bed too long.'

'No. In fact, it's quite diverting for such an ancient woman as me having two young women unsettling the stale air in this old house. Now sit down and have some coffee.'

Leonora and Charlotte were in the middle of their second cups when Lady Bucklebury said, 'On a day as bright as this you should go to Mr Barker's Panorama in Cranbourn Street. They've just changed the view from the Main Circle.'

Charlotte's face flushed with excitement. 'I've just been reading about this in my guidebook. It's the best in the world, and visitors feel they've been transported into the scene of battle or are actually walking in the landscape. Some more sensitive viewers even feel dizzy or faint. I'd love to go!'

Mrs Priddy had just come into the room and greeted everyone before helping herself to a pastry and sitting down. The Countess looked pleased with Charlotte's reaction. 'Good. That will keep you occupied for half the day. But I would like you to be chaperoned by Mrs Priddy as the viewing platforms and the passages to get there are very dimly lit, encouraging all kinds of impertinent behaviour.'

She looked across at Mrs Priddy who nodded. 'I've only seen a small panorama of the view of London when I was young. I think it was shown in a shed in Castle Street to the east of the city. This sounds a most superior experience.'

Lady Bucklebury smiled. 'Well, you need good light to see the panorama at its best. Today's weather is set fair. Apparently a new panorama has just been installed. I've been told it depicts some battle scene, so I hope it's not too gruesome.' She got to her feet and Leonora and Mrs Priddy offered an arm each to help her walk slowly up the stairs to the drawing room. 'I think I need a little rest,' she said as she arrived in the room and settled on the sofa next to the fire, already blazing. 'Now my dears, shall I ask for a chaise to take you there?'

Mrs Priddy was the first to answer. 'Goodness no, my lady, we are all country women and used to walking. It's barely a mile after all. But thank you.' She inclined her head.

It was just after noon when all three women set off to walk to the Leicester Square end of Cranbourn Street where the entrance to the Panorama was situated. In order to avoid the bustle of Bond Street they took a detour through Grosvenor Square. Leonora loved the open gardens and grandeur of the Square with its expanse of sky, grass and trees providing a microcosm of country-side that reminded her of home. As they turned left to walk past the grand façades of the eastern terrace, they noticed a large coach drawn up outside the biggest mansion, its team of magnificent black horses steaming in the afternoon light.

The women approached as shutters were opened and the front door left ajar while luggage and chests were unloaded into the house. Leonora gave a gasp as she recognised the crest on the side of the door of the carriage. She turned to Nanny P, her heart thumping. 'That's the Earl's coach. I thought he never came to Town.'

They hurried past and Mrs Priddy took her arm. "Tis true Lord Rokeby has a house in Grosvenor Square but we don't know that this house is his. He could have lent his coach to someone else? He could have lent his house to another. We'll wait to hear what Lady Bucklebury knows before we jump to conclusions.' She squeezed Leonora's arm in reassurance; Nanny P knew this young woman well enough to know how turbulent her feelings were about Lord Rokeby, feelings she had not yet managed to fully understand.

Soon they were walking through Berkeley Square where Rufus and Livia Dearlove lived at no. 2. Charlotte pointed out the large house in the corner. 'I wonder if his lordship has managed to obtain those invitations for us?'

London was still a novelty filled with thrilling and startling sights. Leonora and Charlotte's eyes were continually caught by the passing show: a dandy in his yellow coat and exaggerated silhouette; young women in enormous bonnets piled with fruit or billowing feathers; fashionable Corinthians driving smart curricles far too fast down Piccadilly, standing to urge their purebred horses on, a long looping whip in hand, a beaver hat pulled low, and the capes on their coats fluttering in the wind. Leonora found the effortless superiority of such men born to power and wealth shamefully attractive.

But the contrasts Leonora and Charlotte found in their first acquaintance with life in London also shocked them: the extravagant splendours of the rich were but the cream on the top of a society where there was also poverty, unimagined by them in their country existence. They had stared in horror at the half-feral children in rags who scavenged with stray dogs for scraps of food, or begged a farthing from passers-by. In the country, most families had a strip of land on which they could grow a few potatoes or root crops, and there was usually a rabbit or bird to be caught for the pot. Their own village was a community in which most of the landowners looked after their tenants, and Reverend and Mrs Mildmay too were diligent in collecting and distributing alms to the poor.

As they walked towards Leicester Square, Charlotte grasped Mrs Priddy's arm, distressed by the sight of wounded ex-soldiers, destitute and disfigured, congregated in small bands in a churchyard. 'Where do these heroes who have fought for their country find comfort and food?' Her voice was urgent.

Mrs Priddy responded with sympathy, 'It is part of the ongoing suffering of wars. The wounded return too often to find themselves homeless and unable to work.'

Charlotte's voice was quiet. 'I wish Lord Rokeby had not settled so much money on me and instead would set up homes and employment for the soldiers who came back wounded from the war.'

Soon they were crossing Leicester Square and queuing up by a small door at the beginning of Cranbourn Street. The tall brick rotunda that housed the Panorama loomed above them. Now that the war had curtailed travel even for the rich who had foregone their Grand Tours, this was the only way to experience the thrill of foreign lands. The excitement was palpable.

The eager customers were informed that in the main gallery, or 'Large Circle' as Mr Barker liked to call it, would be displayed a view of the Battle of Vitoria, the decisive victory the previous year when the Marquess of Wellington had broken the back of the French army in the Peninsular War. The name alone inspired a surge of patriotic pride in English breasts and Leonora and Charlotte joined the excited procession through the dimly lit corridor and up the stairs to the first viewing platform.

Here the emergence from dark to dazzling light was a shock to the senses. Everyone seemed disorientated for a moment. Charlotte exclaimed, 'Look! It's as if we're actually there, watching from a hilltop.' The windowless viewing platform was intentionally kept dark so as to better show the spectacle on the canvas before them, bathed in the natural light flooding down from the glass-domed roof.

Leonora pointed to the painted canvas that encircled them in a vast panorama; an endless vista of distant hazy mountains with at its centre the medieval walled city of Vitoria, its cathedral spires soaring above the plains of the river Zadorra. Everywhere were hundreds of meticulously painted French and British, Spanish and Portuguese soldiers on horseback or with their artillery aimed into the field of battle.

'What's happening here?' Charlotte asked, pointing at a collection of officers on horseback, with Wellington identified in the centre by his long hooked nose. Just as she turned to look for Leonora, she found herself gazing into the face of Captain Ormonde. 'Oh!' She was shocked to see him there.

He smiled, teeth gleaming in the low light. 'Good day to you, Miss Blythe.' He turned to bow to Leonora and Mrs Priddy, murmuring, 'Ladies. The whole of Society will traipse through these doors, so great is the excitement for this new panorama.'

Charlotte realised he was the best person to be a guide to what was depicted of the battle. 'Were you at Vitoria, sir?' she asked.

Captain Ormonde took her elbow and steered her farther along the platform, away from Leonora and Mrs Priddy. He looked down at her, the lack of light making Charlotte aware of the unexpected intimacy of the space. His voice was low. 'I was there, 'tis true. Lord Wellington requested some strategic advice learnt from the debacle of Corunna.'

Leonora, with Nanny P in her wake, hurried to catch up with them, aware of her responsibility and the words of Mr Lockwood. She kept her eyes on Charlotte's new straw bonnet as they were carried on the tide of viewers. Charlotte's admiration for Captain Ormonde grew as he explained the complex troop movements, relayed what the Marquess of Wellington had confided to him – all complimentary – and pointed out where on the field of battle his horse was shot from under him. His narrow eyes were watching her as her warmth of response was reflected in her glowing expression. She tipped her face up to meet his eyes and said with fervour, 'Captain, I have only recently come to consider just what you military men risk and sacrifice to keep us and our country safe. That you are all heroes.'

He inclined his dark head and his eyes appeared black, his voice insinuating. 'Some are more heroic than others, Miss Blythe.'

Charlotte was not going to be disabused of her new-found enthusiasm for military heroes in general. She shook her head and said, 'No, I think anyone who goes to war and faces such terrors is heroic indeed.'

Leonora had caught up with them when she saw Captain Ormonde bend his head and she could just make out his response. 'Some decorated soldiers appear to be heroes fighting for their country when they are really working for the enemy.'

Charlotte was puzzled. 'How can that be, sir? Who could ever manage such deception on the field of battle?'

'You should ask the remaining Rokeby brother; he is a relation of yours now.' He pointed to two English hussars in a huddle in the foreground of the panorama. 'Those cavalry men could be Wellington's exploring officers, as in fact were the Earl and his brother, meant to ride behind enemy lines to bring back information to Lord Wellington. A dangerous mission indeed. But they could just as well have been clandestine spies for Bonaparte taking information of the British troop positions back to the enemy.'

Leonora interrupted with a sharp riposte. 'You are full of insidious words, sir. Why so shabby?' She felt Mrs Priddy's hand squeezing her arm in warning, but her sense of justice recoiled from the thought of Lord Rokeby's reputation sullied by a fellow officer, with no hearing of his defence.

They were standing in the twilight of the viewing platform while the crowds eddied around them, some muttering in irritation. Captain Ormonde turned his dark eyes on Leonora, his charming demeanour having fled. 'Would it not stick in the craw of any fighting man to have one of his fellow officers honoured with the greatest gallantry medal in the land if there was any question over how treacherous his behaviour or his brother's may have been?'

'Might I suggest, Captain Ormonde, that you either take your evidence to the military panel or you desist from sullying the Earl's name.'

Mrs Priddy stepped forward. 'Come, my dears, we should be going.' She turned to Captain Ormonde and smiled. 'We are due back at Bucklebury House, but we hope to see you again.' Charlotte and Leonora offered their hands and bade polite farewells.

'Good day. I will see you at the Hungerford ball. I heard that Lord Dearlove has obtained your invitations.' Captain Ormonde clicked his heels together and bowed.

As they walked home, Mrs Priddy remonstrated with Leonora. 'I really don't think it's wise, my dear, to fight the Earl's battles for him.'

Leonora's spirits were unsettled enough by her own emotions. Having both Rokeby brothers accused of possibly being traitors enraged her. Yet the fact there were rumours, that even Lord Dearlove had mentioned at their musical evening, made her uneasy and all the more emphatic in their defence. She turned to Charlotte and said, 'I think it's despicable for him to spread such scurrilous rumours. And about your own father, Lottie!'

Charlotte sprang to Captain Ormonde's defence. 'The Captain seems to have played an important part as an aide to the Marquess of Wellington. He has not accused my father directly of anything; in fact, he seems as much exercised by the current Earl. Surely an officer and a gentleman would not lie about such a thing?'

This was the first time Charlotte had publicly disagreed with Leonora, who was taken aback. 'Lottie! This is your father and uncle he chooses to defame. Beware of thinking any one person the repository of truth. You can only be disappointed.'

Charlotte tossed her head. 'My father will always be a hero to me and like him, I'm willing to sacrifice myself for the greater good. But I consider Captain Ormonde a hero too.'

Leonora held her tongue, and catching Nanny P's eye, thought to herself that this insistence on the heroic was the effect of too much gothic fiction on young susceptible minds.

* * *

As the women arrived back in Brook Street, the butler took their bonnets and pelisses and said in his gloomy way, 'Her ladyship would like to see you in the drawing room.'

They mounted the stairs and Mrs Priddy said, 'I'll join you later. I need a rest after the day's exertions,' as she continued up the next flight of stairs.

Leonora and Charlotte knocked and entered the drawing room. Lady Bucklebury was sitting in her favourite wing chair by the fire, her thin, blue-veined hands stitching a tapestry that appeared to be of her coat of arms. 'Sit down, my dears.' She waved to the sofa opposite. For the first time, Leonora thought she looked more frail than forbidding. 'Well, tell me, was the Panorama worth the entrance fee?'

'Oh, certainly so, Grandmama. We met Captain Ormonde and he was very interesting, talking about the troop movements.' Charlotte was enthusiastic.

Lady Bucklebury's shrewd eyes missed nothing. 'Don't go setting your sights too low, young miss. I've heard he is a wild young man who has run through his fortune and is casting his line towards many an heiress. I have no intention of your squandering yourself and your fortune on a young reprobate with pockets to let.'

Leonora was pleased by Lady Bucklebury's forthright opinion on the matter and glanced at Charlotte whose eyes were cast down. Unable to contain her curiosity much longer, Leonora asked as nonchalantly as she could, 'Lady Bucklebury, as we walked through Grosvenor Square we noticed trunks being unloaded from the Rokeby coach into a house on the east side. Do you know if the Earl has come to Town?'

The old lady put down her embroidery and met her eyes with her own quizzical gaze. 'I received a note from Alistair yesterday. He's been summoned to receive a posthumous Peninsular Gold Cross on behalf of his brother. I don't know when he will be leaving again for Hasterleigh. He does not care to stay long in Town.'

Leonora tried to keep her face as expressionless as she could, but her heart had begun its breathless rhythm; the room felt hot and she stood up to leave. Lady Bucklebury put out a hand. 'Not so fast, young lady! I have yet to tell you the most important news. Lord Dearlove was true to his word. His charm seems to have worked and I have invitations for you and Charlotte!' She flourished the thick invitation cards with the ducal crown embossed in gilt. 'It looks like it's a masquerade ball, encouraging a greater licence of behaviour. Mrs Priddy will have to accompany you young women as I cannot allow only Miss Appleby to chaperone you, Charlotte.'

Charlotte jumped up, her face alight. 'Oh Grandmama, how exciting! I've never been to a masquerade ball.'

'The Duchess's ball is the smartest and most exclusive of the Season and I think you girls need extra help with dressing your hair. I'll ask my friend Lady Dundas to send one of her maids.'

Leonora escaped upstairs to her room. She did not want to

think about the ball, but longed instead to soothe her soul with music, but the piano-forte was in the drawing room where Lady Bucklebury still sat embroidering. Instead, she threw herself on her bed. How she longed to see Lord Rokeby again, to speak to him, to discover the truth not of Captain Ormonde's terrible slurs, but mostly to know the measure of his feelings for Madame Dupré, an obsession she could not dismiss from her mind.

Charlotte knocked at the door and entered, bubbling with excitement about the ball. Leonora summoned a smile. How much her young friend had gained in confidence and courage since her life had expanded with the knowledge of her parentage; she had found her place in the world.

'Why so glum, Leonora? This is all so diverting, don't you think?'

'Of course it is! We must sort out our most special ball gowns and acquire some masks.'

'Oh, Grandmama has said we can choose from her collection of Venetian masks from her younger days. Once we've chosen our dresses then we can see which ones look most becoming.' And she skipped out the door.

* * *

The day of the Hungerford ball was wet and windy. Charlotte and Leonora were up early but they decided to forgo their walk in Hyde Park, not wishing to spoil their hair that had been carefully curled in rags overnight. Having selected their gowns, gloves, jewellery, dancing shoes and evening cloaks, they discussed with Mrs Priddy and Amy the kind of elaborate hair styles that would be suitable for a more formal ball. Even Leonora had felt her excitement rise. At eleven in the morning, the doorbell rang and George Lockwood was shown into the small sitting room where the two young women, seeking some respite from Lady Bucklebury's forceful character, were pretending to read. They both leapt to their feet, delighted to see him. In a society of artifice and lies, he brought memories of the simple joys of home.

'Good day, Miss Appleby, Miss Blythe.' He bowed and took their hands in turn. His hair was blown by the wind and spots of rain glistened on his immaculate coat.

'We are glad to see you, Mr Lockwood!' Charlotte held onto his hand with enthusiasm.

He turned to them and with a twinkle in his eyes said, 'Would you do me the honour of allowing me to escort you to the Countess of Hungerford's ball tonight? I think we need a Hasterleigh contingent, don't you?'

Leonora said, 'We would be delighted.' Then with her own mischievous gleam added, 'I thought you may be accompanying Lady Livia, whose social attractions are more obvious than ours.'

George Lockwood gave a great hearty laugh. 'That young lady is a honeypot attracting suitors like wasps. She has many admirers buzzing round her head whom she bats away with disdain. I do not intend to be one of them.'

'And I dare say, being chatelaine of Hasterleigh Manor might not provide a large enough stage for someone of her *amour propre*?'

George Lockwood flashed Leonora a sharp look. 'Miss Appleby, I did not know you for a pert lass!' Then he chuckled. ''Tis true, I don't think the Manor is a natural habitat for that rare bird.' Charlotte and Leonora exchanged looks and laughed with him, each still nurturing their own ambitions for the other as the perfect match for this good-natured man, in possession of two estates and in need of a competent wife.

He turned to go, saying, 'I'll collect you at seven in my coach. 'Til then!' He saluted and was soon down the front steps and away.

Preparations for the ball began in the afternoon. Lady Bucklebury's friend, Lady Dundas, had been happy to lend her ladies' maid and as Leonora and Charlotte were beginning to climb into their chemises and stays, Amy knocked on Charlotte's door and entered, accompanied by a woman. 'Miss Blythe, this is Flora Lacey, she's here to help.'

Charlotte had just put on her new Parisian stays, which needed lacing. She looked up and met the maid's gaze; she was modestly dressed in her uniform of a simple dark blue high-necked dress of crisp cotton with a narrow lace trim round the cuffs. Charlotte liked her serene face with striking hazel eyes and approved of the fact she was older and looked more sensible than Amy. 'I'm pleased to meet you, Flora, especially as I'm in need of some help with the lacing.' She smiled.

Charlotte had chosen the most beautiful of the evening gowns Mrs Marmery had made for her. The palest pink gauze over an underlayer of shimmering tiffany silk in oyster looked as iridescent as the inside of a shell. With Flora's help she slipped it over her head and the maid buttoned the tiny pearl buttons up the back. The women stood back and gazed at Charlotte's reflection in the looking glass. They both gasped. 'You are lovely, Miss Blythe!' Flora's words were so heartfelt that Charlotte looked at her more intently. The maid blushed and lowered her eyes. 'I hope I didn't speak out of turn.'

Putting her hand on her arm, Charlotte said, 'Not at all, Flora. It's a very special dress and makes me believe in myself and my future. I've only recently realised that clothes can have such transforming power.' She sat down at the dressing table so that this new maid could arrange her hair in a style Leonora had found in *La Belle Assemblée*. As Flora brushed out the fine fair curls, Charlotte noticed her hands were trembling. 'You have no reason to be nervous. I'm the least particular taskmistress you could find. I'm just grateful that you could help.' She smiled into the looking glass where Flora's eyes met hers.

After an hour of teasing, plaiting and pinning, anchoring strings of seed pearls and small silk flowers into the blonde confection of the style, Charlotte felt lulled by the quiet competence of Flora's fingers. 'You're so good at this. You haven't once pulled my hair or prodded me with a pin.' Again, she caught the maid's eyes in the looking glass and wondered if their brightness was due to tears. Interrupting this thought was a knock at the door and Leonora entered, swishing her skirts as she twirled. Her chestnut curls were swept onto the top of her head with a few tendrils making the style soft and romantic. Amy had added a small plume of silver-grey feathers to complement her dress. 'You look beautiful, Leonora. I love your gown. It's that special silver one you bought from Mrs Marmery, isn't it?'

'Yes. It's my favourite by far.' She was holding a silver mask by its string. 'You look like a rosy pearl, Lottie. You'll be the jewel of the night.'

'And look how beautifully Flora has done my hair.' She stood up and took Leonora's hands and they danced a few turns together. 'We'll both be the belles of the ball.'

'We must hurry. Mr Lockwood will be here in a moment.'

Lady Bucklebury called out to them as they passed the drawing room door. 'Come in, my dears.' They walked over to her chair by the fire, where she sat bright as a bird. Her usually severe expression had softened. 'Goodness! You both look pretty as pictures.' She clasped her hands together. Then her sharp dark eyes settled on Charlotte's naked décolletage, enhanced by the Parisian stays she had insisted her great-granddaughter buy. 'My dear, you need some pearls. Here, take mine.' The Countess unclasped the double strand of pink pearls she always wore with a beautiful large baroque pearl at its centre and handed it to

Leonora for her to fasten round Charlotte's neck. 'Very pretty indeed!' Lady Bucklebury said with satisfaction. 'I hope it's a successful evening. Be on the alert, young misses, and mind what Mrs Priddy says.'

Charlotte put her hands to her throat where she felt the pearls, still warm from her great-grandmother's skin, and tears came to her eyes. It seemed another small gesture of acceptance by the matriarch of this noble family. 'Thank you, Grandmama. I shall care for them greatly.' In a spontaneous gesture, she dashed to the old lady's side and brushed her cheek with a kiss.

'Oh, be gone with you!' was the brusque reply, but Leonora noticed how Lady Bucklebury's posture relaxed and she lost her imperious mien. Charlotte and Leonora bobbed a quick curtsey and ran down the last flight of stairs to where Mrs Priddy waited, already dressed in her warm velvet cloak and gloves, her bonnet on her head.

The front door was opened and there was George Lockwood in the best-fitting jacket his tailor Meyer could construct. Dark blue and of superfine wool, it looked as if it was moulded to his broad shoulders and skimmed close over his muscular arms. His cravat, usually carelessly tied, was pristine, intricately folded and secured with a large diamond pin. Pale pantaloons, so unforgiving on a fleshier man, were beautifully cut to accommodate with elegance Mr Lockwood's athletic thighs. His large feet were somehow reduced to the required almond toe by his shiny black dancing shoes; this was a man happy in his Town clothes now that he had chosen his own tailor who understood how to dress the robust masculine physique.

As George Lockwood removed his hat to greet them, Leonora was gratified to see that no amount of careful ministrations from his valet, armed with brush and pomade, could tame his wayward hair.

Both young women were struck by how good-looking Mr Lockwood appeared. He too seemed transfixed for a moment by the sight of them. His bluff, sunny expression was unexpectedly serious and appraising as he watched Charlotte descend the stairs, her fair hair ringleted, the pearlescent gown falling from her shapely bosom. He put out his gloved hand to take hers. 'Miss Blythe, ladies,' he addressed them all, 'your carriage awaits.'

Mrs Priddy had been watching Charlotte and Mr Lockwood's eyes as this sudden revelation of their attraction to each other occurred. She had wanted it to be her beloved Leonora who caught George Lockwood's imagination and would thus be saved from leaving her childhood home but, although Charlotte and he may not yet have recognised it themselves, Nanny P understood that for them their worlds had shifted, and she was glad.

9

THE GALLANT AND THE PRICE OF GALLANTRY

For those in the highest society of Regency England, noble blood and old money were all that mattered. This was displayed in the possession of extensive acres of parkland and fertile tenant farms encircled by great hunting forests with a magnificent house at the centre. Here resided the power. There was a hierarchy within the aristocracy of which the Duchess of Hungerford was close to the apex. Her mansion in Grosvenor Square was on the opposite terrace from Rokeby House and had been built to show off its owner's fortune and status. In a discreet display of class and long-established wealth, the Hungerford establishment was not ostentatiously embellished. As Leonora and Charlotte entered, with George Lockwood and Mrs Priddy in their wake, they were struck by the grandeur of the building and the modesty of the night's decorations. There was no gold leaf in sight. Whole glasshouses of exotic flowers had not been devastated to conjure one night's scented paradise; instead, there was ivy and the sweet smell of conifer and apple-wood burning in the grates in the many grand fireplaces.

The ballroom was on the first floor, adjoining the drawing

room, and music floated down to the hallway below. Everyone was masked except for Mrs Priddy who, as a chaperone, was excused. As the Hasterleigh party joined the crowd mounting the serpentine stone staircase, Leonora slipped her arm through Mrs Priddy's and Charlotte was left to place her hand on Mr Lockwood's arm. Feeling some protection in the anonymity afforded by a mask, Leonora could not suppress a giggle as she pointed out a particularly portly old nobleman, so corseted he could not bend without creaking. 'Beware, Mr Lockwood, what awaits you if you indulge too much in Cook's famous *boeuf en croûte*,' she said.

George Lockwood patted his trim torso and replied, 'I'm hoping that fashions will be more accommodating by the time I get to that stage.'

Charlotte glanced up into his face and said with a serious expression, 'By then, Mr Lockwood, you'll be deep in country life and barely concerned with what you wear and how you appear.'

He put his gloved hand on hers curled through his arm and replied, 'What a comfortable thought indeed, but my wife may not agree.' His eyes were mischievous in the flickering candlelight.

They arrived in the ballroom to the sight of dancers in the middle of a reel, their gorgeous gowns, jewelled masks and head-dresses captured multiple times in the looking glasses that lined the walls. It felt as if they had entered a kaleidoscope continually turning with fragments of every colour and shape to the exhilarating accompaniment of music. The small string orchestra was playing its heart out and there were claps and cries as the couples in each set parted and came together again.

The guests were from the grandest echelons of Society. Here the stately and elderly rubbed shoulders with the well-behaved young. Jowls and bosoms trembled, feathered caps bobbed and dipped, real jewels sparkled, some even wore their tiaras; the cream of the *haut ton* were out in force and determined on enjoyment.

Mr Lockwood bent his head to murmur to Charlotte, 'Under this one roof is to be found half the wealth of the entire nation.'

The Duchess of Hungerford's guest list was so select that even in masks most people recognised each other. The advent of Leonora and Charlotte as evident newcomers caused some tongues to wag. Any news of an heiress spread like a gorse fire and the combination of unexpected wealth, beauty and noble birth, albeit of rather irregular provenance, added extra frisson to the gossip. It was the first time Charlotte felt the full beam of attention on her and she was taken aback.

The reel came to an end and the couples dispersed with much clapping and chatter. Out of the crowd appeared Captain Ormonde in his full regimentals, handsome and sleek as a panther. Nodding at George Lockwood, he bowed to Charlotte. 'Miss Blythe, what a vision to soothe my war-sick heart. I'm hopeful you may honour me with the next dance?' Once again, his smile dazzled while his eyes remained calculating. It was a compelling combination.

'But sir, you are not meant to be able to identify me. This is a masquerade ball, is it not?'

Her response was arch and Captain Ormonde chuckled, responding perhaps not as flatteringly as she had hoped. 'I recognise you by your companion who appears like Gulliver among the Lilliputians.'

Charlotte turned an uncertain face to George Lockwood, whose arm she still held. A muscle in her companion's jaw twitched but he smiled and said, 'Perhaps, Miss Blythe, I can claim you for the dance after this one?' Charlotte nodded and took Captain Ormonde's proffered hand and followed him to make up the nearest set.

George Lockwood turned to Leonora and muttered, 'I thought the Duchess did not approve of the waltz, but it seems Lord Dearlove has persuaded her otherwise. I just hope it will be no excuse for the Captain's indecorous behaviour should he request a further dance.'

Leonora's face was grave. 'I must admit I have my reasons to be wary of him, but it concerns me you think he may be a fortune hunter with his eyes set on Charlotte when she appears to esteem him so.'

When Charlotte returned to them, breathless and slightly flushed, Mr Lockwood said, 'Let me introduce you to my stepfather.' He led Leonora and Charlotte towards a group of exquisites. Beau Beacham seemed to straddle both the raffish and *haut ton*. His presence was so distinctive that not even his black mask disguised him. Not particularly tall, he nevertheless seemed in perfect physical proportion, made more striking by the cut of his dark coat and silver satin pantaloons. His calves in his evening hose were as elegant as a woman's and his face, no longer young, was still handsome and crowned with an operatic head of grey curls, contrived into fashionable disarray. He was surrounded by a laughing group of fellow dandies, willows amongst whom George Lockwood, despite his fine-tailored evening apparel, looked like a sturdy oak.

'Ladies, my stepfather, Beau Beacham. Sir, may I introduce you to Miss Charlotte Blythe, the Countess of Bucklebury's kin, and Miss Appleby, chatelaine of Hasterleigh Manor.'

Mr Beacham turned from his admiring acolytes and cast his sparkling gaze on Charlotte. The magic word 'Countess' had piqued his interest. He had heard talk too of her fortune. He brought her hand slowly to his lips, his dark eyes continually holding hers. She dropped her gaze and blushed. He murmured,

'Miss Blythe, I am grateful indeed to make your acquaintance. George will look after you, I'm sure.'

Taking Leonora's hand, a roguish look came into his eyes. He recognised her as no longer a green girl and treated her in a more gamesome way. Tucking her hand into his arm, he whisked her off into the ballroom. 'I think I hear the strains of a waltz!' he said, and without hesitation, slipped his arm around her waist and whirled her into the colourful fray.

Leonora gave a small gasp. The waltz was a new and racy dance and still disapproved of in their country dances back home. She had learnt it along with Charlotte but had not had any occasion to practise it in public; to have this stranger clasp her body so close to his seemed extraordinarily intimate. With a pang she realised it was not Beau Beacham, but a distant lord whose arm she wished to have so insistent around her waist.

The music that poured from the orchestra was thrilling. She had never been at a ball where the musicians numbered more than three and to have this octet of harpsichord, flute, violins, hautbois, double bass and English horn made her heart swell. The ballroom itself was awash with candlelight, the walls lined with looking glasses that reflected the scintillas of light and brilliant dresses like a glittering phantasmagoria of movement and colour.

After a few moments, Leonora began to relax and enjoy the exhilaration of waltzing in the arms of a practised dancer. She did not notice Captain Ormonde watching their progress round the floor with dark narrowed eyes. Nor did she see Charlotte in the arms of George Lockwood, confident, not looking anxiously at her feet but up into his face, and managing to converse a little.

Beau Beacham was amusing and rather shocking with his indelicate gossip about various other guests as they danced past. 'Ah, *mon dieu*! That big-bellied *cochon* is the Honourable Lord

Ponsonby and that lady in his arms is no lady. An intimate moment with him, she once told me, was akin to having a wardrobe fall on her with the key still in the lock.' Leonora was astonished that he should talk to her, a young woman he did not know, with such a lack of propriety or discretion, but his laugh at her shocked expression was infectious and she found herself laughing too. The Beau pulled her close to his hip and whirled her into a showy final spin which left her breathless. Music and dancing never failed to stir her heart, even if it was a disreputable charmer, almost old enough to be her father, whose arms held her close.

The first waltz of the night came to a halt with everyone rather giddy and excited. Beau Beacham gave her waist a final squeeze and leaning close, murmured in her ear, 'There is something about you, Miss Appleby, or perhaps your estate, that has excited my George beyond measure. I'm afraid once he moves to Hasterleigh, London will never see him again.'

Leonora extracted herself from his embrace and responded with a smile, 'I don't think the allure is mine, sir, but Mr Lockwood is certainly excited by the land.'

'I find that impossible to understand.' He held her gloved fingers to his lips, appraising her with lustrous eyes, then bowed before returning her to her friends. The orchestra tuned up again just as Lord Dearlove, unmistakeable in his elegance despite a dashing black crystal mask, swept up and grasped Leonora's hand. 'Madame, will you do me the honour of partnering me in this cotillion?' Leonora bowed, not certain if he had recognised her or was just charming to every woman he met. As he led her to the dance, he murmured, 'Your disguise is not very effective, dear Miss Appleby; your resplendent hair gives you away.'

Leonora laughed. He was vain and frittered his life on gambling and pleasure, but he was handsome and there was something appealing about his warmth and lightness of being.

They moved into the circular motion that began the dance. He was a most delightful partner, amusing in his chatter and generous of spirit. She felt entirely easy in his company. As the cotillion ended, he asked her if she needed any refreshment.

Leonora declined with a smile. She was hoping to sit out the next dance and was about to claim a chair at the edge of the ballroom floor when she felt her skin prick, a sensation she had had once before. Someone with an unsettling energy was standing behind her.

'Miss Appleby, may I have the honour of the next dance?' The voice was insinuating and familiar; she could feel his breath on her cheek. She turned to meet the narrow eyes of Captain Ormonde, watching her as he murmured, 'It sounds as if it's a waltz.'

Politeness decreed she could not refuse him, so she placed her hand on his arm as he led her to the dance floor. Captain Ormonde behaved with greater decorum than Beau Beacham and as the music started, they danced at the required formal distance and only on the turns did his arm draw her closer. But his conversation was not as amusing as the Beau's; there was a predatory energy about him. The flash of his legendary smile was indeed charming but always troubling when allied with his cynical manner. He murmured as they danced, 'Miss Blythe is looking very fine tonight. What a difference when a young woman learns she's been born of aristocratic blood.'

Leonora thought this a strangely disobliging comment and changed to a more neutral subject. 'To which regiment do you belong, Captain?'

'The King's Regiment.' He danced them away from the window then added, 'The same as the Rokeby brothers.'

Too late she realised this was not an uncontroversial topic of conversation. Leonora felt the fluttering of alarm. 'I suppose your paths didn't necessarily cross?'

She felt his shoulders stiffen under her fingers. 'Indeed. They were often out of camp. Exploring officers are mostly in enemy territory before reporting their findings back to our commanders.'

There was a hostility in every mention he made of them, and Leonora grew even more uneasy. She met his eyes as he danced her out of the path of another waltzing couple and said, 'Knowing a little of what the Earl of Rokeby has been through has made me full of admiration of all men who go to war.'

The dance had come to an end and Leonora was keen to get away, but he clamped her hand on his arm and she did not want to make a scene. In a low ferocious voice he said, 'I suppose your admiration for military men falls on your local Earl? I presume he told you his brother died in his arms on the field of battle?'

Leonora tried to extract her hand discreetly from his grasp. She was wary as she said, 'He did.'

'Well, rather than trying to save his brother, Alistair Rokeby walked away and left him to die. That way he inherited the estate, the title, everything.'

A protective outrage rose in her breast. She did not want to be heard so lowered her voice, but emotion burst out of her. 'How *dare* you blacken a man's name thus. How can you say such a wicked thing?'

Captain Ormonde met her blazing eyes and answered her with deadly intent. 'Because I was there when his "heroic" brother died and far from cradling him in his arms, Alistair Rokeby was off rutting with one of Boney's army cooks.'

Leonora felt as if she had been punched and gasped with the force of the blow. She walked quickly to the far side of the room just as the music for the next dance was beginning. Her emotions were in such miserable turmoil, she ignored the music, the dancers. Disbelief, jealousy, fear, anger and love were coiled in a deadly ferment. She had witnessed the closeness of Madame Dupré's relationship with Lord Rokeby; indeed, it had haunted her thoughts; could such a dreadful thing be true?

She was gazing sightless on the dark garden when she became aware of a ripple of consternation through the room. The orchestra slithered to a halt and everyone turned to the double doors where a dishevelled figure in black, his great wolfhound by his side, had just entered. For a moment, Leonora stopped breathing.

The Earl of Rokeby was without a mask, wearing only his distinctive eye patch and yet, even fully masked, she would have known him anywhere. His height and natural authority distinguished him. To her he was the most admirable and manly of men and whenever she saw him, her pulse quickened. The dancers had stopped momentarily and Leonora watched him scan the room. A man's voice was heard. 'This is the Duchess's ballroom. Dogs to the stables, my lord!' But Lord Rokeby ignored the instruction, still looking from masked face to masked face, seeking the person he had come for. Leonora heard a woman next to her mutter, 'It's such bad form to parade your wounds at a social event. Look at his face! We want to enjoy ourselves and not be reminded of the war.'

Her companion chimed in. 'And as for his uncouth behaviour bringing his cur...'

Leonora's emotions were so close to the surface she could not stop herself turning to face the woman, turbaned in pink silk with a matching pink feathered mask. In a quiet voice filled with fury she said, 'Madame! It is men like Lord Rokeby who sacrifice their health, even their lives, to keep us safe and able to enjoy such entertainments as these!'

Then Achille suddenly caught a scent and trotted purposefully through the crowd, followed by his master, heading into the press of dancers who parted like the Red Sea. In moments they were by Leonora's side. She felt the dog's wet nose nuzzling her hand and looked up into the tense face of Lord Rokeby. Her knees almost gave way with the shock and emotion of having him so close to her again. The music had started but everyone's eyes in the room had seen his dramatic entrance and wondered what had drawn him here with such urgency.

Taking Leonora's arm, Alistair Rokeby drew her away into the window embrasure farthest from the orchestra. She had recovered some of her equilibrium. 'Lord Rokeby! I thought you could not stomach Town and that nothing would induce you to appear at any event, let alone one like this.'

They moved farther into the recess and he said in a bitter voice, 'You're right, it's not my favoured habitat.'

'Then why here? Why now?'

'I've been summoned to receive my brother's posthumous medal for gallantry. I went to my grandmother's house to find you had left for this pantomime.' He indicated the masked throng with disdain. 'I had to enter the lion's den to find you.' He then took both Leonora's hands and gazed deep into her eyes with an unspoken question she could not fathom. He continued with a throb in his voice, 'Hasterleigh is not the same without you. I could not wait any longer. Achille needs you, my piano-forte has lost its harmony... And I too am strangely unstrung.'

Leonora had spent two weeks longing to see him again, yet not knowing anything about his feelings, about the truth of anything in his life or hers. His declaration of need for her could barely be understood in her current state of anxious unknowing.

Lord Rokeby's voice dropped lower and he was speaking fast,

as if he did not quite believe the *coup de foudre* that had overtaken him so completely. 'Before you, everything seemed black. Achille was all I cared for and the only reason to continue. And then on a muddy lane, you arrived in my life.' He dragged his hand across his brow. 'A country maid with your basket of apples and a pink nose from the cold, but you were a flame to light me through the darkness. Just knowing you were in the world, I began to love life as you did. But it was a love too keen to bear alone.'

Leonora's heart had begun its speeding rhythm that made her tremble, her head grow light and dizzy. Alistair Rokeby squeezed her hands, his words tumbling out. 'But with you gone this long fortnight, I realised it is not enough just to know you're in the world. I want you close to me, day and night.'

This was more than she had even dreamed she would hear from his lips. It was all she had longed for and she returned his grip with a force of feeling that overwhelmed her. But Leonora could not forget the Earl's greeting of Madame Dupré as if she were the only woman in the world for him. What did his impassioned declaration mean alongside that? And Captain Ormonde's malignant words seeped into her mind like an ineradicable stain. The ecstasy at having him close at last, declaring such feelings, became as insubstantial as will-o'-the-wisps in the shadow of the shameful suspicions she could not ignore.

'But my lord, what about Madame Dupré?' She met his gaze with uncertain eyes.

He looked shocked then turned away, his voice short and clipped. 'I have explained her part in my past. You have no reason to bring her into this conversation.'

'But is it the past? She stayed with you at the Abbey, without a chaperone.' Leonora could have bitten her tongue for saying something so mean and provincial-minded, but she had not voiced her fears to anyone, and they had grown in the silence until she could not suppress them any longer.

Lord Rokeby turned back to her, his face once more contorted with strain. 'I've told you already she saved my life. I owe her that affection and respect for eternity. But it is *you*' – his voice cracked with passion – 'who made me want to live again. And that is everything!'

His look was so intense she felt in danger of bursting into flames with the heat of emotion between them. But she had to know if there was any truth in Captain Ormonde's words. 'Forgive my asking, my lord, but did your brother truly die in your arms?'

'What makes you doubt me?' His brow was thunderous.

Leonora met his flashing gaze. 'It's just Captain Ormonde said he was there...' Her words tailed off as she saw the colour flare across Lord Rokeby's cheekbones.

'How can you give any credence to the words of a blackguard and turncoat, and trust them more than mine? How could you? I thought we understood and trusted each other. That we were as one!' Not wishing to be overheard, his voice was quiet but deadly. He was wild with disdain for Ormonde and Leonora felt his cold disappointment spread to her too.

'What was I to think? The Captain said he was there and you left the field with Madame Dupré!' she gasped, angry tears in her eyes, mortified by words she had never meant to say.

Lord Rokeby could not know her vulnerability, the corrosive power of her fear of loss. All he heard was the terrible slur, and her willingness to entertain it. He turned away; even Achille seemed to evade her eyes. 'That is despicable! And it is contemptible to give any credence to what Ormonde says. How can you believe such slander against me? How can you repeat it?' With that he had gone, and Leonora collapsed onto the nearest chair, unable to stand. So great was her dismay and fury with herself for such a betrayal of him that she closed her eyes, wishing she was anywhere but here.

After a while she heard the chair next to hers creak as someone sat down beside her. She opened her eyes and looked straight into the concerned face of George Lockwood. 'Miss Appleby, I wondered if you needed some company. I'm afraid the ballroom has been agog with the Earl's arrival and precipitate departure. May I suggest we dance and look as if we're enjoying ourselves, to still the clacking tongues?'

Despite her wintry heart, Leonora smiled. He was the nicest of men and how perfect for her beloved Charlotte. Suddenly alarmed, she turned and said, 'Where is Charlotte?' She was her responsibility and she noticed Nanny P was no longer eagle-eyed in her chaperonage, having extracted her knitting from her reticule.

'Don't worry about Miss Blythe. She's enjoying herself greatly dancing with Lord Dearlove. He has a certain irresistible charm.' His expression was rueful as they stood up and George Lockwood proffered his arm to Leonora. 'A new quadrille is about to begin and I would be very grateful if you would partner me.'

'Thank you, Mr Lockwood.' Her emotions were still close to the surface and blushing, she blurted out, 'You could not be a better friend.' She managed to put on a passable show as the dancing and chatter continued past midnight. At one point, Leonora was disconcerted to see Charlotte in close conversation with Captain Ormonde, her face unusually downcast. When she approached, both made an effort to look more sanguine and turned away to join a reel.

By the end of the night Leonora was exhausted with the effort of geniality and when she finally took refuge beside Mrs Priddy, she was pleased to see that Charlotte too was ready to leave and had collected George Lockwood to escort them home. All were subdued in the carriage as they made the short journey from Grosvenor Square to Brook Street. The horses trotted round the Square and passed Rokeby House; with a pang Leonora noticed candelabra still burning in the windows and she wondered if Lord Rokeby's spirits were as much out of sorts as hers.

* * *

Leonora awoke the next morning, heavy-hearted and nostalgic for the uncomplicated life that had once been hers. Questions and regrets circled in her fatigued brain like a whirlpool that never comes to rest. Flora brought her a cup of hot chocolate and put it on the table. 'Good morning, Miss Appleby. Amy is unwell so if you need anything, I'll be next door with Miss Blythe.'

Charlotte's heart was also heavy but for different reasons. She was assailed with conflicting feelings about Captain Ormonde and his animosity towards her father and Lord Rokeby. Her inability to reconcile her admiration for the Captain with her pride in her father and his family held her in a painful vice of anxiety. There was a soft knock on her door and not Amy, as she expected, but Flora appeared, carrying a tray. 'Good morning, Miss Blythe,' she said as she offered her a cup of chocolate.

'I'm pleased to see you again,' Charlotte said sitting up, her hair a mess. 'I'm grateful for your skills yesterday, Flora. It's the first time I've felt truly equal to the situation.' She smiled.

'There's a letter for you.' The maid held out a folded and sealed piece of writing paper addressed with a small, neat hand. She then went to draw back one curtain so Charlotte could read.

With a delighted cry, Charlotte took it, saying as she read, 'It's from the Reverend and Mama Mildmay.'

'Did they care for you well?' Flora's question was tentative and barely beyond a whisper.

Charlotte, distracted by reading all the gossip of the village, answered without looking up, 'As well as any parent ever could.' It then occurred to her that Flora's question displayed some unexpected knowledge of her life. She met her eyes, brilliant in the morning light. 'Do you know them, Flora?'

'I met them once.' She had turned away and was drawing the curtains fully back to reveal a sunny day.

'Then you know Hasterleigh?' Charlotte leant forward eagerly; it was so rare to meet other people who knew the village.

'I was very young and it was a long time ago.' She was walking towards the door. 'If you need help with your dressing or your hair, I'll be next door with Miss Appleby.' Charlotte eventually climbed out of bed and padded through to Leonora's room.

She was already up and being laced by Flora into her stays. 'Good morning, Lottie. I hope you slept well.'

'I did. Can I get into your bed?' Charlotte did not wait for a reply but clambered into the mound of feather mattress, bed linen and quilt, grateful for its warmth. 'Flora knows Hasterleigh,' she said.

'It was so long ago I barely remember it,' the maid said hastily, bending her head to focus on lacing the stays. Leonora was suddenly alert. 'Were you working at Rokeby Abbey? Or Oak Hall for the Foplings, perhaps?'

'It was a big house and I was only a girl. My first job. That's all I remember, Miss Appleby.' Flora was flustered. Having helped Leonora into her morning gown she left the room in some haste.

Leonora looked thoughtful and rather troubled. She walked to Charlotte's bedside and took her hand, saying in a quiet voice, 'Lottie, does Flora seem familiar to you? Her hands? Her eyes?'

Charlotte was deep in the folds of the bed and answered sleepily, 'I like how she looks, but familiar, no, I don't think so. Why?'

'I just wondered if she may have been at the Abbey.' Leonora paused; her instinct knew there was more than Flora was willing to say. 'But perhaps her reluctance to recall the time is because of some horror with Sir Roderick Fopling. Stories were rife about his licentious behaviour and servant girls fleeing in the night.'

'You've reminded me. I had a letter from Mama Mildmay.' She paused, aware of the shocking nature of what she was about to impart. 'Sir Roderick was thrown from his horse while out hunting. Dead before they even got to him. A broken neck they think.'

'That is terrible news. Lottie, you should have told me sooner!' Then more equably, she continued, 'But I suppose for a fox-hunting man like him, death would be better than being so incapacitated that he'd never ride again.' Leonora recalled her odd conversation with Hasterleigh's own green witch, who had determined she would marry Curate Fopling. 'Miss Vazey told me before we left for London that Richard Fopling's father was not long for this world.'

Charlotte grasped her hand. 'Do you think she really is a witch?' Her eyes were wide.

'I don't know I believe in witches, although I do think Richard Fopling is some kind of angel.' Leonora laughed. 'I certainly think they're particularly well suited.'

Leonora was sitting on the bed beside Charlotte and in the moment of intimacy and confidences, Charlotte asked one of the questions that had troubled her sleep. 'What was the business Lord Rokeby had with you? He left in such a rage all eyes were upon him.'

Leonora hung her head for a moment. 'Since the death of Captain Worth in Spain I thought my chance of love was lost for ever.' She looked up to meet Charlotte's sympathetic gaze. 'But against all sense and expectation I have awoken to the possibilities of love again.'

'For Lord Rokeby?' Charlotte's eyes flashed with delight.

'I can hardly bring myself to voice such presumption. But yes, I fear my heart is his for ever, even should he care not to receive it.'

There was a bleakness in Leonora's voice that clutched at Charlotte's heart. She put out a hand and grasped hers. 'Why is that presumptuous? Anyone would be lucky indeed to win your affections. Why should he not feel the same?'

Leonora continued in a faltering way, almost disbelieving of the tale herself. 'When I was last at the Abbey with Nanny P, a Frenchwoman arrived and threw herself into his arms. Apparently, she had saved his life on the battlefield and nursed him back to health.' She took a deep breath. 'I'm ashamed to admit it Lottie, but I was filled with jealousy. As if I had any rights over him!'

'So why did he leave the ball last night as if riding a storm?'

'Because I was cloth-eared and did not listen to his own feelings on the matter. Instead, I allowed jealousy and suspicion to speak. I mentioned what Captain Ormonde had told me and he will not forgive me for giving the Captain's words equal weight with his own.'

Charlotte squeezed her friend's hand. 'I sensed Lord Rokeby had touched your heart. But take courage. Love cannot end so easily – and through a misunderstanding too.'

'I can only hope it is a misunderstanding and that his feelings for Madame Dupré go no deeper than respect and gratitude. My head is painfully confused with hope, then despair.' Leonora turned her gaze on Charlotte. 'But tell me, Lottie, why your long face when in the company of Captain Ormonde last night? He seems to have a talent for disruption.'

Charlotte bridled. 'I think him a war hero who has suffered much and is much misunderstood!'

Leonora looked at her intently. 'You sound as if you're susceptible to him yourself?'

'I don't know what I feel. I like his company, his stories are so diverting, and I think him very handsome. But I don't want to marry him.'

Leonora was startled. 'Well then you most certainly must not!'

'He feels ill-used, says a man like him without a fortune would not be able to consider himself a suitor for an heiress like me. That the Earl and his family would never agree to a marriage.'

'Is this why he shows such animosity towards Lord Rokeby?'

Charlotte's fair skin flushed, her own emotions hard to fathom even to herself. She said hesitantly, 'I think he thinks he should right a wrong. He now claims he has evidence that one of the Rokeby brothers was in the pay of Napoleon and his generals. That they are not the heroes everyone thinks they are.'

Leonora felt her outrage flare again. 'He cannot continue to spread such calumny. One brother died for his country, the other has injuries he will carry all his life. Does Captain Ormonde know better than the generals who of their men are the gallant ones?' She leapt to her feet. 'Lord Rokeby is in Town specifically to collect his brother's Army Gold Medal. So few are awarded; if Ormonde truly has evidence to the contrary then he should take it to the authorities.'

'I cannot think other than that my father and Lord Rokeby were heroes.'

'Well, that's what their commanding officers and the world considers them to be.'

'If we were men, and proud and pig-headed enough, we could challenge Captain Ormonde to a duel.' Despite their own troubled spirits, both young women managed to laugh at the vagaries of men. 'But I mean it, Leonora. I am proud to have the blood of heroes in my veins and I will strive to prove myself worthy of them.'

Leonora stood up. 'That can be an onerous burden to bear. Instead, aim to fully live your life, bringing happiness to yourself and others.' She offered her hand. 'Come on, Lottie. Get up and we'll take the horses out for a ride in Hyde Park. That will blow all frowziness away.'

Lady Bucklebury was waiting for them at the breakfast table. 'My dears, tell me about last night. I've heard the gossip already of my disreputable grandson turning up in the Countess's ballroom with his hound. Tsk! So uncouth, but just what I would expect of Alistair. Talk had it he was in search of some unknown lady.' Her eyes were twinkling. 'Do any of you know the identity of the young woman?'

Mrs Priddy had just entered the room and she and Charlotte glanced at Leonora, who almost imperceptibly shook her head. Lady Bucklebury continued in a peevish voice. 'That boy was always so secretive, so havey-cavey about his doings. You recall him when young, don't you, Mrs Priddy?' She turned to where Nanny P had settled into a chair with a cup of coffee.

'I always found Master Alistair a most interesting child, full of spirit and generosity of heart.'

'I'm afraid his father was not as amused. He was more chastised than any child I knew. It pained poor Venetia very much. My daughter felt she had no power to protect him.'

'But his brother could.' Leonora's voice made them all turn to look at her.

Mrs Priddy nodded. 'True enough, but not against everything.' Mrs Priddy's soft face was mournful. 'I counselled he should be allowed greater freedoms with more employment on the estate perhaps. He has such a way with dogs and horses.'

Leonora busied herself spreading jam on her toast but was listening intently to the conversation. Lady Bucklebury's voice became more emphatic. 'As the second son, he could please himself when Charles was alive, but now he's the Earl he has to take his responsibilities seriously. When you inherit a great estate, your life is no longer your own, but has to be lived for the family's greater good.'

Leonora realised with a sinking heart that Lady Bucklebury might as well be reciting the warning to Ophelia against any pretensions towards Prince Hamlet:

His greatness weigh'd, his will is not his own; For he himself is subject to his birth... And therefore must his choice be circumscribed.

Mrs Priddy was quick to smooth the waters. 'I'm sure Lord Rokeby has shouldered his new responsibility already. He's most particular about his stables and bloodstock.'

Lady Bucklebury snorted. 'That's about all he seems particular about.' Then a thought appeared to strike her and she asked, 'Was that high-crested Livia Dearlove at the ball last night?' Without waiting for a reply, she continued in a ruminative tone, 'Now she would make a suitable countess for him, don't you think? Before Alistair went to war, he spent much time with that ne'er-do-well brother of hers and I often wondered if the attraction was not more likely the sister.'

Leonora paused in the process of pouring everyone a second cup of coffee. This unexpected train of thought about Lord Rokeby shook her; Livia Dearlove had not occurred to her as a possible candidate for the post of Countess of Rokeby. In as neutral a manner as she could muster, she said, 'We have entertained Lady Livia at Hasterleigh Manor. She does not seem to be someone entirely at ease in the country.'

With a jolt, Leonora realised that Lady Bucklebury was much more perceptive than she appeared as the old Countess replied with a glint in her eye, 'Mmm, that could be a disadvantage, given Alistair's reclusive habits. Perhaps these Town girls are not ideal marriage material for such a particular bridegroom?' Her mischievous eyes alighted on Leonora's more guarded face, as she mused, 'I certainly think he deserves some happiness after all he's been through, but only an unusual sort of woman could put up with his eccentric character and taste for excess. What think you, Miss Appleby?'

Leonora stood up. 'I wouldn't presume to know, Lady Bucklebury.' She felt the colour rise in her cheeks and changed the subject. 'Just after noon, Charlotte and I are hoping to ride the horses you and the Earl so kindly put at our disposal. It'll exercise them and clear our own heads after last night.'

'Oh, I would like to accompany you, but sadly my equestrian days are long past.' Leonora and Mrs Priddy helped her walk slowly to the door. 'Enjoy yourselves, my dears. Do not break too many hearts, especially not your own.'

* * *

The bright morning had turned into a beautiful early spring afternoon with birds singing in the crisp air. Charlotte and Leonora rode towards the Park, accompanied at a discreet distance by Davy, the Bucklebury groom, who was watchful over the behaviour of the young ladies' horses, but also wary of uninvited approaches by strange men. Leonora had never seen so many people, horses and carriages in one place before, most dressed to be admired in bright silks with gay plumes of feathers waving on their hats. The men were equally showy on their glossy hunters or driving smart painted carriages.

Both young women drew appraising glances, Leonora knew as much for the striking Rokeby horses as for themselves. Minerva sniffed the air, trembling with anticipation of a canter through the trees; Iris was more docile but aware of her beauty and trotted with a proud and easy grace. Leonora felt certain they would meet someone they knew and the thought heightened her spirits. There was excitement in having so many attractive and eligible young men and women gathered into one small space for the Season, a more varied collection of people than she would ever see in a life-time lived contentedly at Hasterleigh. Out of the blur of distant riders, one emerged, unmistakeable for his height and the size of his horse. 'I can see Mr Lockwood ahead.' She turned to Charlotte with a smile.

They had also been spotted and within a minute George Lock-wood, accompanied by Lady Livia and her groom, trotted towards them. 'Why doesn't he see through her artificial charm?' Charlotte muttered under her breath. Leonora looked at her sharply; was she jealous too?

'Hallo, ladies! I had hoped I'd see you in the Park this after-noon.' His eyes met theirs as he continued in his genial way, 'I must say you both look very well indeed after the demands of last night. You know of course, the Honourable Miss Dearlove.' He turned in the saddle to include his companion in his bonhomie.

The women bowed their heads in greeting. Livia Dearlove never failed to put pressure on a bruise. 'My dears, what an exciting night that was,' she purred. 'The Countess's ball has never been so eventful. You do seem to attract a certain raffish element, Miss Appleby.'

Leonora stiffened. She had hoped that her mask had ensued a certain anonymity, but it seemed not. 'It was a most enjoyable ball,' she said in an evasive way.

'Those are possibly amongst the best examples of equine beauty on show today,' George Lockwood said, gazing at the restive mares.

Leonora noticed on the treeline a black horse and rider gallop-ing, with a long-legged hound beside him, slipping in and out of the shadows. Her heart was suddenly pounding in her ears as she realised this was the only person she wanted to see. Without hesi-tating, she turned to Mr Lockwood, Lady Livia and Charlotte and said in a rush, 'Forgive me but I have something to tell that rider.' She gave Minerva her head and Davy spurred his horse in pursuit. She realised that Lord Rokeby was looping through the trees past the Tyburn toll and would end up at the farthest bank of the Serpentine. She set Minerva to head him off and they both arrived breathless at the intersection of paths and pulled their horses up, Jupiter stamping and bridling, and Minerva, recognising her stable mate, whinnying her greeting, and trying to fuss and nuzzle him.

Their riders were less effusive. 'Miss Appleby, good day.' Lord Rokeby's face was stern as he tipped his hat, dismissing Leonora with a brief nod of his head and about to ride on.

'Wait, Lord Rokeby!' The gaze he turned on her was so cold that Leonora faltered. There was too much she wished to say, but only managed the least controversial, 'I wanted to thank you for the loan of such splendid horses.'

'It's my pleasure, Miss Appleby.' He wheeled the mighty Jupiter round and, showing more civility to his grandmother's groom, commended Davy on the excellent condition of his horses. He was about to turn away when he paused and said in a subdued voice, 'I should have told you sooner, perhaps. While my brother was commanding a force in Holland he had to discipline Captain Ormonde for his mistreatment of a young Hollander girl. He was flogged in front of the company as a warning that such behaviour would not be countenanced. Ormonde vowed revenge against us.'

Leonora was shocked and mortified by her own gullibility. 'I'm sorry, Lord Rokeby. That is shameful. I did not know.'

With a hard stare he drawled, 'I have learnt in a dangerous world that knowing who your friends are can be a matter of life and death.' He gazed over her head at some distant horizon. 'In my experience, a friend always thinks the best of you, and endeavours to do the best by you.'

Sudden anger blazed up in Leonora's breast at the unfairness of being condemned as a faithless friend when she had not even known what his feelings were for her. She had been confused by Captain Ormonde's assertions and her own jealousy of Madame Dupré, but now his moral loftiness irked her, for Alistair Rokeby, by his own definition, was proving himself as faithless as he adjudged her to be. Her chin went up and she said, 'Sir, if that's your ideal of friendship, perhaps I can expect you to be the kind of friend to think the best of me, and want what's best for me?'

His gaze snapped back to her face. 'Of course I do. No faithless friend am I, Miss Appleby. Look what I have done for you. Introduced you to my Grandmama, making it possible for you to have the benefit of the Season alongside Charlotte—'

His catalogue of good works was cut short by Leonora. 'By your leave, Lord Rokeby. Having me accompany Charlotte to London has not been in my best interests. If you knew me and were a true friend, then you would have left me to my own contentment in Hasterleigh. That's where I'm happiest.' She could feel her cheeks flushing with emotion as she spoke.

'But what about the chance to marry? All women surely want that?'

With tears pricking her eyes, Leonora said, 'The man I loved who wished to marry me was killed at Fuengirola; why should I choose to marry anyone else? Certainly not a Town dandy who disdains the country and all who live in it!'

His face softened into a smile. 'As you can see, I could never claim to be a Town dandy, but give us gentlemen a chance, Miss Appleby. It's hard to compete with a dead hero.' He caught her eye. 'I should know.' Leonora was surprised by the unexpected tenderness of his expression as he continued, 'We both have unhealed wounds and should treat each other with care.' Then, with the lightest touch, his great black horse leapt forward and the Earl of Rokeby sped away.

Leonora watched him canter around the distant shore of the Serpentine, Jupiter's long tail streaming behind him in the sun. He was right. She should never have doubted him. How clear it was now that Captain Ormonde was out to destroy the Rokeby brothers and she had wielded his perfidious sword for him.

Charlotte trotted up on Iris, closely followed by George Lockwood. 'Leonora, why the haste? His lordship is making a habit of leaving your company at speed. You seem to have an inflammatory effect on him every time you meet.' Her expression was full of mischief.

Leonora could not reveal her mortification and managed a rueful smile, then looked at Mr Lockwood. 'Where's Lady Livia? We haven't chased her away I hope?'

His expression clouded. 'Not at all. I said I must escort Miss Blythe until you returned from your business with the Earl, and she said she had urgent matters to attend to back at Berkeley Square.'

'Well, I have to apologise to you both.' Leonora was shame-faced at how impetuous her behaviour had been, and how discourteous to her companions. She continued, 'I wished to thank Lord Rokeby for the loan of these mares from his stables and I didn't know when I would see him again.' She did not see Charlotte and George Lockwood exchange a knowing glance but leaning forward to pat Minerva's neck, she added, 'I'm getting rather chilled. Would you mind if we turn for home?'

They were trotting in a sedate manner and were approaching Grosvenor Gate when they heard a cry. Turning in the saddle, Leonora saw an outlandish figure cantering towards them. She was obviously a woman, dressed in a striped coat but wearing her full skirt, divided so she could use a man's saddle to ride astride her horse. Her long curling hair was tied back and Leonora recognised her as the woman who haunted her jealous dreams. 'Madame Dupré!'

The Frenchwoman pulled her horse up in a flurry of gravel and grass and leapt off its back as athletically as if she were a man. She approached Leonora with her hand outstretched and a smile on her face. In her heavily accented voice, she cried, 'Ah! *Quelle coïncidence*, Miss Appleby? I had seen Monsieur Alistair's horses and hoped to find it was you.'

Leonora was surprised to be excited to see her again, and yet full of dread; although Alistair Rokeby had declared his love for her, he had never denied that Claudette Dupré was his mistress. She turned to George Lockwood and Charlotte. 'May I introduce you to Madame Dupré. She saved the Earl's life at Corunna. Madame, this is Mr Lockwood and Miss Blythe who both live as neighbours to Rokeby Abbey.' They all bowed their heads in greeting. Then Leonora added, 'Charlotte, if you're happy to be escorted home by Mr Lockwood...' She looked to him for a response on the matter. 'It's such a short ride I hope the absence of my company will not outrage any proprieties. I just need to talk to Madame Dupré.' They waved and set off for Grosvenor Gate.

Davy put a hand up to help Leonora dismount from Minerva and then followed the women at a discreet distance, with the reins of all three horses in his hands. Leonora's cheeks were flushed with emotion as she turned to meet Claudette Dupré's dark eyes. 'Madame, I did not expect to see you in London?' Her heart was hammering at the thought that Claudette Dupré had come in the company of Lord Rokeby and was still living under his protection at Grosvenor Square. Then Leonora noticed the Frenchwoman's mount was closer to a farm horse and not akin to the fine-boned steeds from the Earl's elite stables.

Madame Dupré laughed in her merry, unselfconscious way.

'Ah, I am with the new *ambassadeur* to the Court of King George, le marquis de La Châtre. I manage *la cantine* for him.'

'So you didn't come with Lord Rokeby's entourage?' Leonora could not stop herself blurting out, colouring all the more at how revealing of her deepest hopes and fears this must be.

Madame Dupré recognised her anxiety and grasped her hand with sisterly feeling, saying, 'Miss Appleby, do not fear. Alistair is a brother for me. *C'est vrai,* I've seen him *in extremis* and he has no secret for me, but we are not *amoureux.* This is important, so how you say? We are not the lovers, I promise.'

Her frankness made Leonora gasp, but then relief flooded through her and she was suddenly dizzy with happiness. 'Can you tell me about when you saved his life?'

'Oh! *Quel désastre!* I was busy with the wounded when I see this English with his face sabred, pouring blood, his leg twisted under him. In his arms was another English, but he was close to *fini.* The wound of his stomach was mortal. He could not live. I gave him brandy to suffer less. But this English would not leave. "*Mon frère,* my brother," he said again and again. "Leave me here with him."'

Leonora was immersed in the vividness of the scene and she squeezed Madame Dupré's hand with the force of her feeling. As they walked on in silence, she asked in a quiet voice, 'How did you get Lord Rokeby to safety?'

'We have men with carts to collect wounded and *morts.* They pick him up and put him with the other bodies. He was an officer, so they did not let him to die with the rest of the English but make him prisoner. He was lucky the surgeon see him and save his leg, sew his face too. *Bof! Quel carnage!*' She had stopped, as if over-whelmed with the memory. 'Then I take him to a house to be nursed.'

The clock in Grosvenor Chapel struck three and Madame Dupré was suddenly alert. 'I must go!' She took the reins of her horse from Davy's hands and without help from him, swung herself up into the saddle. Looking into Leonora's upturned face, she said, 'Alistair, your Earl, is special. When they discover he was one of Wellington's *espions* who send information back to the English, they want to shoot him, but he escape to live like a wild animal. That is when he found Achille.' She wheeled her horse around and over her shoulder said, 'Alistair need a special woman to love. I hope you are that one, Miss Appleby, to love him as he deserve.' The extraordinary Frenchwoman then cantered off towards the trees.

Leonora's heart was like the sun which had suddenly emerged from a bank of cloud. She felt her body filled with light. Surely its radiating warmth could be seen in her face? Leonora thought with gratitude of the force of nature that had arrived to upend her life. Madame Dupré had not only saved Lord Rokeby from the battlefield, she had also illuminated Leonora's own life. Blazing like a comet from a different world, she had shown Leonora where her heart belonged. Returning today, she brought the gift of truth and clarity. Leonora knew she must hold this revelation close as she dared to open herself again to love.

* * *

Charlotte arrived home safely and unremarkably in the company of George Lockwood. 'Well, what an eventful afternoon!' she said to him as they pulled their horses up outside the Bucklebury mansion. Mr Lockwood jumped down from Titan then walked round to catch Charlotte as she dismounted. She slipped down into his hands, so large they spanned her waist. He held her in his warm grip and placed her on the ground with deliberate care; even then he did not hurry to release her. Charlotte looked up into his face. 'Thank you, Mr Lockwood.' Then she added, tilting her head, 'Do you think love is in the air?'

Mr Lockwood's half smile made him look as if he knew more than he was admitting. As he led her to the door he said, 'Are you thinking of Miss Appleby and the Earl, perchance? Or more generally? It is spring after all, and the sap is rising.' Then he turned and tipped his hat to her, sprang into the saddle and rode away into the sun, his large silhouette seeming mysterious, yet also consolingly familiar.

There was a letter waiting for her in the hall, addressed to *Miss Blythe* in a distinctive spiky hand she did not recognise. A mixture of excitement and anxiety gripped her as she read.

> *Dear Miss Blythe,*
>   *Would you do me the honour of meeting me tomorrow at Bullock's Museum, the Egyptian Hall, in Piccadilly. At 3 p.m.*
>   *Bring a maid as chaperone rather than Miss Appleby.*
>   *Yours,*
>   *Guy Ormonde*

Charlotte's mind was reeling as she ran upstairs to her room, and cast off her bonnet and pelisse before flinging herself on the bed. Why did Captain Ormonde ask her to meet without Leonora? Was this more business to do with her father's honour? She determined she would be independent and make her own decisions – prove herself a Rokeby in courage and spirit. Considering herself sensible and old enough to go alone, except for the necessary accompaniment of Flora, she scrawled an answering note of acquiescence, sealed it and asked Lady Bucklebury's butler if he could arrange to have it delivered. She did not want to deceive Leonora and was relieved to hear her come in and dash straight up the stairs to the drawing room. In moments, music filled the house, a passionate interpretation of Clementi's Etude played *alle-grissimo* and at full volume. No one could ignore the emotion in her playing.

Mrs Priddy understood Leonora well enough to know that when she heard this cascade of notes played so emphatically, her young charge was in the grip of a tumult of feeling. She entered the room unseen and walked behind Leonora to put a hand lightly on her shoulder. The music stopped abruptly and Leonora leapt up and into her arms. 'Oh, Nanny P, I love him, I love him!' she sobbed. 'I can't believe I am saying this out loud, but my heart is too full. What am I to do?'

Mrs Priddy patted her back. 'My love, why so anguished?'

'Because anyone I love is taken from me. First Mama, then Captain Worth, then Papa. I'm so afraid. To love is too dangerous. There's only you and Charlotte left.'

'Life rushes on and can't be stopped. We have to continue too, Nora; we cannot protect ourselves from sorrow by closing our hearts to love.'

'But I can't bear any more loss.'

Mrs Priddy lifted Leonora's head and looked intently into her tear-stained face. 'If you're worried about losing Lord Rokeby, you must stop now. He's been snatched once from the jaws of death. Now it's his turn to live.' Leonora nodded as Nanny P added, 'And you have no excuse not to live as bravely as he does.'

'But what if I'm not as loved by him as he is beloved by me? I have treated him so ill, have doubted his word. What an insult to a proud and honourable man! What if he despises me after showing such a mean and jealous aspect of myself?'

Mrs Priddy shook her. 'No more of this talk, my dear. We are all fallible before God and all is forgiven by Him!'

Despite her tears, Leonora laughed. 'Now you're sounding just like Curate Fopling!'

'Well, he's a fine young man and you could take some lessons from him.' Mrs Priddy's pale blue eyes twinkled.

Leonora hugged her again. 'I am happy that Charlotte will marry and leave me, but I don't want you to ever leave, my dearest Nanny P.'

'Oh, come now! You know, my love, I won't leave you until you have your own family.' She kissed her on the forehead. 'Now play that lovely tune.'

10

IS AN OFFICER A GENTLEMAN?

Leonora could barely sleep. Old impulses of fear of loss had not yet given way to this new certainty of where her heart belonged. Instead she was restless, locked in fevered jealous dreams. Only as the thin light of dawn seeped through the curtains did she fall into sleep at last. She woke late and drowsy as Flora knocked and entered with a steaming jug of water. 'Good morning, Miss Appleby, may I draw the curtains?'

Leonora struggled to sit, puzzled that Flora was still working in Lady Bucklebury's house. 'Is Amy recovering?'

Flora walked back from the dressing room. 'Her sickness has receded but she still needs rest.'

Leonora watched her. 'Flora, do you remember seeing me at the Manor when you lived in Hasterleigh? Did we ever meet?'

Flora had a newly washed and ironed chemise in her hands and turned away to fold then refold it, not meeting Leonora's eyes. She answered in a neutral voice, 'I think I saw you a couple of times in the lane, Miss Appleby. You were just a girl.' She then placed the chemise on the bed and at the doorway turned to say,

'Miss Charlotte needs help with her hair. If you need me, I'll be with her.'

Charlotte had also had a troubled night, occasioned by Captain Ormonde's note. She knew the sole purpose of the Countess sponsoring her for the Season was to find her a suitable husband, and Guy Ormonde was a most unsuitable match. He lacked a fortune and Lord Rokeby nurtured an old animosity against him that was close to contempt. But she thought him attractive and attentive, admirable too with his tales of military exploits. Her susceptible heart found something thrilling in his roguery, but she could not understand why he was so set against the Earl of Rokeby when she, and the world, considered him the most admirable of humankind.

While she struggled with the conundrum of Captain Ormonde and his motives, her mind returned, like a ship to harbour, to the comfortable figure of George Lockwood. His height and breadth, his cheerful good humour, made her feel safe and at ease. She knew by the way he looked at her that he found her attractive too, although he was warm and civil to all in his orbit, and Charlotte wondered if perhaps everyone had the benefit of his generosity of spirit. She had newly come to the thought that as the daughter of a hero, perhaps she had been born for braver things than comfort and safety? The idea of Mr Lockwood had an even more troubling aspect; if she were to marry him, she would then move into the Manor, Leonora's home, while her friend was displaced to the Lodge. That thought made Charlotte recoil; she did not wish to feel an imposter and a thief.

A light tap woke her from fitful sleep and Flora entered bearing a jug of hot water for her morning's toilette. 'Good morning, Miss Blythe.'

'Good morning, Flora. Would you accompany me to Bullock's Museum this afternoon?'

'Yes, miss, I've been there before. It's full of wonders.'

'I'd forgotten you've lived in London for years.' Charlotte rubbed her eyes and yawned.

'Is Miss Appleby not going with you?'

Charlotte had climbed out of bed and sat at the dressing table where she gazed in dismay at the birds' nest that seemed to have arrived on her head. 'No. I'm meeting a friend who is a captain in the army.'

Flora stood behind her and began to gently brush out the tangles of fine fair hair, a slight frown on her usually serene features. 'Is it Captain Ormonde?'

Charlotte turned to face her. 'Yes, how do you know?'

'I've heard talk of him. Nothing much escapes us maids you know.' Her usually equable face had turned grim as she continued the delicate untangling.

'What do the maids say?' Charlotte's heart lurched with foreboding.

The women caught each other's eyes in the looking glass and with a sudden determination, Flora said, 'I will pass on what the maids say as I don't wish you to be ill-used or compromised. We all warn each other about the men who cannot be trusted. And Captain Ormonde cannot be trusted.' She looked down, embarrassed yet defiant. She continued in a firm, quiet voice, 'It's also rumoured his debts are so extensive and pressing he's threatened with prison or exile.'

Charlotte knew that Flora had broken a golden rule that separated Upstairs from Downstairs; she had offered an opinion on one of her betters, and Charlotte was grateful for her courage. Shocked by both revelations, she accepted that, if true, Captain Ormonde was no longer such a heroic figure, but the news could not deflect her purpose. She had to play the hero now.

'Thank you, Flora. I appreciate your frankness. But I'm afraid it's a matter of my family's honour that I must go.' Flora's clever fingers had just finished sculpting Charlotte's hair into a charming chignon with ringlets round her face, set in rags the night before.

'Just beautiful,' Flora said, almost to herself, and then blushed when she realised she had uttered it out loud.

'You've worked your magic, Flora. Thank you. Shall we meet in the hall at half past the hour of one?'

* * *

Leonora and Mrs Priddy had already left for Hookham's Library when Charlotte dressed carefully in her new walking dress of primrose yellow French cambric, with a pleated collar and a girdle with a clasp of glittering cut steel. She picked up her purple pelisse and new Leghorn bonnet and ran down the stairs to meet Flora. The maid was wearing a pretty dark blue pelisse which looked surprisingly well on her. The garment used to be one of Charlotte's that she had refurbished in the winter with velvet ribbon: when Flora had shown such evident appreciation for her work, she had given it to her.

The afternoon threatened rain, so Lady Bucklebury's butler pressed a large furled umbrella into Flora's hand as they set out to walk to Piccadilly. Charlotte's heart was quickening with anxiety at what may lie ahead. The walk was always interesting and settled her emotions a little; down through Berkeley Square where the children with their nurses bowled hoops and played hopscotch on the paving stones, on through Albermarle and, as they approached the area of St James's, gentlemen in their curricles and on horseback became more numerous. Charlotte felt her beautiful clothes were a form of armour but they also drew attention to her, making her fear she was but an imposter. They turned into the busy throughfare of Piccadilly and there was the unmistakeable Egyptian Hall which never failed to astonish. Charlotte stared with wonder at its incongruity amongst the plain brick façades on either side. The exotic grandeur of the great semi-naked statues above the portico and the ziggurat detail round the windows were so suggestive of an excitingly different culture and an earlier age.

Charlotte paid a shilling each for their tickets and they slipped into the dim interior. It was the perfect place for an assignation, seething as it was with visitors intent on the glass cabinets of curiosities lining the walls, or peering at the exotic stuffed animals in an artificial jungle in a central compound.

Out of the shadows emerged the handsome figure of Captain Ormonde, dressed in his civilian clothes and looking dapper. He bowed over Charlotte's hand and nodded at Flora before drawing her mistress away towards the cabinet on a nearby wall filled with large shells and the skeletons of sea creatures. Flora remained at a discreet distance, but her eyes were intent upon them and her ears strained to hear.

He was formal. 'Miss Blythe, I am pleased to see you. I think what I have to say will be of importance to us both.' Charlotte nodded, her eyes serious as he continued. 'As you know, I've led a soldier's life and did not think it right to ask a wife to make the same sacrifices of absence that I had willingly made.'

Charlotte felt her heart lurch. Was he about to ask her to marry him? she wondered, but he seemed in no hurry to progress that conversation as he began to stroll round the central exhibition, her hand laid on the crook of his arm. Flora walked on the other side of her. He pointed at a giant turtle shell and then stopped by a stuffed mermaid that looked suspiciously like a seal in a wig. 'Captain Cook brought much of this back from his voyages.' Captain Ormonde turned to look at her with his charming smile. 'My travels in Wellington's army introduced me to the world too. I have sought adventure. But now I am back home, you have made me want to live in a different way.'

Ignoring Flora's presence, the Captain grasped Charlotte's hands and said in a low, intense voice, 'Miss Blythe, my sleep has been troubled since I met you. My nights are haunted by dreams of you.' That distinctive smile was lurking even as he spoke, and Charlotte wondered if it was a spontaneous outpouring of feeling or instead had been rehearsed. But despite all her reservations and suspicion of his motives, she could not but be struck by how attractive he was, and how unexpectedly exciting it was to have such unsought power over someone as much a man of the world as the Captain.

She was aware of Flora hovering with a sense of anxiety. Her maid fell back slightly, sensing perhaps what was to come. In a conversational tone, Guy Ormonde said, 'Do you think, Miss Blythe, you could make me the happiest man in the world by consenting to marry me?'

For a moment, Charlotte's breathing stopped. She had been half-expecting this but to actually hear the words was startling to her. 'But sir, we barely know each other.'

'War has taught me that happiness must be grasped where it can.'

'You do know, as I'm underage, Lord Rokeby's permission would be necessary?'

He turned away, his face set hard, a muscle in his jaw pulsing. 'We would never attain it,' he muttered under his breath.

'Then you would have to wait until I was of age.'

'Miss Blythe, I cannot wait.' His voice was low and harsh with urgency. 'There is another way. You can accompany me to the border with Scotland where they have no barriers against love.'

Charlotte was alarmed at the idea. 'I cannot repay my family's generosity with such shameful behaviour!'

His eyes were suddenly narrowed and hard. 'I think you could if it meant saving their honour.'

Charlotte pulled away and looked defiantly up at him. 'How so, sir?'

With a glitter in his eyes and a smile more chilling than charming, he withdrew a piece of paper from his inside pocket. 'Here I have the proof of the Rokeby brothers' treasonous dealing.' He walked over to the waxwork of a pygmy warrior that was particularly well illuminated so that Charlotte could better read. Her heart was pounding as she perused as best she could the paper in his hand. At the head was an official-looking insignia and an engraving of the Napoleonic Imperial Eagle. Below, in black handwriting, were the words: *Les services rendus: 100 Napoléons.* At the bottom of the page was a signature Charlotte could not decipher, and the word *Corunna.*

She looked up at Captain Ormonde, dread tightening her chest. 'What does this mean?'

'This is the receipt for the payment made to the Earl of Rokeby, for services as a spy for Napoleon's army at Corunna.'

In an involuntary protective gesture, Charlotte's hand flew to her throat. 'But he and his brother were exploring officers for Wellington's army,' she weakly protested.

'Exactly! They were dealing with both sides, loyal to neither. As agents for Lord Wellington they were particularly trusted, and so this behaviour was especially treacherous.'

Charlotte could barely comprehend what he was saying. Such crimes even in times of peace were treasonous and demanded the most swingeing of punishments. In a small voice she asked, 'What do you intend to do with it?'

'I will give it to you as a wedding present, to do with as you will.' He gave a sly smile.

'And if I don't agree to accompany you to the Scottish border to marry?'

'Then I will take this to the Secretary of State for War and the Colonies before your father is awarded his posthumous Army Gold Medal for gallantry. I doubt they would wish their highest honour besmirched by a traitor, or indeed the brother of a traitor.'

Flora had been watching from afar this impassioned conversation. Although she could not hear the words above the hubbub of the visitors' voices, it was quite clear that Charlotte was shocked and distressed. The Captain's demeanour too had altered from flattering suitor to something more menacing.

Charlotte realised she had to think fast and remain calm even though her hands were shaking with emotion. Above all, she desired to protect her father's reputation. She wondered if this was a chance for her to prove her bravery, to live up to her Rokeby name. In a voice stronger than she felt she said, 'May I ask, Captain Ormonde, if your determination to marry me is to do with my fortune?'

He looked disconcerted by her frankness then, recovering his sangfroid, responded in a drawl, 'Surely, Miss Blythe, you are not so naive as to think we can live by love alone? Indeed, should love even be necessary? I find it quite gets in the way of rational thought. Instead, you'll find the world revolves around money. I have none, which is really rather a nuisance, and yet you could make us both a good deal happier by sharing what you will have on marriage.' His striking dark eyes had narrowed with the thought and he said under his breath, 'In fact, things have come to such a pretty pass that debtors' prison or exile is my fate.'

Charlotte's heart plummeted. Here was proof of what she had always feared. It was only her fortune he desired, and he had found the perfect way to blackmail her into giving it to him. She determined she would even marry him, if it came to that, and hope for an annulment. Knowing she must do what had to be done, she was prepared to relinquish her chance of love, and her fortune, in the process. 'So, what do you propose?' she asked in the smallest of voices.

Captain Ormonde was suddenly business-like. 'The medal is being awarded in a week. We have no time to lose. I have hired a coach, ready to leave at daybreak from my lodging. Number twelve, South Audley Street, at the Grosvenor Square end. I'll be waiting for you at five in the morning.' His eyes did not leave her face. 'Bring a portmanteau and don't tell a soul, otherwise I'll go straight to the Colonial Office.'

'Can I trust you, Captain Ormonde?' Charlotte looked up into his eyes.

He put out a hand. 'You have my word as an English officer and a gentleman.' Charlotte was glad he did not ask if he could trust her as she had every intention of being as untrustworthy as it was possible to be. The Rokebys were known for their valour and ability to act righteously, without demur or complaint. Their motto after all was *Pietas et Fortitudo*, Duty and Courage. How well she intended to live that now.

Charlotte nodded. 'I will see you tomorrow.'

His charming smile had returned. 'You also have my word that I will treat you as a gentleman should. I will only take you to my bed once we are married. At the posting inns you will be my sister, to allay any suspicion.'

He tipped his hat to Flora who was feigning deep interest in a neighbouring glass cabinet, then took Charlotte's gloved hand and kissed it before turning to go.

* * *

Having returned from Hookham's Library, Leonora and Mrs Priddy walked up the front steps of Bucklebury House and into the antique grandeur of the great hall. Leonora was hoping to see Charlotte in the drawing room but only Lady Bucklebury was there in her chair by the fire. 'My dear, Charlotte has retired to bed looking very peaky.' Leonora started as if to go to her but Lady Bucklebury put a hand out. 'Flora is with her. She has been a godsend to us with Amy so indisposed, but now Amy's recovered, Flora will be able to leave tomorrow. I know dear Lady Dundas is missing her.' She looked intently at Leonora. 'I hope you are well?'

'Lady Bucklebury, thank you, I'm feeling well, just a little tired. I hope you are not too fatigued by having us here?'

The Countess patted the sofa beside her. 'Come, sit. You and Charlotte have added a great deal of interest to my days. I find my painful limbs are eased when I have news of your lives to entertain me. I like to hear the piano-forte played by you both, too.' She then turned to Leonora. 'Tell me, Miss Appleby, is there any young gallant who has captured Charlotte's regard?'

Leonora was unprepared for the question and not wishing to confide too much of Charlotte's affairs, tried to be truthful but vague. 'There are several young men but I'm not certain whether she returns their interest.'

'I hope she's not being too particular. Young gals today talk of love. How jingle-brained they are!' She looked pensively into the fire. 'That other relation I'd like to see settled is my wayward grandson. He's returning to the country soon.' Lady Bucklebury's bird-bright eyes were on Leonora, who attempted to erase any reaction from her expression. Lady Bucklebury put down her embroidery. 'I wish that obstinate boy would settle the succession and beget himself an heir. I know his ruined looks and stormy character make him a challenging choice for a delicately nurtured young woman.' She picked up her canvas again and started stabbing her needle in and out of the fabric, creating a colourful representation in wool of a soaring fish eagle, a salmon in its talons. She continued, 'But now his brother is dead, Alistair is the head of an ancient and noble family, has the Abbey and all those valuable acres. It's not such a bad bargain, I should think?' Her wrinkled old face broke into a smile that combined pride and mischief as once again she caught Leonora's eye.

For the first time Leonora wondered if grandmother and grandson were not more alike than she had first thought. She excused herself, mounted the stairs and knocked on Charlotte's door. Entering, she found the curtains half-drawn and Charlotte propped up in bed, looking pale and rather distraught. 'My dear Lottie, what's caused this?' Leonora took her hand and perched on the edge of the bed.

Charlotte was as evasive as Leonora had been with Lady Bucklebury and it puzzled her to find her young friend so uneasy. 'Has something happened on your walk, or at the museum?'

'No, no. The museum was fascinating. So full of improbable things. There's even a mermaid!'

'Yes, I've heard about that. I think it most likely remains an improbable thing.' Leonora laughed and was relieved to see Charlotte smile.

'I'm just inordinately tired. I think too much excitement.'

'Well, our noble hostess has been asking me about your gentlemen admirers.' Leonora saw Charlotte's startled expression and put out a reassuring hand. 'Don't worry, I was as discreet as I could be.' When Charlotte had relaxed back into the pillows, she continued, 'Do you wish to tell me anything about your feelings for Mr Lockwood and Captain Ormonde, or indeed Lord Dearlove?'

Charlotte shook her head, a flush creeping up her fair skin. 'I'm truly confused. If I were just plain Charlotte Blythe, I would be amazed and delighted if a gentleman like Mr Lockwood showed an interest in me. But now I am part of an eminent family, I feel I have to act for the family's benefit rather than just for my own.' Her voice tailed off.

'Lottie!' Leonora's voice was urgent. 'Just because you now know who your father was does not mean you must deny your own wishes and compromise your happiness. Don't try and please some imaginary arbiter of noble behaviour!'

Charlotte's eyes were bright with tears and she looked away. In a quiet voice she said, 'What of you, Leonora? I think you are in love?' She had been bold in saying such a thing and gave the older woman a shy glance.

'Perhaps I am, but it is of little consequence. Love needs to be returned for it to matter.'

'No, no! How can you say so? You of all people deserve happiness. You're as generous and beautiful as the sun. None of us could live without your warmth.'

'Oh, Lottie.' Leonora felt unexpectedly tearful herself. 'That means much to me, but I'm not certain anyone other than Nanny P and you would agree.'

Charlotte turned serious, her eyes sad in a pale face. 'If I should do anything that shocks you, I hope you'll know it's because I am only trying to do the right thing.'

Leonora wanted to ask her what she meant but as Charlotte turned her back and rolled onto her side, Leonora knew she did not wish to pursue the subject further. Bending over her, she kissed her cheek. 'Dearest, sleep well. And if there's any way I can help, please don't hesitate to ask. I love you as a sister and only want what's best for you.' She heard a small intake of breath, perhaps a sob, and Charlotte's hand sought hers amongst the folds of the coverlet.

* * *

Charlotte could not sleep. Her nerves were strung out with anxiety, not least about having to rise before dawn. She lay amongst her tumbled bedclothes counting the chimes as the clock in the hall struck the hours. She was not certain that what she intended to do was right, but she felt honour-bound to try and get that incriminating piece of paper from Captain Ormonde, at any cost to herself. Most distressing of all was the thought that she was deceiving Leonora. Charlotte had not even begun to consider the enormity of the change in her life if she actually had to marry Captain Ormonde in order to protect her father's reputation. It was a future she could not comprehend and would not consider. Instead, she tried to plan.

She had packed a minimum of clothes and was taking her whole allowance with her so she could pay for a carriage to bring her back to London once she had stolen and destroyed the evidence. Drawing back one curtain so she could watch the darkest hours of night recede, at last she saw the sky grow luminous beyond the trees and rooftops.

She dressed hurriedly, twisted her hair into a loose chignon and tied an everyday bonnet on her head. Her portmanteau was not heavy and she tiptoed down the staircase, careful to avoid the creaking floorboards. Barely able to see in the half-light, she reached the great hallway and slowly eased back the bolts on the front door. Birdsong and the fresh air of morning met her as she stepped into the street. Already the occasional cart was rumbling over the rutted road, horses' hooves clopped and delivery boys clattered down the front steps to the kitchen basements, carrying their deliveries of firewood and vegetables from the country.

Charlotte ran over the cobbles, feeling vulnerable in a world with neither companion nor chaperone beside her. *Honour the purpose*, she exhorted herself. Looking up, she saw the almost-full moon hanging low in the sky, her guide as she reached Grosvenor Square. Here the mansions of the rich still appeared to be slumbering, dark and shuttered as she sped on towards Audley Street, the great moon still lighting her way. Not wanting to draw attention to herself, she slowed her pace to a purposeful walk, keeping close to the railings, slipping in and out of the shadows.

Ahead of her was a dark coach, with a team of four horses, restive in their traces. A man in his long coat stood in the road, alert; Charlotte saw his teeth gleam and knew at once it was Captain Ormonde. They did not embrace. He had promised her he was a gentleman and would not importune her before they had married. Instead, he took her arm. 'Miss Blythe, I'm glad that you have come. You told no one?' She shook her head and he handed her into the carriage. They set off immediately at quite a pace.

Sitting on opposite seats, Charlotte glanced across at Guy Ormonde. His handsome face was brooding, his body tense. He seemed anxious as he glanced at his pocket watch and rapped on the roof to urge the coachman to go faster. For the first time Charlotte realised he was risking his career in the military and the heavy hand of civil law for abducting an underage woman.

This realisation gave Charlotte courage. Like her father, she was behind enemy lines to gain essential information. Valour was in her blood and she was determined to embody it. She sat across from Captain Ormonde and wondered where he had stowed the precious piece of paper. His redingote was double-breasted and tightly buttoned across his chest and he seemed disinclined to relinquish it. Beneath, she suspected his fine-tailored coat had many inside pockets, but he would only remove that when he went to bed at night. She noticed he was watching her with narrowed eyes. 'Are you regretting your decision?' he asked with a sly smile.

Charlotte was uncomfortable under such close scrutiny and turned to look out the window at Sadler's Wells Theatre, busy even at this early hour with cleaners bustling in with their pails and mops, as the horses toiled up the hill to The Angel Inn at Islington. 'No, I'm not regretting anything, apart from deceiving Miss Appleby.'

'Well, we have four days' travel before we arrive at the Borderlands, so I hope you allow yourself to relax more than this. We could play whist?'

'I have my book.' Charlotte withdrew the third volume of *The Heroine* from her reticule and made an attempt to look more settled by sitting in the corner by the window.

'I hope that novel's not putting ideas into your head.' He smirked. 'You know, I like you, Miss Blythe. And you're certainly pretty enough to love. I think you'll make an excellent wife, and I shall contrive to be a good husband to you in return.'

'How much that warms my heart to hear, Captain Ormonde,' she said with a hint of sarcasm. He flashed one of his charming smiles and Charlotte realised his anxiety had receded as they left London behind. He settled back in his seat and tipped his hat over his nose as if he intended to sleep. 'Oh, by the way, don't forget we are travelling as brother and sister. We'll change horses at Barnet; you can get out at the inn there and have a cup of hot chocolate and a bun, if you wish.'

* * *

It was seven in the morning and Leonora was still deeply asleep when she was roused from her dreams by an urgent rap on the door. 'Come in!' she called out in a drowsy voice.

Flora entered the room and even half-asleep, Leonora recognised she was distraught. 'Miss Leonora, my apologies for waking you but Miss Charlotte has gone!'

Leonora sprang upright, all lassitude fled. 'What do you mean, gone?'

'Her room's empty and her portmanteau and a few gowns and under-garments are missing, one of her bonnets too.' The maid stood before Leonora, her hands tightly clasped together, her voice hollow. 'I feared this would happen. I should have slept in her room and stopped her!'

Leonora was out of bed and grasped Flora's arms so that she had to meet her eyes. 'What did you fear would happen?'

'That she would listen to the blandishments of the Captain and run away with him to Scotland to get married.' Flora had tears in her eyes and was trying to hide her face. 'He seemed to put her under some duress. He showed her a piece of paper when we went to the museum.' She walked towards the window and busied herself with the curtains while her shoulders heaved.

Leonora's tumultuous feelings as to what to do next were quelled by a thought so obvious it reverberated in her brain like a clarion. 'Flora, you're Charlotte's mother, are you not?' Her words seemed to shock both women. For a moment time had stilled as Flora stood motionless. Slowly she turned, her face aged with grief. The answer was clear to Leonora. She realised the full poignancy of a young woman, really only a girl, forced to give her baby away, never to see her or contact her again. Leonora could only put out her arms and Flora crumpled into them. When she had stopped shaking with sobs, Leonora asked her, 'Does she know?'

'No. I'm afraid of her knowing.'

'But she'll be so happy to understand who her mother is after eighteen years of wondering. Do not be afraid.'

'Would you tell her, Miss Appleby? I would prefer that, if you could.' Leonora nodded. 'Did you marry, Flora? Has your life been good?'

She nodded. 'I'm married to a good man, Jack Lacey; he's a gardener for Lady Dundas.'

'I'm glad, as will be Charlotte.'

Reeling as she was with Flora's news, unable yet to think of the ramifications, Leonora was overcome with the urgency of saving Charlotte from her fate. 'I must get dressed immediately. We have to be discreet, and certainly cannot tell Lady Bucklebury of Charlotte's disappearance. But I will go to Grosvenor Square to Lord Rokeby who will know what to do. He's her uncle after all.'

Flora's ashen face turned even paler. 'Amy's back to her duties. Shall I ask her to accompany you? After breakfast I must return to Lady Dundas.'

'I'm glad Amy has recovered but we'll miss you, Flora, now more than ever. And I promise when the time's right, I'll tell Charlotte. But most urgent is to stop the scandal of her possible elopement. Can you ask Amy to meet me in the hall in ten minutes?'

Leonora dressed in yesterday's morning gown, quickly plaited her hair and coiled it under her bonnet. She had no time to waste. As she ran down the stairs carrying her shoes, the household was still quiet, except for the murmur of voices from the kitchen. Amy arrived looking pale and flustered. 'Good morning, Amy. I'm so glad you're better. We have to hurry, and to take care we keep this to ourselves.' She looked sternly at the maid's flushing face.

'Yes, Miss Appleby. Haven't said nowt to nobody.' Leonora nodded in approval as they slipped out the door into a different bustling world. She led Amy, threading their way through the delivery carts, and soon they were outside the Rokeby establishment in Grosvenor Square. The shutters were closed and it looked uncared for and unwelcoming. Leonora knew no gentleman could be visited before eleven in the morning, and even that was too early for most. This was the uncouth hour of half past seven when only working people were up, but fear and urgency gave Leonora the temerity to knock on the front door.

She was about to knock again when it swung open to reveal a diminutive housemaid who bobbed a curtsey. 'Could you tell your master Miss Appleby is here to see him? It's a matter of urgency.'

The girl looked doubtful. 'His lordship don't like to be disturbed, specially not this early.'

Leonora felt her chest tighten with anxiety; time was of the essence. 'This is a matter of life and death,' she said with some asperity. She was gratified to see the young girl's eyes widen as she indicated they could wait in the front morning room while she went in search of his lordship's valet. Leonora knew it took hours for most gentlemen to dress and half an hour would be just about sufficient for a slapdash presentation. She was amazed that within ten minutes, the door opened and Alistair Rokeby came into the room followed by Achille. Given that their last meeting had been fractious, Leonora was gratified to see him looking concerned, but also really quite pleased to see her. He was fully dressed, his snowy cravat tied to a passable standard and only his hair still damp and tousled, showing the speed of his dressing.

Leonora looked up, startled and immediately shy. She found his physical presence distracting. 'I didn't expect you so soon, my lord. Apologies for this early intrusion.'

'Turning oneself out in a matter of minutes is one of the advantages of my army training.' His smile was rueful then disappeared as he became business-like. 'You said a matter of life and death propelled you here, Miss Appleby. I'm glad to see you very much alive and well. To what emergency do I owe this unconscionably early wakening?'

'It's Charlotte. She's gone, early this morning. Her maid thinks

she may have been persuaded under some duress to elope with
Captain Ormonde.'

The effect of her words on him was electric. Colour flared into
his cheeks and he strode to the wall as if to punch it. He spoke
through gritted teeth. 'That devil-dog, Ormonde! He's a scape-
gallows who deserves nothing less than death. My poor little
Charlotte.' He slammed out of the room, calling for his groom and
valet. 'Saddle up my fast chaise! Pack my portmanteau for one
night. Ten minutes is all you have!'

When his lordship returned to the room, his dark hair was
standing up, his hands raking through it as if this might ease his
fury. He glanced at Amy, and Leonora knew in the heat of his
distress he was about to say something he did not want a servant
to hear, and so she asked Amy to wait for her in the hall. Lord
Rokeby stood against the fireplace. Almost to himself he said,
'Secrets are always better out. What damage they do.' He turned to
look at Leonora, his face anguished. 'This is my burden of guilt.
Charlotte is my child. For the first time in eighteen years I utter
these words which quite confound me. To protect me from our
father's wrath, my brother took responsibility for my indiscretion,
and he was sent away to war as punishment.'

Leonora felt physically rocked by this latest revelation and
sank back on her chair, but Lord Rokeby was so seized with
remorse he barely noticed, and continued in a rapid low voice,
'Charles rightfully should have stayed at the Abbey and
husbanded the estate. He was the heir and I the expendable one. I
was the wild and reckless son, and I should have paid the price.
But he stepped forward to protect me, as he always had. It was he
who went to the Peninsula instead of me. To be killed on foreign
soil.' His voice had dropped with the terrible weight of it. He cast
an intense look at Leonora. 'How can I live with this guilt and

grief? How can I usurp his destiny and live the life that should have been his?'

Leonora said softly, 'But you have been given by him the gift of a life.' He nodded. 'And Charlotte deserved the truth about her father.'

Alistair Rokeby sighed, 'I know, I've only just realised this now. Only now I'm overwhelmed with the realisation she is *my daughter*. When you live a lie for so long it becomes a kind of truth.'

'And what about her mother's maternal feelings too?'

He looked startled. 'Have you seen her?' When Leonora nodded, he asked, 'Is she well?'

'She is, but she is afraid to tell Charlotte and wants me to, when we find her.'

He shook his head in sorrow. 'We were all so young, she and I were but sixteen, and Charles and I swore to take the truth to our graves. Charlotte's mother agreed to it too. I'm afraid we did not think beyond safeguarding the child's happiness and welfare by placing her with the Reverend and his wife.'

'Well, she could not have been more loved, even while she longed to know something of her family.'

'I know. Now at last I can take up my role as Charlotte's father. But first I have to find her.' He leapt up and strode for the door, followed by Achille. He turned back. 'Miss Appleby, I am grateful to you for bringing your suspicions to me. It's a full moon tonight and I will take advantage of that. For find my daughter I must!'

As he saw Leonora and Amy to the door, his coachman and chaise drew up, harnessed to a team of four gleaming bays. Riding towards them was a large man on a very large horse. 'Mr Lockwood!' Leonora called out.

'Miss Appleby, good morning. Titan demands his exercise, but what are *you* doing out so early?'

Leonora knew that Lord Rokeby had returned to the house to collect his portmanteau. She took the reins of George Lockwood's horse, looked up into his face and said quietly, 'I'm afraid Charlotte left with Captain Ormonde, possibly under some duress, probably heading for the Scottish border.' She spoke quietly and with feeling.

Mr Lockwood's usually benign face turned thunderous. He jumped down from his horse and stood close to Leonora so he could speak without the whole Square hearing. His words burst out of him in a ferocious whisper. 'That scoundrel! I always knew he was a white-livered whipster, a sneaking hell-born rake. My darling Miss Blythe! I must rescue her. How many hours have they been gone?'

Lord Rokeby emerged from his house and greeted George Lockwood with a brusque tip of his hat. Lockwood immediately understood that at this early hour, with a fully harnessed team of four, the Earl would be in pursuit of his niece. 'Sir, I wish to help catch this hellhound. I think we could manage quite well together, you with the carriage to bring Miss Blythe home, while I with a fast horse can travel more quickly.'

Lord Rokeby frowned. He always preferred to act alone but after a few moments' thought, agreed it might be a good plan and make it possible they could catch up with them before dark. 'They have perhaps three hours' advantage on us but due to Ormonde's embarrassed finances, they are probably travelling by hired chaise, changing mere hacks at the posting inns.'

'My horse is strong and powerful with good stamina, but we'll both need to change horses for the journey.'

Lord Rokeby had already worked out their route. 'Ormonde is bound to take the quickest road, the Great North. I have my own horses stabled at Barnet, Hatfield, Baldock. I doubt they can get farther than Alconbury today, where I wager they'll spend the night. We have to catch them there.'

'By God, we will. I don't want that wonderful sweet being in his hands for even one night!' George Lockwood's voice was quivering with outrage and emotion.

Lord Rokeby sought to console him. 'I think Ormonde's treachery is vile enough with his activities during the war. But I hope, when it comes to well-born women, he remembers he is still a gentleman.'

'You have more faith than I, my lord. What dastardly man as he could resist the charms of Miss Blythe if she were in his power?'

Alistair Rokeby was impatient to begin the journey. 'We must go. I'll see you at The George in Barnet. There's a fine hunter there for you and a new team for me.' As he climbed into his chaise, Leonora noticed he had tucked a pistol into the waistband of his breeches. Exhausted, anxious, her nerves strung out, she was reminded of Lord Rokeby's competence and of how dangerous he could be, and a thrill ran through her veins.

11

THE WORK OF HEROES

As the journey wore on, Charlotte's confidence and courage began to seep away. The coach was nothing like as comfortable as the Rokeby one she and Leonora had used for their trip to London. It was cold and the jerky swaying on rusty springs made her queasy. As the light faded, there was little interest in gazing out on the passing countryside and market towns they travelled through. At the coaching inns where they stopped to change horses, there was some excitement in watching the variety of travellers as they bustled about their business, from the poorest country folk with sacks draped over their coats for warmth to the richest and most exquisitely dressed on their way between country estate and London town house.

She had even lost interest in her book. She closed it and it lay heavy in her lap. Captain Ormonde turned his head and watched her. 'It's not too long now before we stop for the night.' He shifted to face her. 'As I said, Miss Blythe, I will treat you in a gentlemanly manner; I trust you will behave like the lady you are and not draw attention to us or attempt to run away. After all, I can ruin both your reputation and your father's in one fell swoop.'

Before he revealed such implacable hostility towards the Earl of Rokeby and his good name, she had thought this brave soldier attractive, even rather distinguished. The idea of marrying him of her own free will had even occurred to her but he had since given up trying to charm her and no longer even gave her the benefit of his smile. Having made it obvious that he needed to marry an heiress to clear his debts and finance a profligate way of life, he offered now only his brooding narrow-eyed demeanour.

Out of the bleakest situations can come absolute clarity and as the twilight deepened, Charlotte was struck with a sudden revelation that altered everything: it was George Lockwood with his warmth and decency who was the heroic one. It was the height of virtue to be so truly himself, generous to others, protective, industrious and fond.

George Lockwood had the gift of constancy and his love would not change, regardless of what Captain Ormonde may demand of her, regardless of what she had to do. In that moment of recognition, Charlotte's heart turned over. How she longed to be enfolded in his arms, pressed against that broad chest, his deep voice laughing. Charlotte knew it was George Lockwood she wished to marry, whether she still had her fortune or not.

She turned back to face Captain Ormonde who was leaning forward, looking alert as the coach drew into the courtyard of The King's Head. This coaching inn was one of the largest and most comfortable of all the ones they had used on their journey north. It looked busy and prosperous, and Charlotte was so hungry and tired she really hoped they had beds for the night. This would be her chance. She was ushered in by Captain Ormonde, and played the part of his meek younger sister. They were shown into a small private parlour at the back of the building overlooking the stables. A welcome fire burned low in the grate. The Captain slung another log on the embers and kicked it into life with his boot, making the flames leap again.

A young countrywoman with cheeks chapped by the cold bustled in to take their orders. 'Mutton stew 'n tatties, all that's left,' she told them in a warm brogue, and soon they were eating a bowl of grey stew with a few crumbling mounds of boiled potatoes like atolls in a greasy sea. Charlotte thought it delicious and was grateful for the accompanying bread to mop up the last of the gravy.

'I like a woman with a healthy appetite,' Captain Ormonde drawled, his voice with an edge of his old seductive humour. Charlotte was counting how many tumblers of ale he drank; he showed no signs of intoxication, but she hoped he would sleep more heavily that night. As the evening wore on, she encouraged him to drink more as she engaged him in desultory conversation, discussing the sights they had seen on the journey and even sharing a laugh. The young blades in their racing curricles, so arrogant and reckless; the farmer whose bristly pig sat up beside him on the seat as he drove his cart home; the mail coach lurched into a ditch, its axle broken and passengers in disarray, their luggage strewn over the road.

Charlotte and Captain Ormonde eventually collected their candles and the young serving woman showed them to two rooms on either side of the landing in the main building. 'Goodnight, Miss Blythe. I hope you sleep well. We have another long day ahead of us.' The Captain bowed and closed his door. Charlotte was desperate for sleep but knew she had to keep awake in order to follow through with her plan. She took the one seat in the room, a hard wooden chair, uncomfortable and cold, and waited. It was past midnight when she removed her shoes and opened the door with utmost care. There were still drinkers in the public bar downstairs, but their voices were muted as she tiptoed across the landing and listened at the Captain's door. She thought she could hear regular heavy breathing.

Her heart in her mouth, Charlotte turned the knob and eased the door open an inch or two. Moonlight flooded the room. On the bed was the prone figure of a sleeping man still in his shirt and breeches but minus his redingote and coat which had been discarded over a chair. She walked with careful step towards them, pausing to check on the sleeping Captain. Slipping her hand into the first pocket in the redingote, then the second and finding nothing, she moved to the fine-tailored superfine coat he wore by day. Charlotte was just about to investigate the first inner pocket when she felt an iron hand grip her wrist. She was so shocked she did not even cry out. Ormonde had sprung from the bed and reached her in one leap. He hissed in her ear, 'Miss Blythe, you really don't think I'm foolish enough to leave such valuable material lying around for just anyone to purloin?' His grip tightened. 'I warned you, if you're intent on double-crossing me, I'll have no compunction in treating you in the most ungentlemanly manner.'

Once again, Charlotte was shocked by his strength and speed, for in one movement he had picked her up and tossed her on the bed. He gripped both her hands as the moonlight gleamed off his face and fell on hers.

She found her voice at last. 'Captain, you're hurting my wrists.' Her heart was pounding as she realised the full extent of her foolishness in thinking she could outwit him when he held every trump, including physical strength.

His body crushed hers as his eyes glittered dangerously. 'You know, Miss Blythe, you have forfeited all respect due to a lady and I no longer have any reason for restraint in my behaviour.' He looked at her, a wolfish smile on his face. 'I quite like the idea of kissing my bride-to-be. What think you?'

Charlotte had been trying to wriggle from under him, but the pressure of his body and the soft lumpy bed trapped her. His breath was on her face, stinking of stew and ale. As he moved his lips towards hers, she twisted suddenly and his kiss landed hard on her cheek. He smelt of sweat and she recoiled, fearful of how powerless she was in a situation to which she had so thoughtlessly agreed. Her resistance and fear seemed to excite him. He muttered, 'Now, Miss Blythe, I'll show you the bargain I'm offering in return for your fortune.' He laughed as his fingers began to ruffle up her skirts.

'No, Captain! Remember your reputation as an officer!' Her voice was hard-edged with panic.

He purred in her ear, 'Ah, but I am no longer a gentleman, my dear.' His fingers had strayed beyond her stocking and had reached her thigh.

Charlotte heard a creak of the floorboard outside the door. She tensed, listening. Captain Ormonde arose from the bed with stealth, suddenly sobered up and as alert as a fox.

* * *

For Lord Rokeby and George Lockwood, the flight north had not been straightforward. Such was George's distress at Charlotte's ordeal, he kept on seeing her in every pretty fair-haired woman along the way. He had just met up with Rokeby at The Queen's Head at Hatfield, where they were due to change horses, when both of them caught sight of a young woman bundled into a carriage and driven away at speed. George was certain it was his beloved in need of immediate rescue. He remounted his tired horse to make chase. After about a mile, the road had cleared enough for him to draw his horse along-side and demand the coachman pull up his horses. He was met by a furious gentleman in a cocked hat and his companion's shocked and angry pair of eyes, brown and sparkling but not Charlotte's.

Apologising profusely, he bowed and wheeled his horse to return to Hatfield, both weary to the bone. The fine hunter he rode was one of Rokeby's best, but fatigue had made them both inattentive and as they approached The Queen's Head for the second time, the horse stumbled and fell to one knee, immediately going lame. George Lockwood walked the last half a mile, leading his limping horse. From then on, the two men travelled together in the Rokeby chaise. As twilight set in, their spirits flagged.

By the time it was fully night, George Lockwood and Lord Rokeby were five miles from Alconbury where they had surmised Ormonde and Charlotte would have to stop for the night. Rather than have to find a roadside tavern to shelter them until dawn, the full moon became the traveller's friend, lighting their way farther along the high road to their goal. Anticipation that the end of their mission was in reach revived George Lockwood's spirits. From a relaxed, easy-going man he had become a knight of legend in his chivalric determination to protect the woman he loved.

This crisis had focussed and crystallised everyone's feelings in the most dramatic fashion. Charlotte discovered her love for George Lockwood; Lord Rokeby, his paternal affections at last and George Lockwood, beguiled for a while by Lady Livia Dearlove's siren-like attraction, had never lost his susceptibility to Charlotte's beauty and down-to-earth allure. Unlike Lady Livia, Charlotte was quite capable of helping birth a lamb, saddle a horse or bake an apple and blackberry pie. Now there was this chance that a blackguardly officer could snatch her from him, his blood surged in his veins. He had been brought up to think he was a failure in his aspirations to be a dandy about Town, as suave as his stepfather, but now for the first time he realised that given a cause, he was born to be a hero and would fulfil this to the hilt.

The coming of night made Charlotte's plight more distressing to him. Sitting opposite Lord Rokeby, he slammed his hand into the window prop of the chaise and said through gritted teeth, 'By Jove, it's outrageous that cur is making Miss Blythe suffer! I'm not a violent man, Rokeby, but I swear I'll plant a facer on his handsome phiz!'

'I've brought my pistol in case he needs a bit more persuasion. I haven't told anyone, but I think it's possibly relevant to the situation; my brother and I were certain he was operating as a spy for Boney's commanders in the Peninsula.' His face was grim. 'As you know, there is no greater treachery. I don't know what, if anything, he has as a hold over Charlotte, but we will find out.' Lord Rokeby's face darkened further. 'If he has compromised her virtue, I swear I'll kill him.'

The thought was unimaginable, but George Lockwood needed to clarify the matter and asked, 'We do know she has gone under duress?'

'Her maid who accompanied her to her meeting with him at the museum was certain that a piece of paper he showed her caused her much distress. This is all we know. Then the next morning, she was gone.'

'For me, nothing can compromise her virtue, it is unimpeachable; she will never be spoiled in my eyes.' George Lockwood seemed so choked with emotion, his lordship looked at him with concern.

'Are you in love with the girl?'

'Of course I am. Who wouldn't be? I loved her from the moment I first saw her at the Manor. But we know such instant affections are impossible, so I denied it and found distractions elsewhere. But it was always her, and only now has it become so damnably clear, and I such a damned fool!'

Alistair Rokeby watched with a strange smile on his lips as his

companion's face registered every emotion from outrage to astonishment and then a fiery passion. He said as if speaking to himself,
'We men are fools when it comes to love.'

As the chaise approached their destination, George Lockwood
was impatient. He had never been surer of anything in his life. He
met Lord Rokeby's questioning gaze. 'Rokeby, as her uncle and
guardian, may I have your permission to ask Miss Blythe to
marry me?'

In a quiet voice, the Earl replied, 'She's not my niece but my
daughter.'

George could not hide his astonishment. 'No! Does she know?'
His first thought had been how the shock of such news would
affect Charlotte.

'Not yet. It was a politic switch of identities with my brother
that happened at her birth, but I should have told her the moment
I returned from France. I deserve every kind of censure for not
doing so.' Alistair Rokeby looked pensive and then addressed
George's request. 'Have you the means to support a wife and
children?'

'Yes, indeed. I have my father's estate in Oxfordshire and his
investments, raising an income of just under ten thousand a year,
and I'm moving to Hasterleigh Manor. That estate has rents of
about five thousand a year. I am very happy to live in the village
and if Miss Blythe should agree to marry me, she will be in close
proximity to you and the Abbey, and to Miss Appleby, of course.'

'Ah, Miss Appleby. What does she feel about having to move
from her childhood home?'

'She has been more than gracious in what seems a fundamen-
tally unfair arrangement.'

'It is what I would expect. I've come to realise what a remarkable woman she is.' Lord Rokeby spoke with a catch of emotion in
his voice.

George Lockwood nodded and said, 'Loved and esteemed in the village, too, so I'm pleased she will not move away but live in the Lodge on the Manor estate. I'll make sure the house is water-tight and warm.'

It was close to one o'clock in the morning as the Rokeby chaise rumbled into the courtyard behind The King's Head tavern. The moonlight was unusually bright, casting mysterious shadows and illuminating the old thatched roof with a silvery sheen that made the ancient building appear otherworldly. Despite the romance of moonlight, the inn was unmistakeably rooted in the real world. George Lockwood led the way to the bar where they were assaulted with the stench of sweat and cheap alcohol and the sight of bleary-eyed sots, some passed out on the settle by the fire. The owner behind the bar looked up, startled; travellers on legitimate business were not expected in the dead of night.

Lord Rokeby strode forward. 'Good evening, sir. A word in private.' His voice was quiet, but it was an order rather than a request. They were led into the same small room where Captain Ormonde and Charlotte had had their meal four hours before. 'I'm Lord Rokeby and my underage daughter has been abducted by a Captain Ormonde; I think they may be here?'

His manner brooked no opposition and the innkeeper blustered, 'Don't blame me, m'lord. 'E said she was 'is sister!' He seemed quite outraged at being so deceived.

'They all say that,' was Lord Rokeby's dry reply. 'Please show me to their rooms?'

The innkeeper at the bottom of the stairs indicated with his hands. 'Gentleman on the left, lady on the right.' Before he had finished speaking, George Lockwood had bounded up the stairs, two at a time, surprisingly light on his feet for such a big man. He knocked on Charlotte's door and when there was no answer, opened it to find the bed empty. Fear and rage swept over him and he turned to barge through the door opposite. There he found a startled Ormonde, standing at the foot of the bed, his shirt untucked, and Charlotte scrambling to her feet, smoothing down her skirts. With a sob she flew into his arms. 'You found me! Thank you, Mr Lockwood.' Her ecstatic face noticed Lord Rokeby who had followed George into the room. 'And you too, my lord. How pleased I am to see you!'

Charlotte turned back to George Lockwood who had been in the saddle most of the day and was exhausted and dusty from the road. She was in disarray and tear-stained, yet they gazed into each other's faces as if they had awoken from a half-sleep and were seeing each other and the world for the first time.

George folded her against his chest, his expression distorted by rage and anguish. 'What has this blackguard done to you?'

'Nothing, Mr Lockwood.'

Captain Ormonde's languid voice cut through the fevered emotion. 'You have rudely interrupted a very pleasant evening with my wife-to-be.'

Charlotte gasped and disentangling herself from his arms, attempted to drag George Lockwood away as he expostulated, 'Despicable cur! How *dare* you!'

Captain Ormonde had recovered his sangfroid and sneered, 'I think you'll find the young lady came with me of her own accord.' Before he finished speaking, a punishing left hook as fast as a serpent's tongue sprang from George Lockwood's forearm and landed in the middle of his smile. The Captain reeled backwards, almost losing his footing.

'How dare you impugn Miss Blythe's honour, you, a man without honour!'

Charlotte rushed forward to take George Lockwood's arm. 'I did go with him of my own volition. He threatened to ruin my father's, my whole family's reputation if I didn't. I thought I could retrieve and destroy the piece of incriminating evidence before we got to Scotland.'

Lord Rokeby stepped forward and in a voice as cold as ice, said, 'Ormonde. Show me this evidence.'

'I will not, my lord.' Captain Ormonde was holding his handkerchief to his nose.

George Lockwood had stripped off his jacket and rolled up his shirtsleeves as if prepared for a fight. The drunken customers downstairs, roused by the commotion, had staggered to the foot of the stairs but the innkeeper barred the way.

Lord Rokeby asked the Captain again, his face distorted by anger and made more intimidating by the contraction of his scar with tension and fatigue. His voice was full of contempt for the man he believed was a traitor to his country, outraged that he should cast such calumny onto his own brother. With some menace, he repeated, 'Show me the evidence that you swore to Miss Blythe would ruin my family's reputation.'

Captain Ormonde drawled, 'I may be a blackguard but I'm not a fool.'

Lord Rokeby whipped the pistol from his waistband and pointed it straight at the Captain's chest. 'I don't think you fool enough to ignore this. I know you as a traitor and will use it if I must.'

Charlotte gasped, 'No!'

Captain Ormonde's face was ashen as he put up his hands in apparent defeat. He turned to his coat and in a split second withdrew not a piece of paper but a duelling pistol. He swung round to face Lord Rokeby but the Earl was faster: he discharged his bullet and it knocked the Captain's gun from his hand before thudding into the wall behind him.

George Lockwood picked up the duelling pistol and removed the shot. Lord Rokeby slipped his weapon back into his pocket.

'I've shown you great indulgence. Now you reveal your evidence or I'll search your effects myself.' Captain Ormonde was beaten at last. He walked to his portmanteau, followed closely by Lord Rokeby, and rummaged through his clothes to reach the leather flap at the bottom, which he lifted to extract a piece of paper. The Earl called over his shoulder for another candle and George Lockwood left Charlotte's side to bring a second flame closer. Rokeby read and then looked up, his face cold with disdain. 'This is a receipt for *your* services to the enemy! It is dastardly to use this lie to coerce Miss Blythe to marry you. I presume so you could claim her fortune?'

Charlotte ran forward to take the paper and read it for herself. Close to tears, she looked from Lord Rokeby to George Lockwood and blurted out, 'What a fool I've been. To put all of you in danger for this! I thought I was saving my father's and his family's name and all I did was shame myself!' She hung her head.

Alistair Rokeby lifted her chin and looked into her tired face, her hair awry, her clothes crumpled and dusty, and he saw her for the first time too. She was so full of impetuous life, so willing to embark on a journey into the unknown when she felt it might bring justice, she was so brave and true. Her fair beauty was not his, but she shared his dark eyes, and he recognised her spirit and courage. His face softened as he folded the paper then placed it in his inside pocket. 'It is you who have been wronged, Miss Blythe, but I think it better I keep this to ensure Captain Ormonde's future behaviour.'

Lord Rokeby turned to the Captain and said with a look of contempt, 'I will not hesitate to use this receipt against you should you ever attempt to compromise my family's honour again. I suggest you emigrate. To the Americas.' Then realising how late it was, he added, 'We all need some sleep before returning to London. Mr Lockwood and I will take your room and you can find a suitable crib in the hay above the horses. Where the coachmen sleep.'

Captain Ormonde quickly picked up his portmanteau and his clothes and as he left, he took Charlotte's hand with a sly smile. 'I apologise for any distress I may have caused you. I must say that it would have been no hardship to be married to you, Miss Blythe. It was not just your fortune that I found attractive. I like a fighting wench!' George Lockwood took a step forward, his fist clenched, but Charlotte held him back. With a ghost of his dashing smile, Captain Ormonde clicked his heels together, saluted her and the two men, and descended the stairs two at a time to head for the stables.

Lord Rokeby said in a voice that was suddenly weary, 'Well, young lady, are you really unhurt? Are your spirits restored?' Charlotte nodded, wrapped in George Lockwood's arms. 'We've all had enough excitement for the night. We will take you home tomorrow in my fast chaise, a much more comfortable conveyance than the bone-shaker you travelled up in.' There was a note of smug pride in his voice. 'Lockwood, you'll travel with us?'

'Thank you, my lord. Until the last stage when I'll collect Titan. He will have had enough of a rest by then.'

'Sleep well, my dear. We have much to discuss on the morrow.' Lord Rokeby squeezed Charlotte's hand with the force of unspoken feeling.

George escorted her across the landing back to her room. He stood on the threshold, both her hands in his. She was gazing into his face, her heart in her eyes. 'Something has changed for ever,' she said in a soft voice, her face gleaming in the moonlight that filled her room with silver. 'I no longer feel so alone knowing you are in the world with me.'

He squeezed her hands between his large warm palms and brought them to his lips to hold there, his blue eyes serious and full of emotion as he met hers. 'My wasted youth is over. But every lonely year has led me closer to you.'

Charlotte took his left hand and kissed his bruised knuckles. 'You are the rarest of spirits, so upright and honourable, as a knight of old.' She longed to be kissed by him but knew he would not take that liberty, not yet, but the longing in his eyes was worth a hundred kisses.

'I need to talk to you, Miss Blythe. May I come by tomorrow evening, when you are home? If that is to your liking.'

'Oh yes, please do, Mr Lockwood.' Her heart was fluttering like a bird.

The intensity of their communion was broken by Lord Rokeby's voice. 'We all must to bed. We're leaving early on the morrow.' George Lockwood and Charlotte broke apart and quietly closed the doors on their separate rooms.

* * *

Leonora and Amy had walked back to Bucklebury House, Leonora's head teeming with thoughts she could not control. They entered the great hallway. Amy had set off for the kitchen with Leonora's exhortation for the necessity of discretion ringing in her ears as Leonora looked up to see Mrs Priddy descending the stairs, her knitting bag in her hands. 'Nora my dear! Where have you been? Where is Charlotte? I've been most concerned.'

Leonora took her arm, steered her into the sitting room at the front and closed the door. 'I don't think you will believe the turn in events. I barely can, and I've had hours to get used to the shocks.'

'Well, don't leave me on tenterhooks. What is it?' Mrs Priddy settled herself on the sofa by the window and patted the seat beside her.

Leonora took a deep breath and said, 'Charlotte's eloped with

Captain Ormonde, under duress we believe. Flora woke me this morning alarmed because she found her young mistress long gone, with a packed portmanteau. Flora thought that Ormonde had some hold over her and was insisting she marry him.'

'You mean she's headed to Scotland?' For the first time, Mrs Priddy seemed concerned. 'Now this is foolish! That's shockingly dishonourable behaviour on the part of the Captain. I never trusted that smile!'

'I immediately went to Berkeley Square to tell Lord Rokeby and he and Mr Lockwood have set out in pursuit.'

Nanny P relaxed. 'Such an early start must have been a rude awakening for Master Alistair. But with him and that young giant in the rescue party, I'm sure Charlotte will soon be home.'

'But Nanny P, this is serious! The Earl took his pistol!' Leonora was haunted by the thought that there would be violence and Lord Rokeby killed or forced into exile.

Mrs Priddy was untroubled. She tutted. 'Don't concern yourself, Nora dear. Men can be cork-brained and think with their fists. Master Alistair was as wild and foolish as they come, but he is older now, and wiser. It will be fine.'

'Well, that was my early morning shock, closely followed by my second.' She looked into Mrs Priddy's face, still barely understanding the full import of everything she had learned in these few hours. 'Flora Lacey, Lady Dundas's maid who came to help when Amy was ill – she's Charlotte's mother! She was the maid at Rokeby Abbey when the Rokeby brothers were running wild.'

Mrs Priddy put down her knitting. 'Well, who'd have thought it? I am surprised by that. I saw her occasionally. She wasn't at the Abbey long but she seemed such a sensible, quiet girl. I always thought it would most likely be one of the laxer girls, of whom there were many!'

'I've been charged with telling Charlotte, when she returns.'

'I don't think it will be too much of a surprise to her.'

'Why do you say that?' Leonora gave Nanny P a quizzical look.

'She knew her mother was a maid, so that's no revelation. And she seemed to get on unusually well with Flora who's a most attractive woman and seems to have lived a blameless life since that early indiscretion. It could be so much worse.'

'There's one final revelation.' Leonora could barely believe her own words, but she had to share the momentous news with her old nanny, so closely involved as she was with everyone. 'Lord Rokeby told me this morning that it is he, not Charles, who is Charlotte's father!'

Nanny P looked unsurprised. 'I've always wondered, and now it makes sense. Charles protected his younger brother, come what may. But poor Alistair, what guilt he must live with over his brother's death.'

Leonora had her head in her hands as she said, 'It's such a cauldron of emotion, of guilt and loss, of grief, hope and desire.'

Mrs Priddy put a hand on her shoulder. 'This is what it is to fully live, dear Nora. You cannot protect yourself from feeling.'

'Can I confide something to you that fills me with such a feeling of fear?'

Mrs Priddy turned a concerned face to her young companion. 'Of course!'

'I can barely allow myself to articulate it out loud...' She paused. 'The thing is, I actually *know* I love Lord Rokeby. And I think he might have some affection for me.'

Mrs Priddy put her small soft hand on Leonora's. 'I know.' Leonora looked at her, startled. 'To someone who understands and loves you as I do, it's been as clear as day since you first met him.'

Leonora's hands flew to her face, her cheeks flaming. 'Oh, no! It cannot have been so obvious. How mortifying! Does he know?'

Mrs Priddy scoffed, 'Of course not! Men are blind, deaf and dumb when it comes to knowing a woman's heart! He's probably worrying that you cannot care for him, that you recoil from his looks.'

'But might he have lost any regard he once had? I have behaved so badly.' Leonora was fearful of entertaining any hope after disappointing him with her own ugly suspicions and jealousy.

'I've known that boy from when he was a baby in skirts. I think he certainly holds you in highest regard. He's been a soldier and not much used to female company and is probably shy too, about his disfigurement. But more than anything he's loyal and does not readily change his mind.'

Leonora sighed and put her head on Mrs Priddy's shoulder.

'Oh, Nanny P, how I long to go home.'

* * *

After an early breakfast, Lord Rokeby checked that Captain Ormonde had already departed before all three climbed into the Rokeby chaise. As they settled in their seats he said, 'This is most irregular that you are not chaperoned, Miss Blythe, but at least I am a close member of your family, which should be protection enough from Society's censure.' For propriety's sake, the men sat together and Charlotte opposite them, still weary from the previous day's alarms. She was vividly aware of them both but only the most desultory conversation passed between them, so tired were they all, so momentous the things that were in their hearts.

George Lockwood disembarked at the last change of horses at Barnet to reclaim Titan and ride him down the Great North Road back into London. Lord Rokeby and Charlotte at last were alone.

As the chaise swung back onto the highway, he crossed to sit beside her. She looked at him, his face pale and drawn, the scar prominent, but she now saw it as an honourable mark of his virtue and valour. He took her hand and said in a low voice. 'Miss Blythe – Charlotte – I have something to tell you and I can only apologise for not doing so sooner, when I first returned from France.'

Charlotte's heart started pounding in her breast. She had had enough emotional reversals already; what shock was about to be delivered now? 'Yes, my lord?' she said, trying to sound unconcerned.

'When you were born, your mother and father were very young and did not know what to do for the best.'

'Being given to Mama Mildmay and the Reverend to be cared for *was* the best. I could not have been more loved.'

'I'm very grateful that that was the case. But my brother Charles and I also made a pact that we swore to keep until death. To protect me from our father's wrath, Charles said he would claim that you were his.'

His face was anguished, and Charlotte's eyes widened as the full import of his words settled into her consciousness. 'You mean that *you* are my father?'

'I am.'

'You're not dead?' Her voice was full of wonder.

'I don't think so,' he said with a rueful expression.

'So I have a real father, someone I can get to know and love?'

He nodded as she threw herself into his arms with a cry. 'I cannot believe that my father has been restored to me. That he is real!' She held him tight against her as if to reassure herself of his bodily presence.

Lord Rokeby was so prepared for hysterics, blame and rejection that he was completely taken aback at her uncomplicated joy at having a real flesh and blood father at last. After initial hesitancy, he hugged her as forcefully as she did him, and they were locked in each other's embrace for a few minutes as the chaise passed on through Highgate and down the hill to Hampstead village. When he extracted himself from her grasp, Alistair Rokeby said, 'Is there anything you need to ask me?'

'There's so much I need to know, but just now I want to sit beside you and let the thought sink in that I am not an orphan.'

'You are definitely not orphaned.'

'I can't wait to tell Leonora my news. I have a father and he is you!' She grasped his hand, the damaged right one, and held it in hers.

'Miss Appleby gave you a mooring in your life, did she not?' Lord Rokeby asked with an anxious frown.

'She is as close as a sister and was always there. I couldn't bear it if she moved away.'

Lord Rokeby's voice surprised her with its urgency. 'That's not likely, surely?'

'If she married, she would move to her husband's property.'

His face looked pained as he took her arm and asked, 'Is there anyone she has in mind?'

Charlotte looked at him, surprised he was so perturbed. Her heart leapt; could it be that he did harbour affections for Leonora after all? That her love would be returned? The conversation was cut short by their arrival at Lady Bucklebury's mansion in Brook Street.

The Earl handed Charlotte out of the chaise and said, 'I know that Miss Appleby has been careful not to alert my grandmother to your escapade, but you've been away for too long. I'll come in with you. Our story is close to the truth, that Ormonde tricked you into accompanying him out of Town and I and Mr Lockwood brought you back.' It was late in the afternoon and they were ushered into the drawing room, both looking travel-worn.

Lady Bucklebury was in her favourite chair by the fire, still working on her tapestry frame, and had reached the eagle's talon. Leonora was reading and Mrs Priddy's knitting needles were flashing. Leonora leapt up as Charlotte entered first. She dashed to her side and embraced her in a fierce hug, then released her, remembering Lady Bucklebury did not know how close she had been to being embroiled in scandal.

Lord Rokeby took charge of the situation and walked forward, tiredness making his limp more pronounced; he gave a quick bow to his grandmother and then kissed her cheek. 'Alistair,' she greeted him with a piercing look, 'where have you and Charlotte been? You both look shockingly disreputable!'

Charlotte stepped forward, feeling this delicate situation needed some word from her. She took Lady Bucklebury's thin arthritic hand and kissed it. 'Grandmama, it's entirely my fault. I was tricked by Captain Ormonde into travelling out of Town with him, but luckily my lord and Mr Lockwood followed and brought me home.'

'Silly gal! You have to learn that Town bucks cannot be trusted!' She seemed to be unbothered by this potential scandal and was distracted by pain. 'Could you help me to my feet, my dear. I feel in need of rest.' Charlotte and Mrs Priddy came forward to attend to her; Alistair Rokeby offered his hand to Leonora and walked her to a distant window overlooking the Square.

She looked into his tired face. His scar was all the more noticeable against the pallor of his skin and she had a sudden longing to trace it with her finger and kiss the slight pucker where it reached his lip. How outrageous this was! she remonstrated to herself.

A frown drew his black brows together. 'Miss Appleby, as you are Charlotte's closest friend, I wanted to tell you that I have made her aware that I am her father. I cannot bear to have you think any worse of me than you already do.'

'You have brought Charlotte back, avoiding scandal and the ruination of her name. For this, anyone who loves her will be eternally grateful.'

The shock of the revelation the previous morning had faded, and Leonora instead was overwhelmed with sympathy for both the brothers and poor Flora, all so young and faced with such censure and fear. 'How did she take the news?'

'She seemed rather pleased to have a live father rather than a dead one.' He managed a smile. 'It quite surprised me. But then the eruption of my fatherly feeling for her has surprised me too.'

Leonora realised that everyone else had left the room and they were alone. 'Perhaps we should go?' She looked up into his face, beloved to her in its damaged asymmetry.

His scar and eye patch were in shadow and his good eye, so dark and full of life, glittered as he met her gaze. 'Miss Appleby, I return to Rokeby Abbey tomorrow.' The strain drained from his expression as he said with some amusement, 'Hasterleigh is not the same without you, you know. My piano-forte is declining into anarchy and its master is more in disarray than usual.' In a spontaneous movement, he grasped her hand and held it to his cheek.

Leonora shivered, her pulse quickening. How different he was from any man she had known; how different from her boyish William Worth whose death had taken her youth with him. Now Alistair Rokeby had reunited her with that hopeful self, and she felt it flare up again like a flame that had survived the storm. She took a deep breath and smiled. 'I have been longing to go home. I very much need to swim and restore the rhythm of my life.'

He looked down at her with his crooked smile. 'It's still too cold to swim. My lake won't have begun to warm up yet.'

'I think I must be a Viking; I can bear the cold quite well.'

He let out a bark of laughter. 'Even if that is true, dear Miss Appleby, you are not to go swimming alone. You promised me that. And I doubt your fabled forebears ever *chose* to swim; their skill was to navigate and travel at speed across the mighty North Sea rather than to plunge into its unforgiving depths.' Lord Rokeby was laughing as he offered his arm and escorted her out of the room. 'Farewell then, my intrepid mermaid. I shall look forward to your return.' He crossed the landing to his grandmother's rooms to take his leave, and after a few minutes bounded down the stairs with unexpected grace, collected his hat and coat, climbed back into his chaise and was gone, leaving Leonora's world strangely bereft.

Charlotte and Mrs Priddy had been sitting talking in the small room beside the kitchen, warmed by the big kitchen range. At the sound of the front door closing, Charlotte called, 'Leonora! Come quickly.' When Leonora entered the room, she was confronted by a radiant Charlotte, her cheeks flushed, her brown eyes sparkling, and although her clothes looked the worse for two days' wear, she showed no sign of the adventures, assaults and revelations of the previous two days.

Charlotte pulled her into the room and closed the door. 'I am in love with George Lockwood, and he is with me! He rescued me from Captain Ormonde by boxing him hard on the nose. I've never seen him so angry, and on my behalf!' Her voice sounded quite thrilled by being the focus of a man's protective violence.

'Well, you couldn't choose a better man to fall in love with, Lottie.'

'That's just what Nanny P said.'

Leonora looked across at her old nanny who was nodding with a knowing smile on her face. 'Charlotte, tell Nanny P your other piece of news.'

'Yes! Almost as exciting is the fact that my papa is not a dead hero but a live one! He is in fact Lord Rokeby, not his brother, and I am so happy to have a father I can know. Such a heroic one too.

You should have seen how brave he and Mr Lockwood were with Captain Ormonde who had brought his own pistol!'

Leonora took her hand and said, 'I'm very glad you feel so blessed. Lord Rokeby is indeed a fine father to have.'

Mrs Priddy had picked up her knitting again and said quietly, 'I'd always thought your father was more likely to be Master Alistair. You have his impetuous nature too, my dear. Charles at heart was quite a sobersides.'

Leonora wondered if the time was right to impart to her friend the next astonishing fact about her parentage. She could not justify keeping it from her any longer. She took Charlotte's hand and drew her to the seat between Mrs Priddy and herself. 'My dear, I have another piece of information for you which I hope will please you equally. You know Flora Lacey?' She paused.

Charlotte's eyes widened. 'Flora is my mother, isn't she?' When Leonora nodded, Charlotte dropped her eyes, her hands clasped tightly in her lap. She didn't speak, although Leonora could see her cheeks grow pink with emotion. Leonora looked with concern at Nanny P who just smiled and nodded.

After what seemed an age, Leonora laid her hand on Charlotte's. 'Is this a great shock to you?' she asked in a quiet voice.

Charlotte looked up, tears in her eyes. 'No. It is consoling. I felt such a connection with Flora. When she was brushing my hair with tenderness, and when she dressed me, it was with such care.' She sobbed and leant across to embrace Leonora and with her voice muffled, she said, 'Then when she met my eyes in the looking glass there was a recognition of something, I knew not what.' She straightened up and looked from Mrs Priddy to Leonora.

Leonora said, 'When she found your bed empty two mornings ago she was so distraught I immediately thought, *she is Charlotte's mother*, and she confirmed it but asked me to be the one to tell you. I think she was afraid of your reaction.'

Charlotte's face was full of concern. 'But I am so pleased. She is familiar to me. How could I wish for a better mother? I have Mama Mildmay and I now have Flora Lacey.' Her face broke into a smile and she reached to take Mrs Priddy's hand and Leonora's. 'Has she been happy, do you know?'

'She says she's married to a good man, a gardener. You must see her and ask her yourself.'

Charlotte appeared overflowing with feeling. 'Perhaps they will come and live with me and George when we marry? He has so many planting schemes.'

Leonora laughed with delight. 'Has he asked you yet?'

'No, but he will. I know he will. And I will say yes!' Charlotte was ecstatic. 'I feel the sun, moon and the stars have all aligned to pour their benison down on me. How could I be any happier?' They hauled Nanny P to her feet so that they could all embrace, laughing with the joy of it. 'And I'm going to go to Beau Beacham's party with him as his betrothed!'

Leonora smiled. 'Mr Lockwood inadvertently has pleased his exacting stepfather, no doubt, by winning the hand of an heiress.'

Charlotte was suddenly serious. 'Do you think my mother would mind living in the same village as Lord Rokeby?'

'It was a different century and they were different people, children playing at life and getting burnt. I don't think it will matter to either of them, especially as she seems happy with Mr Lacey.' Leonora swung Charlotte around. 'Oh, what pleasure this gives me! Lottie, you have found your perfect match and we can all go home! I'm longing for home, as a wave longs for the shore.'

Charlotte giggled, 'And as Mr Lockwood longs for Hasterleigh too. He hates Town life and has only endured it until he found someone to love.' She twirled with joy at knowing that the someone he loved was her. 'How strange, though. We travel all the way to London only to discover that everything we need for happiness is to be found at home.' She hugged Leonora. 'You made all the difference in my passage from green country girl to someone happy to be married, able to run my own household and take my place in Society.' Tears had filled her eyes with the thought of how much richer her life had become with a father and mother alongside the love of the Mildmays. 'And do you really mean it when you say that you've always wanted it to be me to take your place at the Manor? Your family home?'

'Of course, you goose. Who could be better? And I can come and plague you every day, as all your life you've done to me!'

Charlotte looked from Leonora to Mrs Priddy and said, 'You don't need to stay any longer. If you and Nanny P want to leave, I'll travel down with Mr Lockwood once we are betrothed.'

They looked up to see Lady Bucklebury at the door, leaning heavily on her stick and supported by her maid. Leonora and Charlotte jumped up. Leonora came forward. 'Lady Bucklebury, we thought you were resting. Which is the most comfortable chair for you?'

'That higher one by the fire will do well.' Her bird-like frame looked frail as she hobbled across the room.

'I'm sorry Grandmama, if we had known you were no longer resting, we could have joined you in the drawing room and saved you the stairs.' Charlotte looked concerned.

'Oh, don't worry yourself, my dear. It's quite good for me to try the stairs occasionally. I've come to let you know, Charlotte, that Alistair has told me everything. What a naughty boy he was! But I'm glad he has become steadier with age and experience. Are you happy to have him as a father?'

Lady Bucklebury had always been forthright, and Charlotte

flew to her side and knelt so their heads were on the same level. 'I am very happy to have Lord Rokeby as my father. I'm particularly pleased that my father is alive. I felt cheated by fate when I thought he was dead before I could know him.'

Lady Bucklebury patted her arm. 'Well that is a good thing then.' She cast a piercing gaze at Leonora who stood before her. 'Alistair also said I was to give every assistance to you, Miss Appleby, should you need it.'

'It would be very kind if you could lend Mrs Priddy and me your coach to convey us home in the next day or so. Charlotte seems happy for us to leave her in your and Mr Lockwood's care.'

'Of course.' The old lady's face became thoughtful and with a knowing expression, she added, 'If you wished to return home tomorrow, you could join Lord Rokeby in his carriage, much finer and more comfortable than any I could offer. He told me he is heading for Hasterleigh after his usual leisurely breakfast.'

Leonora felt her pulse quicken. She did not even check with Nanny P but said, 'We would be very grateful for that. But Lady Bucklebury, would your grandson be happy to share his conveyance?'

'It was he who suggested it.'

Leonora met Mrs Priddy's bright eyes. 'Well then, we will be delighted. Lady Bucklebury, I will not forget your generous hospitality.' She took her hand. 'Being here under your protection has taught me so much of life and also of myself. Thank you.'

The Countess inclined her head with a smile. 'I felt rather put upon when Alistair asked me to sponsor Charlotte's entry into Society, but I have been surprised myself that I've much enjoyed it. Having you young women in the house, the sound of music being played, your singing, the laughter, all reminded me of past times. It has been a pleasure, my dear. And to see Mrs Priddy again.

Perhaps when you and Charlotte are married, Miss Appleby, I'll come down to Hasterleigh again for a last visit. It has been so many years.'

12

LOVE ME AS YOU ARE BELOVED BY ME

Leonora settled with Mrs Priddy on the seat opposite Lord Rokeby in his luxurious coach. Beside him was Achille. They were on their way home. The carriage was even more handsome than the one he had lent to convey them to London. The seats were upholstered in navy-blue satin with the Rokeby crest embroidered in black and gold, and matching tasselled blinds hung at the windows. In the midst of such elegance, Lord Rokeby cut a striking figure: his good clothes so carelessly worn, his cravat askew, his dark hair ruffled rather than sleekly pomaded, the leather eye patch harsh against his pallor and his scar unmistakeable in the slanting light. Leonora thought he looked magnificent.

As they headed through the busy London streets, the talk was desultory. Mrs Priddy commented on the fashions of some of the more extreme dandies they saw as they crossed St James's. Achille's head poked out the window and caused some consternation to pedestrians who saw him pass. Lord Rokeby watched Nanny P knitting and enquired, 'Mistress Priddy, that looks a most intricate piece of work; what is it and for whom?'

She twinkled back at him. 'My lord, it's an infant's shawl, I don't yet know for whom.' Lord Rokeby lifted an eyebrow. He then turned to Leonora to tell her of his plans to revive the Rokeby estate and prevent the weeds and tares of his unhusbanded acres encroaching on Manor land. Leonora found it hard to meet his gaze as she feared her emotions were so tumultuous they would be written on her face. He looked puzzled by her evasiveness; he settled into the corner and seemed to prepare for sleep. Leonora's nerves were as taut as an overstretched piano string; there was little chance she could succumb even to drowsiness as the coach swayed like a cradle on its well-oiled springs.

By Hounslow, Mrs Priddy's head had fallen onto Leonora's shoulder and she appeared asleep, although Leonora had her suspicions. Achille had also curled up on the fur blanket that covered the floor and closed his eyes. Suddenly alert, Lord Rokeby sat up and in a quiet, urgent voice said, 'Miss Appleby, I have to know. Does my disfigurement cause you distress? In certain lights it's very marked.'

Leonora's eyes flew to his face, her cheeks colouring, appalled that he should think she found anything about him distressing. 'No, no!' She so wanted to put out a hand and grasp one of his but was afraid to wake Nanny P. She longed to blurt out, *I love everything about you. You are embedded in my heart, have reshaped my world, and altered my aspect to the sun.* But instead she said, 'I barely notice it now, Lord Rokeby,' in a voice restrained by fear of the feelings surging through her. However, she wanted to prompt him into saying more. 'Why should it concern you, sir?'

He looked out of the window as if to deflect the emotion in his own words as he said, 'Because everything about you concerns me.' She clasped her hands together to contain her dawning delight as he continued, 'I've told you already that to have my life saved is one thing, but to wish to go on living is quite another. And you have done that for me, Miss Appleby. I now cannot put my hope in any other but you.'

What does this mean? Leonora's heart was beating out a rhythm that she felt sure would wake Nanny P. Lord Rokeby's gaze returned to her as she said in the quietest of voices, 'I thought my chance of love was gone but then I met you. Until that moment I had not known how lonely I have been, how much I longed...' She paused, afraid of revealing so much of her heart.

He leant forward and said softly, 'Say it, Miss Appleby. You need hide nothing from me.'

Leonora took a breath and continued, '...how much I longed for love.' Her face was shining. 'Since that meeting in the lane, thoughts of you have filled my empty dreams and measured my days.'

'Ah, when my coach nearly ran you over?' he murmured, then reaching for her, he gently stripped off her glove and cradled her hand in both of his, his warmth radiating through her. Leonora looked down and held her breath. She felt her soul lay in his grasp. To love and be loved, was that not all there was? A bubble of joy rose in her breast.

He held her hand fast, gripped with his own emotion. 'You've reminded me of who I used to be; my heart, a burnt-out ember, is now aflame and I cannot bear that spark to die.'

Her voice quivered with happiness as she said, 'How can it die, my lord? Once lit, is not the flame of love eternal?'

'That's a lofty thought, Miss Appleby.' He smiled. 'You mean like music and the stars, the wind, waters, and the sky?'

Lord Rokeby released her and looked away as if he feared the force of feeling between them. 'I have travelled Europe and swum its seas. I have been to hell and back.' He met her rapt gaze with a rueful smile. 'And yet my happiness was here all along, in the village where I was born, with the woman who lives in the Manor next door.'

Laughter bubbled out of Leonora as from a released spring. 'We both had to leave in order to find our way home,' she said.

The Earl shifted in his seat and said in a steadier voice, 'I have some of my old regimental friends coming to the Abbey for four days' rest and recuperation.' He caught her eye again and the current of passion flashed between them. 'When they have gone, perhaps, Miss Appleby, you would honour me with your company? With Mrs Priddy too, of course.'

At the sound of her name, Nanny P opened her eyes. 'Oh, goodness. Where are we on the journey, my lord?'

'Just an hour left. We have fresh horses and will soon be home.'

They fell into silence. At the sight of the familiar hedgerows and trees, Leonora knew that round the next corner the village would be in sight, nestling in its fold in the Downs. Achille had also woken up and stood at the window close to her, sniffing the air. Spring had truly arrived, with apple blossom in the orchards and cowslips in the fields. The green verges were abundant too with bluebells and wood anemones, campion, celandine and the mysterious medieval sleeves of lords-and-ladies pressing up through the grass. Excitement rose in Leonora's breast. She was home.

As the carriage drew up in front of the portico of the Manor, Lord Rokeby handed down both women. Mrs Priddy led the way, but he held Leonora back. Her hand was still ungloved, and he entwined his fingers with hers in a fleeting gesture of intimacy that left her breathless. He bowed his head and said with quiet intent, 'My spirit rests at last now you are home.' His glance was suddenly shy. 'When my friends have left, may I send for you?'

Leonora nodded, her heart too full to trust her voice. The

Rokeby coach turned in the drive and his lordship tipped his hat as he climbed back into its plush interior. Leonora noticed his limp and her heart was touched. Here was a man prepared to give his life for his country. And this hero was hers.

The Earl sat back in the seat with a sigh. He looked down at his right hand where the middle finger had been torn away by a French artillery shot. Could Miss Appleby really love such an imperfect figure of a man? And yet he could not now envision life without her.

A sense of necessity and desire gripped his spirit. The force of will and endeavour that had characterised his life now made Alistair Rokeby impatient to grasp every precious second left to him, to live fully with his new countess by his side. Already more relaxed now that she was within reach, he inhaled the breezy scent of the country that fizzed in his lungs. What happiness to relinquish the clanging city, the soot-laden air, the press of people and the posturing coxcombs and coquettes, for this sweet green land and the only woman he loved.

Even the burden of guilt for his brother's death, and the sense he was an imposter sitting on the ancestral seat, began to shift its oppressive weight. Alistair Rokeby sighed with satisfaction as his carriage started the descent to the Abbey. He had spent too long wishing he had never agreed to that schoolboy pact, carrying for ever the conviction that it should have been him to die in a foreign field. But even these years of regret faded with the promise of a new life; he had survived and must now honour his felled brother by living that life to the hilt. Lord Rokeby exhaled as if for the first time and felt this breath as freedom. For this, for Leonora, for love, he would give all he had been and could be, and the thought soothed his soul.

As the coach pulled up in front of the ancient building, Lord Rokeby climbed out and looked up at the atmospheric ruin looming into the blue above, with the welcoming house nestled in beside it, and was overcome with emotion. He wished he could see his brother again and say thank you. But this could never be, and Alistair Rokeby straightened his shoulders and entered the ancestral home he loved with new gratitude and at last a sense of right.

* * *

Leonora and Nanny P settled in the room by the kitchen to sort out the menus for the week ahead. 'I don't know when we will be transferring to the Lodge, but I think Mr Lockwood will soon be wishing to move in here and prepare for his new bride.' As Leonora spoke those words for the first time, she felt a fillip in her heart. How much she had hoped it would be Charlotte taking her place as the chatelaine of her beloved house, but now it was about to happen, she could not quite erase the underlying pulse of loss.

Mrs Priddy looked across at her with an anxious frown. 'Oh Nora, it'll be a wrench I know, but you will be moving soon to an even more beautiful place, will you not?' Her eyes had dropped again to the list of meals in her lap.

Before Leonora could answer with a laugh that she was presuming a great deal, there was a tap at the door and Milly entered with a message from Cook. 'Curate Fopling has sent across a haunch of venison to welcome you home, so she can cook that any day this week.'

'Thank you, Milly.' Leonora looked across at Mrs Priddy. 'What a thoughtful gesture.'

Milly hesitated and then blurted out, 'All the female servants at the Abbey, apart from Mistress Plum, the cook, have been given four days off-duty, Miss.' Nanny P met Leonora's startled glance but Leonora would not reveal any of her shock to Milly, whom she could see was already agog with lurid speculation.

'Thank you for that information, but I'm afraid the Manor cannot do without you.' Milly left, closing the door behind her. Leonora felt unable to express her sudden fears, even to her old nanny. She said in an equable voice, 'Lord Rokeby told me some of his military friends were visiting for a few days. He did say they were rather a wild set. Perhaps he didn't care to have his servants upset by their language and drunkenness?' But a cold trickle of foreboding deflated some of the ecstasy in her heart.

The next days were unseasonably hot and sultry with a threat of thunder. Leonora longed to reacquaint herself with the beautiful lake and plunge in for a swift, exhilarating swim. But she did not wish to visit it when Lord Rokeby's friends were in residence. As she was walking past the Vicarage, Mrs Mildmay rushed out, a letter in her hand. 'Charlotte is due home tomorrow! I'm busy devising a special welcome dinner for her; would you and Mrs Priddy come too?'

'Of course, it will be so good to hear her news.' Leonora took Mrs Mildmay's hands and squeezed them.

Mrs Mildmay then imparted a less happy piece of news. 'Oh, but have you also heard? The village gossips are clacking; they say things at the Abbey are as bad as the days when the old Earl was still alive.'

Leonora found her heart so constricted she could hardly breathe. 'No?'

'Well, a carriage full of ladies of uncertain repute was seen on its way into the Abbey drive. The old Earl would throw wild parties for his friends. Lord knows what those young sons were exposed to!' Mrs Mildmay's hand fluttered to her face but there was a certain glee in her eyes. Leonora felt as if a blade had pierced her soul. What a fool she was to think she knew Lord Rokeby's heart. What a fool to think it belonged just to her, with neither beauty, fortune, nor noble blood to distinguish her.

She turned away, so that Mrs Mildmay would not see how stricken she was. In a muffled voice she said as brightly as possible, 'I will look forward to seeing Charlotte again. Until tomorrow!'

The following day dawned even hotter, with no overnight storm to clear the air. Leonora's spirit was oppressed. She returned to her packing now that George Lockwood would be taking up residence at last. This was a melancholy task as she wrapped in paper and put into boxes the Delft porcelain her mother had collected and loved, her own books, the miniature portraits of her ancestors, her jewellery and clothes. Overcome with heat and growing despair, Leonora decided to walk to the orchard to collect some wild flowers to welcome Charlotte home.

In the shade of the lane, her spirits revived. There were so many flowers in the verges she hardly needed to walk as far as the orchard to collect a big bunch of bluebells, cow parsley and wood anemones, inhaling their heady scent as she turned for home. Passing the wall of the Rokeby estate, Leonora heard distant shouts and laughter; the higher timbre of female voices floated towards her like sirens. She climbed over the broken-down wall that she and Charlotte used on their clandestine visits to the lake. Irresistibly drawn onwards despite her dread, she walked with careful stealth over the mossy ground, her heart pounding. Soon she came to the fringe of the woodland and looked down on the lake – her lake.

Five men – some bare-chested, having stripped off their shirts, others barefoot, with their breeches wet to the knees – were chasing four women in the flimsiest of chemises, their hair loose down their backs. They squealed, flitting in and out of the shade at the water's edge. Leonora was appalled. There was her majestic oak tree, her lake, all treated with scant regard by these careless, libidinous friends of Lord Rokeby's. She strained her eyes in search of him but could not see his dark-haired figure amongst them. She gasped, recognising one of the bare-chested men as Rufus Dearlove just as he caught a young woman in his arms, kissing her as she giggled, and his hands moved up beneath her chemise. She wriggled free and he set off in pursuit again as she pirouetted to flick water at him with her toe.

Leonora turned away in a terrible confusion of feeling: shame that she was clandestinely prying on a scene she was never meant to see; horror that this licentious party was hosted by the man she thought loved her alone; shock at the jealousy and misery that gripped her spirit. How much she hated this feeling and hated what she had become: a sneaky, overwrought woman, humiliated by her presumptuous hopes and marked by ignorance.

Leonora scrambled back over the wall, pulled sticky grass from her skirts, and hurried home. She put the flowers into a jug of water and ran upstairs to throw herself on the bed and allow herself to cry.

Eventually, she recovered herself, splashed her face with cold water, and slipped into one of her favourite evening gowns, made by her and Nanny P in emerald tiffany. She could not resist a wry smile as she was taken aback by her image in the looking glass, noticing how green the fabric made her hazel eyes appear, how flaming her hair. She hoped her unhappy, jealous heart was not as evident to others. Leonora brushed and rearranged her hair and for good measure, slipped a pink satin rose into the waves she had managed to secure into a passable chignon.

She and Mrs Priddy set out to walk up through the adjoining Vicarage garden, scents of spring flowers hanging in the humid air. As they entered the house, they were greeted by a radiant Charlotte who flew into Leonora's arms. 'Oh, Leonora, I have told Mama Mildmay and the Reverend everything. They are so happy too that I have a father who lives, and my mother also. I saw her at Lady Dundas's.' Charlotte reached for Mrs Mildmay's hand. 'She wants to meet my family who cared for me and in time, will come with her husband to live in the Gardener's Cottage at the Manor.' Charlotte slipped her arm through George Lockwood's and said with utmost tenderness, 'But most gratifying of all is my Mr Lockwood, my...' she hesitated, her fair skin colouring at the thought of the intimacy of using his name. '...my George. How can I not be happy when the man I love loves me?'

Leonora looked up into his beaming face. How at home he seemed, dressed in his comfortable country clothes, smiling down into the beautiful, flushed face of the woman he had chosen for life's adventure. Leonora could envision them in ten years' time, affectionate and indulgent parents to their family of small children clustered round the table, and she smiled. This was just what her much-loved Hasterleigh Manor needed, a new young family to love and care for it as she had done.

Leonora's own pallor and lack of vitality was unnoticed in the general light of happiness that spilled from Charlotte and George Lockwood as they sat together at the head of the table while a good roast goose was carved and eaten. There was ceaseless chatter and laughter as Charlotte and Mama Mildmay caught up on the village gossip, the deaths and newborn babies, the welcome news that Richard Fopling, not his father, would be managing the Fopling estate, with a more benign hand. George Lockwood added, to laughter, that Beau Beacham had been so charmed by his newly betrothed that he had commended his stepson for the first time in his life for his unrivalled good taste.

Nanny P was sitting next to Leonora and she realised something was troubling her. She slipped her hand under the lacy tablecloth to take Leonora's and give it an encouraging squeeze. Leonora roused herself to take greater part in the discussions and add something to the night's celebrations. She caught Charlotte's eye and raised her glass to toast her. 'From the moment I first met

Mr Lockwood, I determined he should marry Charlotte so that it would be her who took my place at the Manor. And I could not be more delighted this has come to pass. Who else but she can grace this place and make Mr Lockwood happy?' Everyone round the table raised their glasses to drink to Charlotte's and Mr Lockwood's health, laughing and grateful that Leonora had been so magnanimous about giving up her family home.

Leonora and Mrs Priddy left early to return to the Manor and bed. As they walked through the warm scented night, Mrs Priddy took Leonora's hand. 'My dear, I know something is troubling you, and it's no longer just about losing the Manor. Tell me.'

'Oh, Nanny P, I can't, not yet. It's just I've had a harsh awakening to the folly of dreams. And my foolishness in believing in them.'

'We are never foolish to believe in dreams, my dear. Only sometimes to act on them is not wise. Come on now, you're hot and tired.' She patted Leonora's arm and Leonora hugged her.

'Oh, Nanny P, how would I ever have got by when my mother died if it hadn't been for you? Then when Captain Worth—' her voice broke with a stifled sob '—when he was killed, I couldn't see a way forward. But you have always been by my side. Thank you,' she said in a muffled voice as she buried her face in her old nanny's shoulder.

The spell of stifling heat did not break. Leonora arose from fitful sleep to dress in her lightest white muslin. She had been tempted to leave off her stays but felt that would be going a bit far into déshabillé, especially as George Lockwood was in the house. He had suggested she take as long as she wished to move into the Lodge as he still had a thatcher there sorting out the roof ridge where birds had nested.

Everyone's nerves were frayed by the unseasonable heat. Leonora's hair had curled into damp tendrils against her forehead, and she sought the cellar as the coolest place in the house, deciding to pack the china there into boxes. She heard a knock on the front door and a gentleman's voice talking to Milly.

As Leonora emerged from the cool dark, she was hit by a blast of heat and dazzled for a moment by the sun. There, in dark silhouette, was a man she knew well. 'Lord Dearlove!' she cried and took his hands, before she remembered she had seen him cavorting half-naked by the lake and was feeling very cross with him, and Lord Rokeby too. 'Would you like to come in?' she asked in a less welcoming tone.

Rufus Dearlove looked as handsome and untroubled as he always did, particularly now his forehead and cheekbones were burnished by the sun. 'Miss Appleby, I'm on my way back to my estate but did not wish to leave Berkshire before wishing you well.'

'Have you been visiting in the vicinity, my lord?' she asked with an ingenuous smile.

'Yes. The most bang-up reunion of us old soldiers at the Abbey. Rokeby certainly knows how to throw a good party.'

'I thought he did not much care for society.'

'Well then, something must have loosened m'lord's stays and upped his spirits.' The young buck laughed, little knowing the volcanoes of passion he was unloosing in Leonora's breast.

She hated herself for asking, but she was held tight in the toils of fear and jealousy. 'So, a gathering of you men with no ladies present?'

Lord Dearlove did not even look sheepish as he replied in his sunny way, 'No, no ladies at all. A few days of eating, drinking and gambling into the night. It's restored our energy and good humour. But I must be going if I'm to get back home before nightfall.' Leonora followed him to his curricle and nodded at his groom. As he swung himself into the driving seat he said, 'Oh, congratulations to young Miss Blythe. That George Lockwood is a fine man, rich too. My sister Livia was rather taken with him but is now betrothed to that cod's head Cholmodley.' He was irrepressible as he snorted with laughter. 'An absolute fool but well-oiled, thirty thousand a year from his northern estate. But she won't be happy exiled to the wastes of Northumberland, so far from London.'

'Please offer her my regards and congratulations.' Leonora was surprised how weak her voice sounded. His lordship then tipped his hat, wheeled his magnificent pair of black horses and set them off in a brisk trot as he drove his curricle back to the lane in a flurry of dust. Leonora was now hot, sticky and dusty and her mood was not improved.

She returned to her toil in the cellar and had been busy for about an hour when she heard a horse's hooves trot up to their door, followed by a rap. No one seemed to be available to answer the call and so she emerged from her cool dark sanctuary and opened the door to Roddy, Lord Rokeby's chief groom. He offered her a note, addressed to *Miss Appleby* in black ink in a large cursive hand she recognised with a jolt. 'M'lord said I should wait for a reply.' Leonora's heart was hammering as she unfolded it and under the gilded Rokeby crest, read:

Would my favourite and best piano-forte tuner be able to attend Rokeby Abbey at two tomorrow?

And it was signed with a flourish, *R*.

After enduring days of heat, fevered speculation and distress, his facetious tone was the last straw. Leonora grasped a piece of her own writing paper from the table in the hall and scrawled:

No. I'm afraid she would not.
    I suggest you find yourself a more amusing and complaisant p-f tuner.

And she signed with her own flourish, *LA*.

She folded it, not bothering with a wax seal, and handed it back to the groom. Leonora was seething with an anger she did not fully understand. After so many years of grief, when she had struggled for self-reliance, armouring her vulnerability with a steel band around her heart, she had finally offered it again to a man. Was she so hurt because he appeared to have treated her gift with scant regard? She removed her apron and catching sight of herself in the looking glass in the hall, was astonished by how untidy her hair was and how pink her cheeks, flushed with the heat of the day and the emotion of the hour. She had just managed to clean the dust of the cellar from her face, her hair still damp and tendrilled round her face, when there was the sound of cantering hooves.

Leonora went to the front door and there stood the Earl, his face dark, his hair wild. He was coatless, just wearing his shirt and breeches, and he too was flushed with the heat, sweat standing out on his forehead and glistening on his exposed collarbone. Achille came panting up and pushed through into the shade of the house. 'Lord Rokeby, to what do I owe this visit?' Leonora asked with a cold voice.

He flourished her note. 'To what do I owe this rude riposte? Why the sulky tone?'

'I'm not sulking, I'm irritated and disappointed.'

'How so?' he said, raking his hand through his hair, making it even wilder.

'Perhaps your behaviour with your friends over the last days might give you a clue,' she said, horrified at the edge of sarcasm in her voice. He took a step towards her, fury in his face, and Leonora realised this argument was being conducted in full hearing of the servants. 'Come into the morning room, my lord. I don't think we need to advertise our disagreements to the world.'

She closed the door behind them and he whirled around to face her. 'Pray tell me, Miss Appleby, how do you know how I behave with my friends?' His face contorted with anger and incomprehension. 'Did you come and visit me? Or were you by chance spying?'

Leonora recoiled from his words for he was right, and she felt suddenly very much in the wrong. She scrabbled for an explanation that did not implicate her. 'The whole village was agog!' she said.

He was contemptuous. 'So you prefer to hark to the clacking of old wives' tongues than to trust in my character?'

'How could I not? A carriage full of women was reported as being seen in your drive.' Her own outrage was on stronger ground as she saw him blink in shock.

'So I'm now guilty of entertaining a carriage-load of harlots, am I? Did it not occur to you this may have had nothing to do with me?' He had paced in his lopsided way to the window and back, then turned and said in an exasperated voice, 'If a friend of mine, a comrade in arms, chooses to invite some of his female friends, do you expect me to humiliate him, and them, by barring their entry? I'd hope you would have done as I did and treated them with respect.'

Leonora was still upset, not least by the desecration of her favourite swimming spot that these visitors had prevented her from visiting. 'If it was all so respectable, my lord, why were these friends cavorting in semi-undress around my—I mean *your*—lake?'

His visage suddenly lightened with amusement or triumph, she was not sure which. 'Ah ha! So you *were* spying! Miss Appleby, you are back to your old trespassing ways. You say you are disappointed in me, well I am disappointed in you.' His voice continued, more in sorrow, 'Why not think the best of me? And if you could not do that, then ask for an explanation. I thought you knew my heart.' In an involuntary movement, his hand went to his chest. 'But perhaps I was mistaken in that too? Instead, you damn me, again unheard.' Leonora hung her head. Lord Rokeby was right. She had jumped to conclusions that had hurt them both.

'You had not fully declared yourself to me. What was I to think? How was I to know this was a lark thought up by one of your gentlemen friends and not something you had organised for your own gratification?'

'I'm sorry you have been concerned, but I'd hoped you would be less quick to judge.' He was still frosty.

In a quiet voice she asked, 'Was the war comrade you mention Lord Dearlove by any chance?'

Alistair Rokeby met her eyes with lofty hauteur. 'I do not intend to answer that. Dearlove is an officer and a gentleman, as am I, and I will not deign to tattle like a fishwife.'

Leonora thought, *That spoilt Rufus Dearlove may be an officer and a gentleman but he's left you with this mess.* She looked at the distinguished, irascible man who stood before her and he turned his head to meet her gaze, a softer, sorrowful expression on his face.

'I thought I'd met in you, Miss Appleby, the love I'd waited for all my life, but I fear that you do not feel the same certainty. Instead, you offer so suspicious a mind, thinking the worst and rushing to judgement.' He then flared up with indignation. 'You admonish me for my behaviour – and you're not even my wife!'

In any other situation, Leonora would have laughed. To hear him admit to having thought of marrying her just a week ago would have filled her disbelieving heart with joy. But that innocent time had passed. Overcome by distress at her own behaviour and suffocated by the heat, Leonora snapped, her eyes flashing, 'Your wife? What presumption, my lord! Why on earth would I wish to marry you?'

Alistair Rokeby looked stricken. Even Achille gazed at her with an aghast expression. His lordship turned on his heel and walked straight for the door, his hound at his heel. Leonora was appalled at what she had said, how opposite it was to any truth she felt, and yet she had uttered the unsayable and it could not be undone. She dashed after him, but he was mounted on Jupiter and they were disappearing at a fast trot down the drive towards home.

Unbearably agitated by the emotion of the day, Leonora rushed back into the house and opened her piano-forte. She banged out the most clamorous of the Clementi sonatinas. The house rang with the notes and Mrs Priddy bustled in, her hands over her ears. 'Nora dear, can you play a little more quietly? You'll make my head break!'

Leonora rose from the stool and walked across to sit beside her old nanny. 'I'm sorry. I've just been such a fool and I don't know what to do to try and make it right.'

Mrs Priddy looked at her and asked, 'I presume this involves Alistair Rokeby?'

'I've done such damage not trusting him, not trusting myself. Oh, Nanny P, I've been so afraid of loving anyone again, fearing that my heart asks more than life can give.'

'It's not surprising my dear, given the deaths you've had to endure.'

Leonora took her hand. 'I can't bear the risk of loss. Or never finding love again. And yet I think my own stupidity has thrown Lord Rokeby's trust and affection back in his face.'

Mrs Priddy put her arm around Leonora and said in her motherly way, 'I think you'll feel much better after a night's sleep. And so will Master Alistair.'

'What will make me feel better is a swim. I've been longing to slip into that cold water since we've been home. I'll ask Charlotte to come with me early when Lord Rokeby's still abed.'

'These last days may have been hot, but that lake water will still be winter-cold. Take care not to stay in too long.'

'I think I'll go round to the Vicarage and ask Lottie.' Leonora stood up and kissed her on the cheek. 'Thank you for always being on my side, Nanny P.' Leonora ran into their garden; the moon was growing brighter in the dusky sky and the birdsong had ceased as the birds roosted for the night. She swung through the connecting garden gate and started walking towards the house when she heard low laughter. Peering through the dim light she saw, in the distance, the pergola of roses and honeysuckle, with Charlotte and George Lockwood sitting on a garden seat, their hands intertwined and heads bent close.

Leonora felt she was intruding and was about to turn and go when Charlotte looked up and called, 'Leonora, come and join us.'

Leonora shook her head, smiling, as she walked towards them. 'I don't want to disturb you.'

'You're not. Mama Mildmay doesn't know I'm out here without a chaperone, so you can be her.' Charlotte laughed and threw back her head to look up into George Lockwood's face, his eyes gleaming in the moonlight.

'I really can't stay. I just came to ask you, Lottie, if you would accompany me swimming tomorrow early, about nine?'

Charlotte cast a smile at her betrothed and said, 'I could manage noon, but Mr Lockwood—George,' she corrected herself shyly, 'George and I were going to ride round the estate just after breakfast.'

George Lockwood stirred and got to his feet. 'We could always postpone our ride until the afternoon?' He looked down at the woman he loved.

Charlotte had gained so much in confidence that she was

perfectly happy to go against both him and her dearest friend and answered, 'It's going to be another really hot day, I'd much rather we rode early. Do you mind, dear George, and you too, Leonora? We could swim the following morning?' Her face was questioning.

Leonora kissed Charlotte. 'Thank you. I'll think about that offer. Sleep well, my dear. Isn't it good to be home?'

'Oh yes! It's where the heart is. Now with Mr Lockwood here, my heart is with him.'

As Leonora turned to go, she put out a hand to George Lockwood. 'I haven't congratulated you on finding the sweetest, most competent and generous-hearted wife you could hope for.' Over her shoulder she added, 'The garden door will be open for you when you return.' They waved and Leonora walked back through the Manor gardens with the sound of their soft voices murmuring on the scented air.

The night was hot and heavy but Leonora was so exhausted by the day, she was quickly enfolded in a deep and dreamless sleep where no shame, jealousy, hope or fear of loss could follow. Even the insistent moon and its attendant stars did not penetrate the dark oblivion. She awoke with a start to a world wreathed in mist; it was the softest of mornings. The call of the lake and its reviving dark waters could no longer be resisted. She knew she had promised everyone she would never swim alone but all she needed was a quick dip, then she'd be out and home for breakfast. No one would be any the wiser.

Leonora slipped into her bathing dress of blue calico. She had followed the pattern and used a good strong fabric so it wouldn't cling when wet, but high-necked, full-length and covering her arms, it was almost too hot for the day. She threw her plain green pelisse over the top and stepped out into the warm morning. The mist was clearing but the light was still milky as she clambered over the wall into the Abbey estate. She trod her old path down through the trees, bright with spring foliage. Excited birds were rustling in the branches and rummaging through the moss and dead leaves.

Emerging from shadow into the sun, the new grass springy beneath her feet, Leonora felt at peace at last, as if only the elemental forces of water and air, life and love, truly mattered. In the clarity of this moment all the petty everyday concerns were as nothing. As if to mark this revelation, a blackbird in the tree above her poured out its liquid song as she ran down through the dew to her favourite oak tree by the water's edge.

Leonora's heart was beating fast; how she had longed for this since last October when Diggory Shrubb had banished her and Charlotte from the lake. It was astounding to think how entirely her world had altered since she had last stood in this place, but here the lake lay before her, unchanging and beyond understanding, its water merged with sky, with no ripple to disturb its glassy surface.

She tossed off her pelisse and changed her shoes for canvas swimming pumps. Her hair was already swept upwards in a tight chignon as she waded into the shallows. The intense cold made her gasp, and the heat of the air made the contrast all the more shocking. As she breasted off into the inky black, exhilaration began to rise at her silky passage through the water. Leonora could feel her heart pounding in her chest and knew she should not stay too long, but the mysterious centre of the lake was seductive; she could not leave it undisturbed.

Leonora swam through the filaments of mist before slipping onto her back for a minute to gaze upwards into the sky where newly arrived swallows were inscribing airy curlicues in the blue. She could feel the cold beginning to work itself into her limbs and turned to swim for shore. As her left leg trailed into the deeper recesses of the lake she was filled with dread as something caught her by the hem of her garment. She tugged as vigorously as she could, but the fabric held fast. She tried kicking her legs to break free, but the toe of her canvas shoe hit something hard and pointed. With rising panic, Leonora realised she may have been caught in the branch of a petrified tree, part of the woodland that was flooded when the lake was first created. She had strayed into the part Lord Rokeby had warned was out of bounds for this very reason. She had broken every rule.

She felt her limbs grow weaker as she struggled. Her fingers lost all their dexterity as she tried to unloose her buttons. Perhaps she could wriggle free of the dress? But so quickly had the cold entered her body that she barely had the strength to reach her back, let alone manage to slip the buttons through the loops. She started to call for help but as her voice echoed over the water, Leonora feared there would be no one abroad this early to hear her. Where was Diggory Shrubb when she needed him? she wondered bleakly. How headstrong and foolish she had been to come alone, how impatient and obstinate in her determination to swim in her precious lake. She should have waited for Charlotte.

Leonora could not feel her limbs and keeping her head above water was increasingly difficult. She called out again, more weakly, and put up an arm to wave, but even the smallest movement took more energy than she had. Suddenly, there was a young man with a dog emerging from the woods. Was this a hallucination? she wondered. Then, as the sun caught the unmistakeable flame of his red hair, she recognised Silas Sproat and a spark of hope was ignited.

'Silas!' she called, 'Silas!' Her cry was feeble and took an almighty effort.

He seemed to have heard her and raced to the shore. 'Miss Appleby, is that you?'

'Yes, Silas. Quickly! My dress is caught. I can't move.'

'I can't swim, missus!' His voice was panicked.

'Get help!' And she watched him set off running up the broad ride towards the Abbey.

Leonora could feel her body closing down. She knew she could not resist this cold much longer before losing consciousness. Barely able to prevent her eyes closing and her head slipping under the water, she lost track of time. Her life began to pass before her: her darling mama smiling, with sunlight in her hair, holding out her arms; her favourite pony, Meg; her father; then brave William Worth so handsome in his regimental colours; Nanny P as a young woman, lifting her onto her lap; then a dark turbulent lord galloping, galloping on his black horse. With a sob she felt herself slipping away.

'Miss Appleby, Miss Appleby! Hold on!' The voice seemed to come from far away. Was it still part of a dying dream? 'Miss Appleby!' With enormous effort, she opened her eyes to see that dark-haired lord gallop up on Jupiter and before he'd reined his great steed in, he threw himself from the saddle. Alistair Rokeby was barely dressed, his nightshirt stuffed into his breeches; he hadn't even pulled on his boots. He dived into the water and in an instant was surging towards her, a knife between his teeth. Without saying a word, he dived down to where her dress was caught and she felt the knife sawing through the hem. She was free but incapable of movement. He grasped her round the waist and started to propel them back to land.

Leonora could not speak, her teeth were chattering so much. Unconcerned by propriety when a life was in the balance, Lord Rokeby hitched up Leonora's skirt so she could sit astride in his saddle, her naked legs almost blue as they hung down against Jupiter's glossy flanks. He sprang up behind to sit on Jupiter's rump, with his arm around Leonora's waist to keep her from falling. Then he drove Jupiter into a canter.

Leonora's mind slipped in and out of reality; she did not quite know where she was but she knew she was safe. The arms tight around her belonged to the man she loved; she felt his warmth pressed against the frigid cold of her back. When they reached the Abbey, Lord Rokeby dismounted and she almost fell into his arms. He called for his groom. 'Help me carry Miss Appleby into the drawing room where there are remnants of last night's fire. Then take the curricle and collect Mrs Priddy from the Manor. Tell her to bring some warm clothes.'

The two men laid her gently on the sofa by the fire; her body was limp and her lips, blue. Lord Rokeby chafed her hands. 'Miss Appleby, don't slip into sleep. Nanny P will soon be here. You don't want to alarm her.' His voice was urgent, his face, distraught. Roddy left to collect Mrs Priddy and Lord Rokeby called for Mistress Plum, his cook, his most capable female servant, to come and remove Leonora's sodden bathing dress.

Despite his damaged leg he ran up the stairs and returned with the only piece of his mother's clothing he had kept, her ermine-lined opera cloak, together with the wolfskin cover from his own bed. The cook was just undoing the buttons of Leonora's gown when he entered. 'I'll leave you to this, Mistress Plum. I must also change. Dress Miss Appleby in my mother's cloak then cover her with the fur blanket. I'll be back in five minutes. I'll put your kettle on the stove. We'll need warm drinks.'

Alistair Rokeby was gripped by the same fear he had endured when his brother was cradled in his arms, his life slipping away in front of his eyes. The second person he loved more than life itself was here in his house, her own life hanging by a thread. He stripped off his clothes and dressed quickly in a clean shirt and breeches. He did not have time to shave and his face was grey with worry and the night's stubble. All that concerned him was to return to Leonora as quickly as possible.

Lord Rokeby re-entered his drawing room to find his cook brushing Leonora's hair off her forehead and chafing her hands while she lay under his wolfskin blanket, colour slowly returning to her face. 'Thank you, Mistress Plum. I will take over until Mrs Priddy arrives. Could you bring us two cups of hot chocolate, please?'

Leonora's eyes flickered open and she smiled before closing them again as she murmured, 'Lord Rokeby, I apologise for all this trouble.'

He fell to his knees beside her. 'Thank God you have come back to me. How could I live without you?' Leonora had just the energy to place her hand on his cheek and gently stroke the curling hair at his temples. He took her hands in consternation. 'You're still so cold. Do you feel warmth returning at all? May I check your feet?' Leonora nodded and he slipped his hand under the wolfskin to cradle her feet in his warm hands. 'Good, they seem less chilled.'

Leonora shivered with the thrill of his touch. She opened her eyes to meet his intense gaze. His words were close to a murmur, so terrible were the memories that assailed him. 'When I first found you, your eyes had that distant glassy look I have seen too many times before. In that moment, nothing mattered but you and securing you to life.' He dropped his head to kiss her feet, before covering them again carefully and tucking them in the skirt of his mother's cloak with the heavy fur bedcover over the top. He sprang up to place another log on the fire. On such a warm day the room seemed almost unbearably hot, but colour was seeping back into Leonora's skin. Her lips were no longer blue.

Mistress Plum appeared with two bowls of hot chocolate and Mrs Priddy followed her into the room. 'Oh Nora, what have you been up to? Let me see you.' She sat down heavily in the chair next to the sofa and leant across to take her hand. 'Good, you're warming up. I'm not surprised, this room is like a furnace.' She stood up to remove her pelisse and bonnet and then turned to Lord Rokeby. 'Well? What's been going on, my lord?'

'Miss Appleby was swimming in the lake when she got entangled in the branches of the petrified forest at the eastern end. That village lad, Silas Sproat, poaching no doubt, came tearing up to the Abbey, yelling. Got me from my bed. Our greatest thanks are due to him. Not many people are brave enough to demand I rouse myself from sleep at such an unconscionable hour.' He smiled.

'And how did you rescue her?' Mrs Priddy had grasped both of Leonora's hands.

'I dived down to where the hem of her dress was entangled and cut it free.'

'Well, thank the Lord she is safe.' She picked up the bowl of hot chocolate and said, 'Nora, I think you need some sustenance. Can you sit up?'

As Leonora struggled to sit, Alistair Rokeby put his arm around her back. Her old nanny handed her the hot chocolate and she sipped from the bowl. It was the first time Lord Rokeby had seen anyone but his mother wear the beautiful cream velvet and ermine cloak that now set off Leonora's colouring. He smiled. 'My mama's garment becomes you well, Miss Appleby. I shall have to give it to you.'

The chocolate and the warmth had revived her and she smiled. 'I have never worn anything so soft and luxurious.' She pulled it closer round her face. Then she added, 'Why not have your chocolate too, my lord? You won't have had any breakfast and saving me from the icy lake is a rude awakening, I'm sure.'

Mrs Priddy stood up. 'I'm far too hot by the fire.' She went to sit by the window and settled down with her knitting. 'I've nearly finished, just the last piece of scalloped edging to go.'

Lord Rokeby took her seat and gazed with some concern at

Leonora. 'Are you really feeling stronger?' He took her hand and felt her pulse. 'You are warmer, 'tis true. You cannot be in the army as long as I have been and not learn to read the vital signs.'

Leonora would not let his hand go. 'I apologise for trespassing and spying on your friends and their party. And for being so reproving when really, I had no right or reason. It's a presumptuous conceit I have that the lake is special and is mine.' She did not add *and a presumptuous conceit that you too are mine.*

Lord Rokeby smiled. 'I also must apologise for the behaviour of my friends. I was not pleased, but perhaps am indulgent of men who have been to war and seen the worst of humankind.'

'I know. How can I ever know what you have suffered.'

'I think you understand, though, how my music has consoled and healed me.' They still held each other's hands. 'But only you have made me value the life that was snatched from death. Now I want to live that life with you.'

Leonora was still weak and her emotions close to the surface. She laid her head on his knee, and he bent his face to put his cheek on hers. Drawing strength from his warmth, she straightened up and said, 'Do you remember my first visit here? My showing you the musical phrase you had forgotten?'

'How could I not? The air between us vibrated with some connection I could not fathom. But I resisted. For what had I to offer any woman? A broken body and a haunted mind.'

Leonora leaned forward to touch his face. 'But I'm not just any woman, my lord.' Her face was serious. 'And that forgotten melody came back to you, did it not? And the music was released again to flow on.'

''Tis true. Like that splintered arpeggio; you showed me where the notes belonged and how to complete the composition.'

'So, less haunted now, my lord?' With an anxious question in her eyes, she met his mischievous gaze.

He gave her a roguish smile. 'Not so haunted, but mightily distracted by the thought that you are naked under that cloak.' He looked at her, her eyes dancing, her cheeks flushed from the roaring fire. She put a finger to her lips and checked where her old nanny sat.

'She's fallen asleep,' she whispered.

'Our dear Nanny P always seems to drowse off when she's meant to be chaperoning us. Are we really that tedious?'

Leonora laughed. 'No, but I think she's very diplomatic.' He put out his hands and helped Leonora to her feet. She looked down at the beautiful ermine-lined cloak fixed across her body with kitchen twine. 'As you can see, your kindly cook has trussed me like a haunch of venison. I think she knows her master's susceptibilities well.'

He chuckled. 'She should by now. But I have never before had to rescue a headstrong beauty from *my* lake!' He took her into his arms, bundled up in velvet and ermine, and said in a more serious voice, 'A beauty who then threatened to break my heart by leaving me alone in this world.'

'If my déshabillé so disconcerts you, my lord, I can go upstairs and get dressed in the clothes Nanny P has brought from the Manor.' She looked up into his face with a teasing light in her eyes.

'No, it's much more fun to see if I can unwrap this charming parcel.' He pulled at the bow in the twine his cook had tied at the front, and the makeshift string belt fell to the floor.

Leonora giggled and clutched the edges of the cloak together. 'Have a care, Lord Rokeby! As you once pointed out to me, we are not even married!'

'Well, Miss Appleby, as you once told me, nothing would induce you to marry me. I wondered if there were anything I could do or say that might persuade you otherwise?'

Leonora gazed up at his rough, scarred face, shadowed with

the night's stubble. She glanced across at where Mrs Priddy slept and feeling unaccustomedly provocative, slipped her arms round his neck. 'Do you think you might kiss me, Lord Rokeby?'

He looked down into her expectant face, a peculiar, guarded expression on his. With a voice no longer teasing he said, 'Before you agree to marry me, even to kiss me, I want you to know the full extent of the damaged man you profess to love.' He released her and took a step backwards, and in one deft movement he stripped off his shirt.

Leonora gasped at the sight of his lean, muscled torso bisected by a long shocking wound. From his left shoulder to his right hip bone was a jagged raised scar. Watching her face, he turned his back and there was a comet-shaped gouge across his shoulder blade, and scattered pitted holes from grapeshot.

His voice was matter-of-fact but Leonora sensed the air between them electric with emotion. He continued, 'That was the shot that deflected off my shoulder and took my finger instead of my life. The sabre cut that opened my chest was wielded by one of Napoleon's elite Old Guard, still wearing his bearskin. Such men don't usually leave their adversaries alive.' He turned back to face her, his expression soft and uncertain. 'As you see, it is not a pretty sight.'

Leonora put out her hand and traced the scar with her finger. 'I see it as part of your beauty and the courage in which you live your life. How could I think otherwise?'

Alistair Rokeby put his damaged right hand over her small pale one and pressed it against his chest. 'There is one other disfigurement I have to show you.' With his gaze steady on her, he slipped off his eye patch. Leonora had become so used to the scar that ran across his face she had grown to barely notice it. It was part of the gallant landscape that distinguished him. She now saw the full extent of that French sabre's damage and her spirit recoiled. The raised gash that ran from his temple continued across his eyelid to his jaw. His lordship's eye had been saved but was milky and sightless. It was a shock to see his face so ravaged and she felt her knees give way. He had been watching her closely and murmured, 'Do not be ashamed of recoiling. I would find my look repellent if I hadn't become so used to it by now.'

'No, no! Never repellent. Never anything but beloved.'

He still held her from him. 'Can you really love such a grotesque carved-up man as this?'

Tenderness welled in Leonora's breast and she flew into his arms. 'How could I not love every inch of you? Your character and heroism are inscribed on your body and I embrace them with pride and love.' She stretched up on tiptoe to gently kiss the puckered corner of his mouth, then with a small moan he moved his head and their mouths met, at first with the faintest brush of their lips and then with the urgency of long pent-up desire. The opera cloak had fallen open and Leonora's bare breasts were pressed against his naked chest. The intimacy was astounding to her. She had never felt so close to anyone in her life, not certain where her flesh ended and his began, aware only of the warmth, the hard insistent strength of his body and the soft pulsating joy of hers.

There was a stir in the window and they looked across at Mrs Priddy who had just woken. They sprung apart. Nanny P said, 'My dear, you look quite restored to health. In fact, more bonny than I've seen you for ages.' She stood, holding up the large lacy shawl she had been knitting for months. 'It's finished at last!'

Leonora had hurriedly closed the cloak over her body and walked towards her old nanny. Lord Rokeby slipped his shirt back on, tucking it roughly into his breeches. He replaced his eye patch and with Achille by his side, walked to stand with Leonora and Mrs Priddy. They both put out their hands to touch the shawl. He said, 'This is beautiful, Nanny P. Now you have to tell us who it's for.'

Her blue eyes twinkled. 'It's for either your or Charlotte's baby, whoever first arrives.'

'But neither of us are yet married.'

'Well, I suggest you hurry up, then,' was her unruffled reply.

Leonora took her hand. 'My dearest Nanny P, I have relied on you as a mother for so many years, so you must be the first to know.' She looked up at Alistair Rokeby, her face aglow. 'I think Lord Rokeby has just asked me to marry him and if that is so, then I have agreed.'

Lord Rokeby stepped forward to embrace them both. 'Of course I've asked Miss Appleby—Leonora, to marry me. And of course she has agreed, as you, Nanny P, always knew she would. And I hope you will move with her into the Abbey as soon as we are man and wife.' With a smile that was full of mischief he continued, 'As Leonora and I are no longer young, we will need help with our new baby.'

Leonora protested with a laugh. 'How ungallant, my lord!'

He slipped an arm around her waist, pulled her close and continued, 'We have both stared death in the face and need now to grasp hold of life. Time is fast fleeing and happiness so precious; if I have learnt anything, it is that we can rely on very little. My life with Leonora begins on this auspicious day.'

He took her hand and turned to Mrs Priddy. 'Before you and Leonora return to the Manor, may I have your permission to take my future countess upstairs to help her dress?'

This scandalous request did not shock Mrs Priddy who merely looked unruffled and offered no objection. 'Since I first knew you, Master Alistair, convention has never constrained you. And in my dearest Nora, you have found yourself a woman who can match you in independence of spirit.'

'You mean we are *both* laws unto ourselves?' Leonora smiled, turning her old nanny's favourite description of the Earl back on her.

'Indeed, I don't think anything I might say would change either of you.'

Alistair Rokeby bowed his head in thanks and took Leonora's hand. She looked at him, her heart beginning to race. Nanny P had warned her he was a law unto himself, but what did the wild Earl have in mind?

'Lord Rokeby—Alistair.' Saying his given name out loud was another moment of thrilling intimacy. 'Alistair, Alistair,' she sighed, 'when were you ever a lady's maid?'

He bowed his head and smiled. 'I am willing to learn.' Then his expression turned serious. 'But first, I have shown you my scars and you have promised to love them as you love me. It seems only fair that you show me your scars too. Then I can assure you of my passion for you in your entirety.'

Leonora and Alistair walked into the hall where he picked up the portmanteau Mrs Priddy had brought and led Leonora up the great oak stairs. Achille tried to follow them, but Alistair turned and sent him back to the drawing room. Alistair Rokeby led Leonora into the master bedroom where a great four-poster bed – the bedclothes in disarray, exited as it had been that morning in a hurry – stood in stately splendour in the middle of the room. Putting down the portmanteau he took Leonora into his arms and murmured in her ear, 'Come now, my Lady Rokeby, let's start with that small mark on your neck. If I'm to marry you, I fear it needs closer scrutiny.'

Leonora wriggled out of his embrace and standing opposite him, her head proud, she said, 'As you so ungallantly pointed out, I'm no longer a young miss. I hope, Lord Rokeby, you will not think less of me for being so bold?'

He chuckled. 'My beautiful, headstrong, rule-breaking, most dear Lady R, I would expect no less of you. I think we should begin as we mean to go on.'

Leonora laughed with the delicious naughtiness of it. 'So, it's this mark on my neck?' She tilted her head to expose her throat and slipped the ermine cloak from her shoulders. 'I hope you will love my imperfections as I love yours, my lord?' As he walked towards her, she put her hand to his cheek and with the greatest tenderness, slipped his eye patch from his face. 'Thus, all defences gone.' Her eyes never left his as she slowly let the ermine cloak fall to the floor.

With a sharp intake of breath, Alistair Rokeby gasped, 'Oh, Leonora!' She walked into his arms, and he scooped her up and carried her to his disorderly bed. Laying her down amongst the pillows, he gazed at her with an expression on his face she had never seen before.

Excited and shy, Leonora pulled a sheet over herself and feeling rather breathless, said, 'Lord Rokeby, you are meant to be helping me dress!'

'I am... but not quite yet.' He bent his head and deflected her laughing protestations with a kiss.

EPILOGUE

Hasterleigh had never seen such a celebration in the last hundred years. It was June and the whole village was invited to the Earl of Rokeby's marriage to Miss Leonora Appleby. The Abbey doors and windows had been flung open, the floors swept, the magnificent drawing room painted a celadon green to reflect the vista beyond the full-length windows of parterre and rolling grass sward leading to the glittering lake. The house was filled to overflowing with flowers from the orchard and meadows, and roses from the Vicarage, Manor and every village garden.

It had been a summer of weddings and Leonora's was the last and the largest, mingling Society grandees with the villagers and tenant farmers. Lady Bucklebury kept her promise and travelled down to attend her grandson's celebration, bearing her ancestral diamond tiara as a present for Leonora. 'Every countess deserves a crown,' she said with a smile.

Charlotte and George Lockwood had married the previous month in a smaller ceremony that filled the Manor with flowers and laughter. Charlotte had effortlessly assumed her role as wife and chatelaine of the house but was equally as interested in George's plans for his arboretum, spending days with him tramping across the hundred-acre field, marking the planting positions for each tree, to return to the Manor windblown, her cheeks glowing from the sun.

Curate Fopling and his new wife Rose had insisted on a modest ceremony followed by a wedding feast amongst the trees. On assuming control of the Fopling estate, the first thing Richard and Rose had done was remove every trace of the ferocious animal and mantraps, and this party was a celebration of the woodland returning to its natural sense of sanctuary and beauty. It had been decided that Leonora and Lord Rokeby would lead the main dance through the trees, with Achille, sporting a red cravat, bounding beside them.

Until she was married and could move into Rokeby Abbey as the new Countess of Rokeby, Leonora, with Mrs Priddy, continued to live for a few more weeks in the guest wing of the Manor. During the day, Mrs Priddy made herself useful to Charlotte with her household managing skills, and every afternoon Leonora slipped from the Manor to go swimming in the lake, and there she met Alistair Rokeby. Together they dived into the cool dark waters to set out for the mysterious island in the centre that seemed to shimmer like a mirage on the cloud-reflecting surface of the lake. The Earl loved swimming as much as Leonora did and they played together like dolphins diving and gambolling in the silky water.

On the day of her wedding, Leonora wore a dress specially commissioned from Mrs Marmery of Windsor and was astonished how the pearly gauze, lace and ribbon enhanced her russet hair, making her translucent skin glow. Was it just the dress or was it happiness? she wondered as she luxuriated in the pleasure of her new-found beauty. At their first sight of each other, her noble husband seemed mesmerised by her presence. As soon as the ceremony was over, he caught her round the waist and whisked her behind a particularly tall flower arrangement and buried his face in her hair, inhaling her scent, as she slipped her bare arms around his neck. He murmured against her skin, 'I am lost as a flame is lost in light.'

Leonora lifted his head and kissed him. 'But you're still a flame, my darling Lord Rokeby.'

He was kissing her throat. 'You certainly inflame my passion, Leonora.' She threaded her fingers through his hair as he continued, 'How long before we can decorously excuse ourselves from our party so I can take my delectable new Countess to my bed?'

She giggled with pleasure at the thought. 'Not until we have bidden goodnight to our last guests. Your grandmother is here, don't forget.'

Alistair Rokeby whispered in her ear, 'She certainly would approve. Surely we won't be missed during one of those interminable reels?' His arm was tight round her waist, holding her to him. Laughing, Leonora wriggled free and they walked, their arms entwined, to take their place at the head of their wedding feast.

After the food had been eaten, the speeches made, and the dancing had become more abandoned as the night wore on, Alistair Rokeby took his wife's hand. With his other, he grasped two glasses and a bottle of champagne and led her through to the gallery to stand before the portrait of his brother, Charles. Handing a glass to Leonora, he took one for himself and together they looked up at the handsome dark youth, magnificent in his full hussar regalia, in easy control of his rearing warhorse, with Rokeby Abbey in the misty distance.

'Charles, meet the new Countess. She more than fills dear

Mama's shoes and fills my heart to overflowing.' He raised his glass and quaffed the champagne in one draught.

Leonora turned to her husband and said shyly, 'Alistair, you may want to tell your brother too that a possible new heir is already on his way.'

He swung round to face her, his expression sparkling with disbelief and joy. 'Are you sure?'

'As sure as I can be this early.' Her eyes were shining.

'So all that clandestine swimming together in your favourite lake has borne fruit!' He laughed, then gave a triumphant shout and swept her off her feet in front of the imperious portrait. 'See, Charles! See what a naughty, minxy wife I have!'

Leonora was laughing in his arms. 'So we're not too old after all!'

'No, indeed. Not too old at all.' He kissed her full on the lips. 'Wait!' he said, his face filled with delight. 'This means it will be our baby who will be awarded Nanny P's christening shawl.'

'How could it have gone to anyone else? It's a work of love made by someone who has loved me all my life.' Leonora's expression was ecstatic as she extricated herself from his arms. 'But let's not tell her or anyone until a respectable time has elapsed.'

'You've got it all worked out, haven't you? My darling Lady Rokeby.'

'Only to protect your reputation,' she protested.

Alistair Rokeby laughed. 'Of that, I'm past caring. Let them call me the Wicked Earl for seducing Hasterleigh's favourite maiden before I even married her!'

Leonora put a finger across his lips, her eyes mischievous. 'A maiden no longer, my lord; now a woman, and with child.'

He hugged her close. 'Thank you for loving me, Leonora. The house is alive again. *I* am alive again, and the Abbey once more will echo with laughter and childish chatter, all because of you.'

He took her hand. 'But now, my utterly irresistible Lady of the Lake, I wish to share with you the even greater pleasures of love on dry land.' He led her down the gallery past the watching ancestors and up the staircase to the first floor, where the noble Rokeby bed awaited.

ACKNOWLEDGEMENTS

After a lifetime of being a sensible lady biographer, just three years ago I was seized with the delight of writing novels set in the Regency. Initially written for my own enjoyment, I was lucky to have my heroic agent Jim Gill of United Agents read *The Marriage Season* and declare, *There's something here for everyone*! My second big stroke of luck came when he sold it, with Amber Garvey's help, to Boldwood Books, one of the most exciting, dynamic – and award-winning – new entrants to the publishing world. Gratifyingly, they wished me to go on writing in the same vein and *An Unsuitable Heiress* and *A Scandalous Match* followed in quick succession, and now here is *A Lady's Fortune*. I have been astounded by how many wonderful readers have read my books and, of course, it is you who make everything possible: your support is never taken for granted and my gratitude is unwavering.

But before a book gets to be offered to the world, there is the publishing engine; the intelligent, heart-felt efficiency of Boldwood Books with its moving genius at the centre – Amanda Ridout, Chief Bold Woman – of which my super editor, Sarah Ritherdon, is another. Sarah's unerring eye for continuity, plausibility of character or action and any florid excess is invaluable in making my tender offering a better book. Candida Bradford's emotionally intelligent insights and sense of style add immensely to her copy-editing skills and finally Christina de Caix-Curtis, with her superb discriminating eye and linguistic skills, polishes the book for human consumption.

Embellished with its beautiful cover, thanks to the artistry of Alice Moore, it is handed to the brilliant production team, and then on to Nia Beynon and Claire Fenby and their inspired cohorts who use their magical powers of sales and promotion to propel the book to the most important element in this process – the readers! The fantastic collegiate team at Boldwood is now too numerous to mention in person, but my gratitude and thanks to you all.

Every writer needs her own support network of family and friends. Thanks are always due to my dearest husband, Nick, who is the gateway to every language under the sun and is forced to read my books first. Other first readers are my beloved sister Ka and long-distance friend, Jennifer Larson, a Heyer aficionada, intellectual and writer herself who gives me invaluable feedback from across the Atlantic. With *A Lady's Fortune*, Emma Orchard, another Heyer expert and writer of Regency historical novels herself, generously offered to read my raw manuscript and gave a hugely helpful overview. I have never met Emma but such is the camaraderie of fellow authors – and especially fellow Boldwood authors – that one will offer her invaluable time to critique a first draft of another!

My wonderful friends and family have supported my writing all the way. There are too many to name but at random: my precious sisters, sisters-in-law and nieces (at least one brother-in-law loves my books too); Stef, writing friend and cheerleader from schooldays; Annette, expert on horses and their behaviour (who has ridden side-saddle herself and experienced many a bolting prancer) and loyal supporter in everything; Yvonne who enthusiastically presses my books on friends and customers; all the lovely people who have written to me to say how much they enjoyed my work and so many, many more.

Thanks are finally due to my beloved children, Ben and Lily, who have put up with me throughout their lives, since I was writing biographies while they slept (when it was possible to put your youngsters to bed at six in the evening) to now when I'm writing romantic historical fiction and they have much-loved families of their own. Heartfelt thanks too to my stepdaughter, Sophia, and her wonderful family who are always interested, entertaining and supportive. All these and their children are more precious than any books on my shelf!

But if any readers have got this far, it is to you that I owe the greatest thanks. Thank you for buying, reading and giving your time to write wonderful reviews or rate the book on Amazon. It is so touching and encouraging too to get your letters, emails and messages of support on Twitter. Thank you for making it all worthwhile.

ABOUT THE AUTHOR

Jane Dunn is an historian and biographer and the author of seven acclaimed biographies, including Daphne du Maurier and her Sisters and the Sunday Times and NYT bestseller, Elizabeth & Mary: Cousins, Rivals, Queens. She lives in Berkshire with her husband, the linguist Nicholas Ostler.

Sign up to Jane Dunn's mailing list for news, competitions and updates on future books.

Follow Jane on social media here:

 x.com/JaneDunnAuthor

ALSO BY JANE DUNN

You're cordially invited to

The Scandal Sheet

The home of swoon-worthy historical romance from the Regency to the Victorian era!

Warning: may contain spice 🌶️

Sign up to the newsletter
https://bit.ly/thescandalsheet

Boldwood

Boldwood Books is an award-winning fiction publishing company seeking out the best stories from around the world.

Find out more at www.boldwoodbooks.com

Join our reader community for brilliant books, competitions and offers!

Follow us
@BoldwoodBooks
@TheBoldBookClub

Sign up to our weekly deals newsletter

https://bit.ly/BoldwoodBNewsletter